Praise for Ken Follett
and his bestselling novels

"Masterful . . . plot and counterplot, treachery, cunning and killing . . . keep you on the edge every moment."

—*Associated Press*

"Razor-sharp . . . harrowing . . . a cleverly crafted, easily read novel!"

—*The Dallas Times*

"Follett's great strength is his female characters—they are smart, strong, independent, and when they love a man, by golly, he knows the game is up."

—*People*

"An absolutely terrific thriller, so pulse-pounding, so ingenious in its plotting, and so frighteningly realistic that you simply cannot stop reading."

—*Publishers Weekly*

"Can Follett write! . . . He outclasses his competitors!"

—*Newsday*

Books by Ken Follett

THE
KEY TO
REBECCA

Ken Follett

A SIGNET BOOK

SIGNET
Published by New American Library, a division of
Penguin Putnam Inc., 375 Hudson Street,
New York, New York 10014, U.S.A.
Penguin Books Ltd, 27 Wrights Lane,
London W8 5TZ, England
Penguin Books Australia Ltd, Ringwood,
Victoria, Australia
Penguin Books Canada Ltd, 10 Alcorn Avenue,
Toronto, Ontario, Canada M4V 3B2
Penguin Books (N.Z.) Ltd, 182–190 Wairau Road,
Auckland 10, New Zealand

Penguin Books Ltd, Registered Offices:
Harmondsworth, Middlesex, England

Published by Signet, an imprint of New American Library,
a division of Penguin Putnam Inc.
A hardcover edition was published by William Morrow and Company, Inc.

Published also in a Plume edition.

First Signet Printing, September 1981
48 47 46 45 44 43 42

REGISTERED TRADEMARK—MARCA REGISTRADA

Printed in the United States of America

PUBLISHER'S NOTE
This is a work of fiction. Names, characters, places, and incidents either are the
product of the author's imagination or are used fictitiously, and any resemblance
to actual persons, living or dead, events, or locales is entirely coincidental.

TO ROBIN McGIBBON

"Our spy in Cairo is the greatest hero of them all."
        —ERWIN ROMMEL, September 1942

(Quoted by Anthony Cave Brown in *Bodyguard of Lies*)

PART ONE

——————

TOBRUK

1

The last camel collapsed at noon.

It was the five-year-old white bull he had bought in Gialo, the youngest and strongest of the three beasts, and the least ill-tempered: he liked the animal as much as a man could like a camel, which is to say that he hated it only a little.

They climbed the leeward side of a small hill, man and camel planting big clumsy feet in the inconstant sand, and at the top they stopped. They looked ahead, seeing nothing but another hillock to climb, and after that a thousand more, and it was as if the camel despaired at the thought. Its forelegs folded, then its rear went down, and it couched on top of the hill like a monument, staring across the empty desert with the indifference of the dying.

The man hauled on its nose rope. Its head came forward and its neck stretched out, but it would not get up. The man went behind and kicked its hindquarters as hard as he could, three or four times. Finally he took out a razor-sharp curved Bedouin knife with a narrow point and stabbed the camel's rump. Blood flowed from the wound but the camel did not even look around.

The man understood what was happening. The very tissues of the animal's body, starved of nourishment, had simply stopped working, like a machine that has run out of fuel. He had seen camels collapse like this on the outskirts of an oasis, surrounded by life-giving foliage which they ignored, lacking the energy to eat.

There were two more tricks he might have tried. One was to pour water into its nostrils until it began to drown; the other to light a fire under its hindquarters. He could not spare the water for one nor the firewood for the other, and besides neither method had a great chance of success.

It was time to stop, anyway. The sun was high and fierce. The long Saharan summer was beginning, and the midday temperature would reach 110 degrees in the shade.

Without unloading the camel, the man opened one of his bags and took out his tent. He looked around again, automatically: there was no shade or shelter in sight—one place was as bad as another. He pitched his tent beside the dying camel, there on top of the hillock.

He sat cross-legged in the open end of the tent to make his tea. He scraped level a small square of sand, arranged a few precious dry twigs in a pyramid and lit the fire. When the kettle boiled he made tea in the nomad fashion, pouring it from the pot into the cup, adding sugar, then returning it to the pot to infuse again, several times over. The resulting brew, very strong and rather treacly, was the most revivifying drink in the world.

He gnawed at some dates and watched the camel die while he waited for the sun to pass overhead. His tranquillity was practiced. He had come a long way in this desert, more than a thousand miles. Two months earlier he had left El Agela, on the Mediterranean coast of Libya, and traveled due south for five hundred miles, via Gialo and Kufra, into the empty heart of the Sahara. There he had turned east and crossed the border into Egypt unobserved by man or beast. He had traversed the rocky wasteland of the Western Desert and turned north near Kharga; and now he was not far from his destination. He knew the desert, but he was afraid of it—all intelligent men were, even the nomads who lived all their lives here. But he never allowed that fear to take hold of him, to panic him, to use up his nervous energy. There were always catastrophes: mistakes in navigation that made you miss a well by a couple of miles; water bottles that leaked or burst; apparently healthy camels that got sick a couple of days out. The only response was to say *Inshallah*: It is the will of God.

Eventually the sun began to dip toward the west. He looked at the camel's load, wondering how much of it he could carry. There were three small European suitcases, two heavy and one light, all important. There was a little bag of clothes, a sextant, the maps, the food and the water bottle. It was already too much: he would have to abandon the tent, the tea set, the cooking pot, the almanac and the saddle.

He made the three cases into a bundle and tied the clothes, the food and the sextant on top, strapping the lot together with a length of cloth. He could put his arms through the cloth straps and carry the load like a rucksack on his back. He slung the goatskin water bag around his neck and let it dangle in front.

It was a heavy load.

Three months earlier he would have been able to carry it all day then play tennis in the evening, for he was a strong man; but the desert had weakened him. His bowels were water, his skin was a mass of sores, and he had lost twenty or thirty pounds. Without the camel he could not go far.

Holding his compass in his hand, he started walking.

He followed the compass wherever it led, resisting the temptation to divert around the hills, for he was navigating by dead reckoning over the final miles, and a fractional error could take him a fatal few hundred yards astray. He settled into a slow, long-strided walk. His mind emptied of hopes and fears and he concentrated on the compass and the sand. He managed to forget the pain of his ravaged body and put one foot in front of the other automatically, without thought and therefore without effort.

The day cooled into evening. The water bottle became lighter around his neck as he consumed its contents. He refused to think about how much water was left: he was drinking six pints a day, he had calculated, and he knew there was not enough for another day. A flock of birds flew over his head, whistling noisily. He looked up, shading his eyes with his hand, and recognized them as Lichtenstein's sandgrouse, desert birds like brown pigeons that flocked to water every morning and evening. They were heading the same way as he was, which meant he was on the right track, but he knew they could fly fifty miles to water, so he could take little encouragement from them.

Clouds gathered on the horizon as the desert cooled. Behind him, the sun sank lower and turned into a big yellow balloon. A little later a white moon appeared in a purple sky.

He thought about stopping. Nobody could walk all night. But he had no tent, no blanket, no rice and no tea. And he was sure he was close to the well: by his reckoning he should have been there.

He walked on. His calm was deserting him now. He had set his strength and his expertise against the ruthless desert, and it began to look as if the desert would win. He thought again of the camel he had left behind, and how it had sat on the hillock, with the tranquillity of exhaustion, waiting for death. He would not wait for death, he thought: when it became inevitable he would rush to meet it. Not for him the hours of agony and encroaching madness—that would be undignified. He had his knife.

The thought made him feel desperate, and now he could no longer repress the fear. The moon went down, but the landscape was bright with starlight. He saw his mother in the distance, and she said: "Don't say I never warned you!" He heard a railway train that chugged along with his heartbeat, slowly. Small rocks moved in his path like scampering rats. He smelled roast lamb. He breasted a rise and saw, close by, a red glow of the fire over which the meat had been roasted, and a small boy beside it gnawing the bones. There were the tents around the fire, the hobbled camels grazing the scattered thorns, and the wellhead beyond. He walked into the hallucination. The people in the dream looked up at him, startled. A tall man stood up and spoke. The traveler pulled at his howli, partially unwinding the cloth to reveal his face.

The tall man stepped forward, shocked, and said, "My cousin!"

The traveler understood that this was not, after all, an illusion; and he smiled faintly and collapsed.

When he awoke he thought for a moment that he was a boy again, and that his adult life had been a dream.

Someone was touching his shoulder and saying "Wake up, Achmed," in the tongue of the desert. Nobody had called him Achmed for years. He realized he was wrapped in a coarse blanket and lying on the cold sand, his head swathed in a howli. He opened his eyes to see the gorgeous sunrise like a straight rainbow against the flat black horizon. The icy morning wind blew into his face. In that instant he experienced again all the confusion and anxiety of his fifteenth year.

He had felt utterly lost, that first time he woke up in the desert. He had thought *My father is dead,* and then *I have a new father.* Snatches from the Surahs of the Koran had run through his head, mixed with bits of the Creed which his mother still taught him secretly, in German. He remembered the recent sharp pain of his adolescent circumcision, followed by the cheers and rifle shots of the men as they congratulated him on at last becoming one of them, a true man. Then there had been the long train journey, wondering what his desert cousins would be like, and whether they would despise his pale body and his city ways. He had walked briskly out of the railway station and seen the two Arabs, sitting beside their camels in the dust of the station yard, wrapped in traditional robes which covered them from head to foot except for the slit in the howli which revealed only their dark, unreadable eyes. They had taken him to the well. It had been terrifying: nobody had spoken to him, except in gestures. In the evening he had realized that these people had *no toilets,* and he became desperately embarrassed. In the end he had been forced to ask. There was a moment of silence, then they all burst out laughing. It transpired that they had thought he could not speak their language, which was why everyone had tried to communicate with him in signs; and that he had used a baby word in asking about toilet arrangements, which made it funnier. Someone had explained to him about walking a little way beyond the circle of tents and squatting in the sand, and after that he had not been so frightened, for although these were hard men they were not unkind.

All these thoughts had run through his mind as he looked at his first desert sunrise, and they came back again twenty years later, as fresh and as painful as yesterday's bad memories, with the words "Wake up, Achmed."

He sat up abruptly, the old thoughts clearing rapidly like the morning clouds. He had crossed the desert on a vitally important mission. He had found the well, and it had not been a hallucination: his cousins were here, as they always were at this time of the year. He had collapsed with exhaustion, and they had wrapped him in blankets and let him sleep by the fire. He suffered a sudden sharp panic as he thought of his precious baggage—had he still been carrying it when he arrived?—then he saw it, piled neatly at his feet.

Ishmael was squatting beside him. It had always been like
this: throughout the year the two boys had spent together in
the desert, Ishmael had never failed to wake first in the
morning. Now he said: "Heavy worries, cousin."

Achmed nodded. "There is a war."

Ishmael proffered a tiny jeweled bowl containing water.
Achmed dipped his fingers in the water and washed his eyes.
Ishmael went away. Achmed stood up.

One of the women, silent and subservient, gave him tea.
He took it without thanking her and drank it quickly. He ate
some cold boiled rice while the unhurried work of the encampment went on around him. It seemed that this branch of
the family was still wealthy: there were several servants,
many children and more than twenty camels. The sheep
nearby were only a part of the flock—the rest would be grazing a few miles away. There would be more camels, too.
They wandered at night in search of foliage to eat, and although they were hobbled they sometimes went out of sight.
The young boys would be rounding them up now, as he and
Ishmael had done. The beasts had no names, but Ishmael
knew each one individually, and its history. He would say:
"This is the bull my father gave to his brother Abdel in the
year many women died, and the bull became lame so my
father gave Abdel another and took this one back, and it still
limps, see?" Achmed had come to know camels well, but he
had never quite adopted the nomad attitude to them: he had
not, he remembered, lit a fire underneath his dying white yesterday. Ishmael would have.

Achmed finished his breakfast and went back to his baggage. The cases were not locked. He opened the top one, a
small leather suitcase; and when he looked at the switches
and dials of the compact radio neatly fitted into the rectangular case he had a sudden vivid memory like a movie: the bus-
tling frantic city of Berlin; a tree-lined street called the
Tirpitzufer; a four-story sandstone building; a maze of hall-
ways and staircases; an outer office with two secretaries; an
inner office, sparsely furnished with desk, sofa, filing cabinet,
small bed and on the wall a Japanese painting of a grinning
demon and a signed photograph of Franco; and beyond the
office, on a balcony overlooking the Landwehr Canal, a pair

of dachshunds and a prematurely white-haired admiral who said: "Rommel wants me to put an agent into Cairo."

The case also contained a book, a novel in English. Idly, Achmed read the first line: "Last night I dreamt I went to Manderley again." A folded sheet of paper fell out from between the leaves of the book. Carefully, Achmed picked it up and put it back. He closed the book, replaced it in the case, and closed the case.

Ishmael was standing at his shoulder. He said: "Was it a long journey?"

Achmed nodded. "I came from El Agela, in Libya." The names meant nothing to his cousin. "I came from the sea."

"From the sea!"

"Yes."

"Alone?"

"I had some camels when I started."

Ishmael was awestruck: even the nomads did not make such long journeys, and he had never seen the sea. He said: "But why?"

"It is to do with this war."

"One gang of Europeans fighting with another over who shall sit in Cairo—what does this matter to the sons of the desert?"

"My mother's people are in the war," Achmed said.

"A man should follow his father."

"And if he has two fathers?"

Ishmael shrugged. He understood dilemmas.

Achmed lifted the closed suitcase. "Will you keep this for me?"

"Yes." Ishmael took it. "Who is winning the war?"

"My mother's people. They are like the nomads—they are proud, and cruel, and strong. They are going to rule the world."

Ishmael smiled. "Achmed, you always did believe in the desert lion."

Achmed remembered: he had learned, in school, that there had once been lions in the desert, and that it was possible a few of them remained, hiding in the mountains, living off deer and fennec fox and wild sheep. Ishmael had refused to believe him. The argument had seemed terribly important then, and they had almost quarreled over it. Achmed grinned. "I still believe in the desert lion," he said.

The two cousins looked at one another. It was five years since the last time they had met. The world had changed. Achmed thought of the things he could tell: the crucial meeting in Beirut in 1938, his trip to Berlin, his great coup in Istanbul . . . None of it would mean anything to his cousin—and Ishmael was probably thinking the same about the events of *his* last five years. Since they had gone together as boys on the pilgrimage to Mecca they had loved each other fiercely, but they never had anything to talk about.

After a moment Ishmael turned away, and took the case to his tent. Achmed fetched a little water in a bowl. He opened another bag, and took out a small piece of soap, a brush, a mirror and a razor. He stuck the mirror in the sand, adjusted it, and began to unwind the howli from around his head.

The sight of his own face in the mirror shocked him.

His strong, normally clear forehead was covered with sores. His eyes were hooded with pain and lined in the corners. The dark beard grew matted and unkempt on his fine-boned cheeks, and the skin of his large hooked nose was red and split. He parted his blistered lips and saw that his fine, even teeth were filthy and stained.

He brushed the soap on and began to shave.

Gradually his old face emerged. It was strong rather than handsome, and normally wore a look which he recognized, in his more detached moments, to be faintly dissolute; but now it was simply ravaged. He had brought a small phial of scented lotion across hundreds of miles of desert for this moment, but now he did not put it on because he knew it would sting unbearably. He gave it to a girl-child who had been watching him, and she ran away, delighted with her prize.

He carried his bag into Ishmael's tent and shooed out the women. He took off his desert robes and donned a white English shirt, a striped tie, gray socks and a brown checked suit. When he tried to put on the shoes he discovered that his feet had swollen: it was agonizing to attempt to force them into the hard new leather. However, he could not wear his European suit with the improvised rubber-tire sandals of the desert. In the end he slit the shoes with his curved knife and wore them loose.

He wanted more: a hot bath, a haircut, cool soothing cream for his sores, a silk shirt, a gold bracelet, a cold bottle of champagne and a warm soft woman. For those he would have to wait.

When he emerged from the tent the nomads looked at him as if he were a stranger. He picked up his hat and hefted the two remaining cases—one heavy, one light. Ishmael came to him carrying a goatskin water bottle. The two cousins embraced.

Achmed took a wallet from the pocket of his jacket to check his papers. Looking at the identity card, he realized that once again he was Alexander Wolff, age thirty-four, of Villa les Oliviers, Garden City, Cairo, a businessman, race— European.

He put on his hat, picked up his cases and set off in the cool of the dawn to walk across the last few miles of desert to the town.

The great and ancient caravan route, which Wolff had followed from oasis to oasis across the vast empty desert, led through a pass in the mountain range at last merged with an ordinary modern road. The road was like a line drawn on the map by God, for on one side were the yellow, dusty, barren hills, and on the other were lush fields of cotton squared off with irrigation ditches. The peasants, bent over their crops, wore galabiyas, simple shifts of striped cotton, instead of the cumbersome protective robes of the nomads. Walking north on the road, smelling the cool damp breeze off the nearby Nile, observing the increasing signs of urban civilization, Wolff began to feel human again. The peasants dotted about the fields came to seem less like a crowd. Finally he heard the engine of a car, and he knew he was safe.

The vehicle was approaching him from the direction of Assyut, the town. It came around a bend and into sight, and he recognized it as a military jeep. As it came closer he saw the British Army uniforms of the men in it, and he realized he had left behind one danger only to face another.

Deliberately he made himself calm. I have every right to be here, he thought. I was born in Alexandria. I am Egyptian by nationality. I own a house in Cairo. My papers are all genuine. I am a wealthy man, a European and a German spy behind enemy lines—

The jeep screeched to a halt in a cloud of dust. One of the men jumped out. He had three cloth pips on each shoulder of his uniform shirt: a captain. He looked terribly young, and walked with a limp.

The captain said: "Where the devil have you come from?"

Wolff put down his cases and jerked a thumb back over his shoulder. "My car broke down on the desert road."

The captain nodded, accepting the explanation instantly: it would never have occurred to him, or to anyone else, that a European might have walked here from Libya. He said: "I'd better see your papers, please."

Wolff handed them over. The captain examined them, then looked up. Wolff thought: There has been a leak from Berlin, and every officer in Egypt is looking for me; or they have changed the papers since last time I was here, and mine are out of date; or—

"You look about all in, Mr. Wolff," the captain said. "How long have you been walking?"

Wolff realized that his ravaged appearance might get some useful sympathy from another European. "Since yesterday afternoon," he said with a weariness that was not entirely faked. "I got a bit lost."

"You've been out here all *night*?" The captain looked more closely at Wolff's face. "Good Lord, I believe you have. You'd better have a lift with us." He turned to the jeep. "Corporal, take the gentleman's cases."

Wolff opened his mouth to protest, then shut it again abruptly. A man who had been walking all night would be only too glad to have someone take his luggage. To object would not only discredit his story, it would draw attention to the bags. As the corporal hefted them into the back of the jeep, Wolff realized with a sinking feeling that he had not even bothered to lock them. How could I be so stupid? he thought. He knew the answer. He was still in tune with the desert, where you were lucky to see other people once a week, and the last thing they wanted to steal was a radio transmitter that had to be plugged in to a power outlet. His senses were alert to all the wrong things: he was watching the movement of the sun, smelling the air for water, measuring the distances he was traveling, and scanning the horizon as if searching for a lone tree in whose shade he could rest during the heat of the day. He had to forget all that now, and think instead of policemen and papers and locks and lies.

He resolved to take more care, and climbed into the jeep.

The captain got in beside him and said to the driver: "Back into town."

Wolff decided to bolster his story. As the jeep turned in the dusty road he said: "Have you got any water?"

"Of course." The captain reached beneath his seat and pulled up a tin bottle covered in felt, like a large whiskey flask. He unscrewed the cap and handed it to Wolff.

Wolff drank deeply, swallowing at least a pint. "Thanks," he said, and handed it back.

"Quite a thirst you had. Not surprising. Oh, by the way— I'm Captain Newman." He stuck out his hand.

Wolff shook it and looked more closely at the man. He *was* young—early twenties, at a guess—and fresh-faced, with a boyish forelock and a ready smile; but there was in his demeanor that weary maturity that comes early to fighting men. Wolff asked him: "Seen any action?"

"Some." Captain Newman touched his own knee. "Did the leg at Cyrenaica, that's why they sent me to this one-horse town." He grinned. "I can't honestly say I'm panting to get back into the desert, but I'd like to be doing something a bit more positive than this, minding the shop hundreds of miles from the war. The only fighting we ever see is between the Christians and the Moslems in the town. Where does your accent come from?"

The sudden question, unconnected with what had gone before, took Wolff by surprise. It had surely been intended to, he thought: Captain Newman was a sharp-witted young man. Fortunately Wolff had a prepared answer. "My parents were Boers who came from South Africa to Egypt. I grew up speaking Afrikaans and Arabic." He hesitated, nervous of overplaying his hand by seeming too eager to explain. "The name Wolff is Dutch, originally; and I was christened Alex after the town where I was born."

Newman seemed politely interested. "What brings you here?"

Wolff had prepared for that one, too. "I have business interests in several towns in Upper Egypt." He smiled. "I like to pay them surprise visits."

They were entering Assyut. By Egyptian standards it was a large town, with factories, hospitals, a Muslim university, a famous convent and some sixty thousand inhabitants. Wolff was about to ask to be dropped at the railway station when Newman saved him from that error. "You need a garage," the captain said. "We'll take you to Nasif's: he has a tow truck."

Wolff forced himself to say: "Thank you." He swallowed drily. He was still not thinking hard enough or fast enough. I wish I could pull myself together, he thought; it's the damn desert, it's slowed me down. He looked at his watch. He had time to go through a charade at the garage and still catch the daily train to Cairo. He considered what he would do. He would have to go into the place, for Newman would watch. Then the soldiers would drive away. Wolff would have to make some inquiries about car parts or something, then take his leave and walk to the station.

With luck, Nasif and Newman might never compare notes on the subject of Alex Wolff.

The jeep drove through the busy, narrow streets. The familiar sights of an Egyptian town pleased Wolff: the gay cotton clothes, the women carrying bundles on their heads, the officious policemen, the sharp characters in sunglasses, the tiny shops spilling out into the rutted streets, the stalls, the battered cars and the overloaded asses. They stopped in front of a row of low mud-brick buildings. The road was half blocked by an ancient truck and the remains of a cannibalized Fiat. A small boy was working on a cylinder block with a wrench, sitting on the ground outside the entrance.

Newman said: "I'll have to leave you here, I'm afraid; duty calls."

Wolff shook his hand. "You've been very kind."

"I don't like to dump you this way," Newman continued. "You've had a bad time." He frowned, then his face cleared. "Tell you what—I'll leave Corporal Cox to look after you."

Wolff said: "It's kind, but really—"

Newman was not listening. "Get the man's bags, Cox, and look sharp. I want you to take care of him—and don't you leave anything to the wogs, understand?"

"Yes, sir!" said Cox.

Wolff groaned inwardly. Now there would be more delay while he got rid of the corporal. Captain Newman's kindness was becoming a nuisance—could that possibly be intentional?

Wolff and Cox got out, and the jeep pulled away. Wolff walked into Nasif's workshop, and Cox followed, carrying the cases.

Nasif was a smiling young man in a filthy galabiya, working on a car battery by the light of an oil lamp. He spoke to them in English. "You want to rent a beautiful automobile? My brother have Bentley—"

Wolff interrupted him in rapid Egyptian Arabic. "My car has broken down. They say you have a tow truck."

"Yes. We can leave right away. Where is the car?"

"On the desert road, forty or fifty miles out. It's a Ford. But we're not coming with you." He took out his wallet and gave Nasif an English pound note. "You'll find me at the Grand Hotel by the railway station when you return."

Nasif took the money with alacrity. "Very good! I leave immediately!"

Wolff nodded curtly and turned around. Walking out of the workshop with Cox in tow, he considered the implications of his short conversation with Nasif. The mechanic would go out into the desert with his tow truck and search the road for the car. Eventually he would return to the Grand Hotel to confess failure. He would learn that Wolff had left. He would consider he had been reasonably paid for his wasted day, but that would not stop him telling all and sundry the story of the disappearing Ford and its disappearing driver. The likelihood was that all this would get back to Captain Newman sooner or later. Newman might not know quite what to make of it all, but he would certainly feel that here was a mystery to be investigated.

Wolff's mood darkened as he realized that his plan of slipping unobserved into Egypt might have failed.

He would just have to make the best of it. He looked at his watch. He still had time to catch the train. He would be able to get rid of Cox in the lobby of the hotel, then get something to eat and drink while he was waiting, if he was quick.

Cox was a short, dark man with some kind of British regional accent which Wolff could not identify. He looked about Wolff's age, and as he was still a corporal he was probably not too bright. Following Wolff across the Midan el-Mahatta, he said: "You know this town, sir?"

"I've been here before," Wolff replied.

They entered the Grand. With twenty-six rooms it was the larger of the town's two hotels. Wolff turned to Cox. "Thank you, Corporal. I think you could get back to work now."

"No hurry, sir," Cox said cheerfully. "I'll carry your bags upstairs."

"I'm sure they have porters here—"

"Wouldn't trust 'em, sir, if I were you."

The situation was becoming more and more like a nightmare or a farce, in which well-intentioned people pushed him into increasingly senseless behavior in consequence of one small lie. He wondered again whether this was entirely accidental, and it crossed his mind with terrifying absurdity that perhaps they knew everything and were simply toying with him.

He pushed the thought aside and spoke to Cox with as much grace as he could muster. "Well, thank you."

He turned to the desk and asked for a room. He looked at his watch: he had fifteen minutes left. He filled in the form quickly, giving an invented address in Cairo—there was a chance Captain Newman would forget the true address on the identity papers, and Wolff did not want to leave a reminder.

A Nubian porter led them upstairs to the room. Wolff tipped him off at the door. Cox put the cases down on the bed.

Wolff took out his wallet: perhaps Cox expected a tip too. "Well, Corporal," he began, "you've been very helpful—"

"Let me unpack for you, sir," Cox said. "Captain said not to leave anything to the wogs."

"No, thank you," Wolff said firmly. "I want to lie down right now."

"You go ahead and lie down," Cox persisted generously. "It won't take me—"

"Don't open that!"

Cox was lifting the lid of the case. Wolff reached inside his jacket, thinking *Damn the man* and *Now I'm blown* and *I should have locked it* and *Can I do this quietly?* The little corporal stared at the neat stacks of new English pound notes which filled the small case. He said: "Jesus Christ, you're loaded!" It crossed Wolff's mind, even as he stepped forward, that Cox had never seen so much money in his life. Cox began to turn, saying: "What do you want with all that—" Wolff pulled the wicked curved Bedouin knife, and it glinted in his hand as his eyes met Cox's, and Cox flinched and opened his mouth to shout; and then the razor-sharp blade sliced deep into the soft flesh of his throat, and his shout of fear came as a bloody gurgle and he died; and Wolff felt nothing, only disappointment.

2

It was May, and the khamsin was blowing, a hot dusty wind from the south. Standing under the shower, William Vandam had the depressing thought that this would be the only time he would feel cool all day. He turned off the water and dried himself rapidly. His body was full of small aches. He had played cricket the day before, for the first time in years. General Staff Intelligence had got up a team to play the doctors from the field hospital—spies versus quacks, they had called it—and Vandam, fielding on the boundary, had been run ragged as the medics hit the Intelligence Department's bowling all over the park. Now he had to admit he was not in good condition. Gin had sapped his strength and cigarettes had shortened his wind, and he had too many worries to give the game the fierce concentration it merited.

He lit a cigarette, coughed and started to shave. He always smoked while he was shaving—it was the only way he knew to relieve the boredom of the inevitable daily task. Fifteen years ago he had sworn he would grow a beard as soon as he got out of the Army, but he was still in the Army.

He dressed in the everyday uniform: heavy sandals, socks, bush shirt and the khaki shorts with the flaps that could be let down and buttoned below the knee for protection against mosquitoes. Nobody ever used the flaps, and the younger officers usually cut them off, they looked so ridiculous.

There was an empty gin bottle on the floor beside the bed. Vandam looked at it, feeling disgusted with himself: it was the first time he had taken the damn bottle to bed with him. He picked it up, replaced the cap and threw the bottle into the wastebasket. Then he went downstairs.

Gaafar was in the kitchen, making tea. Vandam's servant was an elderly Copt with a bald head and a shuffling walk, and pretensions to be an English butler. That he would never be, but he had a little dignity and he was honest, and Vandam had not found those qualities to be common among Egyptian house servants.

Vandam said: "Is Billy up?"

"Yes, sir, he's coming down directly."

Vandam nodded. A small pan of water was bubbling on the stove. Vandam put an egg in to boil and set the timer. He cut two slices from an English-type loaf and made toast. He buttered the toast and cut it into fingers, then he took the egg out of the water and decapitated it.

Billy came into the kitchen and said: "Good morning, Dad."

Vandam smiled at his ten-year-old son. "Morning. Breakfast is ready."

The boy began to eat. Vandam sat opposite him with a cup of tea, watching. Billy often looked tired in the mornings recently. Once upon a time he had been infallibly daisy-fresh at breakfast. Was he sleeping badly? Or was his metabolism simply becoming more like an adult's? Perhaps it was just that he was staying awake late, reading detective stories under the sheet by the light of a flashlight.

People said Billy was like his father, but Vandam could not see the resemblance. However, he could see traces of Billy's mother: the gray eyes, the delicate skin and the faintly supercilious expression which came over his face when someone crossed him.

Vandam always prepared his son's breakfast. The servant was perfectly capable of looking after the boy, of course, and most of the time he did; but Vandam liked to keep this little ritual for himself. Often it was the only time he was with Billy all day. They did not talk much—Billy ate and Vandam smoked—but that did not matter: the important thing was that they were together for a while at the start of each day.

After breakfast Billy brushed his teeth while Gaafar got out Vandam's motorcycle. Billy came back wearing his school cap, and Vandam put on his uniform cap. As they did every day, they saluted each other. Billy said: "Right, sir—let's go and win the war."

Then they went out.

Major Vandam's office was at Gray Pillars, one of a group of
buildings surrounded by barbed-wire fencing which made up
GHQ Middle East. There was an incident report on his desk
when he arrived. He sat down, lit a cigarette and began to
read.

The report came from Assyut, three hundred miles south,
and at first Vandam could not see why it had been marked
for Intelligence. A patrol had picked up a hitchhiking European who had subsequently murdered a corporal with a
knife. The body had been discovered last night, almost as
soon as the corporal's absence was noted, but several hours
after the death. A man answering the hitchhiker's description
had bought a ticket to Cairo at the railway station, but by the
time the body was found the train had arrived in Cairo and
the killer had melted into the city.

There was no indication of motive.

The Egyptian police force and the British Military Police
would be investigating already in Assyut, and their colleagues
in Cairo would, like Vandam, be learning the details this
morning. What reason was there for Intelligence to get involved?

Vandam frowned and thought again. A European is picked
up in the desert. He says his car has broken down. He checks
into a hotel. He leaves a few minutes later and catches a
train. His car is not found. The body of a soldier is discovered that night in the hotel room.

Why?

Vandam got on the phone and called Assyut. It took the
army camp switchboard a while to locate Captain Newman,
but eventually they found him in the arsenal and got him to
a phone.

Vandam said: "This knife murder almost looks like a
blown cover."

"That occurred to me, sir," said Newman. He sounded a
young man. "That's why I marked the report for Intelligence."

"Good thinking. Tell me, what was your impression of the
man?"

"He was a big chap—"

"I've got your description here—six foot, twelve stone, dark hair and eyes—but that doesn't tell me what he was *like*."

"I understand," Newman said. "Well, to be candid, at first I wasn't in the least suspicious of him. He looked all in, which fitted with his story of having broken down on the desert road, but apart from that he seemed an upright citizen: a white man, decently dressed, quite well spoken with an accent he said was Dutch, or rather Afrikaans. His papers were perfect—I'm still quite sure they were genuine."

"But . . . ?"

"He told me he was checking on his business interests in Upper Egypt."

"Plausible enough."

"Yes, but he didn't strike me as the kind of man to spend his life investing in a few shops and small factories and cotton farms. He was much more the assured cosmopolitan type: if he had money to invest it would probably be with a London stockbroker or a Swiss bank. He just wasn't a small-timer . . . It's very vague, sir, but do you see what I mean?"

"Indeed." Newman sounded a bright chap, Vandam thought. What was he doing stuck out in Assyut?

Newman went on: "And then it occurred to me that he had, as it were, just appeared in the desert, and I didn't really know where he might have come from . . . so I told poor old Cox to stay with him, on the pretense of helping him, to make sure he didn't do a bunk before we had a chance to check his story. I should have arrested the man, of course, but quite honestly, sir, at the time I had only the most slender suspicion—"

"I don't think anyone's blaming you, Captain," said Vandam. "You did well to remember the name and address from the papers. Alex Wolff, Villa les Oliviers, Garden City, right?"

"Yes, sir."

"All right, keep me in touch with any developments at your end, will you?"

"Yes, sir."

Vandam hung up. Newman's suspicions chimed with his own instincts about the killing. He decided to speak to his immediate superior. He left his office, carrying the incident report.

General Staff Intelligence was run by a brigadier with the title of Director of Military Intelligence. The DMI had two deputies: DDMI(O)—for Operational—and DDMI(I)—for Intelligence. The deputies were colonels. Vandam's boss, Lieutenant Colonel Bogge, came under the DDMI(I). Bogge was responsible for personnel security, and most of his time was spent administering the censorship apparatus. Vandam's concern was security leaks by means other than letters. He and his men had several hundred agents in Cairo and Alexandria; in most clubs and bars there was a waiter who was on his payroll, he had an informant among the domestic staffs of the more important Arab politicians, King Farouk's valet worked for Vandam, and so did Cairo's wealthiest thief. He was interested in who was talking too much, and who was listening; and among the listeners, Arab nationalists were his main target. However, it seemed possible that the mystery man from Assyut might be a different kind of threat.

Vandam's wartime career had so far been distinguished by one spectacular success and one great failure. The failure took place in Turkey. Rashid Ali had escaped there from Iraq. The Germans wanted to get him out and use him for propaganda; the British wanted him kept out of the limelight; and the Turks, jealous of their neutrality, wanted to offend nobody. Vandam's job had been to make sure Ali stayed in Istanbul, but Ali had switched clothes with a German agent and slipped out of the country under Vandam's nose. A few days later he was making propaganda speeches to the Middle East on Nazi radio. Vandam had somewhat redeemed himself in Cairo. London had told him they had reason to believe there was a major security leak there, and after three months of painstaking investigation Vandam had discovered that a senior American diplomat was reporting to Washington in an insecure code. The code had been changed, the leak had been stopped up and Vandam had been promoted to major.

Had he been a civilian, or even a peacetime soldier, he would have been proud of his triumph and reconciled to his defeat, and he would have said: "You win some, you lose some." But in war an officer's mistakes killed people. In the aftermath of the Rashid Ali affair an agent had been murdered, a woman, and Vandam was not able to forgive himself for that.

He knocked on Lieutenant Colonel Bogge's door and walked in. Reggie Bogge was a short, square man in his fifties, with an immaculate uniform and brilliantined black hair. He had a nervous, throat-clearing cough which he used when he did not know quite what to say, which was often. He sat behind a huge curved desk—bigger than the DMIs—going through his in tray. Always willing to talk rather than work, he motioned Vandam to a chair. He picked up a bright-red cricket ball and began to toss it from hand to hand. "You played a good game yesterday," he said.

"You didn't do badly yourself," Vandam said. It was true: Bogge had been the only decent bowler on the Intelligence team, and his slow googlies had taken four wickets for forty-two runs. "But are we winning the war?"

"More bloody bad news, I'm afraid." The morning briefing had not yet taken place, but Bogge always heard the news by word of mouth beforehand. "We expected Rommel to attack the Gazala Line head on. Should have known better—fellow never fights fair and square. He went around our southern flank, took the Seventh Armored's headquarters, and captured General Messervy."

It was a depressingly familiar story, and Vandam suddenly felt weary. "What a shambles," he said.

"Fortunately he failed to get through to the coast, so the divisions on the Gazala Line didn't get isolated. Still . . ."

"Still, when are we going to *stop* him?"

"He won't get much farther." It was an idiotic remark: Bogge simply did not want to get involved in criticism of generals. "What have you got there?"

Vandam gave him the incident report. "I propose to follow this one through myself."

Bogge read the paper and looked up, his face blank. "I don't see the point."

"It looks like a blown cover."

"Uh?"

"There's no motive for the murder, so we have to speculate," Vandam explained. "Here's one possibility: the hitch-hiker was not what he said he was, and the corporal discovered that fact, and so the hitchhiker killed the corporal."

"Not what he said he was—you mean he was a spy?" Bogge laughed. "How d'you suppose he got to Assyut—by parachute? Or did he walk?"

That was the trouble with explaining things to Bogge, thought Vandam: he had to ridicule the idea, as an excuse for not thinking of it himself. "It's not impossible for a small plane to sneak through. It's not impossible to cross the desert, either."

Bogge sailed the report through the air across the vast expanse of his desk. "Not very likely, in my view," he said. "Don't waste any time on that one."

"Very good, sir." Vandam picked up the report from the floor, suppressing the familiar frustrated anger. Conversations with Bogge always turned into points-scoring contests, and the smart thing to do was not to play. "I'll ask the police to keep us informed of their progress—copies of memos, and so on, just for the file."

"Yes." Bogge never objected to making people send him copies for the file: it enabled him to poke his finger into things without taking any responsibility. "Listen, how about arranging some cricket practice? I noticed they had nets and a catching boat there yesterday. I'd like to lick our team into shape and get some more matches going."

"Good idea."

"See if you can organize something, will you?"

"Yes, sir." Vandam went out.

On the way back to his own office, he wondered what was so wrong with the administration of the British Army that it could promote to lieutenant colonel a man as empty-headed as Reggie Bogge. Vandam's father, who had been a corporal in the first war, had been fond of saying that British soldiers were "lions led by donkeys." Sometimes Vandam thought it was still true. But Bogge was not merely dull. Sometimes he made bad decisions because he was not clever enough to make good decisions; but mostly, it seemed to Vandam, Bogge made bad decisions because he was playing some other game, making himself look good or trying to be superior or something, Vandam did not know what.

A woman in a white hospital coat saluted him and he re

turned the salute absent-mindedly. The woman said: "Major Vandam, isn't it?"

He stopped and looked at her. She had been a spectator at the cricket match, and now he remembered her name. "Dr. Abuthnot," he said. "Good morning." She was a tall, cool woman of about his age. He recalled that she was a surgeon—highly unusual for a woman, even in wartime—and that she held the rank of captain.

She said: "You worked hard yesterday."

Vandam smiled. "And I'm suffering for it today. I enjoyed myself, though."

"So did I." She had a low, precise voice and a great deal of confidence. "Shall we see you on Friday?"

"Where?"

"The reception at the Union."

"Ah." The Anglo-Egyptian Union, a club for bored Europeans, made occasional attempts to justify its name by holding a reception for Egyptian guests. "I'd like that. What time?"

"Five o'clock, for tea."

Vandam was professionally interested: it was an occasion at which Egyptians might pick up service gossip, and service gossip sometimes included information useful to the enemy. "I'll come," he said.

"Splendid. I'll see you there." She turned away.

"I look forward to it," Vandam said to her back. He watched her walk away, wondering what she wore under the hospital coat. She was trim, elegant and self-possessed: she reminded him of his wife.

He entered his office. He had no intention of organizing a cricket practice, and he had no intention of forgetting about the Assyut murder. Bogge could go to hell. Vandam would go to work.

First he spoke again to Captain Newman, and told him to make sure the description of Alex Wolff got the widest possible circulation.

He called the Egyptian police and confirmed that they would be checking the hotels and flophouses of Cairo today.

He contacted Field Security, a unit of the prewar Canal Defense Force, and asked them to step up their spot checks on identity papers for a few days.

He told the British paymaster general to keep a special watch for forged currency.

He advised the wireless listening service to be alert for a new, local transmitter; and thought briefly how useful it would be if the boffins ever cracked the problem of locating a radio by monitoring its broadcasts.

Finally he detailed a sergeant on his staff to visit every radio shop in Lower Egypt—there were not many—and ask them to report any sales of parts and equipment which might be used to make or repair a transmitter.

Then he went to the Villa les Oliviers.

The house got its name from a small public garden across the street where a grove of olive trees was now in bloom, shedding white petals like dust on to the dry, brown grass.

The house had a high wall broken by a heavy, carved wooden gate. Using the ornamentation for footholds, Vandam climbed over the gate and dropped on the other side to find himself in a large courtyard. Around him the white-washed walls were smeared and grubby, their windows blinded by closed, peeling shutters. He walked to the center of the courtyard and looked at the stone fountain. A bright-green lizard darted across the dry bowl.

The place had not been lived in for at least a year.

Vandam opened a shutter, broke a pane of glass, reached through to unfasten the window, and climbed over the sill into the house.

It did not look like the home of a European, he thought as he walked through the dark cool rooms. There were no hunting prints on the walls, no neat rows of bright-jacketed novels by Agatha Christie and Dennis Wheatley, no three-piece suite imported from Maples or Harrods. Instead the place was furnished with large cushions and low tables, handwoven rugs and hanging tapestries.

Upstairs he found a locked door. It took him three or four minutes to kick it open. Behind it there was a study.

The room was clean and tidy, with a few pieces of rather luxurious furniture: a wide, low divan covered in velvet, a hand-carved coffee table, three matching antique lamps, a bear-skin rug, a beautifully inlaid desk and a leather chair.

On the desk were a telephone, a clean white blotter, an

ivory-handled pen and a dry inkwell. In the desk drawer
Vandam found company reports from Switzerland, Germany
and the United States. A delicate beaten-copper coffee service
gathered dust on the little table. On a shelf behind the desk
were books in several languages: nineteenth-century French
novels, the Shorter Oxford Dictionary, a volume of what appeared to Vandam to be Arabic poetry, with erotic illustra-
tions, and the Bible in German.

There were no personal documents.

There were no letters.

There was not a single photograph in the house.

Vandam sat in the soft leather chair behind the desk and
looked around the room. It was a masculine room, the home
of a cosmopolitan intellectual, a man who was on the one
hand careful, precise and tidy and on the other hand sensitive
and sensual.

Vandam was intrigued.

A European name, a totally Arabic house. A pamphlet
about investing in business machines, a book of Arab verse.
An antique coffee jug and a modern telephone. A wealth of
information about a character, but not a single clue which
might help find the man.

The room had been carefully cleaned out.

There should have been bank statements, bills from tradesmen, a birth certificate and a will, letters from a lover and
photographs of parents or children. The man had collected all
those things and taken them away, leaving no trace of his
identity, as if he knew that one day someone would come
looking for him.

Vandam said aloud: "Alex Wolff, who are you?"

He got up from the chair and left the study. He walked
through the house and across the hot, dusty courtyard. He
climbed back over the gate and dropped into the street.
Across the road an Arab in a green-striped galabiya sat
cross-legged on the ground in the shade of the olive trees,
watching Vandam incuriously. Vandam felt no impulse to explain that he had broken into the house on official business:
the uniform of a British officer was authority enough for just
about anything in this town. He thought of the other sources
from which he could seek information about the owner of
this house: municipal records, such as they were; local trades-

men who might have delivered there when the place was occupied; even the neighbors. He would put two of his men on
to it, and tell Bogge some story to cover up. He climbed onto
his motorcycle and kicked it into life. The engine roared enthusiastically, and Vandam drove away.

3

Full of anger and despair Wolff sat outside his home and watched the British officer drive away.

He remembered the house as it had been when he was a boy, loud with talk and laughter and life. There by the great carved gate there had always been a guard, a black-skinned giant from the south, sitting on the ground, impervious to the heat. Each morning a holy man, old and almost blind, would recite a chapter from the Koran in the courtyard. In the cool of the arcade on three sides the men of the family would sit on low divans and smoke their hubble-bubbles while servant boys brought coffee in long-necked jugs. Another black guard stood at the door to the harem, behind which the women grew bored and fat. The days were long and warm, the family was rich and the children were indulged.

The British officer, with his shorts and his motorcycle, his arrogant face and his prying eyes hidden in the shadow of the peaked uniform cap, had broken in and violated Wolff's childhood. Wolff wished he could have seen the man's face, for he would like to kill him one day.

He had thought of this place all through his journey. In Berlin and Tripoli and El Agela, in the pain and exhaustion of the desert crossing, in the fear and haste of his flight from Assyut, the villa had represented a safe haven, a place to rest and get clean and whole again at the end of the voyage. He had looked forward to lying in the bath and sipping coffee in the courtyard and bringing women home to the great bed.

Now he would have to go away and stay away.

He had remained outside all morning, alternately walking the street and sitting under the olive trees, just in case Captain Newman should have remembered the address and sent somebody to search the house; and he had bought a galabiya in the souk beforehand, knowing that if someone did come they would be looking for a European, not an Arab.

It had been a mistake to show genuine papers. He could see that with hindsight. The trouble was, he mistrusted Abwehr forgeries. Meeting and working with other spies he had heard horror stories about crass and obvious errors in the documents made by German Intelligence: botched printing, inferior-quality paper, even misspellings of common English words. In the spy school where he had been sent for his wireless cipher course the current rumor had been that every policeman in England knew that a certain series of numbers on a ration card identified the holder as a German spy.

Wolff had weighed the alternatives and picked what seemed the least risky. He had been wrong, and now he had no place to go.

He stood, picked up his cases and began to walk.

He thought of his family. His mother and his stepfather were dead, but he had three stepbrothers and a stepsister in Cairo. It would be hard for them to hide him. They would be questioned as soon as the British realized the identity of the owner of the villa, which might be today; and while they might tell lies for his sake, their servants would surely talk. Furthermore, he could not really trust them, for when his stepfather had died, Alex as the oldest son had got the house as well as a share of the inheritance, although he was European and an adopted, rather than natural, son. There had been some bitterness, and meetings with lawyers; Alex had stood firm and the others had never really forgiven him.

He considered checking in to Shepheard's Hotel. Unfortunately the police were sure to think of that, too: Shepheard's would by now have the description of the Assyut murderer. The other major hotels would have it soon. That left the pensions. Whether they were warned depended on how thorough the police wanted to be. Since the British were involved, the police might feel obliged to be meticulous. Still, the managers of small guest houses were often too busy to pay a lot of attention to nosy policemen.

He left the Garden City and headed downtown. The streets were even more busy and noisy than when he had left Cairo. There were countless uniforms—not just British but Australian, New Zealand, Polish, Yugoslav, Palestinian, Indian and Greek. The slim, pert Egyptian girls in their cotton frocks and heavy jewelry competed successfully with their red-faced, dispirited European counterparts. Among the older women it seemed to Wolff that fewer wore the traditional black robe and veil. The men still greeted one another in the same exuberant fashion, swinging their right arms outward before bringing their hands together with a loud clap, shaking hands for at least a minute or two while grasping the shoulder of the other with the left hand and talking excitedly. The beggars and peddlers were out in force, taking advantage of the influx of naïve Europeans. In his galabiya Wolff was immune, but the foreigners were besieged by cripples, women with fly-encrusted babies, shoeshine boys and men selling everything from secondhand razor blades to giant fountain pens guaranteed to hold six months' supply of ink.

The traffic was worse. The slow, verminous trams were more crowded than ever, with passengers clinging precariously to the outside from a perch on the running board, crammed into the cab with the driver and sitting cross-legged on the roof. The buses and taxis were no better: there seemed to be a shortage of vehicle parts, for so many of the cars had broken windows, flat tires and ailing engines, and were lacking headlights or windshield wipers. Wolff saw two taxis—an elderly Morris and an even older Packard—which had finally stopped running and were now being drawn by donkeys. The only decent cars were the monstrous American limousines of the wealthy pashas and the occasional prewar English Austin. Mixing with the motor vehicles in deadly competition were the horse-drawn gharries, the mule carts of the peasants, and the livestock—camels, sheep and goats— which were banned from the city center by the most unenforceable law on the Egyptian statute book.

And the noise—Wolff had forgotten the noise.

The trams rang their bells continuously. In traffic jams all the cars hooted all the time, and when there was nothing to hoot at they hooted on general principles. Not to be outdone, the drivers of carts and camels yelled at the tops of their voices. Many shops and all cafés blared Arab music from cheap radios turned to full volume. Street vendors called continually and pedestrians told them to go away. Dogs barked and circling kites screamed overhead. From time to time it would all be swamped by the roar of an airplane.

This is my town, Wolff thought; they can't catch me here.

There were a dozen or so well-known pensions catering for tourists of different nationalities: Swiss, Austrian, German, Danish and French. He thought of them and rejected them as too obvious. Finally he remembered a cheap lodging house run by nuns at Bulaq, the port district. It catered mainly for the sailors who came down the Nile in steam tugs and feluccas laden with cotton, coal, paper and stone. Wolff could be sure he would not get robbed, infected or murdered, and nobody would think to look for him there.

As he headed out of the hotel district the streets became a little less crowded, but not much. He could not see the river itself, but occasionally he glimpsed, through the huddled buildings, the high triangular sail of a felucca.

The hostel was a large, decaying building which had once been the villa of some pasha. There was now a bronze crucifix over the arch of the entrance. A black-robed nun was watering a tiny bed of flowers in front of the building. Through the arch Wolff saw a cool quiet hall. He had walked several miles today, with his heavy cases: he looked forward to a rest.

Two Egyptian policemen came out of the hostel.

Wolff took in the wide leather belts, the inevitable sunglasses and the military haircuts in a swift glance, and his heart sank. He turned his back on the men and spoke in French to the nun in the garden. "Good day, Sister."

She unbent from her watering and smiled at him. "Good day." She was shockingly young. "Do you want lodgings?"

"No lodgings. Just your blessing."

The two policemen approached, and Wolff tensed, preparing his answers in case they should question him, considering which direction he should take if he had to run away; then they went past, arguing about a horse race.

"God bless you," said the nun.

Wolff thanked her and walked on. It was worse than he had imagined. The police must be checking *everywhere*. Wolff's feet were sore now, and his arms ached from carrying the luggage. He was disappointed, and also a little indignant, for everything in this town was notoriously haphazard, yet it seemed they were mounting an efficient operation just for him. He doubled back, heading for the city center again. He was beginning to feel as he had in the desert, as if he had been walking forever without getting anywhere.

In the distance he saw a familiar tall figure: Hussein Fahmy, an old school friend. Wolff was momentarily paralyzed. Hussein would surely take him in, and perhaps he could be trusted; but he had a wife, and three children, and how would one explain to them that Uncle Achmed was coming to stay, but it was a secret, they must not mention his name to their friends . . . How, indeed, would Wolff explain it all to Hussein himself? Hussein looked in Wolff's direction, and Wolff turned quickly and crossed the road, darting behind a tram. Once on the opposite pavement he went quickly down an alley without looking back. No, he could not seek shelter with old school friends.

He emerged from the alley into another street, and realized he was close to the German School. He wondered if it were still open: a lot of German nationals in Cairo had been interned. He walked toward it, then saw, outside the building, a Field Security patrol checking papers. He turned about quickly and headed back the way he had come.

He had to get off the streets.

He felt like a rat in a maze—every way he turned he was blocked. He saw a taxi, a big old Ford with steam hissing out from under its hood. He hailed it and jumped in. He gave the driver an address and the car jerked away in third gear, apparently the only gear that worked. On the way they stopped twice to top up the boiling radiator, and Wolff skulked in the back seat, trying to hide his face.

The taxi took him to Coptic Cairo, the ancient Christian ghetto.

He paid the driver and went down the steps to the entrance. He gave a few piasters to the old woman who held the great wooden key, and she let him in.

It was an island of darkness and quiet in the stormy sea of Cairo. Wolff walked its narrow passages, hearing faintly the low chanting from the ancient churches. He passed the school and the synagogue and the cellar where Mary was supposed to have brought the baby Jesus. Finally he went into the smallest of the five churches.

The service was about to begin. Wolff put down his precious cases beside a pew. He bowed to the pictures of saints on the wall, then approached the altar, knelt and kissed the hand of the priest. He returned to the pew and sat down.

The choir began to chant a passage of scripture in Arabic. Wolff settled into his seat. He would be safe here until darkness fell. Then he would try his last shot.

The Cha-Cha was a large open-air nightclub in a garden beside the river. It was packed, as usual. Wolff waited in the queue of British officers and their girls while the safragis set up extra tables on trestles in every spare inch of space. On the stage a comic was saying: "Wait till Rommel gets to Shepheard's—that will hold him up."

Wolff finally got a table and a bottle of champagne. The evening was warm and the stage lights made it worse. The audience was rowdy—they were thirsty, and only champagne was served, so they quickly got drunk. They began to shout for the star of the show, Sonja el-Aram.

First they had to listen to an overweight Greek woman sing "I'll See You in My Dreams" and "I Ain't Got Nobody" (which made them laugh). Then Sonja was announced. However, she did not appear for a while. The audience became noisier and more impatient as the minutes ticked by. At last, when they seemed to be on the verge of rioting, there was a roll of drums, the stage lights went off and silence descended.

When the spotlight came on Sonja stood still in the center of the stage with her arms stretched skyward. She wore diaphanous trousers and a sequined halter, and her body was powdered white. The music began—drums and a pipe—and she started to move.

Wolff sipped champagne and watched, smiling. She was still the best.

She jerked her hips slowly, stamping one foot and then the other. Her arms began to tremble, then her shoulders moved and her breasts shook; and then her famous belly rolled hypnotically. The rhythm quickened. She closed her eyes. Each part of her body seemed to move independently of the rest. Wolff felt, as he always did, as every man in the audience did, that he was alone with her, that her display was just for him, and that this was not an act, not a piece of show-

business wizardry, but that her sensual writhings were compulsive, she did it because she had to, she was driven to a
sexual frenzy by her own voluptuous body. The audience was
tense, silent, perspiring, mesmerized. She went faster and
faster, seeming to be transported. The music climaxed with a
bang. In the instant of silence that followed Sonja uttered a
short, sharp cry; then she fell backward, her legs folded
beneath her, her knees apart, until her head touched the
boards of the stage. She held the position for a moment, then
the lights went out. The audience rose to their feet with a
roar of applause.

The lights came up, and she was gone.

Sonja never took encores.

Wolff got out of his seat. He gave a waiter a pound—three
months' wages for most Egyptians—to lead him backstage.
The waiter showed him the door to Sonja's dressing room,
then went away.

Wolff knocked on the door.

"Who is it?"

Wolff walked in.

She was sitting on a stool, wearing a silk robe, taking off
her makeup. She saw him in the mirror and spun around to
face him.

Wolff said: "Hello, Sonja."

She stared at him. After a long moment she said: "You
bastard."

She had not changed.

She was a handsome woman. She had glossy black hair,
long and thick; large, slightly protruding brown eyes with
lush eyelashes; high cheekbones which saved her face from
roundness and gave it shape; an arched nose, gracefully arrogant; and a full mouth with even white teeth. Her body was
all smooth curves, but because she was a couple of inches
taller than average she did not look plump.

Her eyes flashed with anger. "What are you doing here?
Where did you go? What happened to your face?"

Wolff put down his cases and sat on the divan. He looked
up at her. She stood with her hands on her hips, her chin
thrust forward, her breasts outlined in green silk. "You're
beautiful," he said.

"Get out of here."

He studied her carefully. He knew her too well to like or dislike her: she was part of his past, like an old friend who remains a friend, despite his faults, just because he has always been there. Wolff wondered what had happened to Sonja in the years since he had left Cairo. Had she got married, bought a house, fallen in love, changed her manager, had a baby? He had given a lot of thought, that afternoon in the cool, dim church, to how he should approach her; but he had reached no conclusions, for he was not sure how she would be with him. He was still not sure. She appeared angry and scornful, but did she mean it? Should he be charming and full of fun, or aggressive and bullying, or helpless and pleading?

"I need help," he said levelly.

Her face did not change.

"The British are after me," he went on. "They're watching my house, and all the hotels have my description. I've nowhere to sleep. I want to move in with you."

"Go to hell," she said.

"Let me tell you why I walked out on you."

"After two years no excuse is good enough."

"Give me a minute to explain. For the sake of . . . all that."

"I owe you nothing." She glared at him a moment longer, then she opened the door. He thought she was going to throw him out. He watched her face as she looked back at him, holding the door. Then she put her head outside and yelled: "Somebody get me a drink!"

Wolff relaxed a little.

Sonja came back inside and closed the door. "A minute," she said to him.

"Are you going to stand over me like a prison guard? I'm not dangerous." He smiled.

"Oh yes you are," she said, but she went back to her stool and resumed working on her face.

He hesitated. The other problem he had mulled over during the long afternoon in the Coptic church had been how to explain why he had left her without saying good-bye and never contacted her since. Nothing less than the truth sounded convincing. Reluctant as he was to share his secret, he had to tell her, for he was desperate and she was his only hope.

He said: "Do you remember I went to Beirut in nineteen thirty-eight?"

"No."

"I brought back a jade bracelet for you."

Her eyes met his in the mirror. "I don't have it anymore."

He knew she was lying. He went on: "I went there to see a German army officer called Heinz. He asked me to work for Germany in the coming war. I agreed."

She turned from her mirror and faced him, and now he saw in her eyes something like hope.

"They told me to come back to Cairo and wait until I heard from them. Two years ago I heard. They wanted me to go to Berlin. I went. I did a training course, then I worked in the Balkans and the Levant. I went back to Berlin in February for briefing on a new assignment. They sent me here—"

"What are you telling me?" she said incredulously. "You're a *spy?*"

"Yes."

"I don't believe you."

"Look." He picked up a suitcase and opened it. "This is a radio, for sending messages to Rommel." He closed it again and opened the other. "This is my financing."

She stared at the neat stacks of notes. "My God!" she said. "It's a *fortune.*"

There was a knock at the door. Wolff closed the case. A waiter came in with a bottle of champagne in a bucket of ice. Seeing Wolff, he said: "Shall I bring another glass?"

"No," Sonja said impatiently. "Go away."

The waiter left. Wolff opened the wine, filled the glass, gave it to Sonja, then took a long drink from the bottle.

"Listen," he said. "Our army is winning in the desert. We can help them. They need to know about the British strength—numbers of men, which divisions, names of commanders, quality of weapons and equipment and—if possible—battle plans. We're here, in Cairo; we can find these things out. Then, when the Germans take over, we will be heroes."

"We?"

"You can help me. And the first thing you can do is give

me a place to live. You hate the British, don't you? You want
to see them thrown out?"

"I would do it for anyone but you." She finished her champagne and refilled her glass.

Wolff took the glass from her hand and drank. "Sonja. If I
had sent you a postcard from Berlin the British would have
thrown you in jail. You must not be angry, now that you
know the reasons why." He lowered his voice. "We can bring
those old times back. We'll have good food and the best
champagne, new clothes and beautiful parties and an American car. We'll go to Berlin, you've always wanted to dance in
Berlin, you'll be a star there. Germany is a new *kind* of nation—we're going to rule the world, and you can be a
princess. We—" He paused. None of this was getting through
to her. It was time to play his last card. "How is Fawzi?"

Sonja lowered her eyes. "She left, the bitch."

Wolff set down the glass, then he put both hands to Sonja's
neck. She looked up at him, unmoving. With his thumbs under her chin he forced her to stand. "I'll find another Fawzi
for us," he said softly. He saw that her eyes were suddenly
moist. His hands moved over the silk robe, descending her
body, stroking her flanks. "I'm the only one who understands
what you need." He lowered his mouth to hers, took her lip
between his teeth, and bit until he tasted blood.

Sonja closed her eyes. "I hate you," she moaned.

In the cool of the evening Wolff walked along the towpath
beside the Nile toward the houseboat. The sores had gone
from his face and his bowels were back to normal. He wore a
new white suit, and he carried two bags full of his favorite
groceries.

The island suburb of Zamalek was quiet and peaceful. The
raucous noise of central Cairo could be heard only faintly
across a wide stretch of water. The calm, muddy river lapped
gently against the houseboats lined along the bank. The boats,
all shapes and sizes, gaily painted and luxuriously fitted out,
looked pretty in the late sunshine.

Sonja's was smaller and more richly furnished than most.
A plank led from the path to the top deck, which was open
to the breeze but shaded from the sun by a green-and-white
striped canopy. Wolff boarded the boat and went down the

ladder to the interior. It was crowded with furniture: chairs and divans and tables and cabinets full of knickknacks. There was a tiny kitchen in the prow. Floor-to-ceiling curtains of maroon velvet divided the space in two, closing off the bedroom. Beyond the bedroom, in the stern, was a bathroom.

Sonja was sitting on a cushion painting her toenails. It was extraordinary how slovenly she could look, Wolff thought. She wore a grubby cotton dress, her face looked drawn and her hair was uncombed. In half an hour, when she left for the Cha-Cha Club, she would look like a dream.

Wolff put his bags on a table and began to take things out. "French champagne . . . English marmalade . . . German sausage . . . quail's eggs . . . Scotch salmon . . ."

Sonja looked up, astonished. "Nobody can find things like that—there's a war on."

Wolff smiled. "There's a little Greek grocer in Qulali who remembers a good customer."

"Is he safe?"

"He doesn't know where I'm living—and besides, his shop is the only place in North Africa where you can get caviar."

She came across and dipped into a bag. "Caviar!" She took the lid off the jar and began to eat with her fingers. "I haven't had caviar since—"

"Since I went away," Wolff finished. He put a bottle of champagne in the icebox. "If you wait a few minutes you can have cold champagne with it."

"I can't wait."

"You never can." He took an English-language newspaper out of one of the bags and began to look through it. It was a rotten paper, full of press releases, its war news censored more heavily than the BBC broadcasts which everyone listened to, its local reporting even worse—it was illegal to print speeches by the official Egyptian opposition politicians. "Still nothing about me in here," Wolff said. He had told Sonja of the events in Assyut.

"They're always late with the news," she said through a mouthful of caviar.

"It's not that. If they report the murder they need to say what the motive was—or, if they don't, people will guess. The British don't want people to suspect that the Germans have spies in Egypt. It looks bad."

She went into the bedroom to change. She called through the curtain: "Does that mean they've stopped looking for you?" ·

"No. I saw Abdullah in the souk. He says the Egyptian police aren't really interested, but there's a Major Vandam who's keeping the pressure on." Wolff put down the newspaper, frowning. He would have liked to know whether Vandam was the officer who had broken into the Villa les Oliviers. He wished he had been able to look more closely at that man, but from across the street the officer's face, shaded by the peaked cap, had been a dark blank.

Sonja said: "How does Abdullah know?"

"I don't know." Wolff shrugged. "He's a thief, he hears things." He went to the icebox and took out the bottle. It was not really cold enough, but he was thirsty. He poured two glasses. Sonja came out, dressed: as he had anticipated, she was transformed, her hair perfect, her face lightly but cleverly made up, wearing a sheer cherry-red dress and matching shoes.

A couple of minutes later there were footsteps on the gangplank and a knock at the hatch. Sonja's taxi had arrived. She drained her glass and left. They did not say hello and goodbye to one another.

Wolff went to the cupboard where he kept the radio. He took out the English novel and the sheet of paper bearing the key to the code. He studied the key. Today was May 28. He had to add 42—the year—to 28 to arrive at the page number in the novel which he must use to encode his message. May was the fifth month, so every fifth letter on the page would be discounted.

He decided to send HAVE ARRIVED. CHECKING IN. ACKNOWLEDGE. Beginning at the top of page 70 of the book, he looked along the line of print for the letter H. It was the tenth character, discounting every fifth letter. In his code it would therefore be represented by the tenth letter of the alphabet, J. Next he needed an A. In the book, the third letter after the H was an A. The A of HAVE would therefore be represented by the third letter of the alphabet, C. There were special ways of dealing with rare letters, like X.

This type of code was a variation on the one-time pad, the only kind of code which was unbreakable in theory and in practice. To decode the message a listener had to have both the book and the key.

When he had encoded his message he looked at his watch. He was to transmit at midnight. He had a couple of hours before he needed to warm up the radio. He poured another glass of champagne and decided to finish the caviar. He found a spoon and picked up the pot. It was empty. Sonja had eaten it all.

The runway was a strip of desert hastily cleared of camel thorn and large rocks. Rommel looked down as the ground came up to meet him. The Storch, a light aircraft used by German commanders for short trips around the battlefield, came down like a fly, its wheels on the ends of long, spindly front legs. The plane stopped and Rommel jumped out.

The heat hit him first, then the dust. It had been relatively cool, up in the sky; now he felt as if he had stepped into a furnace. He began to perspire immediately. As soon as he breathed in, a thin layer of sand coated his lips and the end of his tongue. A fly settled on his big nose, and he brushed it away.

Von Mellenthin, Rommel's Ic—intelligence officer—ran toward him across the sand, his high boots kicking up dusty clouds. He looked agitated. "Kesselring's here," he said.

"*Auch, das noch.*" said Rommel. "That's all I need."

Kesselring, the smiling field marshal, represented everything Rommel disliked in the German armed forces. He was a General Staff officer, and Rommel hated the General Staff; he was a founder of the Luftwaffe, which had let Rommel down so often in the desert war; and he was—worst of all—a snob. One of his acid comments had gotten back to Rommel. Complaining that Rommel was rude to his subordinate officers, Kesselring had said: "It might be worth speaking to him about it, were it not that he's a Wuerttemberger." Wuerttemberg was the provincial state where Rommel was born, and the remark epitomized the prejudice Rommel had been fighting all his career.

He stumped across the sand toward the command vehicle, with von Mellenthin in tow. "General Cruewell has been captured," von Mellenthin said. "I had to ask Kesselring to take over. He's spent the afternoon trying to find out where you were."

"Worse and worse," Rommel said sourly.

They entered the back of the command vehicle, a huge truck. The shade was welcome. Kesselring was bent over a map, brushing away flies with his left hand while tracing a line with his right. He looked up and smiled. "My dear Rommel, thank heaven you're back," he said silkily.

Rommel took off his cap. "I've been fighting a battle," he grunted.

"So I gather. What happened?"

Rommel pointed to the map. "This is the Gazala Line." It was a string of fortified "boxes" linked by minefields which ran from the coast at Gazala due south into the desert for fifty miles. "We made a dogleg around the southern end of the line and hit them from behind."

"Good idea. What went wrong?"

"We ran out of gasoline and ammunition." Rommel sat down heavily, suddenly feeling very tired. "Again," he added. Kesselring, as commander in chief (South), was responsible for Rommel's supplies, but the field marshal seemed not to notice the implied criticism.

An orderly came in with mugs of tea on a tray. Rommel sipped his. There was sand in it.

Kesselring spoke in a conversational tone. "I've had the unusual experience, this afternoon, of taking the role of one of your subordinate commanders."

Rommel grunted. There was some piece of sarcasm coming, he could tell. He did not want to fence with Kesselring now, he wanted to think about the battle.

Kesselring went on: "I found it enormously difficult, with my hands tied by subordination to a headquarters that issued no orders and could not be reached."

"I was at the heart of the battle, giving my orders on the spot."

"Still, you might have stayed in touch."

"That's the way the British fight," Rommel snapped. "The generals are miles behind the lines, staying in touch. But I'm winning. If I'd had my supplies, I'd be in Cairo now."

"You're not going to Cairo," Kesselring said sharply. "You're going to Tobruk. There you'll stay until I've taken Malta. Such are the Fuehrer's orders."

"Of course." Rommel was not going to reopen that argument; not yet. Tobruk was the immediate objective. Once that fortified port was taken, the convoys from Europe—inadequate though they were—could come directly to the front line, cutting out the long journey across the desert which used so much gasoline. "And to reach Tobruk we have to break the Gazala Line."

"What's your next step?"

"I'm going to fall back and regroup." Rommel saw Kesselring raise his eyebrows: the field marshal knew how Rommel hated to retreat.

"And what will the enemy do?" Kesselring directed the question to von Mellenthin, who as Ic was responsible for detailed assessment of the enemy position.

"They will chase us, but not immediately," said von Mellenthin. "They are always slow to press an advantage, fortunately. But sooner or later they will try a breakout."

Rommel said: "The question is, when and where?"

"Indeed," von Mellenthin agreed. He seemed to hesitate, then said, "There is a little item in today's summaries which will interest you. The spy checked in."

"The spy?" Rommel frowned. "Oh, him!" Now he remembered. He had flown to the Oasis of Gialo, deep in the Libyan desert, to brief the man finally before the spy began a long marathon walk. Wolff, that was his name. Rommel had been impressed by his courage, but pessimistic about his chances. "Where was he calling from?"

"Cairo."

"So he got there. If he's capable of that, he's capable of anything. Perhaps he can foretell the breakout."

Kesselring broke in: "My God, you're not relying on spies now, are you?"

"I'm not relying on anyone!" Rommel said. "I'm the one upon whom everything else relies."

"Good." Kesselring was unruffled, as always. "Intelligence is never much use, as you know; and intelligence from spies is the worst kind."

"I agree," Rommel said more calmly. "But I have a feeling this one could be different."

"I doubt it," said Kesselring.

4

Elene Fontana looked at her face in the mirror and thought: I'm twenty-three, I must be losing my looks.

She leaned closer to the glass and examined herself carefully, searching for signs of deterioration. Her complexion was perfect. Her round brown eyes were as clear as a mountain pool. There were no wrinkles. It was a childish face, delicately modeled, with a look of waiflike innocence. She was like an art collector checking on his finest piece: she thought of the face as *hers*, not as *her*. She smiled, and the face in the mirror smiled back at her. It was a small, intimate smile, with a hint of mischief about it: she knew it could make a man break out into a cold sweat.

She picked up the note and read it again.

Thursday

My dear Elene,

I'm afraid it is all over. My wife has found out. We have patched things up, but I've had to promise never to see you again. Of course you can stay in the flat, but I can't pay the rent anymore. I'm so sorry it happened this way—but I suppose we both knew it could not last forever. Good luck.

Your,
Claud.

Just like that, she thought.
She tore up the note and its cheap sentiments. Claud was a

44

fat, half-French and half-Greek businessman who owned
three restaurants in Cairo and one in Alexandria. He was cultured and jolly and kind, but when it came to the crunch he
cared nothing for Elene.

He was the third in six years.

It had started with Charles, the stockbroker. She had been
seventeen years old, penniless, unemployed and frightened to
go home. Charles had set her up in the flat and visited her
every Tuesday night. She had thrown him out after he offered
her to his brother as if she were a dish of sweetmeats. Then
there had been Johnnie, the nicest of the three, who wanted
to divorce his wife and marry Elene: she had refused. Now
Claud, too, had gone.

She had known from the start there was no future in it.

It was her fault as much as theirs that the affairs broke up.
The ostensible reasons—Charles's brother, Johnnie's proposal,
Claud's wife—were just excuses, or maybe catalysts. The real
cause was always the same: Elene was unhappy.

She contemplated the prospect of another affair. She knew
how it would be. For a while she would live on the little nest
egg she had in Barclays Bank in the Shari Kasr-el-Nil—she
always managed to save, when she had a man. Then she
would see the balance slowly going down, and she would take
a job in a dance troupe, kicking up her legs and wiggling her
bottom in some club for a few days. Then . . . She looked
into the mirror and through it, her eyes unfocusing as she
visualized her fourth lover. Perhaps he would be an Italian,
with flashing eyes and glossy hair and perfectly manicured
hands. She might meet him in the bar of the Metropolitan
Hotel, where the reporters drank. He would speak to her,
then offer her a drink. She would smile at him, and he would
be lost. They would make a date for dinner the next day. She
would look stunning as she walked into the restaurant on his
arm. All heads would turn, and he would feel proud. They
would have more dates. He would give her presents. He
would make a pass at her, then another: his third would be
successful. She would enjoy making love with him—the intimacy, the touching, the endearments—and she would make
him feel like a king. He would leave her at dawn, but he would
be back that evening. They would stop going to restaurants together—"too risky," he would say—but he would

spend more and more time at the flat, and he would begin to pay the rent and the bills. Elene would then have everything she wanted: a home, money and affection. She would begin to wonder why she was so miserable. She would throw a tantrum if he arrived half an hour late. She would go into a black sulk if he so much as mentioned his wife. She would complain that he no longer gave her presents, but accept them nonchalantly when he did. The man would be irritated but he would be unable to leave her, for by this time he would be eager for her grudging kisses, greedy for her perfect body; and she would still make him feel like a king in bed. She would find his conversation boring; she would demand from him more passion than he was able to give; there would be rows. Finally the crisis would come. His wife would get suspicious, or a child would fall ill, or he would have to take a six-month business trip, or he would run short of money. And Elene would be back where she was now: drifting, alone, disreputable—and a year older.

Her eyes focused, and she saw again her face in the mirror. Her face was the cause of all this. It was because of her face that she led this pointless life. Had she been ugly, she would always have yearned to live like this, and never discovered its hollowness. You led me astray, she thought; you deceived me, you pretended I was somebody else. You're not my face, you're a mask. You should stop trying to run my life.

I'm not a beautiful Cairo socialite, I'm a slum girl from Alexandria.

I'm not a woman of independent means, I'm the next thing to a whore.

I'm not Egyptian, I'm Jewish.

My name is not Elene Fontana. It's Abigail Asnani.

And I want to go home.

The young man behind the desk at the Jewish Agency in Cairo wore a yarmulke. Apart from a wisp of beard, his cheeks were smooth. He asked for her name and address. Forgetting her resolution, she called herself Elene Fontana.

The young man seemed confused. She was used to this: most men got a little flustered when she smiled at them. He said: "Would you— I mean, do you mind if I ask you why you want to go to Palestine?"

"I'm Jewish," she said abruptly. She could not explain her life to·this boy. "All my family are dead. I'm wasting my life." The first part was not true, but the second part was.

"What work would you do in Palestine?"

She had not thought of that. "Anything."

"It's mostly agricultural labor."

"That's fine."

He smiled gently. He was recovering his composure. "I mean no offense, but you don't look like a farmhand."

"If I didn't want to change my life, I wouldn't want to go to Palestine."

"Yes." He fiddled with his pen. "What work do you do now?"

"I sing, and when I can't get singing I dance, and when I can't get dancing I wait on tables." It was more or less true. She had done all three at one time or another, although dancing was the only one she did successfully, and she was not brilliant at that. "I told you, I'm wasting my life. Why all the questions? Is Palestine accepting only college graduates now?"

"Nothing like that," he said. "But it's very tough to get in. The British have imposed a quota, and all the places are taken by refugees from the Nazis."

"Why didn't you tell me that before?" she said angrily.

"Two reasons. One is that we can get people in illegally. The other . . . the other takes a little longer to explain. Would you wait a minute? I must telephone someone."

She was still angry with him for questioning her before he told her there were no places. "I'm not sure there's any point in my waiting."

"There is, I promise you. It's quite important. Just a minute or two."

"Very well."

He went into a back room to phone. Elene waited impatiently. The day was warming up, and the room was poorly ventilated. She felt a little foolish. She had come here impulsively, without thinking through the idea of emigration. Too many of her decisions were made like that. She might have guessed they would ask her questions; she could have prepared her answers. She could have come dressed in something a little less glamorous.

The young man came back. "It's so warm," he said. "Shall we go across the street for a cold drink?"

So that was the game, she thought. She decided to put him down. She gave him an appraising look, then said: "No. You're much too young for me."

He was terribly embarrassed. "Oh, please don't misunderstand me. There's someone I want you to meet, that's all."

She wondered whether to believe him. She had nothing to lose, and she was thirsty. "All right."

He held the door for her. They crossed the street, dodging the rickety carts and broken-down taxis, feeling the sudden blazing heat of the sun. They ducked under a striped awning and stepped into the cool of a café. The young man ordered lemon juice; Elene had gin and tonic.

She said: "You can get people in illegally."

"Sometimes." He took half his drink in one gulp. "One reason we do it is if the person is being persecuted. That's why I asked you some questions."

"I'm not being persecuted."

"The other reason is if people have done a lot for the cause, some way."

"You mean I have to earn the right to go to Palestine?"

"Look, maybe one day all Jews will have the right to go there to live. But while there are quotas there have to be criteria."

She was tempted to ask: Who do I have to sleep with? But she had misjudged him that way once already. All the same, she thought he wanted to use her somehow. She said: "What do I have to do?"

He shook his head. "I can't make a bargain with you. Egyptian Jews can't get into Palestine, except for special cases, and you're not a special case. That's all there is to it."

"What are you trying to tell me, then?"

"You can't go to Palestine, but you can still fight for the cause."

"What, exactly, did you have in mind?"

"The first thing we have to do is defeat the Nazis."

She laughed. "Well, I'll do my best!"

He ignored that. "We don't like the British much, but any

enemy of Germany's is a friend of ours, so at the moment—strictly on a temporary basis—we're working with British Intelligence. I think you could help them."

"For God's sake! How?"

A shadow fell across the table, and the young man looked up. "Ah!" he said. He looked back at Elene. "I want you to meet my friend Major William Vandam."

He was a tall man, and broad: with those wide shoulders and mighty legs he might once have been an athlete, although now, Elene guessed, he was close to forty and just beginning to go a little soft. He had a round, open face topped by wiry brown hair which looked as if it might curl if it were allowed to grow a little beyond the regulation length. He shook her hand, sat down, crossed his legs, lit a cigarette and ordered gin. He wore a stern expression, as if he thought life was a very serious business and he did not want anybody to start fooling around.

Elene thought he was a typical frigid Englishman.

The young man from the Jewish Agency asked him: "What's the news?"

"The Gazala Line is holding, but it's getting very fierce out there."

Vandam's voice was a surprise. English officers usually spoke with the upper-class drawl which had come to symbolize arrogance for ordinary Egyptians. Vandam spoke precisely but softly, with rounded vowels and a slight burr on the *r*: Elene had a feeling this was the trace of a country accent, although she could not remember how she knew.

She decided to ask him. "Where do you come from, Major?"

"Dorset. Why do you ask?"

"I was wondering about your accent."

"Southwest of England. You're observant. I thought I had no accent."

"Just a trace."

He lit another cigarette. She watched his hands. They were long and slender, rather at odds with the rest of his body; the nails were well manicured and the skin was white except for the deep amber stains where he held his cigarette.

The young man took his leave. "I'll let Major Vandam ex-

plain everything to you. I hope you will work with him; I believe it's very important."

Vandam shook his hand and thanked him, and the young
man went out.

Vandam said to Elene: "Tell me about yourself."

"No," she said. "You tell me about *your*self."

He raised an eyebrow at her, faintly startled, a little
amused and suddenly not at all frigid. "All right," he said after a moment. "Cairo is full of officers and men who know
secrets. They know our strengths, our weaknesses and our
plans. The enemy wants to know those secrets. We can be
sure that at any time the Germans have people in Cairo trying to get information. It's my job to stop them."

"That simple."

He considered. "It's simple, but it's not easy."

He took everything she said seriously, she noticed. She
thought it was because he was humorless, but all the same
she rather liked it: men generally treated her conversation
like background music in a cocktail bar, a pleasant enough
but largely meaningless noise.

He was waiting. "It's your turn," he said.

Suddenly she wanted to tell him the truth. "I'm a lousy
singer and a mediocre dancer, but sometimes I find a rich
man to pay my bills."

He said nothing, but he looked taken aback.

Elene said: "Shocked?"

"Shouldn't I be?"

She looked away. She knew what he was thinking. Until
now he had treated her politely, as if she were a respectable
woman, one of his own class. Now he realized he had been
mistaken. His reaction was completely predictable, but all the
same she felt bitter. She said: "Isn't that what most women
do, when they get married—find a man to pay the bills?"

"Yes," he said gravely.

She looked at him. The imp of mischief seized her. "I just
turn them around a little faster than the average housewife."

Vandam burst out laughing. Suddenly he looked a different
man. He threw back his head, his arms and legs spread sideways, and all the tension went out of his body. When the
laugh subsided he was relaxed, just briefly. They grinned at
one another. The moment passed, and he crossed his legs

again. There was a silence. Elene felt like a schoolgirl who has been giggling in class.

Vandam was serious again. "My problem is information," he said. "Nobody tells an Englishman anything. That's where you come in. Because you're Egyptian, you hear the kind of gossip and street talk that never comes my way. And because you're Jewish, you'll pass it to me. I hope."

"What kind of gossip?"

"I'm interested in anyone who's curious about the British Army." He paused. He seemed to be wondering how much to tell her. "In particular . . . At the moment I'm looking for a man called Alex Wolff. He used to live in Cairo and he has recently returned. He may be hunting for a place to live, and he probably has a lot of money. He is certainly making inquiries about British forces."

Elene shrugged. "After all that buildup I was expecting to be asked to do something much more dramatic."

"Such as?"

"I don't know. Waltz with Rommel and pick his pockets."

Vandam laughed again. Elene thought: I could get fond of that laugh.

He said: "Well, mundane though it is, will you do it?"

"I don't know." But I do know, she thought; I'm just trying to prolong the interview, because I'm enjoying myself.

Vandam leaned forward. "I need people like you, Miss Fontana." Her name sounded silly when he said it so politely. "You're observant, you have a perfect cover and you're obviously intelligent; please excuse me for being so direct—"

"Don't apologize, I love it," she said. "Keep talking."

"Most of my people are not very reliable. They do it for the money, whereas you have a better motive—"

"Wait a minute," she interrupted. "I want money, too. What does the job pay?"

"That depends on the information you bring in."

"What's the minimum?"

"Nothing."

"That's a little less than what I was hoping for."

"How much do you want?"

"You might be a gentleman and pay the rent of my flat." She bit her lip: it sounded so tarty, put like that.

"How much?"

"Seventy-five a month."

Vandam's eyebrows rose. "What have you got, a palace?"

"Prices have gone up. Haven't you heard? It's all these English officers desperate for accommodation."

"Touché." He frowned. "You'd have to be awfully useful to justify seventy-five a month."

Elene shrugged. "Why don't we give it a try?"

"You're a good negotiator." He smiled. "All right, a month's trial."

Elene tried not to look triumphant. "How do I contact you?"

"Send me a message." He took a pencil and a scrap of paper from his shirt pocket and began to write. "I'll give you my address and phone number, at GHQ and at home. As soon as I hear from you I'll come to your place."

"All right." She wrote down her address, wondering what the major would think of her flat. "What if you're seen?"

"Will it matter?"

"I might be asked who you are."

"Well, you'd better not tell the truth."

She grinned. "I'll say you're my lover."

He looked away. "Very well."

"But you'd better act the part." She kept a straight face. "You must bring armfuls of flowers and boxes of chocolates."

"I don't know—"

"Don't Englishmen give their mistresses flowers and chocolates?"

He looked at her unblinkingly. She noticed that he had gray eyes. "I don't know," he said levelly. "I've never had a mistress."

Elene thought: I stand corrected. She said: "Then you've got a lot to learn."

"I'm sure. Would you like another drink?"

And now I'm dismissed, she thought. You're a little too much, Major Vandam: there's a certain self-righteousness about you, and you rather like to be in charge of things; you're so masterful. I may take you in hand, puncture your vanity, do you a little damage.

"No, thanks," she said. "I must go."

He stood up. "I'll look forward to hearing from you."

She shook his hand and walked away. Somehow she had the feeling that he was not watching her go.

Vandam changed into a civilian suit for the reception at the Anglo-Egyptian Union. He would never have gone to the Union while his wife was alive: she said it was "plebby." He told her to say "plebeian" so that she would not sound like a county snob. She said she was a county snob, and would he kindly stop showing off his classical education.

Vandam had loved her then and he did now.

Her father was a fairly wealthy man who became a diplomat because he had nothing better to do. He had not been pleased at the prospect of his daughter marrying a postman's son. He was not much mollified when he was told that Vandam had gone to a minor public school (on a scholarship) and London University, and was considered one of the most promising of his generation of junior army officers. But the daughter was adamant in this as in all things, and in the end the father had accepted the match with good grace. Oddly enough, on the one occasion when the fathers met they got on rather well. Sadly, the mothers hated each other and there were no more family gatherings.

None of it mattered much to Vandam; nor did the fact that his wife had a short temper, an imperious manner and an ungenerous heart. Angela was graceful, dignified and beautiful. For him she was the epitome of womanhood, and he thought himself a lucky man.

The contrast with Elene Fontana could not have been more striking.

He drove to the Union on his motorcycle. The bike, a BSA 350, was very practical in Cairo. He could use it all the year round, for the weather was almost always good enough; and he could snake through the traffic jams that kept cars and taxis waiting. But it was a rather quick machine, and it gave him a secret thrill, a throwback to his adolescence, when he had coveted such bikes but had not been able to buy one. Angela had loathed it—like the Union, it was plebby—but for once Vandam had resolutely defied her.

The day was cooling when he parked at the Union. Passing the clubhouse, he looked through a window and saw a snooker game in full swing. He resisted the temptation and walked on to the lawn.

He accepted a glass of Cyprus sherry and moved into the crowd, nodding and smiling, exchanging pleasantries with people he knew. There was tea for the teetotal Muslim guests, but not many had turned up. Vandam tasted the sherry and wondered whether the barman could be taught to make a martini.

He looked across the grass to the neighboring Egyptian Officers' Club, and wished he could eavesdrop on conversations there. Someone spoke his name, and he turned to see the woman doctor. Once again he had to think before he could remember her name. "Dr. Abuthnot."

"We might be informal here," she said. "My name is Joan."

"William. Is your husband here?"

"I'm not married."

"Pardon me." Now he saw her in a new light. She was single and he was a widower, and they had been seen talking together in public three times in a week: by now the English colony in Cairo would have them practically engaged. "You're a surgeon?" he said.

She smiled. "All I do these days is sew people up and patch them—but yes, before the war I was a surgeon."

"How did you manage that? It's not easy for a woman."

"I fought tooth and nail." She was still smiling, but Vandam detected an undertone of remembered resentment. "You're a little unconventional yourself, I'm told."

Vandam thought himself to be utterly conventional. "How so?" he said with surprise.

"Bringing up your child yourself."

"No choice. If I had wanted to send him back to England, I wouldn't have been able to: you can't get a passage unless you're disabled or a general."

"But you didn't want to."

"No."

"That's what I mean."

"He's my son," Vandam said. "I don't want anyone else to bring him up—nor does he."

"I understand. It's just that some fathers would think it ... unmanly."

He raised his eyebrows at her, and to his surprise she blushed. He said: "You're right, I suppose. I'd never thought of it that way."

"I'm ashamed of myself, I've been prying. Would you like another drink?"

Vandam looked into his glass. "I think I shall have to go inside in search of a real drink."

"I wish you luck." She smiled and turned away.

Vandam walked across the lawn to the clubhouse. She was an attractive woman, courageous and intelligent, and she had made it clear she wanted to know him better. He thought: Why the devil do I feel so indifferent to her? All these people are thinking how well matched we are—and they're right.

He went inside and spoke to the bartender. "Gin. Ice. One olive. And *a few drops* of very dry vermouth."

The martini when it came was quite good, and he had two more. He thought again of the woman Elene. There were a thousand like her in Cairo—Greek, Jewish, Syrian and Palestinian as well as Egyptian. They were dancers for just as long as it took to catch the eye of some wealthy roué. Most of them probably entertained fantasies of getting married and being taken back to a large house in Alexandria or Paris or Surrey, and they would be disappointed.

They all had delicate brown faces and feline bodies with slender legs and pert breasts, but Vandam was tempted to think that Elene stood out from the crowd. Her smile was devastating. The idea of her going to Palestine to work on a farm was, at first sight, ridiculous; but she had tried, and when that failed she had agreed to work for Vandam. On the other hand, retailing street gossip was easy money, like being a kept woman. She was probably the same as all the other dancers: Vandam was not interested in that kind of woman, either.

The martinis were beginning to take effect, and he was afraid he might not be as polite as he should to the ladies when they came in, so he paid his bill and went out.

He drove to GHQ to get the latest news. It seemed the day had ended in a standoff after heavy casualties on both sides—rather more on the British side. It was just bloody demoralizing, Vandam thought: we had a secure base, good supplies, superior weapons and greater numbers; we planned thoughtfully and we fought carefully, and we never damn well won anything. He went home.

Gaafar had prepared lamb and rice. Vandam had another drink with his dinner. Billy talked to him while he ate. Today's geography lesson had been about wheat farming in Canada. Vandam would have liked the school to teach the boy something about the country in which he lived.

After Billy went to bed Vandam sat alone in the drawing room, smoking, thinking about Joan Abuthnot and Alex Wolff and Erwin Rommel. In their different ways they all threatened him. As night fell outside, the room came to seem claustrophobic. Vandam filled his cigarette case and went out.

The city was as much alive now as at any time during the day. There were a lot of soldiers on the streets, some of them very drunk. These were hard men who had seen action in the desert, had suffered the sand and the heat and the bombing and the shelling, and they often found the wogs less grateful than they should be. When a shopkeeper gave short change or a restaurant owner overcharged or a barman refused to serve drunks, the soldiers would remember seeing their friends blown up in the defense of Egypt, and they would start fighting and break windows and smash the place up. Vandam understood why the Egyptians were ungrateful—they did not much care whether it was the British or the Germans who oppressed them—but still he had little sympathy for the Cairo shopkeepers, who were making a fortune out of the war.

He walked slowly, cigarette in hand, enjoying the cool night air, looking into the tiny open-fronted shops, refusing to buy a cotton shirt made-to-measure-while-you-wait, a leather handbag for the lady or a secondhand copy of a magazine called *Saucy Snips*. He was amused by a street vendor who had filthy pictures in the left-hand side of his jacket and crucifixes in the right. He saw a bunch of soldiers collapse with laughter at the sight of two Egyptian policemen patrolling the street hand in hand.

He went into a bar. Outside of the British clubs it was wise to avoid the gin, so he ordered zibib, the aniseed drink which turned cloudy with water. At ten o'clock the bar closed, by mutual consent of the Muslim Wafd government and the

a

kill-joy provost marshal. Vandam's vision was a little blurred when he left.

He headed for the Old City. Passing a sign saying OUT OF BOUNDS TO TROOPS he entered the Birka. In the narrow streets and alleys the women sat on steps and leaned from windows, smoking and waiting for customers, chatting to the military police. Some of them spoke to Vandam, offering their bodies in English, French and Italian. He turned into a little lane, crossed a deserted courtyard and entered an unmarked open doorway.

He climbed the staircase and knocked at a door on the first floor. A middle-aged Egyptian woman opened it. He paid her five pounds and went in.

In a large, dimly lit inner room furnished with faded luxury, he sat on a cushion and unbuttoned his shirt collar. A young woman in baggy trousers passed him the nargileh. He took several deep lungfuls of hashish smoke. Soon a pleasant feeling of lethargy came over him. He leaned back on his elbows and looked around. In the shadows of the room there were four other men. Two were pashas—wealthy Arab landowners—sitting together on a divan and talking in low, desultory tones. A third, who seemed almost to have been sent to sleep by the hashish, looked English and was probably an officer like Vandam. The fourth sat in the corner talking to one of the girls. Vandam heard snatches of conversation and gathered that the man wanted to take the girl home, and they were discussing a price. The man was vaguely familiar, but Vandam, drunk and now doped too, could not get his memory in gear to recall who he was.

One of the girls came over and took Vandam's hand. She led him into an alcove and drew the curtain. She took off her halter. She had small brown breasts. Vandam stroked her cheek. In the candlelight her face changed constantly, seeming old, then very young, then predatory, then loving. At one point she looked like Joan Abuthnot. But finally, as he entered her, she looked like Elene.

5

Alex Wolff wore a galabiya and a fez and stood thirty yards from the gate of GHQ—British headquarters—selling paper fans which broke after two minutes of use.

The hue and cry had died down. He had not seen the British conducting a spot check on identity papers for a week. This Vandam character could not keep up the pressure indefinitely.

Wolff had gone to GHQ as soon as he felt reasonably safe. Getting into Cairo had been a triumph; but it was useless unless he could exploit the position to get the information Rommel wanted—and quickly. He recalled his brief interview with Rommel in Gialo. The Desert Fox did not look foxy at all. He was a small, tireless man with the face of an aggressive peasant: a big nose, a downturned mouth, a cleft chin, a jagged scar on his left cheek, his hair cut so short that none showed beneath the rim of his cap. He had said: "Numbers of troops, names of divisions, in the field and in reserve, state of training. Numbers of tanks, in the field and in reserve, state of repair. Supplies of ammunition, food and gasoline. Personalities and attitudes of commanding officers. Strategic and tactical intentions. They say you're good, Wolff. They had better be right."

It was easier said than done.

There was a certain amount of information Wolff could get just by walking around the city. He could observe the uniforms of the soldiers on leave and listen to their talk, and that told him which troops had been where and when they were going back. Sometimes a sergeant would mention statistics of dead and wounded, or the devastating effect of the

88-millimeter guns—designed as antiaircraft weapons—which the Germans had fitted to their tanks. He had heard an army mechanic complain that thirty-nine of the fifty new tanks which arrived yesterday needed major repairs before going into service. All this was useful information which could be sent to Berlin, where Intelligence analysts would put it together with other snippets in order to form a big picture. But it was not what Rommel wanted.

Somewhere inside GHQ there were pieces of paper which said things like: "After resting and refitting, Division A, with 100 tanks and full supplies, will leave Cairo tomorrow and join forces with Division B at the C Oasis in preparation for the counterattack west of D next Saturday at dawn."

It was those pieces of paper Wolff wanted.

That was why he was selling fans outside GHQ.

For their headquarters the British had taken over a number of the large houses—most of them owned by pashas—in the Garden City suburb. (Wolff was grateful that the Villa les Oliviers had escaped the net.) The commandeered homes were surrounded by a barbed-wire fence. People in uniform were passed quickly through the gate, but civilians were stopped and questioned at length while the sentries made phone calls to verify credentials.

There were other headquarters in other buildings around the city—the Semiramis Hotel housed something called British Troops in Egypt, for example—but this was GHQ Middle East, the powerhouse. Wolff had spent a lot of time, back in the Abwehr spy school, learning to recognize uniforms, regimental identification marks and the faces of literally hundreds of senior British officers. Here, several mornings running, he had observed the large staff cars arriving and had peeked through the windows to see colonels, generals, admirals, squadron leaders and the commander in chief, Sir Claude Auchinleck, himself. They all looked a little odd, and he was puzzled until he realized that the pictures of them which he had burned into his brain were in black and white, and now he was seeing them for the first time in color.

The General Staff traveled by car, but their aides walked. Each morning the captains and majors arrived on foot, carrying their little briefcases. Toward noon—after the regular morning conference, Wolff presumed—some of them left, still carrying their briefcases.

Each day Wolff followed one of the aides.

Most of the aides worked at GHQ, and their secret papers would be locked up in the office at the end of the day. But these few were men who had to be at GHQ for the morning conference, but had their own offices in other parts of the city; and they had to carry their briefing papers with them in between one office and another. One of them went to the Semiramis. Two went to the barracks in the Nasr-el-Nil. A fourth went to an unmarked building in the Shari Suleiman Pasha.

Wolff wanted to get into those briefcases.

Today he would do a dry run.

Waiting under the blazing sun for the aides to come out, he thought about the night before, and a smile curled the corners of his mouth below the newly-grown mustache. He had promised Sonja that he would find her another Fawzi. Last night he had gone to the Birka and picked out a girl at Madame Fahmy's establishment. She was not a Fawzi—*that* girl had been a real enthusiast—but she was a good temporary substitute. They had enjoyed her in turn, then together; then they had played Sonja's weird, exciting games ... It had been a long night.

When the aides came out, Wolff followed the pair that went to the barracks.

A minute later Abdullah emerged from a café and fell into step beside him.

"Those two?" Abdullah said.

"Those two."

Abdullah was a fat man with a steel tooth. He was one of the richest men in Cairo, but unlike most rich Arabs he did not ape the Europeans. He wore sandals, a dirty robe and a fez. His greasy hair curled around his ears and his fingernails were black. His wealth came not from land, like the pashas', nor from trade, like the Greeks'. It came from crime.

Abdullah was a thief.

Wolff liked him. He was sly, deceitful, cruel, generous, and always laughing: for Wolff he embodied the age-old vices and virtues of the Middle East. His army of children, grandchildren, nephews, nieces and second cousins had been burgling houses and picking pockets in Cairo for thirty years. He had tentacles everywhere: he was a hashish wholesaler, he had influence with politicians, and he owned half the houses in the Birka, including Madame Fahmy's. He lived in a large crumbling house in the Old City with his four wives.

They followed the two officers into the modern city center. Abdullah said: "Do you want one briefcase, or both?"

Wolff considered. One was a casual theft; two looked organized. "One," he said.

"Which?"

"It doesn't matter."

Wolff had considered going to Abdullah for help after the discovery that the Villa les Oliviers was no longer safe. He had decided not to. Abdullah could certainly have hidden Wolff away somewhere—probably in a brothel—more or less indefinitely. But as soon as he had Wolff concealed, he would have opened negotiations to sell him to the British. Abdullah divided the world in two: his family and the rest. He was utterly loyal to his family and trusted them completely; he would cheat everyone else and expected them to try to cheat him. All business was done on the basis of mutual suspicion. Wolff found this worked surprisingly well.

They came to a busy corner. The two officers crossed the road, dodging the traffic. Wolff was about to follow when Abdullah put a hand on his arm to stop him.

"We'll do it here," Abdullah said.

Wolff looked around, observing the buildings, the pavement, the road junction and the street vendors. He smiled slowly, and nodded. "It's perfect," he said.

They did it the next day.

Abdullah had indeed chosen the perfect spot for the snatch. It was where a busy side street joined a main road. On the corner was a café with tables outside, reducing the pavement to half its width. Outside the café, on the side of the main road, was a bus stop. The idea of queueing for the bus had never really caught on in Cairo despite sixty years of British domination, so those waiting simply milled about on the already crowded pavement. On the side street it was a little clearer, for although the café had tables out here too, there was no bus stop. Abdullah had observed this little shortcoming, and had put it right by detailing two acrobats to perform on the street there.

Wolff sat at the corner table, from where he could see along both the main road and the side street, and worried about the things that might go wrong.

The officers might not go back to the barracks today.

They might go a different way.

They might not be carrying their briefcases.

The police might arrive too early and arrest everyone on the scene.

The boy might be grabbed by the officers and questioned.

Wolff might be grabbed by the officers and questioned.

Abdullah might decide he could earn his money with less trouble simply by contacting Major Vandam and telling him he could arrest Alex Wolff at the Café Nasif at twelve noon today.

Wolff was afraid of going to prison. He was more than afraid, he was terrified. The thought of it brought him out in a cold sweat under the noonday sun. He could live without good food and wine and girls, if he had the vast wild emptiness of the desert to console him; and he could forego the freedom of the desert to live in a crowded city if he had the urban luxuries to console him: but he could not lose both. He had never told anyone of this: it was his secret nightmare. The idea of living in a tiny, colorless cell, among the scum of the earth (and all of them men), eating bad food, never seeing the blue sky or the endless Nile or the open plains . . . panic touched him glancingly even while he contemplated it. He pushed it out of his mind. It was not going to happen.

At eleven forty-five the large, grubby form of Abdullah waddled past the café. His expression was vacant but his small black eyes looked around sharply, checking his arrangements. He crossed the road and disappeared from view.

At five past twelve Wolff spotted two military caps among the massed heads in the distance.

He sat on the edge of his chair.

The officers came nearer. They were carrying their briefcases.

Across the street a parked car revved its idling engine.

A bus drew up to the stop, and Wolff thought: Abdullah

can't possibly have arranged *that*: it's a piece of luck, a bonus.

The officers were five yards from Wolff.

The car across the street pulled out suddenly. It was a big black Packard with a powerful engine and soft American springing. It came across the road like a charging elephant, motor screaming in low gear, regardless of the main road traffic, heading for the side street, its horn blowing continuously. On the corner, a few feet from where Wolff sat, it plowed into the front of an old Fiat taxi.

The two officers stood beside Wolff's table and stared at the crash.

The taxi driver, a young Arab in a Western shirt and a fez, leaped out of his car.

A young Greek in a mohair suit jumped out of the Packard.

The Arab said the Greek was the son of a pig.

The Greek said the Arab was the back end of a diseased camel.

The Arab slapped the Greek's face and the Greek punched the Arab on the nose.

The people getting off the bus, and those who had been intending to get on it, came closer.

Around the corner, the acrobat who was standing on his colleague's head turned to look at the fight, seemed to lose his balance, and fell into his audience.

A small boy darted past Wolff's table. Wolff stood up, pointed at the boy and shouted at the top of his voice: "Stop, thief!"

The boy dashed off. Wolff went after him, and four people sitting near Wolff jumped up and tried to grab the boy. The child ran between the two officers, who were staring at the fight in the road. Wolff and the people who had jumped up to help him cannoned into the officers, knocking both of them to the ground. Several people began to shout "Stop, thief!" although most of them had no idea who the alleged thief was. Some of the newcomers thought it must be one of the fighting drivers. The crowd from the bus stop, the acrobats' audience, and most of the people in the café surged forward and began to attack one or other of the drivers—Arabs assuming the Greek was the culprit and everyone else assuming it was

the Arab. Several men with sticks—most people carried
sticks—began to push into the crowd, beating on heads at
random in an attempt to break up the fighting which was entirely counterproductive. Someone picked up a chair from the
café and hurled it into the crowd. Fortunately it overshot and
went through the windshield of the Packard. However the
waiters, the kitchen staff and the proprietor of the café now
rushed out and began to attack everyone who swayed,
stumbled or sat on their furniture. Everyone yelled at everyone else in five languages. Passing cars halted to watch the
melee, the traffic backed up in three directions, and every
stopped car sounded its horn. A dog struggled free of its
leash and started biting people's legs in a frenzy of excitement. Everyone got off the bus. The brawling crowd became
bigger by the second. Drivers who had stopped to watch the
fun regretted it, for when the fight engulfed their cars they
were unable to move away (because everyone else had
stopped too) and they had to lock their doors and roll up
their windows while men, women and children, Arabs and
Greeks and Syrians and Jews and Australians and Scotsmen,
jumped on their roofs and fought on their hoods and fell on
their running boards and bled all over their paintwork. Somebody fell through the window of the tailor's shop next to the
café, and a frightened goat ran into the souvenir shop which
flanked the café on the other side and began to knock down
all the tables laden with china and pottery and glass. A baboon came from somewhere—it had probably been riding the
goat, in a common form of street entertainment—and ran
across the heads in the crowd, nimble-footed, to disappear in
the direction of Alexandria. A horse broke free of its harness
and bolted along the street between the lines of cars. From a
window above the café a woman emptied a bucket of dirty
water into the melee. Nobody noticed.

At last the police arrived.

When people heard the whistles, suddenly the shoves and
pushes and insults which had started their own individual
fights seemed a lot less important. There was a scramble to
get away before the arrests began. The crowd diminished rapidly. Wolff, who had fallen over early in the proceedings,
picked himself up and strolled across the road to watch the
dénouement. By the time six people had been handcuffed it

was all over, and there was no one left fighting except for an old woman in black and a one-legged beggar feebly shoving each other in the gutter. The café proprietor, the tailor and the owner of the souvenir shop were wringing their hands and berating the police for not coming sooner while they mentally doubled and trebled the damage for insurance purposes.

The bus driver had broken his arm, but all the other injuries were cuts and bruises.

There was only one death; the goat had been bitten by the dog and consequently had to be destroyed.

When the police tried to move the two crashed cars, they discovered that during the fight the street urchins had jacked up the rear ends of both vehicles and stolen the tires.

Every single light bulb in the bus had also disappeared.

And so had one British Army briefcase.

Alex Wolff was feeling pleased with himself as he walked briskly through the alleys of Old Cairo. A week ago the task of prizing secrets out of GHQ had seemed close to impossible. Now it looked as if he had pulled it off. The idea of getting Abdullah to orchestrate a street fight had been brilliant.

He wondered what would be in the briefcase.

Abdullah's house looked like all the other huddled slums. Its cracked and peeling façade was irregularly dotted with small misshapen windows. The entrance was a low doorless arch with a dark passage beyond. Wolff ducked under the arch, went along the passage and climbed a stone spiral staircase. At the top he pushed through a curtain and entered Abdullah's living room.

The room was like its owner—dirty, comfortable and rich. Three small children and a puppy chased each other around the expensive sofas and inlaid tables. In an alcove by a window an old woman worked on a tapestry. Another woman was drifting out of the room as Wolff walked in: there was no strict Muslim separation of the sexes here, as there had been in Wolff's boyhood home. In the middle of the floor Abdullah sat cross-legged on an embroidered cushion with a baby in his lap. He looked up at Wolff and smiled broadly. "My friend, what a success we have had!"

Wolff sat on the floor opposite him. "It was wonderful," he said. "You're a magician."

"Such a riot! And the bus arriving at just the right moment—and the baboon running away . . ."

Wolff looked more closely at what Abdullah was doing. On the floor beside him was a pile of wallets, handbags, purses and watches. As he spoke he picked up a handsome tooled leather wallet. He took from it a wad of Egyptian banknotes, some postage stamps and a tiny gold pencil, and put them somewhere under his robe. Then he put down the wallet, picked up a handbag and began to rifle through that.

Wolff realized where they had come from. "You old rogue," he said. "You had your boys in the crowd picking pockets."

Abdullah grinned, showing his steel tooth. "To go to all that trouble and then steal only one briefcase . . ."

"But you have got the briefcase."

"Of course."

Wolff relaxed. Abdullah made no move to produce the case. Wolff said: "Why don't you give it to me?"

"Immediately," Abdullah said. Still he did nothing. After a moment he said: "You were to pay me another fifty pounds on delivery."

Wolff counted out the notes and they disappeared beneath the grubby robe. Abdullah leaned forward, holding the baby to his chest with one arm, and with the other reached under the cushion he was sitting on and pulled out the briefcase.

Wolff took it from him and examined it. The lock was broken. He felt cross: surely there should be a limit to duplicity. He made himself speak calmly. "You've opened it already."

Abdullah shrugged. He said: "*Maaleesh.*" It was a conveniently ambiguous word which meant both "Sorry" and "So what?"

Wolff sighed. He had been in Europe too long; he had forgotten how things were done at home.

He lifted the lid of the case. Inside was a sheaf of ten or twelve sheets of paper closely typewritten in English. As he began to read someone put a tiny coffee cup beside him. He glanced up to see a beautiful young girl. He said to Abdullah "Your daughter?"

Abdullah laughed. "My wife."

Wolff took another look at the girl. She seemed about fourteen years old. He turned his attention back to the papers.

He read the first, then with growing incredulity leafed through the rest.

He put them down. "Dear God," he said softly. He started to laugh.

He had stolen a complete set of barracks canteen menus for the month of June.

Vandam said to Colonel Bogge: "I've issued a notice reminding officers that General Staff papers are not to be carried about the town other than in exceptional circumstances."

Bogge was sitting behind his big curved desk, polishing the red cricket ball with his handkerchief. "Good idea," he said. "Keep chaps on their toes."

Vandam went on: "One of my informants, the new girl I told you about—"

"The tart."

"Yes." Vandam resisted the impulse to tell Bogge that "tart" was not the right word for Elene. "She heard a rumor that the riot had been organized by Abdullah—"

"Who's he?"

"He's a kind of Egyptian Fagin, and he also happens to be an informant, although selling me information is the least of his many enterprises."

"For what purpose was the riot organized, according to this rumor?"

"Theft."

"I see." Bogge looked dubious.

"A lot of stuff was stolen, but we have to consider the possibility that the main object of the exercise was the briefcase."

"A conspiracy!" Bogge said with a look of amused skepticism. "But what would this Abdullah want with our canteen menus, eh?" He laughed.

"He wasn't to know what the briefcase contained. He may simply have assumed that they were secret papers."

"I repeat the question," Bogge said with the air of a father patiently coaching a child. "What would he want with secret papers?"

"He may have been put up to it."

"By whom?"

"Alex Wolff."

"Who?"

"The Assyut knife man."

"Oh, now really, Major, I thought we had finished with all that."

Bogge's phone rang, and he picked it up. Vandam took the opportunity to cool off a little. The truth about Bogge, Vandam reflected, was probably that he had no faith in himself, no trust in his own judgment; and, lacking the confidence to make real decisions, he played one-upmanship, scoring points off people in a smart-alec fashion to give himself the illusion that he *was* clever after all. Of course Bogge had no idea whether the briefcase theft was significant or not. He might have listened to what Vandam had to say and then made up his own mind; but he was frightened of that. He could not engage in a fruitful discussion with a subordinate, because he spent all his intellectual energy looking for ways to trap you in a contradiction or catch you in an error or pour scorn on your ideas; and by the time he had finished making himself feel superior that way the decision had been taken, for better or worse and more or less by accident, in the heat of the exchange.

Bogge was saying: "Of course, sir, I'll get on it right away." Vandam wondered how he coped with superiors. The colonel hung up. He said: "Now, then, where were we?"

"The Assyut murderer is still at large," Vandam said. "It may be significant that soon after his arrival in Cairo a General Staff officer is robbed of his briefcase."

"Containing canteen menus."

Here we go again, Vandam thought. With as much grace as he could muster he said: "In Intelligence, we don't believe in coincidence, do we?"

"Don't lecture me, laddie. Even if you were right—and I'm sure you're not—what could we do about it, other than issue the notice you've sent out?"

"Well. I've talked to Abdullah. He denies all knowledge of Alex Wolff, and I think he's lying."

"If he's a thief, why don't you tip off the Egyptian police about him?"

And what would be the point of that? thought Vandam.

He said: "They know all about him. They can't arrest him because too many senior officers are making too much money from his bribes. But we could pull him in and interrogate him, sweat him a little. He's a man without loyalty, he'll change sides at the drop of a hat—"

"General Staff Intelligence does not pull people in and sweat them, Major—"

"Field Security can, or even the military police."

Bogge smiled. "If I went to Field Security with this story of an Arab Fagin stealing canteen menus I'd be laughed out of the office."

"But—"

"We've discussed this long enough, Major—too long, in fact."

"For Christ's sake—"

Bogge raised his voice. "I don't believe the riot was organized, I don't believe Abdullah intended to steal the briefcase, and I don't believe Wolff is a Nazi spy. Is that clear?"

"Look, all I want—"

"Is that *clear?*"

"Yes, sir."

"Good. Dismissed."

Vandam went out.

6

I am a small boy. My father told me how old I am, but I forgot. I will ask him again next time he comes home. My father is a soldier. The place he goes to is called a Sudan. A Sudan is a long way away.

I go to school. I learn the Koran. The Koran is a holy book. I also learn to read and write. Reading is easy, but it is difficult to write without making a mess. Sometimes I pick cotton or take the beasts to drink.

My mother and my grandmother look after me. My grandmother is a famous person. Practically everyone in the whole world comes to see her when they are sick. She gives them medicines made of herbs.

She gives me treacle. I like it mixed with curdled milk. I lie on top of the oven in my kitchen and she tells me stories. My favorite story is the ballad of Zahran, the hero of Denshway. When she tells it, she always says that Denshway is nearby. She must be getting old and forgetful, because Denshway is a long way away. I walked there once with Abdel and it took us all morning.

Denshway is where the British were shooting pigeons when one of their bullets set fire to a barn. All the men of the village come running to find out who had started the fire. One of the soldiers was frightened by the sight of all the strong men of the village running toward him, so he fired at them. There was a fight between the soldiers and the villagers. Nobody won the fight, but the soldier who had fired on the barn was killed. Soon more soldiers came and arrested all the men in the village.

The soldiers made a thing out of wood called a scaffold. I

don't know what a scaffold is but it is used to hang people. I don't know what happens to people when they are hanged. Some of the villagers were hanged and the others were flogged. I know about flogging. It is the worst thing in the world, even worse than hanging, I should think.

Zahran was the first to be hanged, for he had fought the hardest against the soldiers. He walked to the scaffold with his head high, proud that he had killed the man who set fire to the barn.

I wish I were Zahran.

I have never seen a British soldier, but I know that I hate them.

My name is Anwar el-Sadat, and I am going to be a hero.

Sadat fingered his mustache. He was rather pleased with it. He was only twenty-two years old, and in his captain's uniform he looked a bit like a boy soldier: the mustache made him seem older. He needed all the authority he could get, for what he was about to propose was—as usual—faintly ludicrous. At these little meetings he was at pains to talk and act as if the handful of hotheads in the room really were going to throw the British out of Egypt any day now.

He deliberately made his voice a little deeper as he began to speak. "We have all been hoping that Rommel would defeat the British in the desert and so liberate our country." He looked around the room: a good trick, that, in large or small meetings, for it made each one think Sadat was talking to him personally. "Now we have some very bad news. Hitler has agreed to give Egypt to the Italians."

Sadat was exaggerating: this was not news, it was a rumor. Furthermore most of the audience knew it to be a rumor. However, melodrama was the order of the day, and they responded with angry murmurs.

Sadat continued: "I propose that the Free Officers Movement should negotiate a treaty with Germany, under which we would organize an uprising against the British in Cairo, and they would guarantee the independence and sovereignty of Egypt after the defeat of the British." As he spoke the risibility of the situation struck him afresh: here he was, a peasant boy just off the farm, talking to half a dozen discontented subalterns about negotiations with the German Reich.

And yet, who else would represent the Egyptian people? The British were conquerors, the Parliament was a puppet and the King was a foreigner.

There was another reason for the proposal, one which would not be discussed here, one which Sadat would not admit to himself except in the middle of the night: Abdel Nasser had been posted to the Sudan with his unit, and his absence gave Sadat a chance to win for himself the position of leader of the rebel movement.

He pushed the thought out of his mind, for it was ignoble. He had to get the others to agree to the proposal, then to agree to the means of carrying it out.

It was Kemel who spoke first. "But will the Germans take us seriously?" he asked. Sadat nodded, as if he too thought that was an important consideration. In fact he and Kemel had agreed beforehand that Kemel should ask this question, for it was a red herring. The real question was whether the Germans could be trusted to keep to any agreement they made with a group of unofficial rebels: Sadat did *not* want the meeting to discuss that. It was unlikely that the Germans would stick to their part of the bargain; but if the Egyptians did rise up against the British, and if they were then betrayed by the Germans, they would see that nothing but independence was good enough—and perhaps, too, they would turn for leadership to the man who had organized the uprising. Such hard political realities were not for meetings such as this: they were too sophisticated, too calculating. Kemel was the only person with whom Sadat could discuss tactics. Kemel was a policeman, a detective with the Cairo force, a shrewd, careful man: perhaps police work had made him cynical.

The others began to talk about whether it would work. Sadat made no contribution to the discussion. Let them talk, he thought; it's what they really like to do. When it came to action they usually let him down.

As they argued, Sadat recalled the failed revolution of the previous summer. It had started with the sheik of al-Azhar, who had preached: "We have nothing to do with the war." Then the Egyptian Parliament, in a rare display of independence, had adopted the policy: "Save Egypt from the scourge of war." Until then the Egyptian Army had been fighting side by side with the British Army in the desert, but now the British ordered the Egyptians to lay down their arms and withdraw. The Egyptians were happy to withdraw but did not want to be disarmed. Sadat saw a heaven-sent opportunity to foment strife. He and many other young officers refused to hand in their guns and planned to march on Cairo. To Sadat's great disappointment, the British immediately yielded and let them keep their weapons. Sadat continued to try to fan the spark of rebellion into the flame of revolution, but the British had outmaneuvered him by giving way. The march on Cairo was a fiasco: Sadat's unit arrived at the assembly point but nobody else came. They washed their vehicles, sat down, waited awhile, then went on to their camp.

Six months later Sadat had suffered another failure. This time it centered on Egypt's fat, licentious, Turkish King. The British gave an ultimatum to King Farouk: either he was to instruct his Premier to form a new, pro-British government, or he was to abdicate. Under pressure the King summoned Mustafa el-Nahas Pasha and ordered him to form a new government. Sadat was no royalist, but he was an opportunist: he announced that this was a violation of Egyptian sovereignty, and the young officers marched to the palace to salute the King in protest. Once again Sadat tried to push the rebellion further. His plan was to surround the palace in token defense of the King. Once again, he was the only one who turned up.

He had been bitterly disappointed on both occasions. He had felt like abandoning the whole rebel cause: let the Egyptians go to hell their own way, he had thought in the moments of blackest despair. Yet those moments passed, for he knew the cause was right and he knew he was smart enough to serve it well.

"But we haven't any means of contacting the Germans." It was Imam speaking, one of the pilots. Sadat was pleased that they were already discussing *how to* do it rather than *whether to*.

Kemel had the answer to the question. "We might send the message by plane."

"Yes!" Imam was young and fiery. "One of us could go up on a routine patrol and then divert from the course and land behind German lines."

One of the older pilots said: "On his return he would have to account for his diversion—"

"He could not come back at all," Imam said, his expression turning forlorn as swiftly as it had become animated.

Sadat said quietly: "He could come back with Rommel."

Imam's eyes lit up again. and Sadat knew that the young pilot was seeing himself and Rommel marching into Cairo at the head of an army of liberation. Sadat decided that Imam should be the one to take the message.

"Let us agree on the text of the message," Sadat said democratically. Nobody noticed that such a clear decision had not been required on the question of whether a message should be sent at all. "I think we should make four points. One: We are honest Egyptians who have an organization within the Army. Two: Like you, we are fighting the British. Three: We are able to recruit a rebel army to fight on your side. Four: We will organize an uprising against the British in Cairo, if you will in return guarantee the independence and sovereignty of Egypt after the defeat of the British." He paused. With a frown, he added: "I think perhaps we should offer them some token of our good faith."

There was a silence. Kemel had the answer to this question, too, but it would look better coming from one of the others.

Imam rose to the occasion. "We could send some useful military information along with the message."

Kemel now pretended to oppose the idea. "What sort of information could *we* get? I can't imagine—"

"Aerial photographs of British positions."

"How is that possible?"

"We can do it on a routine patrol, with an ordinary camera."

Kemel looked dubious. "What about developing the film?"

"Not necessary," Imam said excitedly. "We can just send the film."

"Just one film?"

"As many as we like."

Sadat said: "I think Imam is right." Once again they were discussing the practicalities of an idea instead of its risks. There was only one more hurdle to jump. Sadat knew from bitter experience that these rebels were terribly brave until the moment came when they really had to stick their necks out. He said: "That leaves only the question of which of us will fly the plane." As he spoke he looked around the room, letting his eyes rest finally on Imam.

After a moment's hesitation. Imam stood up.

Sadat's eyes blazed with triumph.

Two days later Kemel walked the three miles from central Cairo to the suburb where Sadat lived. As a detective inspector, Kemel had the use of an official car whenever he wanted it. but he rarely used one to go to rebel meetings, for security reasons. In all probability his police colleagues would be sympathetic to the Free Officers Movement; still, he was not in a hurry to put them to the test.

Kemel was fifteen years older than Sadat, yet his attitude to the younger man was one almost of hero worship. Kemel shared Sadat's cynicism, his realistic understanding of the levers of political power; but Sadat had something more, and that was a burning idealism which gave him unlimited energy and boundless hope.

Kemel wondered how to tell him the news.

The message to Rommel had been typed out, signed by Sadat and all the leading Free Officers except the absent Nasser and sealed in a big brown envelope. The aerial photographs of British positions had been taken. Imam had taken off in his Gladiator, with Baghdadi following in a second plane. They had touched down in the desert to pick up Kemel. who had given the brown envelope to Imam and climbed into Baghdadi's plane. Imam's face had been shining with youthful idealism.

Kemel thought: How will I break it to Sadat?

It was the first time Kemel had flown. The desert, so featureless from ground level, had been an endless mosaic of shapes and patterns: the patches of gravel, the dots of vegetation and the carved volcanic hills. Baghdadi said: "You're going to be cold," and Kemel thought he was joking—the desert was like a furnace—but as the little plane climbed the temperature dropped steadily, and soon he was shivering in his thin cotton shirt.

After a while both planes had turned due east, and Baghdadi spoke into his radio, telling base that Imam had veered off course and was not replying to radio calls. As expected, base told Baghdadi to follow Imam. This little pantomime was necessary so that Baghdadi, who was to return, should not fall under suspicion.

They flew over an army encampment. Kemel saw tanks, trucks, field guns and jeeps. A bunch of soldiers waved: they must be British, Kemel thought. Both planes climbed. Directly ahead they saw signs of battle: great clouds of dust, explosions and gunfire. They turned to pass to the south of the battlefield.

Kemel had thought: We flew over a British base, then a battlefield—next we should come to a German base.

Ahead, Imam's plane lost height. Instead of following, Baghdadi climbed a little more—Kemel had the feeling that the Gladiator was near its ceiling—and peeled off to the south. Looking out of the plane to the right, Kemel saw what the pilots had seen: a small camp with a cleared strip marked as a runway.

Approaching Sadat's house, Kemel recalled how elated he had felt, up there in the sky above the desert, when he realized they were behind German lines, and the treaty was almost in Rommel's hands.

He knocked on the door. He still did not know what to tell Sadat.

It was an ordinary family house, rather poorer than Kemel's home. In a moment Sadat came to the door, wearing a galabiya and smoking a pipe. He looked at Kemel's face, and said immediately: "It went wrong."

"Yes." Kemel stepped inside. They went into the little room Sadat used as a study. There were a desk, a shelf of books and some cushions on the bare floor. On the desk an army pistol lay on top of a pile of papers.

They sat down. Kemel said: "We found a German camp with a runway. Imam descended. Then the Germans started to fire on his plane. It was an English plane, you see—we never considered that."

Sadat said: "But surely, they could see he was not hostile—he did not fire, did not drop bombs—"

"He just kept on going down," Kemel went on. "He waggled his wings, and I suppose he tried to raise them on the radio; anyway they kept firing. The tail of the plane took a hit."

"Oh, God."

"He seemed to be going down very fast. The Germans stopped firing. Somehow he managed to land on his wheels. The plane seemed to bounce. I don't think Imam could control it any longer. Certainly he could not slow down. He went off the hard surface and into a patch of sand; the port wing hit the ground and snapped; the nose dipped and plowed into the sand; then the fuselage fell on the broken wing."

Sadat was staring at Kemel, blank-faced and quite still, his pipe going cold in his hand. In his mind Kemel saw the plane lying broken in the sand, with a German fire truck and ambulance speeding along the runway toward it, followed by ten or fifteen soldiers. He would never forget how, like a blossom opening its petals, the belly of the plane had burst skyward in a riot of red and yellow flame.

"It blew up," he told Sadat.

"And Imam?"

"He could not possibly live through such a fire."

"We must try again," Sadat said. "We must find another way to get a message through."

Kemel stared at him, and realized that his brisk tone of voice was phony. Sadat tried to light his pipe, but the hand holding the match was shaking too much. Kemel looked closely, and saw that Sadat had tears in his eyes.

"The poor boy," Sadat whispered.

7

Wolff was back at square one: he knew where the secrets were, but he could not get at them.

He might have stolen another briefcase the way he had taken the first, but that would begin to look, to the British, like a conspiracy. He might have thought of another way to steal a briefcase, but even that might lead to a security clampdown. Besides, one briefcase on one day was not enough for his needs: he had to have regular, unimpeded access to secret papers.

That was why he was shaving Sonja's pubic hair.

Her hair was black and coarse, and it grew very quickly. Because she shaved it regularly she was able to wear her translucent trousers without the usual heavy, sequined G-string on top. The extra measure of physical freedom—and the persistent and accurate rumor that she had nothing on under the trousers—had helped to make her the leading belly dancer of the day.

Wolff dipped the brush into the bowl and began to lather her.

She lay on the bed, her back propped up by a pile of pillows, watching him suspiciously. She was not keen on this, his latest perversion. She thought she was not going to like it.

Wolff knew better.

He knew how her mind worked, and he knew her body better than she did, and he wanted something from her.

He stroked her with the soft shaving brush and said: "I've thought of another way to get into those briefcases."

"What?"

He did not answer her immediately. He put down the

brush and picked up the razor. He tested its sharp edge with his thumb, then looked at her. She was watching him with horrid fascination. He leaned closer, spread her legs a little more, put the razor to her skin, and drew it upward with a light, careful stroke.

He said: "I'm going to befriend a British officer."

She did not answer: she was only half listening to him. He wiped the razor on a towel. With one finger of his left hand he touched the shaved patch, pulling down to stretch the skin, then he brought the razor close.

"Then I'll bring the officer here," he said.

Sonja said: "Oh, no."

He touched her with the edge of the razor and gently scraped upward.

She began to breathe harder.

He wiped the razor and stroked again once, twice, three times.

"Somehow I'll get the officer to bring his briefcase."

He put his finger on her most sensitive spot and shaved around it. She closed her eyes.

He poured hot water from a kettle into a bowl on the floor beside him. He dipped a flannel into the water and wrung it out.

"Then I'll go through the briefcase while the officer is in bed with you."

He pressed the hot flannel against her shaved skin.

She gave a sharp cry like a cornered animal: "Ahh, God!"

Wolff slipped out of his bathrobe and stood naked. He picked up a bottle of soothing skin oil, poured some into the palm of his right hand, and knelt on the bed beside Sonja; then he anointed her pubis.

"I won't," she said as she began to writhe.

He added more oil, massaging it into all the folds and crevices. With his left hand he held her by the throat, pinning her down. "You will."

His knowing fingers delved and squeezed, becoming less gentle.

She said: "No."

He said: "Yes."

She shook her head from side to side. Her body wriggled, helpless in the grip of intense pleasure. She began to shudder, and finally she said: "Oh. Oh. Oh. Oh. Oh. Oh!" Then she relaxed.

Wolff would not let her stop. He continued to stroke her smooth, hairless skin while with his left hand he pinched her brown nipples. Unable to resist him, she began to move again.

She opened her eyes and saw that he, too, was aroused. She said: "You bastard, stick it in me."

He grinned. The sense of power was like a drug. He lay over her and hesitated, poised.

She said: "Quickly!"

"Will you do it?"

"Quickly!"

He let his body touch hers, then paused again. "Will you do it?"

"Yes! Please!"

"Aaah," Wolff breathed, and lowered himself to her.

She tried to go back on it afterward, of course.

"That kind of promise doesn't count," she said.

Wolff came out of the bathroom wrapped in a big towel. He looked at her. She was lying on the bed, still naked, eating chocolates from a box. There were moments when he was almost fond of her.

He said: "A promise is a promise."

"You promised to find us another Fawzi." She was sulking. She always did after sex.

"I brought that girl from Madame Fahmy's," Wolff said.

"She wasn't another Fawzi. Fawzi didn't ask for ten pounds every time, and she didn't go home in the morning."

"All right. I'm still looking."

"You didn't promise to *look*, you promised to *find*."

Wolff went into the other room and got a bottle of champagne out of the icebox. He picked up two glasses and took them back into the bedroom. "Do you want some?"

"No," she said. "Yes."

He poured and handed her a glass. She drank some and took another chocolate. Wolff said: "To the unknown British officer who is about to get the nicest surprise of his life."

"I won't go to bed with an Englishman," Sonja said. "They smell bad and they have skins like slugs and I hate them."

"That's why you'll do it—because you hate them. Just imagine it: while he's screwing you and thinking how lucky he is, I'll be reading his secret papers."

Wolff began to dress. He put on a shirt which had been made for him in one of the tiny tailor shops in the Old City—a British uniform shirt with captain's pips on the shoulders.

Sonja said: "What are you wearing?"

"British officer's uniform. They don't talk to foreigners, you know."

"You're going to pretend to be British?"

"South African, I think."

"But what if you slip up?"

He looked at her. "I'll probably be shot as a spy."

She looked away.

Wolff said: "If I find a likely one, I'll take him to the Cha-Cha." He reached into his shirt and drew his knife from its underarm sheath. He went close to her and touched her naked shoulder with its point. "If you let me down, I'll cut your lips off."

She looked into his face. She did not speak, but there was fear in her eyes.

Wolff went out.

Shepheard's was crowded. It always was.

Wolff paid off his taxi, pushed through the pack of hawkers and dragomans outside, mounted the steps and went into the foyer. It was packed with people: Levantine merchants holding noisy business meetings, Europeans using the post office and the banks, Egyptian girls in their cheap gowns and British officers—the hotel was out of bounds to Other Ranks. Wolff passed between two larger-than-life bronze ladies holding lamps and entered the lounge. A small band played nondescript music while more crowds, mostly European now, called constantly for waiters. Negotiating the divans and marble-topped tables Wolff made his way through to the long bar at the far end.

Here it was a little quieter. Women were banned, and serious drinking was the order of the day. It was here that a lonely officer would come.

Wolff sat at the bar. He was about to order champagne,

then he remembered his disguise and asked for whiskey and water.

He had given careful thought to his clothes. The brown shoes were officer pattern and highly polished; the khaki socks were turned down at exactly the right place; the baggy brown shorts had a sharp crease; the bush shirt with captain's pips was worn outside the shorts, not tucked in; the flat cap was just slightly raked.

He was a little worried about his accent. He had his story ready to explain it—the line he had given Captain Newman, in Assyut, about having been brought up in Dutch-speaking South Africa—but what if the officer he picked up was a South African? Wolff could not distinguish English accents well enough to recognize a South African.

He was more worried about his knowledge of the Army. He was looking for an officer from GHQ, so he would say that he himself was with BTE—British Troops in Egypt— which was a separate and independent outfit. Unfortunately he knew little else about it. He was uncertain what BTE did and how it was organized, and he could not quote the name of a single one of its officers. He imagined a conversation:

"How's old Buffy Jenkins?"

"Old Buffy? Don't see much of him in my department."

"Don't see much of him? He runs the show! Are we talking about the same BTE?"

Then again:

"What about Simon Frobisher?"

"Oh, Simon's the same, you know."

"Wait a minute—someone said he'd gone back home. Yes, I'm sure he has—how come you didn't know?"

Then the accusations, and the calling of the military police, and the fight, and finally the jail.

Jail was the only thing that really frightened Wolff. He pushed the thought out of his mind and ordered another whiskey.

A perspiring colonel came in and stood at the bar next to Wolff's stool. He called to the barman: *"Ezma!"* It meant "Listen," but all the British thought it meant "Waiter." The colonel looked at Wolff.

Wolff nodded politely and said: "Sir."

"Cap off in the bar, Captain," said the colonel. "What are you thinking of?"

Wolff took off his cap, cursing himself silently for the error. The colonel ordered beer. Wolff looked away.

There were fifteen or twenty officers in the bar, but he recognized none of them. He was looking for any one of the eight aides who left GHQ each midday with their briefcases. He had memorized the face of each one, and would recognize them instantly. He had already been to the Metropolitan Hotel and the Turf Club without success, and after half an hour in Shepheard's he would try the Officers' Club, the Gezira Sporting Club and even the Anglo-Egyptian Union. If he failed tonight he would try again tomorrow: sooner or later he was sure to bump into at least one of them.

Then everything would depend on his skill.

His scheme had a lot going for it. The uniform made him one of them, trustworthy and a comrade. Like most soldiers they were probably lonely and sex-starved in a foreign country. Sonja was undeniably a very desirable woman—to look at, anyway—and the average English officer was not well armored against the wiles of an Oriental seductress.

And anyway, if he was unlucky enough to pick an aide smart enough to resist temptation, he would have to drop the man and look for another.

He hoped it would not take that long.

In fact it took him five more minutes.

The major who walked in was a small man, very thin, and about ten years older than Wolff. His cheeks had the broken veins of a hard drinker. He had bulbous blue eyes, and his thin sandy hair was plastered to his head.

Every day he left GHQ at midday and walked to an unmarked building in the Shari Suleiman Pasha—carrying his briefcase.

Wolff's heart missed a beat.

The major came up to the bar, took off his cap, and said: "*Ezmal* Scotch. No ice. Make it snappy." He turned to Wolff. "Bloody weather," he said conversationally.

"Isn't it always, sir?" Wolff said.

"Bloody right. I'm Smith, GHQ."

"How do you do, sir," Wolff said. He knew that, since Smith went from GHQ to another building every day, the major could not really be at GHQ; and he wondered briefly why the man should lie about it. He put the thought aside for the moment and said: "I'm Slavenburg, BTE."

"Jolly good. Get you another?"

It was proving even easier than he had expected to get into conversation with an officer. "Very kind of you, sir," Wolff said.

"Ease up on the sirs. No bull in the bar, what?"

"Of course." Another error.

"What'll it be?"

"Whiskey and water, please."

"Shouldn't take water with it if I were you. Comes straight out of the Nile, they say."

Wolff smiled. "I must be used to it."

"No gippy tummy? You must be the only white man in Egypt who hasn't got it."

"Born in Africa, been in Cairo ten years." Wolff was slipping into Smith's abbreviated style of speech. I should have been an actor, he thought.

Smith said: "Africa, eh? I thought you had a bit of an accent."

"Dutch father, English mother. We've got a ranch in South Africa."

Smith looked solicitous. "It's rough for your father, with Jerry all over Holland."

Wolff had not thought of that. "He died when I was a boy," he said.

"Bad show." Smith emptied his glass.

"Same again?" Wolff offered.

"Thanks."

Wolff ordered more drinks. Smith offered him a cigarette: Wolff refused.

Smith complained about the poor food, the way bars kept running out of drinks, the rent of his flat and the rudeness of Arab waiters. Wolff itched to explain that the food was poor because Smith insisted on English rather than Egyptian dishes, that drinks were scarce because of the European war, that rents were sky-high because of the thousands of foreigners like Smith who had invaded the city, and that the waiters were rude to him because he was too lazy or arrogant to learn a few phrases of courtesy in their language. Instead

of explaining he bit his tongue and nodded as if he sympa-
thized.

In the middle of this catalogue of discontent Wolff looked
past Smith's shoulder and saw six military policemen enter
the bar.

Smith noticed his change of expression and said: "What's
the matter—seen a ghost?"

There was an army MP, a navy MP in white leggings, an
Australian, a New Zealander, a South African and a tur-
baned Gurkha. Wolff had a crazy urge to run for it. What
would they ask him? What would he say?

Smith looked around, saw the MPs and said: "The usual
nightly picket—looking for drunken officers and German
spies. This is an officers' bar, they won't disturb us. What's
the matter—you breaking bounds or something?"

"No, no." Wolff improvised hastily: "The navy man looks
just like a chap I knew who got killed at Halfaya." He continued to stare at the picket. They appeared very businesslike
with their steel hats and holstered pistols. Would they ask to
see papers?

Smith had forgotten them. He was saying: "And as for the
servants . . . Bloody people. I'm bloody sure my man's been
watering the gin. I'll find him out though. I've filled an empty
gin bottle with zibi—you know, that stuff that turns cloudy
when you add water? Wait till he tries to dilute that. He'll
have to buy a whole new bottle and pretend nothing happened. Haha! Serve him right."

The officer in charge of the picket walked over to the
colonel who had told Wolff to take off his hat. "Everything in
order, sir?" the MP said.

"Nothing untoward," the colonel replied.

"What's the matter with you?" Smith said to Wolff. "I say,
you are entitled to those pips, aren't you?"

"Of course." Wolff said. A drop of perspiration ran into
his eyes, and he wiped it away with a too-rapid gesture.

"No offense intended," Smith said. "But, you know, Shepheard's being off limits to Other Ranks, it's not unknown for
subalterns to sew a few pips on their shirts just to get in
here."

Wolff pulled himself together. "Look here, sir, if you'd care
to check—"

"No, no, no," Smith said hastily.

"The resemblance was rather a shock."

"Of course, I understand. Let's have another drink. *Ezma!*"

The MP who had spoken to the colonel was taking a long look around the room. His armband identified him as the assistant provost marshal. He looked at Wolff. Wolff wondered whether the man remembered the description of the Assyut knife murderer. Surely not. Anyway, they would not be looking for a British officer answering the description. And Wolff had grown a mustache to confuse the issue. He forced himself to meet the MP's eyes, then let his gaze drift casually away. He picked up his drink, sure the man was still staring at him.

Then there was a clatter of boots and the picket went out.

By an effort Wolff prevented himself from shaking with relief. He raised his glass in a determinedly steady hand and said: "Cheers."

They drank. Smith said: "You know this place. What's a chap to do in the evening, other than drink in Shepheard's bar?"

Wolff pretended to consider the question. "Have you seen any belly dancing?"

Smith gave a disgusted snort. "Once. Some fat wog wiggling her hips."

"Ah. Then you ought to see the real thing."

"Should I?"

"Real belly dancing is the most erotic thing you've ever seen."

There was an odd light in Smith's eyes. "Is that so?"

Wolff thought: Major Smith, you are just what I need. He said: "Sonja is the best. You must try to see her act."

Smith nodded. "Perhaps I shall."

"Matter of fact, I was toying with the idea of going on to the Cha-Cha Club myself. Care to join me?"

"Let's have another drink first," said Smith.

Watching Smith put away the liquor Wolff reflected that the major was, at least on the surface, a highly corruptible man. He seemed bored, weak-willed and alcoholic. Provided he was normally heterosexual, Sonja would be able to seduce him easily. (Damn, he thought, she had better do her stuff.) Then they would have to find out whether he had in his briefcase anything more useful than menus. Finally they would have to find a way to get the secrets out of him. There were too many maybes and too little time.

He could only go step by step, and the first step was to get Smith in his power.

They finished their drinks and set out for the Cha-Cha. They could not find a taxi, so they took a gharry, a horse-drawn open carriage. The driver mercilessly whipped his elderly horse.

Smith said: "Chap's a bit rough on the beast."

"Isn't he," Wolff said, thinking: You should see what we do to camels.

The club was crowded and hot, again. Wolff had to bribe a waiter to get a table.

Sonja's act began moments after they sat down. Smith watched Sonja while Wolff watched Smith. In minutes the major was drooling.

Wolff said: "Good, isn't she?"

"Fantastic," Smith replied without looking around.

"Matter of fact, I know her slightly," Wolff said. "Shall I ask her to join us afterwards?"

This time Smith did look around. "Good Lord!" he said. "Would you?"

The rhythm quickened. Sonja looked out across the crowded floor of the club. Hundreds of men feasted their eyes greedily on her magnificent body. She closed her eyes.

The movements came automatically: the sensations took over. In her imagination she saw the sea of rapacious faces staring at her. She felt her breasts shake and her belly roll and her hips jerk, and it was as if someone else was doing it to her, as if all the hungry men in the audience were manipulating her body. She went faster and faster. There was no artifice in her dancing, not any more; she was doing it for herself. She did not even follow the music—it followed her. Waves of excitement swept her. She rode the excitement, dancing, until she knew she was on the edge of ecstasy, knew she only had to jump and she would be flying. She hesitated on the brink. She spread her arms. The music climaxed with a bang. She uttered a cry of frustration and fell backward, her legs folded beneath her, her thighs open to the audience, until her head hit the stage. Then the lights went out.

It was always like that.

In the storm of applause she got up and crossed the darkened stage to the wings. She walked quickly to her dressing room, head down, looking at no one. She did not want their words or their smiles. They did not understand. Nobody knew how it was for her, nobody knew what she went through every night when she danced.

She took off her shoes, her filmy pantaloons and her sequined halter, and put on a silk robe. She sat in front of the mirror to remove her makeup. She always did this immediately, for the makeup was bad for the skin. She had to look after her body. Her face and throat were getting that fleshy look again, she observed. She would have to stop eating chocolates. She was already well past the age at which women began to get fat. Her age was another secret the audience must never discover. She was almost as old as her father had been when he died. Father . . .

He had been a big, arrogant man whose achievements never lived up to his hopes. Sonja and her parents had slept together in a narrow hard bed in a Cairo tenement. She had never felt so safe and warm since those days. She would curl up against her father's broad back. She could remember the close familiar smell of him. Then, when she should have been asleep, there had been another smell, something that excited her unaccountably. Mother and father would begin to move in the darkness, lying side by side; and Sonja would move with them. A few times her mother realized what was happening. Then her father would beat her. After the third time they made her sleep on the floor. Then she could hear them but could not share the pleasure: it seemed so cruel. She blamed her mother. Her father was willing to share, she was sure; he had known all along what she had been doing. Lying on the floor, cold, excluded, listening, she had tried to enjoy it at a distance, but it had not worked. Nothing had worked since then, until the arrival of Alex Wolff . . .

She had never spoken to Wolff about that narrow bed in the tenement, but somehow he understood. He had an instinct for the deep needs that people never acknowledged. He and the girl Fawzi had re-created the childhood scene for Sonja, and it had worked.

He did not do it out of kindness, she knew. He did these things so that he could use people. Now he wanted to use her to spy on the British. She would do almost anything to spite the British—anything but go to bed with them . . .

There was a knock on the door of her dressing room. She called: "Come in."

One of the waiters entered with a note. She nodded dismissal at the boy and unfolded the sheet of paper. The message said simply: "Table 41. Alex."

She crumpled the paper and dropped it on the floor. So he had found one. That was quick. His instinct for weakness was working again.

She understood him because she was like him. She, too, used people—although less cleverly than he did. She even used him. He had style, taste, high-class friends and money; and one day he would take her to Berlin. It was one thing to be a star in Egypt, and quite another in Europe. She wanted to dance for the aristocratic old generals and the handsome young Storm Troopers; she wanted to seduce powerful men and beautiful white girls; she wanted to be queen of the cabaret in the most decadent city in the world. Wolff would be her passport. Yes, she was using him.

It must be unusual, she thought, for two people to be so close and yet to love each other so little.

He *would* cut her lips off.

She shuddered, stopped thinking about it and began to dress. She put on a white gown with wide sleeves and a low neck. The neckline showed off her breasts while the skirt slimmed her hips. She stepped into white high-heeled sandals. She fastened a heavy gold bracelet around each wrist, and around her neck she hung a gold chain with a teardrop pendant which lay snugly in her cleavage. The Englishman would like that. They had the most coarse taste.

She took a last look at herself in the mirror and went out into the club.

A zone of silence went with her across the floor. People fell quiet as she approached and then began to talk about her when she had passed. She felt as if she were inviting mass rape. Onstage it was different: she was separated from them by an invisible wall. Down here they could touch her, and they all wanted to. They never did, but the danger thrilled her.

She reached table 41 and both men stood up.

Wolff said: "Sonja, my dear, you were magnificent, as always."

She acknowledged the compliment with a nod.

"Allow me to introduce Major Smith."

Sonja shook his hand. He was a thin, chinless man with a fair mustache and ugly, bony hands. He looked at her as if she were an extravagant dessert which had just been placed before him.

Smith said: "Enchanted, absolutely."

They sat down. Wolff poured champagne. Smith said: "Your dancing was splendid, mademoiselle, just splendid. Very . . . artistic."

"Thank you."

He reached across the table and patted her hand. "You're very lovely."

And you're a fool, she thought. She caught a warning look from Wolff: he knew what was in her mind. "You're very kind, Major," she said.

Wolff was nervous, she could tell. He was not sure whether she would do what he wanted. In truth she had not yet decided.

Wolff said to Smith: "I knew Sonja's late father."

It was a lie, and Sonja knew why he had said it. He wanted to remind her.

Her father had been a part-time thief. When there was work he worked, and when there was none he stole. One day he had tried to snatch the handbag of a European woman in the Shari el-Koubri. The woman's escort had made a grab for Sonja's father, and in the scuffle the woman had been knocked down, spraining her wrist. She was an important woman, and Sonja's father had been flogged for the offense. He had died during the flogging.

Of course, it was not supposed to kill him. He must have had a weak heart, or something. The British who administered the law did not care. The man had committed the crime, he had been given the due punishment and the punishment had killed him: one wog less. Sonja, twelve years old,

had been heartbroken. Since then she had hated the British
with all her being.

Hitler had the right idea but the wrong target, she believed.
It was not the Jews whose racial weakness infected the
world—it was the British. The Jews in Egypt were more or
less like everyone else: some rich, some poor, some good,
some bad. But the British were uniformly arrogant, greedy
and vicious. She laughed bitterly at the high-minded way in
which the British tried to defend Poland from German op-
pression while they themselves continued to oppress Egypt.

Still, for whatever reasons, the Germans were fighting the
British, and that was enough to make Sonja pro-German.

She wanted Hitler to defeat, humiliate and ruin Britain.

She would do anything she could to help.

She would even seduce an Englishman.

She leaned forward. "Major Smith," she said, "you're a
very attractive man."

Wolff relaxed visibly.

Smith was startled. His eyes seemed about to pop out of
his head. "Good Lord!" he said. "Do you think so?"

"Yes, I do, Major."

"I say, I wish you'd call me Sandy."

Wolff stood up. "I'm afraid I've got to leave you. Sonja,
may I escort you home?"

Smith said: "I think you can leave that to me, Captain."

"Yes, sir."

"That is, if Sonja . . ."

Sonja batted her eyelids. "Of course, Sandy."

Wolff said: "I hate to break up the party, but I've got an
early start."

"Quite all right," Smith told him. "You just run along."

As Wolff left a waiter brought dinner. It was a European
meal—steak and potatoes—and Sonja picked at it while
Smith talked to her. He told her about his successes in the
school cricket team. He seemed to have done nothing spectacular since then. He was very boring.

Sonja kept remembering the flogging.

He drank steadily through dinner. When they left he was
weaving slightly. She gave him her arm, more for his benefit
than for hers. They walked to the houseboat in the cool night

air. Smith looked up at the sky and said: "Those stars . . . beautiful." His speech was a little thick.

They stopped at the houseboat. "Looks pretty," Smith said.

"It's rather nice," Sonja said. "Would you like to see inside?"

"Rather."

She led him over the gangplank, across the deck, and down the stairs.

He looked around, wide-eyed. "I must say, it's very luxurious."

"Would you like a drink?"

"Very much."

Sonja hated the way he said "very" all the time. He slurred the *r* and pronounced it "vey." She said: "Champagne, or something stronger?"

"A drop of whiskey would be nice."

"Do sit down."

She gave him his drink and sat close to him. He touched her shoulder, kissed her cheek, and roughly grabbed her breast. She shuddered. He took that as a sign of passion, and squeezed harder.

She pulled him down on top of her. He was very clumsy: his elbows and knees kept digging into her. He fumbled beneath the skirt of her dress.

She said: "Oh, Sandy, you're so strong."

She looked over his shoulder and saw Wolff's face. He was on deck, kneeling down and watching through the hatch, laughing soundlessly.

8

William Vandam was beginning to despair of ever finding Alex Wolff. The Assyut murder was almost three weeks in the past, and Vandam was no closer to his quarry. As time went by the trail got colder. He almost wished there would be another briefcase snatch, so that at least he would know what Wolff was up to.

He knew he was becoming a little obsessed with the man. He would wake up in the night, around 3 A.M. when the booze had worn off, and worry until daybreak. What bothered him was something to do with Wolff's *style*: the sideways manner in which he had slipped into Egypt, the suddenness of the murder of Corporal Cox, the ease with which Wolff had melted into the city. Vandam went over these things, again and again, all the time wondering why he found the case so fascinating.

He had made no real progress, but he had gathered some information, and the information had fed his obsession—fed it not as food feeds a man, making him satisfied, but as fuel feeds a fire, making it burn hotter.

The Villa les Oliviers was owned by someone called Achmed Rahmha. The Rahmhas were a wealthy Cairo family. Achmed had inherited the house from his father, Gamal Rahmha, a lawyer. One of Vandam's lieutenants had dug up the record of a marriage between Gamal Rahmha and one Eva Wolff, widow of Hans Wolff, both German nationals; and then adoption papers making Hans and Eva's son Alex the legal child of Gamal Rahmha . . .

Which made Achmed Rahmha a German, and explained

how he got legitimate Egyptian papers in the name of Alex Wolff.

Also in the records was a will which gave Achmed, or Alex, a share of Gamal's fortune, plus the house.

Interviews with all surviving Rahmhas had produced nothing. Achmed had disappeared two years ago and had not been heard from since. The interviewer had come back with the impression that the adopted son of the family was not much missed.

Vandam was convinced that when Achmed disappeared he had gone to Germany.

There was another branch of the Rahmha family, but they were nomads, and no one knew where they could be found. No doubt, Vandam thought, they had helped Wolff somehow with his reentry into Egypt.

Vandam understood that now. Wolff could not have come into the country through Alexandria. Security was tight at the port: his entry would have been noted, he would have been investigated, and sooner or later the investigation would have revealed his German antecedents, whereupon he would have been interned. By coming from the south he had hoped to get in unobserved and resume his former status as a born-and-bred Egyptian. It had been a piece of luck for the British that Wolff had run into trouble in Assyut.

It seemed to Vandam that that was the last piece of luck they had had.

He sat in his office, smoking one cigarette after another, worrying about Wolff.

The man was no low-grade collector of gossip and rumor. He was not content, as other agents were, to send in reports based on the number of soldiers he saw in the street and the shortage of motor spares. The briefcase theft proved he was after top-level stuff, and he was capable of devising ingenious ways of getting it. If he stayed at large long enough he would succeed sooner or later.

Vandam paced the room—from the coat stand to the desk, around the desk for a look out of the window, around the other side of the desk, and back to the coat stand.

The spy had his problems, too. He had to explain himself to inquisitive neighbors, conceal his radio somewhere, move about the city and find informants. He could run out of money, his radio could break down, his informants could betray him or someone could quite accidentally discover his secret. One way or another, traces of the spy had to appear.

The cleverer he was, the longer it would take.

Vandam was convinced that Abdullah, the thief, was involved with Wolff. After Bogge refused to have Abdullah arrested, Vandam had offered a large sum of money for Wolff's whereabouts. Abdullah still claimed to know nothing of anyone called Wolff, but the light of greed had flickered in his eyes.

Abdullah might not know where Wolff could be found—Wolff was surely careful enough to take that precaution with a notoriously dishonest man—but perhaps Abdullah could find out. Vandam had made it clear that the money was still on offer. Then again, once Abdullah had the information he might simply go to Wolff, tell him of Vandam's offer and invite him to bid higher.

Vandam paced the room.

Something to do with *style*. Sneaking in; murder with a knife; melting away; and . . . Something else went with all that. Something Vandam knew about, something he had read in a report or been told in a briefing. Wolff might almost have been a man Vandam had known, long ago, but could no longer bring to mind. Style.

The phone rang.

He picked it up. "Major Vandam."

"Oh, hello, this is Major Calder in the paymaster's office."

Vandam tensed. "Yes?"

"You sent us a note, a couple of weeks ago, to look out for forged sterling. Well, we've found some."

That was it—that was the trace. "Good!" Vandam said.

"Rather a lot, actually," the voice continued.

Vandam said: "I need to see it as soon as possible."

"It's on its way. I'm sending a chap round—he should be there soon."

"Do you know who paid it in?"

"There's been more than one lot, actually, but we've got some names for you."

"Marvelous. I'll ring you back when I've seen the notes. Did you say Calder?"

"Yes." The man gave his phone number. "We'll speak later, then."

Vandam hung up. Forged sterling—it fitted: this could be the breakthrough. Sterling was no longer legal tender in Egypt. Officially Egypt was supposed to be a sovereign country. However, sterling could always be exchanged for Egyptian money at the office of the British paymaster general. Consequently people who did a lot of business with foreigners usually accepted pound notes in payment.

Vandam opened his door and shouted along the hall. "Jakes!"

"Sir!" Jakes shouted back equally loudly.

"Bring me the file on forged banknotes."

"Yes, sir!"

Vandam stepped to the next office and spoke to his secretary. "I'm expecting a package from the paymaster. Bring it in as soon as it comes, would you?"

"Yes, sir."

Vandam went back into his office. Jakes appeared a moment later with a file. The most senior of Vandam's team, Jakes was an eager, reliable young man who would follow orders to the letter, as far as they went, then use his initiative. He was even taller than Vandam, thin and black-haired, with a somewhat lugubrious look. He and Vandam were on terms of easy formality: Jakes was very scrupulous about his salutes and sirs, yet they discussed their work as equals, and Jakes used bad language with great fluency. Jakes was very well connected, and would almost certainly go further in the Army than Vandam would.

Vandam switched on his desk light and said: "Right, show me a picture of Nazi-style funny money."

Jakes put down the file and flicked through it. He extracted a sheaf of glossy photographs and spread them on the desk. Each print showed the front and back of a banknote, somewhat larger than actual size.

Jakes sorted them out. "Pound notes, fivers, tenners and twenties."

Black arrows on the photographs indicated the errors by which the forgeries might be identified.

The source of the information was counterfeit money taken from German spies captured in England. Jakes said:

"You'd think they'd know better than to give their spies funny money."

Vandam replied without looking up from the pictures. "Espionage is an expensive business, and most of the money is wasted. Why should they buy English currency in Switzerland when they can make it themselves? A spy has forged papers, he might as well have forged money. Also, it has a slightly damaging effect on the British economy if it gets into circulation. It's inflationary, like the government printing money to pay its debts."

"Still, you'd think they would have cottoned on by now to the fact that we're catching the buggers."

"Ah—but when we catch 'em, we make sure the Germans don't *know* we've caught 'em."

"All the same, I hope our spies aren't using counterfeit Reichmarks."

"I shouldn't think so. We take Intelligence rather more seriously than they do, you know. I wish I could say the same about tank tactics."

Vandam's secretary knocked and came in. He was a bespectacled twenty-year-old corporal. "Package from the paymaster, sir."

"Good show!" Vandam said.

"If you'd sign the slip, sir."

Vandam signed the receipt and tore open the envelope. It contained several hundred pound notes.

Jakes said: "Bugger me!"

"They told me there were a lot," Vandam said. "Get a magnifying glass, Corporal, on the double."

"Yes, sir."

Vandam put a pound note from the envelope next to one of the photographs and looked for the identifying error.

He did not need the magnifying glass.

"Look, Jakes."

Jakes looked.

The note bore the same error as the one in the photograph.

"That's it, sir," said Jakes.

"Nazi money, made in Germany," said Vandam. "*Now* we're on his trail."

Lieutenant Colonel Reggie Bogge knew that Major Vandam

was a smart lad, with the kind of low cunning one sometimes finds among the working class; but the major was no match for the likes of Bogge.

That night Bogge played snooker with Brigadier Povey, the Director of Military Intelligence, at the Gezira Sporting Club. The brigadier was shrewd, and he did not like Bogge all that much, but Bogge thought he could handle him.

They played for a shilling a point, and the brigadier broke.

While they played, Bogge said: "Hope you don't mind talking shop in the club, sir."

"Not at all," said the brigadier.

"It's just that I don't seem to get a chance to leave m'desk in the day."

"What's on your mind?" the brigadier chalked his cue.

Bogge potted a red ball and lined up the pink. "I'm pretty sure there's a fairly serious spy at work in Cairo." He missed the pink.

The brigadier bent over the table. "Go on."

Bogge regarded the brigadier's broad back. A little delicacy was called for here. Of course the head of a department was responsible for that department's successes, for it was only well-run departments which had successes, as everyone knew; nevertheless it was necessary to be subtle about how one took the credit. He began: "You remember a corporal was stabbed in Assyut a few weeks ago?"

"Vaguely."

"I had a hunch about that, and I've been following it up ever since. Last week a General Staff aide had his briefcase pinched during a street brawl. Nothing very remarkable about that, of course, but I put two and two together."

The brigadier potted the white. "Damn," he said. "Your shot."

"I asked the paymaster general to look out for counterfeit English money. Lo and behold, he found some. I had my boys examine it. Turns out to have been made in Germany."

"Aha!"

Bogge potted a red, the blue and another red, then he missed the pink again.

"I think you've left me rather well off," said the brigadier, scrutinizing the table through narrowed eyes. "Any chance of tracing the chap through the money?"

"It's a possibility. We're working on that already."

"Pass me that bridge, will you?"

"Certainly."

The brigadier laid the bridge on the baize and lined up his shot.

Bogge said: "It's been suggested that we might instruct the paymaster to continue to accept the forgeries, in case he can bring in any new leads." The suggestion had been Vandam's, and Bogge had turned it down. Vandam had argued—something that was becoming wearyingly familiar—and Bogge had had to slap him down. But it was an imponderable, and if things turned out badly Bogge wanted to be able to say he had consulted his superiors.

The brigadier unbent from the table and considered. "Rather depends how much money is involved, doesn't it?"

"Several hundred pounds so far."

"It's a lot."

"I feel it's not really necessary to continue to accept the counterfeits, sir."

"Jolly good." The brigadier pocketed the last of the red balls and started on the colors.

Bogge marked the score. The brigadier was ahead, but Bogge had got what he came for.

"Who've you got working on this spy thing?" the brigadier asked.

"Well, I'm handling it myself basically—"

"Yes, but which of your majors are you using?"

"Vandam, actually."

"Ah, Vandam. Not a bad chap."

Bogge did not like the turn the conversation was taking. The brigadier did not really understand how careful you had to be with the likes of Vandam: give them an inch and they would take the Empire. The Army *would* promote these people above their station. Bogge's nightmare was to find himself taking orders from a postman's son with a Dorset accent. He said: "Vandam's got a bit of a soft spot for the wog, unfortunately; but as you say, he's good enough in a plodding sort of fashion."

"Yes." The brigadier was enjoying a long break, potting the colors one after another. "He went to the same school as I. Twenty years later, of course."

Bogge smiled. "He was a scholarship boy, though, wasn't he, sir?"

"Yes," said the brigadier. "So was I." He pocketed the black.

"You seem to have won, sir," said Bogge.

The manager of the Cha-Cha Club said that more than half his customers settled their bills in sterling, he could not possibly identify who payed in which currency, and even if he could he did not know the names of more than a few regulars.

The chief cashier of Shepheard's Hotel said something similar.

So did two taxi drivers, the proprietor of a soldiers' bar and the brothel keeper Madame Fahmy.

Vandam was expecting much the same story from the next location on his list, a shop owned by one Mikis Aristopoulos.

Aristopoulos had changed a large amount of sterling, most of it forged, and Vandam imagined his shop would be a business of considerable size, but it was not so. Aristopoulos had a small grocery store. It smelled of spices and coffee but there was not much on the shelves. Aristopoulos himself was a short Greek of about twenty-five years with a wide, white-toothed smile. He wore a striped apron over his cotton trousers and white shirt.

He said: "Good morning, sir. How can I help you?"

"You don't seem to have much to sell," Vandam said.

Aristopoulos smiled. "If you're looking for something particular, I may have it in the stock room. Have you shopped here before, sir?"

So that was the system: scarce delicacies in the back room for regular customers only. It meant he might know his clientele. Also, the amount of counterfeit money he had exchanged probably represented a large order, which he would remember.

Vandam said: "I'm not here to buy. Two days ago you took one hundred and forty-seven pounds in English money to the British paymaster general and exchanged it for Egyptian currency."

Aristopoulos frowned and looked troubled. "Yes . . ."

"One hundred and twenty-seven pounds of that was counterfeit—forged—no good."

Aristopoulos smiled and spread his arms in a huge shrug. "I am sorry for the paymaster. I take the money from English, I give it back to English . . . What can I do?"

"You can go to jail for passing counterfeit notes."

Aristopoulos stopped smiling. "Please. This is not justice. How could I know?"

"Was all that money paid to you by one person?"

"I don't know—"

"Think!" Vandam said sharply. "Did anyone pay you one hundred and twenty-seven pounds?"

"Ah . . . yes! Yes!" Suddenly Aristopoulos looked hurt. "A very respectable customer. One hundred twenty-six pounds ten shillings."

"His name?" Vandam held his breath.

"Mr. Wolff—"

"Ahhh."

"I am so shocked. Mr. Wolff has been a good customer for many years, and no trouble with paying, never."

"Listen," Vandam said, "did you deliver the groceries?"

"No."

"*Damn.*"

"We offered to deliver, as usual, but this time Mr. Wolff—"

"You usually deliver to Mr. Wolff's home?"

"Yes, but this time—"

"What's the address?"

"Let me see. Villa les Oliviers, Garden City."

Vandam banged his fist on the counter in frustration. Aristopoulos looked a little frightened. Vandam said: "You haven't delivered there recently, though."

"Not since Mr. Wolff came back. Sir, I am very sorry that this bad money has passed through my innocent hands. Perhaps something can be arranged . . . ?"

"Perhaps," Vandam said thoughtfully.

"Let us drink coffee together."

Vandam nodded. Aristopoulos led him into the back room. The shelves here were well laden with bottles and tins, most of them imported. Vandam noticed Russian caviar, American canned ham and English jam. Aristopoulos poured thick strong coffee into tiny cups. He was smiling again.

Aristopoulos said: "These little problems can always be worked out between friends."

They drank coffee.

Aristopoulos said: "Perhaps, as a gesture of friendship, I could offer you something from my store. I have a little stock of French wine—"

"No, no—"

"I can usually find some Scotch whiskey when everyone else in Cairo has run out—"

"I'm not interested in *that* kind of arrangement," Vandam said impatiently.

"Oh!" said Aristopoulos. He had become quite convinced that Vandam was seeking a bribe.

"I want to find Wolff," Vandam continued. "I need to know where he is living now. You said he was a regular customer?"

"What sort of stuff does he buy?"

"Much champagne. Also some caviar. Coffee, quite a lot. Foreign liquor. Pickled walnuts, garlic sausage, brandied apricots . . ."

"Hm." Vandam drank in this incidental information greedily. What kind of a spy spent his funds on imported delicacies? Answer: one who was not very serious. But Wolff *was* serious. It was a question of style. Vandam said: "I was wondering how soon he is likely to come back."

"As soon as he runs out of champagne."

"All right. When he does, I must find out where he lives."

"But, sir, if he again refuses to allow me to deliver . . . ?"

"That's what I've been thinking about. I'm going to give you an assistant."

Aristopoulos did not like that idea. "I want to help you, sir, but my business is private—"

"You've got no choice," Vandam said. "It's help me, or go to jail."

"But to have an English officer working here in my shop—"

"Oh, it won't be an English officer." He would stick out like a sore thumb, Vandam thought, and probably scare Wolff away as well. Vandam smiled. "I think I know the ideal person for the job."

That evening after dinner Vandam went to Elene's apartment, carrying a huge bunch of flowers, feeling foolish.

She lived in a graceful, spacious old apartment house near the Place de l'Opéra. A Nubian concierge directed Vandam to the third floor. He climbed the curving marble staircase which occupied the center of the building and knocked on the door of 3A.

She was not expecting him, and it occurred to him suddenly that she might be entertaining a man friend.

He waited impatiently in the corridor, wondering what she would be like in her own home. This was the first time he had been here. Perhaps she was out. Surely she had plenty to do in the evenings—

The door opened.

She was wearing a yellow cotton dress with a full skirt, rather simple but almost thin enough to see through. The color looked very pretty against her light-brown skin. She gazed at him blankly for a moment, then recognized him and gave her impish smile.

She said: "Well, hello!"

"Good evening."

She stepped forward and kissed his cheek. "Come in."

He went inside and she closed the door.

"I wasn't expecting the kiss," he said.

"All part of the act. Let me relieve you of your disguise."

He gave her the flowers. He had the feeling he was being teased.

"Go in there while I put these in water," she said.

He followed her pointing finger into the living room and looked around. The room was comfortable to the point of sensuality. It was decorated in pink and gold and furnished with deep soft seats and a table of pale oak. It was a corner room with windows on two sides, and now the evening sun shone in and made everything glow slightly. There was a thick rug of brown fur on the floor that looked like bearskin. Vandam bent down and touched it: it was genuine. He had a sudden, vivid picture of Elene lying on the rug, naked and writhing. He blinked and looked elsewhere. On the seat beside him was a book which she had, presumably, been reading when he knocked. He picked up the book and sat on the seat. It was warm from her body. The book was called

Stamboul Train. It looked like cloak-and-dagger stuff. On the wall opposite him was a rather modern-looking painting of a society ball: all the ladies were in gorgeous formal gowns and all the men were naked. Vandam went and sat on the couch beneath the painting so that he would not have to look at it. He thought it peculiar.

She came in with the flowers in a vase, and the smell of wistaria filled the room. "Would you like a drink?"

"Can you make martinis?"

"Yes. Smoke if you want to."

"Thank you." She knew how to be hospitable, Vandam thought. He supposed she had to, given the way she earned her living. He took out his cigarettes. "I was afraid you'd be out."

"Not this evening." There was an odd note in her voice when she said that, but Vandam could not figure it out. He watched her with the cocktail shaker. He had intended to conduct the meeting on a businesslike level, but he was not able to, for it was she who was conducting it. He felt like a clandestine lover.

"Do you like this stuff?" He indicated the book.

"I've been reading thrillers lately."

"Why?"

"To find out how a spy is supposed to behave."

"I shouldn't think you——" He saw her smiling, and realized he was being teased again. "I never know whether you're serious."

"Very rarely." She handed him a drink and sat down at the opposite end of the couch. She looked at him over the rim of her glass. "To espionage."

He sipped his martini. It was perfect. So was she. The mellow sunshine burnished her skin. Her arms and legs looked smooth and soft. He thought she would be the same in bed as she was out of it: relaxed, amusing and game for anything. Damn. She had had this effect on him last time, and he had gone on one of his rare binges and ended up in a wretched brothel.

"What are you thinking about?" she said.

"Espionage."

She laughed: it seemed that somehow she knew he was lying. "You must love it," she said.

Vandam thought: How does she do this to me? She kept him always off balance, with her teasing and her insight, her innocent face and her long brown limbs. He said: "Catching spies can be very satisfying work, but I don't love it."

"What happens to them when you've caught them?"

"They hang, usually."

"Oh."

He had managed to throw her off balance for a change. She shivered. He said: "Losers generally die in wartime."

"Is that why you don't love it—because they hang?"

"No. I don't love it because I don't always catch them."

"Are you proud of being so hardhearted?"

"I don't think I'm hardhearted. We're trying to kill more of them than they can kill us." He thought: How did I come to be defending myself?

She got up to pour him another drink. He watched her walk across the room. She moved gracefully—like a cat, he thought; no, like a kitten. He looked at her back as she stooped to pick up the cocktail shaker, and he wondered what she was wearing beneath the yellow dress. He noticed her hands as she poured the drink: they were slender and strong. She did not give herself another martini.

He wondered what background she came from. He said: "Are your parents alive?"

"No," she said abruptly.

"I'm sorry," he said. He knew she was lying.

"Why did you ask me that?"

"Idle curiosity. Please forgive me."

She leaned over and touched his arm lightly, brushing his skin with her fingertips, a caress as gentle as a breeze. "You apologize too much." She looked away from him, as if hesitating; and then, seeming to yield to an impulse, she began to tell him of her background.

She had been the eldest of five children in a desperately poor family. Her parents were cultured and loving people— "My father taught me English and my mother taught me to wear clean clothes," she said—but the father, a tailor, was ultraorthodox and had estranged himself from the rest of the Jewish community in Alexandria after a doctrinal dispute with the ritual slaughterer. When Elene was fifteen years old her father began to go blind. He could no longer work as a tailor—but he would neither ask nor accept help from the "back-sliding" Alexandrian Jews. Elene went as a live-in maid to a British home and sent her wages to her family. From that point on, her story was one which had been repeated, Vandam knew, time and again over the last hundred years in the homes of the British ruling class: she fell in love with the son of the house, and he seduced her. She had been fortunate in that they had been found out before she became pregnant. The son was sent away to university and Elene was paid off. She was terrified to return home to tell her father she had been fired for fornication—and with a gentile. She lived on her payoff, continuing to send home the same amount of cash each week, until the money ran out. Then a lecherous businessman whom she had met at the house had set her up in a flat, and she was embarked upon her life's work. Soon afterward her father had been told how she was living, and he made the family sit shiva for her.

"What is shiva?" Vandam asked.

"Mourning."

Since then she had not heard from them, except for a message from a friend to tell her that her mother had died.

Vandam said: "Do you hate your father?"

She shrugged. "I think it turned out rather well." She spread her arms to indicate the apartment.

"But are you happy?"

She looked at him. Twice she seemed about to speak and then said nothing. Finally she looked away. Vandam felt she was regretting the impulse that had made her tell him her life story. She changed the subject. "What brings you here tonight, Major?"

Vandam collected his thoughts. He had been so interested in her—watching her hands and her eyes as she spoke of her past—that he had forgotten for a while his purpose. "I'm still looking for Alex Wolff," he began. "I haven't found him, but I've found his grocer."

"How did you do that?"

He decided not to tell her. Better that nobody outside Intelligence should know that German spies were betrayed by their forged money. "That's a long story," he said. "The important thing is, I want to put someone inside the shop in case he comes back."

"Me."

"That's what I had in mind."

"Then, when he comes in, I hit him over the head with a bag of sugar and guard the unconscious body until you come along."

Vandam laughed. "I believe you would," he said. "I can just see you leaping over the counter." He realized how much he was relaxing, and resolved to pull himself together before he made a fool of himself.

"Seriously, what do I have to do?" she said.

"Seriously, you have to discover where he lives."

"How?"

"I'm not sure." Vandam hesitated. "I thought perhaps you might befriend him. You're a very attractive woman—I imagine it would be easy for you."

"What do you mean by 'befriend'?"

"That's up to you. Just as long as you get his address."

"I see." Suddenly her mood had changed, and there was bitterness in her voice. The switch astonished Vandam: she was too quick for him to follow her. Surely a woman like Elene would not be offended by this suggestion? She said: "Why don't you just have one of your soldiers follow him home?"

"I may have to do that, if you fail to win his confidence. The trouble is, he might realize he was being followed and shake off the tail—then he would never go back to the grocer's, and we would have lost our advantage. But if you can persuade him, say, to invite you to his house for dinner, then we'll get the information we need without tipping our hand. Of course, it might not work. Both alternatives are risky. But I prefer the subtle approach."

"I understand that."

Of course she understood, Vandam thought; the whole thing was as plain as day. What the devil was the matter with her? She was a strange woman: at one moment he was quite enchanted by her, and at the next he was infuriated. For the first time it crossed his mind that she might refuse to do what he was asking. Nervously he said: "Will you help me?"

She got up and filled his glass again, and this time she took another drink herself. She was very tense, but it was clear she was not willing to tell him why. He always felt very annoyed with women in moods like this. It would be a damn nuisance if she refused to cooperate now.

At last she said: "I suppose it's no worse than what I've been doing all my life."

"That's what I thought," said Vandam with relief.

She gave him a very black look.

"You start tomorrow," he said. He gave her a piece of paper with the address of the shop written on it. She took it without looking at it. "The shop belongs to Mikis Aristopoulos," he added.

"How long do you think this will take?" she said.

"I don't know." He stood up. "I'll get in touch with you every few days, to make sure everything's all right—but you'll contact me as soon as he makes an appearance, won't you?"

"Yes."

Vandam remembered something. "By the way, the shopkeeper thinks we're after Wolff for forgery. Don't talk to him about espionage."

"I won't."

The change in her mood was permanent. They were no longer enjoying each other's company. Vandam said: "I'll leave you to your thriller."

She stood up. "I'll see you out."

They went to the door. As Vandam stepped out, the tenant of the neighboring flat approached along the corridor. Vandam had been thinking of this moment, in the back of his mind, all evening, and now he did what he had been determined not to do. He took Elene's arm, bent his head and kissed her mouth.

Her lips moved briefly in response. He pulled away. The neighbor passed by. Vandam looked at Elene. The neighbor unlocked his door, entered his flat and closed the door behind him. Vandam released Elene's arm.

She said: "You're a good actor."

"Yes," he said. "Good-bye." He turned away and strolled briskly down the corridor. He should have felt pleased with his evening's work, but instead he felt as if he had done something a little shameful. He heard the door of her apartment bang shut behind him.

Elene leaned back against the closed door and cursed William Vandam.

He had come into her life, full of English courtesy, asking her to do a new kind of work and help win the war; and then he had told her she must go whoring again.

She had really believed he was going to change her life. No more rich businessmen, no more furtive affairs, no more dancing or waiting on tables. She had a worthwhile job, something she believed in, something that mattered. Now it turned out to be the same old game.

For seven years she had been living off her face and her body, and now she wanted to stop.

She went into the living room to get a drink. His glass was there on the table, half empty. She put it to her lips. The drink was warm and bitter.

At first she had not liked Vandam: he had seemed a stiff, solemn, dull man. Then she had changed her mind about him. When had she first thought there might be another, different man beneath the rigid exterior? She remembered: it had been when he laughed. That laugh intrigued her. He had done it again tonight, when she said she would hit Wolff over the head with a bag of sugar. There was a rich vein of fun deep, deep inside him, and when it was tapped the laughter bubbled up and took over his whole personality for a moment. She suspected that he was a man with a big appetite for life—an appetite which he had firmly under control, too firmly. It made Elene want to get under his skin, to make him be himself. That was why she teased him, and tried to make him laugh again.

That was why she had kissed him, too.

She had been curiously happy to have him in her home, sitting on her couch, smoking and talking. She had even thought how nice it would be to take this strong, innocent man to bed and show him things he never dreamed of. Why did she like him? Perhaps it was that he treated her as a person, not as a girlie. She knew he would never pat her bottom and say: "Don't you worry your pretty little head . . ."

And he had spoiled it all. Why was she so bothered by this thing with Wolff? One more insincere act of seduction would do her no harm. Vandam had more or less said that. And in saying so, he had revealed that he regarded her as a whore.

That was what had made her so mad. She wanted his esteem, and when he asked her to "befriend" Wolff, she knew she was never going to get it, not really. Anyway the whole thing was foolish: the relationship between a woman such as she and an English officer was doomed to turn out like all Elene's relationships—manipulation on one side, dependence on the other and respect nowhere. Vandam would always see her as a whore. For a while she had thought he might be different from all the rest, but she had been wrong.

And she thought: But why do I mind so much?

Vandam was sitting in darkness at his bedroom window in the middle of the night, smoking cigarettes and looking out at the moonlit Nile, when a memory from his childhood sprang, fully formed, into his mind.

He is eleven years old, sexually innocent, physically still a child. He is in the terraced gray brick house where he has always lived. The house has a bathroom, with water heated by the coal fire in the kitchen below: he has been told that this makes his family very fortunate, and he must not boast about it; indeed, when he goes to the new school, the posh school in Bournemouth, he must pretend that he thinks it is perfectly normal to have a bathroom and hot water coming out of the taps. The bathroom has a water closet too. He is going there now to pee. His mother is in there, bathing his sister, who is seven years old, but they won't mind him going in to pee, he has done it before, and the other toilet is a long cold walk down the garden. What he has forgotten is that his cousin is also being bathed. She is eight years old. He walks into the bathroom. His sister is sitting in the bath. His cousin is standing, about to come out. His mother holds a towel. He looks at his cousin.

She is naked, of course. It is the first time he has seen any girl other than his sister naked. His cousin's body is slightly plump, and her skin is flushed with the heat of the water. She is quite the loveliest sight he has ever seen. He stands inside the bathroom doorway looking at her with undisguised interest and admiration.

He does not see the slap coming. His mother's large hand seems to come from nowhere. It hits his cheek with a loud clap. She is a good hitter, his mother, and this is one of her best efforts. It hurts like hell, but the shock is even worse than the pain. Worst of all is that the warm sentiment which had engulfed him has been shattered like a glass window.

"Get out!" his mother screams, and he leaves, hurt and humiliated.

Vandam remembered this as he sat alone watching the Egyptian night, and he thought, as he had thought at the time it happened: Now why did she do that?

9

In the early morning the tiled floor of the mosque was cold to Alex Wolff's bare feet. The handful of dawn worshipers was lost in the vastness of the pillared hall. There was a silence, a sense of peace, and a bleak gray light. A shaft of sunlight pierced one of the high narrow slits in the wall, and at that moment the muezzin began to cry:

"Allahu akbar! Allahu akbar! Allahu akbar! Allahu akbar!"

Wolff turned to face Mecca.

He was wearing a long robe and a turban, and the shoes in his hand were simple Arab sandals. He was never quite sure why he did this. He was a True Believer only in theory. He had been circumcised according to Islamic doctrine, and he had completed the pilgrimage to Mecca; but he drank alcohol and ate pork, he never paid the zakat tax, he never observed the fast of Ramadan and he did not pray every day, let alone five times a day. But every so often he felt the need to immerse himself, just for a few minutes, in the familiar, mechanical ritual of his stepfather's religion. Then, as he had done today, he would get up while it was still dark, and dress in traditional clothes, and walk through the cold quiet streets of the city to the mosque his father had attended, and perform the ceremonial ablutions in the forecourt, and enter in time for the first prayers of the new day.

He touched his ears with his hands, then clasped his hands in front of him, the left within the right. He bowed, then knelt down. Touching his forehead to the floor at appropriate moments, he recited the el-fatha:

"In the name of God the merciful and compassionate.

112

Praise be to God, the lord of the worlds, the merciful and compassionate, the Prince of the day of judgment; Thee we serve, and to Thee we pray for help; lead us in the right way, the way of those to whom Thou hast shown mercy, upon whom no wrath resteth, and who go not astray."

He looked over his right shoulder, then his left, to greet the two recording angels who wrote down his good and bad acts.

When he looked over his left shoulder, he saw Abdullah.

Without interrupting his prayer the thief smiled broadly, showing his steel tooth.

Wolff got up and went out. He stopped outside to put on his sandals, and Abdullah came waddling after him. They shook hands.

"You are a devout man, like myself," Abdullah said. "I knew you would come, sooner or later, to your father's mosque."

"You've been looking for me?"

"Many people are looking for you."

Together they walked away from the mosque. Abdullah said: "Knowing you to be a True Believer, I could not betray you to the British, even for so large a sum of money; so I told Major Vandam that I knew nobody by the name of Alex Wolff, or Achmed Rahmha."

Wolff stopped abruptly. So they were still hunting him. He had started to feel safe—too soon. He took Abdullah by the arm and steered him into an Arab café. They sat down.

Wolff said: "He knows my Arab name."

"He knows all about you—except where to find you."

Wolff felt worried, and at the same time intensely curious. "What is this major like?" he asked.

Abdullah shrugged. "An Englishman. No subtlety. No manners. Khaki shorts and a face the color of a tomato."

"You can do better than that."

Abdullah nodded. "This man is patient and determined. If I were you, I should be afraid of him."

Suddenly Wolff *was* afraid.

He said: "What has he been doing?"

"He has found out all about your family. He has talked to all your brothers. They said they knew nothing of you."

The café proprietor brought each of them a dish of mashed fava beans and a flat loaf of coarse bread. Wolff broke his bread and dipped it into the beans. Flies began to gather around the bowls. Both men ignored them.

Abdullah spoke through a mouthful of food. "Vandam is offering one hundred pounds for your address. Ha! As if we would betray one of our own for money."

Wolff swallowed. "Even if you knew my address."

Abdullah shrugged. "It would be a small thing to find out."

"I know," Wolff said. "So I am going to tell you, as a sign of my faith in your friendship. I am living at Shepheard's Hotel."

Abdullah looked hurt. "My friend, I know this is not true. It is the first place the British would look—"

"You misunderstand me." Wolff smiled. "I am not a guest there. I work in the kitchens, cleaning pots, and at the end of the day I lie down on the floor with a dozen or so others and sleep there."

"So cunning!" Abdullah grinned: he was pleased with the idea and delighted to have the information. "You hide under their very noses!"

"I know you will keep this secret," Wolff said. "And, as a sign of my gratitude for your friendship, I hope you will accept from me a gift of one hundred pounds."

"But this is not necessary—"

"I insist."

Abdullah sighed and gave in reluctantly. "Very well."

"I will have the money sent to your house."

Abdullah wiped his empty bowl with the last of his bread. "I must leave you now," he said. "Allow me to pay for your breakfast."

"Thank you."

"Ah! But I have come with no money. A thousand pardons—"

"It's nothing," Wolff said. "*Alallah*—in God's care."

Abdullah replied conventionally: "*Allah yisallimak*—may God protect thee." He went out.

Wolff called for coffee and thought about Abdullah. The thief would betray Wolff for a lot less than a hundred pounds, of course. What had stopped him so far was that he did not know Wolff's address. He was actively trying to discover it—that was why he had come to the mosque. Now he would attempt to check on the story about living in the

kitchens of Shepheard's. This might not be easy, for of course
no one would admit that staff slept on the kitchen floor—
indeed Wolff was not at all sure it was true—but he had to
reckon on Abdullah discovering the lie sooner or later. The
story was no more than a delaying tactic; so was the bribe.
However, when at last Abdullah found out that Wolff was
living on Sonja's houseboat, he would probably come to
Wolff for more money instead of going to Vandam.

The situation was under control—for the moment.

Wolff left a few millièmes on the table and went out.

The city had come to life. The streets were already
jammed with traffic, the pavements crowded with vendors
and beggars, the air full of good and bad smells. Wolff made
his way to the central post office to use a telephone. He
called GHQ and asked for Major Smith.

"We have seventeen of them," the operator told him. "Have
you got a first name?"

"Sandy."

"That will be Major Alexander Smith. He's not here at the
moment. May I take a message?"

Wolff had known the major would not be at GHQ—it was
too early. "The message is: Twelve noon today at Zamalek.
Would you sign it: S. Have you got that?"

"Yes, but if I may have your full—"

Wolff hung up. He left the post office and headed for
Zamalek.

Since Sonja had seduced Smith, the major had sent her a
dozen roses, a box of chocolates, a love letter and two hand-
delivered messages asking for another date. Wolff had forbid-
den her to reply. By now Smith was wondering whether he
would ever see her again. Wolff was quite sure that Sonja was
the first beautiful woman Smith had ever slept with. After a
couple of days of suspense Smith would be desperate to see
her again, and would jump at any chance.

On the way home Wolff bought a newspaper, but it was
full of the usual rubbish. When he got to the houseboat Sonja
was still asleep. He threw the rolled-up newspaper at her to
wake her. She groaned and turned over.

Wolff left her and went through the curtains back into the
living room. At the far end, in the prow of the boat, was a
tiny open kitchen. It had one quite large cupboard for

brooms and cleaning materials. Wolff opened the cupboard door. He could just about get inside if he bent his knees and ducked his head. The catch of the door could be worked only from the outside. He searched through the kitchen drawers and found a knife with a pliable blade. He thought he could probably work the catch from inside the cupboard by sticking the knife through the crack of the door and easing it against the spring-loaded bolt. He got into the cupboard, closed the door and tried it. It worked.

However, he could not see through the doorjamb.

He took a nail and a flatiron and banged the nail through the thin wood of the door at eye level. He used a kitchen fork to enlarge the hole. He got inside the cupboard again and closed the door. He put his eye to the hole.

He saw the curtains part, and Sonja came into the living room. She looked around, surprised that he was not there. She shrugged, then lifted her nightdress and scratched her belly. Wolff suppressed a laugh. She came across to the kitchen, picked up the kettle and turned on the tap.

Wolff slipped the knife into the crack of the door and worked the catch. He opened the door, stepped out and said: "Good morning."

Sonja screamed.

Wolff laughed.

She threw the kettle at him, and he dodged. He said: "It's a good hiding place, isn't it?"

"You terrified me, you bastard," she said.

He picked up the kettle and handed it to her. "Make the coffee," he told her. He put the knife in the cupboard, closed the door and went to sit down.

Sonja said: "What do you need a hiding place for?"

"To watch you and Major Smith. It's very funny—he looks like a passionate turtle."

"When is he coming?"

"Twelve noon today."

"Oh, no. Why so early in the morning?"

"Listen. If he's got anything worthwhile in that briefcase, then he certainly isn't allowed to go wandering around the city with it in his hand. He should take it straight to his office and lock it in the safe. We mustn't give him time to do that—the whole thing is useless unless he brings his case here.

What we want is for him to come rushing here straight from GHQ. In fact, if he gets here late and without his briefcase, we're going to lock up and pretend you're out—then next time he'll know he has to get here fast."

"You've got it all worked out, haven't you?"

Wolff laughed. "You'd better start getting ready. I want you to look irresistible."

"I'm always irresistible." She went through to the bedroom.

He called after her: "Wash your hair." There was no reply.

He looked at his watch. Time was running out. He went around the houseboat hiding traces of his own occupation, putting away his shoes, his razor, his toothbrush and his fez. Sonja went up on deck in a robe to dry her hair in the sun. Wolff made the coffee and took her a cup. He drank his own, then washed his cup and put it away. He took out a bottle of champagne, put it in a bucket of ice and placed it beside the bed with two glasses. He thought of changing the sheets, then decided to do it after Smith's visit, not before. Sonja came down from the deck. She dabbed perfume on her thighs and between her breasts. Wolff took a last look around. All was ready. He sat on a divan by a porthole to watch the towpath.

It was a few minutes after noon when Major Smith appeared. He was hurrying, as if afraid to be late. He wore his uniform shirt, khaki shorts, socks and sandals, but he had taken off his officer's cap. He was sweating in the midday sun.

He was carrying his briefcase.

Wolff grinned with satisfaction.

"Here he comes," Wolff called. "Are you ready?"

"No."

She was trying to rattle him. She would be ready. He got into the cupboard, closed the door, and put his eye to the peephole.

He heard Smith's footsteps on the gangplank and then on the deck. The major called: "Hello?"

Sonja did not reply.

Looking through the peephole, Wolff saw Smith come down the stairs into the interior of the boat.

"Is anybody there?"

Smith looked at the curtains which divided off the bedroom. His voice was full of the expectation of disappointment. "Sonja?"

The curtains parted. Sonja stood there, her arms lifted to hold the curtains apart. She had put her hair up in a complex pyramid as she did for her act. She wore the baggy trousers of filmy gauze, but at this distance her body was visible through the material. From the waist up she was naked except for a jeweled collar around her neck. Her brown breasts were full and round. She had put lipstick on her nipples.

Wolff thought: Good girl!

Major Smith stared at her. He was quite bowled over. He said: "Oh, dear. Oh, good Lord. Oh, my soul."

Wolff tried not to laugh.

Smith dropped his briefcase and went to her. As he embraced her, she stepped back and closed the curtains behind his back.

Wolff opened the cupboard door and stepped out.

The briefcase lay on the floor just this side of the curtains. Wolff knelt down, hitching up his galabiya, and turned the case over. He tried the catches. The case was locked.

Wolff whispered: "*Lieber Gott.*"

He looked around. He needed a pin, a paper clip, a sewing needle, something with which to pick the locks. Moving quietly, he went to the kitchen area and carefully pulled open a drawer. Meat skewer, too thick; bristle from a wire brush, too thin; vegetable knife, too broad . . . In a little dish beside the sink he found one of Sonja's hair clips.

He went back to the case and poked the end of the clip into the keyhole of one of the locks. He twisted and turned it experimentally, encountered a kind of springy resistance, and pressed harder.

The clip broke.

Again Wolff cursed under his breath.

He glanced reflexively at his wristwatch. Last time Smith had screwed Sonja in about five minutes. I should have told her to make it last, Wolff thought.

He picked up the flexible knife he had been using to open the cupboard door from the inside. Gently, he slid it into one of the catches on the briefcase. When he pressed, the knife bent.

He could have broken the locks in a few seconds, but he

did not want to, for then Smith would know that his case had been opened. Wolff was not afraid of Smith, but he wanted the major to remain oblivious to the real reason for the seduction: if there was valuable material in the case, Wolff wanted to open it regularly.

But if he could not open the case, Smith would always be useless.

What would happen if he broke the locks? Smith would finish with Sonja, put on his pants, pick up his case and realize it had been opened. He would accuse Sonja. The houseboat would be blown unless Wolff killed Smith. What would be the consequences of killing Smith? Another British soldier murdered, this time in Cairo. There would be a terrific manhunt. Would they be able to connect the killing with Wolff? Had Smith told anyone about Sonja? Who had seen them together in the Cha-Cha Club? Would inquiries lead the British to the houseboat?

It would be risky—but the worst of it would be that Wolff would be without a source of information, back at square one.

Meanwhile his people were fighting a war out there in the desert, and they needed information.

Wolff stood silent in the middle of the living room, racking his brains. He had thought of something, back there, which gave him his answer, and now it had slipped his mind. On the other side of the curtain, Smith was muttering and groaning. Wolff wondered if he had his pants off yet—

His pants off, that was it.

He would have the key to his briefcase in his pocket.

Wolff peeped between the curtains. Smith and Sonja lay on the bed. She was on her back, eyes closed. He lay beside her, propped up on one elbow, touching her. She was arching her back as if she were enjoying it. As Wolff watched, Smith rolled over, half lying on her, and put his face to her breasts.

Smith still had his shorts on.

Wolff put his head through the curtains and waved an arm, trying to attract Sonja's attention. He thought: Look at me, woman! Smith moved his head from one breast to the other. Sonja opened her eyes, glanced at the top of Smith's head, stroked his brilliantined hair, and caught Wolff's eye.

He mouthed: Take off his pants.

She frowned, not understanding.

Wolff stepped through the curtains and mimed removing pants.

Sonja's face cleared as enlightenment dawned.

Wolff stepped back through the curtains and closed them silently, leaving only a tiny gap to look through.

He saw Sonja's hands go to Smith's shorts and begin to struggle with the buttons of the fly. Smith groaned. Sonja rolled her eyes upward, contemptuous of his credulous passion. Wolff thought: I hope she has the sense to throw the shorts this way.

After a minute Smith grew impatient with her fumbling, rolled over, sat up and took them off himself. He dropped them over the end of the bed and turned back to Sonja.

The end of the bed was about five feet away from the curtain.

Wolff got down on the floor and lay flat on his belly. He parted the curtains with his hands and inched his way through, Indian fashion.

He heard Smith say: "Oh, God, you're so beautiful."

Wolff reached the shorts. With one hand he carefully turned the material over until he saw a pocket. He put his hand in the pocket and felt for a key.

The pocket was empty.

There was the sound of movement from the bed. Smith grunted. Sonja said: "No, lie still."

Wolff thought: Good *girl*.

He turned the shorts over until he found the other pocket. He felt in it. That, too, was empty.

There might be more pockets. Wolff grew reckless. He felt the garment, searching for hard lumps that might be metal. There were none. He picked up the shorts—

A bunch of keys lay beneath them.

Wolff breathed a silent sigh of relief.

The keys must have slipped out of the pocket when Smith dropped the shorts on the floor.

Wolff picked up the keys and the shorts and began to inch backward through the curtains.

Then he heard footsteps on deck.

Smith said: "Good God, what's that!" in a high-pitched voice.

"Hush!" Sonja said. "Only the postman. Tell me if you like this . . ."

"Oh, yes."

Wolff made it through the curtains and looked up. The postman was placing a letter on the top step of the stairs, by the hatch. To Wolff's horror the postman saw him and called out: *"Sabah el-kheir*—good morning!"

Wolff put a finger to his lips for silence, then lay his cheek against his hand to mime sleep, then pointed to the bedroom.

"Your pardon!" the postman whispered.

Wolff waved him away.

There was no sound from the bedroom.

Had the postman's greeting made Smith suspicious? Probably not, Wolff decided: a postman might well call good morning even if he could see no one, for the fact that the hatch was open indicated that someone was at home.

The lovemaking noises in the next room resumed, and Wolff breathed more easily.

He sorted through the keys, found the smallest, and tried it in the locks of the case.

It worked.

He opened the other catch and lifted the lid. Inside was a sheaf of papers in a stiff cardboard folder. Wolff thought: No more menus, please. He opened the folder and looked at the top sheet.

He read:

OPERATION ABERDEEN

1. Allied forces will mount a major counterattack at dawn on 5 June.

2. The attack will be two-pronged . . .

Wolff looked up from the papers. "My God," he whispered. "This is it!"

He listened. The noises from the bedroom were louder now. He could hear the springs of the bed, and he thought the boat itself was beginning to rock slightly. There was not much time.

The report in Smith's possession was detailed. Wolff was

not sure exactly how the British chain of command worked, but presumably the battles were planned in detail by General Ritchie at desert headquarters then sent to GHQ in Cairo for approval by Auchinleck. Plans for more important battles would be discussed at the morning conferences, which Smith obviously attended in some capacity. Wolff wondered again which department it was that was housed in the unmarked building in the Shari Suleiman Pasha to which Smith returned each afternoon; then he pushed the thought aside. He needed to make notes.

He hunted around for pencil and paper, thinking: I should have done this beforehand. He found a writing pad and a red pencil in a drawer. He sat down by the briefcase and read on.

The main Allied forces were besieged in an area they called the Cauldron. The June 5 counterattack was intended to be a breakout. It would begin at 0520 with the bombardment, by four regiments of artillery, of the Aslagh Ridge, on Rommel's eastern flank. The artillery was to soften up the opposition in readiness for the spearhead attack by the infantry of the 10th Indian Brigade. When the Italians had breached the line at Aslagh Ridge, the tanks of the 22nd Armored Brigade would rush through the gap and capture Sidi Muftah while the 9th Indian Brigade followed through and consolidated.

Meanwhile the 32nd Army Tank Brigade, with infantry support, would attack Rommel's northern flank at Sidra Ridge.

When he came to the end of the report Wolff realized he had been so absorbed that he had heard, but had not taken notice of, the sound of Major Smith reaching his climax. Now the bed creaked and a pair of feet hit the floor.

Wolff tensed.

Sonja said: "Darling, pour some champagne."

"Just a minute—"

"I want it now."

"I feel a bit silly with me pants off, m'dear."

Wolff thought: Christ, he wants his pants.

Sonja said: "I like you undressed. Drink a glass with me before you put your clothes on."

"Your wish is my command."

Wolff relaxed. She may bitch about it, he thought, but she does what I want!

He looked quickly through the rest of the papers, determined that he would not be caught now: Smith was a wonderful find, and it would be a tragedy to kill the goose the first time it laid a golden egg. He noted that the attack would employ four hundred tanks, three hundred and thirty of them with the eastern prong and only seventy with the northern; that Generals Messervy and Briggs were to establish a combined headquarters; and that Auchinleck was demanding—a little peevishly, it seemed—thorough reconnaissance and close cooperation between infantry and tanks.

A cork popped loudly as he was writing. He licked his lips, thinking: I could use some of that. He wondered how quickly Smith could drink a glass of champagne. He decided to take no chances.

He put the papers back in the folder and the folder back in the case. He closed the lid and keyed the locks. He put the bunch of keys in a pocket of the shorts. He stood up and peeped through the curtain.

Smith was sitting up in bed in his army-issue underwear with a glass in one hand and a cigarette in the other, looking pleased with himself. The cigarettes must have been in his shirt pocket: it would have been awkward if they had been in his shorts.

At the moment Wolff was within Smith's field of view. He took his face away from the tiny gap between the curtains, and waited. He heard Sonja say: "Pour me some more, please." He looked through again. Smith took her glass and turned away to the bottle. His back was now to Wolff. Wolff pushed the shorts through the curtains and put them on the floor. Sonja saw him and raised her eyebrows in alarm. Wolff withdrew his arm. Smith handed Sonja the glass.

Wolff got into the cupboard, closed the door and eased himself to the floor. He wondered how long he would have to wait before Smith left. He did not care: he was jubilant. He had struck gold.

It was half an hour before he saw, through the peephole, Smith come into the living room, wearing his clothes again. By this time Wolff was feeling very cramped. Sonja followed Smith, saying: "Must you go so soon?"

"I'm afraid so," he said."It's a very awkward time for me, you see." He hesitated. "To be perfectly frank, I'm not actually supposed to carry this briefcase around with me. I had the very devil of a job to come here at noon.You see, I have to go from GHQ straight to my office. Well, I didn't do that today—I was desp rately afraid I might miss you if I came late. I told my office I was lunching at GHQ, and told the chaps at GHQ I was lunching at my office. However, next time I'll go to my office, dump the briefcase, and come on here—if that's all right with you, my little poppet."

Wolff thought: For God's sake, Sonja, say something!

She said: "Oh, but, Sandy, my housekeeper comes every afternoon to clean—we wouldn't be alone."

Smith frowned. "Damn. Well, we'll just have to meet in the evenings."

"But I have to work—and after my act, I have to stay in the club and talk to the customers. And I couldn't sit at your table every night: people would gossip."

The cupboard was very hot and stuffy. Wolff was perspiring heavily.

Smith said: "Can't you tell your cleaner not to come?"

"But darling, I couldn't clean the place myself—I wouldn't know how."

Wolff saw her smile, then she took Smith's hand and placed it between her legs. "Oh, Sandy, say you'll come at noon."

It was much more than Smith could withstand. "Of course I will, my darling," he said.

They kissed, and at last Smith left. Wolff listened to the footsteps crossing the deck and descending the gangplank, then he got out of the cupboard.

Sonja watched with malicious glee as he stretched his aching limbs. "Sore?" she said with mock sympathy.

"It was worth it," Wolff said. "You were wonderful."

"Did you get what you wanted?"

"Better than I could have dreamed."

Wolff cut up bread and sausage for lunch while Sonja took a bath. After lunch he found the English novel and the key to the code, and drafted his signal to Rommel. Sonja went to the racetrack with a crowd of Egyptian friends: Wolff gave her fifty pounds to bet with.

In the evening she went to the Cha-Cha Club and Wolff sat at home drinking whiskey and reading Arab poetry. As midnight approached, he set up the radio.

At exactly 2400 hours, he tapped out his call sign, Sphinx. A few seconds later Rommel's desert listening post, or Horch Company, answered. Wolff sent a series of V's to enable them to tune in exactly, then asked them what his signal strength was. In the middle of the sentence he made a mistake, and sent a series of E's—for Error—before beginning again. They told him his signal was maximum strength and made GA for Go Ahead. He made a KA to indicate the beginning of his message; then, in code, he began: "Operation Aberdeen. . . ."

At the end he added AR for Message Finished and K for Over. They replied with a series of R's, which meant: "Your message has been received and understood."

Wolff packed away the radio, the core book and the key, then he poured himself another drink.

All in all, he thought he had done incredibly well.

10

The signal from the spy was only one of twenty or thirty reports on the desk of von Mellenthin, Rommel's Ic—intelligence officer—at seven o'clock on the morning of June 4. There were several other reports from listening units: infantry had been heard talking to tanks *au clair*; field headquarters had issued instructions in low-grade codes which had been deciphered overnight; and there was other enemy radio traffic which, although indecipherable, nevertheless yielded hints about enemy intentions simply because of its location and frequency. As well as radio reconnaissance there were the reports from the Ics in the field, who got information from captured weapons, the uniforms of enemy dead, interrogation of prisoners and simply looking across the desert and *seeing* the people they were fighting. Then there was aerial reconnaissance, a situation report from an order-of-battle expert and a summary—just about useless—of Berlin's current assessment of Allied intentions and strength.

Like all field intelligence officers, von Mellenthin despised spy reports. Based on diplomatic gossip, newspaper stories and sheer guesswork, they were wrong at least as often as they were right, which made them effectively useless.

He had to admit that this one *looked* different.

The run-of-the-mill secret agent might report: "9th Indian Brigade have been told they will be involved in a major battle in the near future," or: "Allies planning a breakout from the Cauldron in early June," or: "Rumors that Auchinleck will be replaced as commander in chief." But there was nothing indefinite about this report.

The spy, whose call sign was Sphinx, began his message:

Changes in the closing prices from 4 p.m. the previous day.

March 20, 2021

YTD %Chg	52-Week Hi	Lo	Stock	Sym	Yld %	PE	Last	Net Chg
25.16	32.64	7.98	CanNaturalRes	CNQ	5.0	dd	30.10	0.52
9.17	385.87	180.12	CanPacRlwy	CP	0.8	28	378.48	-5.27
13.29	24.22	15.46	Canon	CAJ	2.9	40	21.99	0.29
39.81	5.60	11.30	CanopyGrowth	CGC	...	dd	34.45	1.08
27.90	134.70	39.90	CapitalOne	COF	1.3	25	126.43	-1.88
31.40	58.58	7.75	Capri	CPRI	...	dd	55.19	-0.35
9.56	59.46	39.05	CardinalHealth	CAH	3.3	13	58.68	0.40
0.60	161.54	97.55	Carlisle	CSL	1.3	27	157.12	-1.90
16.03	37.81	17.35	Carlyle	CG	2.7	40	36.48	0.11
41.05	136.43	43.14	CarMax	KMX	...	29	133.24	-1.32
33.70	30.12	7.80	Carnival	CCL	...	dd	28.96	0.69
28.87	25.19	7.33	Carnival	CUK	0.0	dd	24.15	0.37
8.46	41.94	11.50	CarrierGlobal	CARR	1.2	18	40.91	-0.09
12.39	323.39	26.35	Carvana	CVNA	...	dd	269.22	6.41
1.86	127.68	37.15	Catalent	CTLT	...	59	106.01	2.01
23.77	237.78	90.64	Caterpillar	CAT	1.8	41	225.29	-5.39
13.62	152.60	60.33	Celanese	CE	1.8	9	147.64	-1.03
29.59	7.59	1.55	Cemex	CX	0.0	dd	6.70	-0.19
32.45	8.57	1.56	CenovusEnergy	CVE	0.7	dd	8	0.13
7.01	74.70	44.81	Centene	CNC	...	21	64.24	0.67
2.87	25.39	11.68	CenterPointEner	CNP	2.9	dd	22.26	0.32
-12.88	7.75	2.96	CentraisElBras	EBR	...	7	6.09	-0.04
-22.13	111.93	38.90	CeridianHCM	CDAY	...	dd	82.98	0.27
-8.32	84.20	53.08	Cerner	CERN	1.2	28	71.95	0.21
14.74	303.79	97.23	CharlesRiverLabs	CRL	...	40	286.68	-1.60
-4.81	681.71	364.67	CharterComms	CHTR	...	41	629.74	0.35
-12.21	139.26	83.72	CheckPoint	CHKP	...	20	116.68	0.59
1.51	115.21	29.23	Chegg	CHGG	...	dd	91.69	1.34
18.71	77.11	29.25	CheniereEnergy	LNG	...	dd	71.26	-0.22
23.72	44.63	21	CheniereEnerPtrs	CQP	5.9	20	43.61	0.24
22.42	112.70	52.97	Chevron	CVX	5.0	dd	103.38	-0.74
-8.19	120	29.16	Chewy	CHWY	dd	...	82.53	5.02
17.48	26.19	15.80	ChinaEastrnAir	CEA	...	dd	25.27	-0.51
-4.25	13.63	8.63	ChinaLifeIns	LFC	4.2	9	10.59	0.05
19.48	58.40	38.18	ChinaPetrol	SNP	6.2	12	53.29	-1.18
29.71	39.96	18.45	ChinaSoAirlines	ZNH	...	dd	38.46	-0.36
2.49	1564.91	551.21	Chipotle	CMG	...	74	1421.20	-8.16
3.45	179.01	92.04	Chubb	CB	2.0	21	159.23	-8.90
0.52	40.25	34.72	ChunghwaTel	CHT	2.7	27	38.82	-0.06
-4.75	98.96	59.36	Church&Dwight	CHD	1.2	27	83.09	0.83
23.31	258.32	69	ChurchillDowns	CHDN	0.3	dd	240.20	1.17
4.86	61.52	32.77	Ciena	CIEN	...	21	55.42	0.17
16.85	248.39	126	Cigna	CI	1.6	11	243.26	-0.56
22.47	108.99	46.07	CincinnatiFin	CINF	2.4	13	108.14	-1.01
-5.77	369.20	154.33	Cintas	CTAS	0.9	37	333.05	-4.18
9.45	49.74	33.74	CiscoSystems	CSCO	3.0	21	48.98	0.18
18.41	76.13	34.67	Citigroup	C	2.8	15	73.01	-0.83
24.55	47.56	19.13	CitizensFin	CFG	3.2	40	44.54	-0.84
2.67	173.56	111.26	CitrixSystems	CTXS	1.1	33	133.57	2.07
-12.79	33.55	16.01	Clarivate	CLVT	...	dd	25.91	-0.14
14.22	18.77	3.01	Cleveland-Cliffs	CLF	0.0	dd	16.63	-0.06
-7.82	239.87	161.11	Clorox	CLX	2.4	19	186.13	1.66
-5.66	95.77	19.53	Cloudflare	NET	...	dd	71.69	1.27
-7.35	54.93	36.27	Coca-Cola	KO	3.1	28	50.81	0.24
3.91	54.55	28.35	Coca-Cola Euro	CCEP	3.9	41	51.75	-0.11
-1.29	101.82	36.51	Cognex	CGNX	0.3	80	79.25	-0.78
-6.59	82.73	40.01	CognizantTech	CTSH	1.3	30	76.55	0.15
12.31	86.41	58.49	ColgatePalm	CL	2.4	24	74.98	-1.09
5.84	58.59	31.70	Comcast A	CMCSA	1.8	24	55.46	-0.41
24.15	73.73	25.80	Comerica	CMA	3.9	21	69.35	-1.28
20.79	83.06	43.34	CommerceBcshrs	CBSH	1.3	27	79.36	-0.56
7.90	7.24	1.02	CiaSiderurgica	SID	...	43	6.42	-0.15
4.38	39.34	24.86	ConagraBrands	CAG	2.9	17	37.85	-0.73
31.53	61.14	20.84	ConocoPhillips	COP	3.3	dd	52.60	-0.78
0.04	90	62.03	ConEd	ED	4.3	22	72.30	0.08
7.14	242.62	104.28	ConstBrands A	STZ	1.3	26	234.70	3.63
-2.08	32.85	15.06	ContextLogic	WISH	...	dd	17.86	0.60
83.13	32.39	6.90	ContinentalRscs	CLR	0.0	dd	26.59	1.21
5.70	401.92	237.71	Cooper	COO	0.0	8	384.02	5.24
16.23	130.96	55.69	Copart	CPRT	...	36	106.59	-2.42
14.67	42.55	17.44	Corning	GLW	2.3	86	41.20	-0.11
21.57	47.98	21.11	Corteva	CTVA	1.1	52	47.07	0.11
11.43	952.76	500.24	CoStar	CSGP	...	137	818.66	13.15
12.71	393.15	278.42	Costco	COST	0.9	34	328.91	5.93
26.61	377.00	147	CoupaSoftware	COUP	...	dd	248.73	-0.72
...	69	42.70	Coupang	CPNG	...	dd	49.17	-1.00
10.50	172.12	110.47	Credicorp	BAP	5.9	128	146.79	-0.87
2.19	14.95	6.67	CreditSuisse	CS	0.9	12	13.08	-0.02
0.82	129.91	31.08	Cree	CREE	...	dd	104.67	-1.53
-8.12	251.28	46.01	CrowdStrike	CRWD	...	dd	194.63	4.42

...ned up its wealth-management subsidia...

Invest in C

...eijing, after
...nuary 2020
access to
sector for
...ons.

...ent builds
agreed in
J.P. Morgan
...nt and the
they would
...duct devel-
...stor educa-
...t the strong
...bute to the
...a's financial
Hui, execu-
...esident of
Bank and
...e group's

...erate China Merchants
is one of the country's
commercial lenders
wealth-management s
...iary managed the equ
of $377 billion at the
2020, up 12% from the
...ous year, according
bank's annual report.

China Merchants F
the clear leader amo
country's banks for we
...lated business, analy
Citigroup said in Janua
note to clients, they sai
...rives a higher propor
revenues from wealth r
...ment and manages a
pool of assets for in...
...investors than any of t...

"Operation Aberdeen." He gave the date of the attack, the brigades involved and their specific roles, the places they would pounce, and the tactical thinking of the planners.

Von Mellenthin was not convinced, but he was interested.

As the thermometer in his tent passed the 100-degree mark he began his routine round of morning discussions. In person, by field telephone and—rarely—by radio, he talked to the divisional Ics, the Luftwaffe liaison officer for aerial reconnaissance, the Horch Company liaison man and a few of the better brigade Ics. To all of these men he mentioned the 9th and 10th Indian Brigades, the 22nd Armored Brigade, and the 32nd Army Tank Brigade. He told them to look out for these brigades. He also told them to watch for battle preparations in the areas from which, according to the spy, the counterthrust would come. They would also observe the enemy's observers: if the spy were right, there would be increased aerial reconnaissance by the Allies of the positions they planned to attack, namely Aslagh Ridge, Sidra Ridge and Sidi Muftah. There might be increased bombing of those positions, for the purpose of softening up, although this was such a giveaway that most commanders would resist the temptation. There might be *de*creased bombing, as a bluff, and this too could be a sign.

These conversations also enabled the field Ics to update their overnight reports. When they were finished von Mellenthin wrote *his* report for Rommel, and took it to the command vehicle. He discussed it with the chief of staff, who then presented it to Rommel.

The morning discussion was brief, for Rommel had made his major decisions and given his orders for the day during the previous evening. Besides, Rommel was not in a reflective mood in the mornings: he wanted action. He tore around the desert, going from one front-line position to another in his staff car or his Storch aircraft, giving new orders, joking with the men and taking charge of skirmishes—and yet, although he constantly exposed himself to enemy fire, he had not been wounded since 1914. Von Mellenthin went with him today, taking the opportunity to get his own picture of the front-line situation, and making his personal assessment of the Ics who were sending in his raw material: some were overcautious, omitting all unconfirmed data, and others exaggerated in order to get extra supplies and reinforcements for their units.

In the early evening, when at last the thermometer showed a fall, there were more reports and conversations. Von Mellenthin sifted the mass of detail for information relating to the counterattack predicted by Sphinx.

The Ariete Armored—the Italian division occupying the Aslagh Ridge—reported increased enemy air activity. Von Mellenthin asked them whether this was bombing or reconnaissance, and they said reconnaissance: bombing had actually ceased.

The Luftwaffe reported activity in no-man's-land which might, or might not, have been an advance party marking out an assembly point.

There was a garbled radio intercept in a low-grade cipher in which the something Indian Brigade requested urgent clarification of the morning's something (orders?) with particular reference to the timing of something artillery bombardment. In British tactics, von Mellenthin knew, artillery bombardment generally preceded an attack.

The evidence was building.

Von Mellenthin checked his card index for the 32nd Army Tank Brigade and discovered that they had recently been sighted at Rigel Ridge—a logical position from which to attack Sidra Ridge.

The task of an Ic was an impossible one: to forecast the enemy's moves on the basis of inadequate information. He looked at the signs, he used his intuition and he gambled.

Von Mellenthin decided to gamble on Sphinx.

At 1830 hours he took his report to the command vehicle. Rommel was there with his chief of staff Colonel Bayerlein and Kesselring. They stood around a large camp table looking at the operations map. A lieutenant sat to one side ready to take notes.

Rommel had taken his cap off, and his large, balding head appeared too big for his small body. He looked tired and thin. He suffered recurring stomach trouble, von Mellenthin knew, and was often unable to eat for days. His normally pudgy face had lost flesh, and his ears seemed to stick out more than usual. But his slitted dark eyes were bright with enthusiasm and the hope of victory.

Von Mellenthin clicked his heels and formally handed over the report, then he explained his conclusions on the map. When he had done Kesselring said: "And all this is based on the report of a spy, you say?"

"No, Field Marshal," von Mellenthin said firmly. "There are confirming indications."

"You can find confirming indications for anything," Kesselring said.

Out of the corner of his eye von Mellenthin could see that Rommel was getting cross.

Kesselring said: "We really can't plan battles on the basis of information from some grubby little secret agent in Cairo."

Rommel said: "I am inclined to believe this report."

Von Mellenthin watched the two men. They were curiously balanced in terms of power—curiously, that was, for the Army, where hierarchies were normally so well defined. Kesselring was C in C South, and outranked Rommel, but Rommel did not take orders from him, by some whim of Hitler's. Both men had patrons in Berlin—Kesselring, the Luftwaffe man, was Goering's favorite, and Rommel produced such good publicity that Goebbels could be relied upon to support him. Kesselring was popular with the Italians, whereas Rommel always insulted them. Ultimately Kesselring was more powerful, for as a field marshal he had direct access to Hitler, while Rommel had to go through Jodl; but this was a card Kesselring could not afford to play too often. So the two men quarreled; and although Rommel had the last word here in the desert, back in Europe—von Mellenthin knew—Kesselring was maneuvering to get rid of him.

Rommel turned to the map. "Let us be ready, then, for a two-pronged attack. Consider first the weaker, northern prong. Sidra Ridge is held by the Twenty-first Panzer Division with antitank guns. Here, in the path of the British advance, is a minefield. The panzers will lure the British into the minefield and destroy them with antitank fire. If the spy is right, and the British throw only seventy tanks into this assault, the Twenty-first Panzers should deal with them quickly and be free for other action later in the day."

He drew a thick forefinger down across the map. "Now consider the second prong, the main assault, on our eastern

flank. This is held by the Italian Army. The attack is to be
led by an Indian brigade. Knowing those Indians, and knowing our Italians, I assume the attack will succeed. I therefore
order a vigorous riposte.

"One: The Italians will counterattack from the west. Two:
The Panzers, having repelled the other prong of the attack at
Sidra Ridge, will turn about and attack the Indians from the
north. Three: Tonight our engineers will clear a gap in the
minefield at Bir el-Harmat, so that the Fifteenth Panzers can
make a swing to the south, emerge through the gap, and attack the British forces from the rear."

Von Mellenthin, listening and watching, nodded appreciation. It was a typical Rommel plan, involving rapid switching
of forces to maximize their effect, an encircling movement,
and the surprise appearance of a powerful division where it
was least expected, in the enemy's rear. If it all worked, the
attacking Allied brigades would be surrounded, cut off and
wiped out.

If it all worked.

If the spy was right.

Kesselring said to Rommel: "I think you could be making
a big mistake."

"That's your privilege," Rommel said calmly.

Von Mellenthin did not feel calm. If it worked out badly,
Berlin would soon hear about Rommel's unjustified faith in
poor intelligence; and von Mellenthin would be blamed for
supplying that intelligence. Rommel's attitude to subordinates
who let him down was savage.

Rommel looked at the note-taking lieutenant. "Those, then,
are my orders for tomorrow." He glared defiantly at Kesselring.

Von Mellenthin put his hands in his pockets and crossed
his fingers.

Von Mellenthin remembered that moment when, sixteen days
later, he and Rommel watched the sun rise over Tobruk.

They stood together on the escarpment northeast of El
Adem, waiting for the start of the battle. Rommel was wearing the goggles he had taken from the captured General
O'Connor, the goggles which had become a kind of trademark of his. He was in top form: bright-eyed, lively and con-

fident. You could almost hear his brain tick as he scanned the landscape and computed how the battle might go.

Von Mellenthin said: "The spy was right."

Rommel smiled. "That's exactly what I was thinking."

The Allied counterattack of June 5 had come precisely as forecast, and Rommel's defense had worked so well that it had turned into a counter-counterattack. Three of the four Allied brigades involved had been wiped out, and four regiments of artillery had been captured. Rommel had pressed his advantage remorselessly. On June 14 the Gazala Line had been broken and today, June 20, they were to besiege the vital coastal garrison of Tobruk.

Von Mellenthin shivered. It was astonishing how cold the desert could be at five o'clock in the morning.

He watched the sky.

At twenty minutes past five the attack began.

A sound like distant thunder swelled to a deafening roar as the Stukas approached. The first formation flew over, dived toward the British positions, and dropped their bombs. A great cloud of dust and smoke arose, and with that Rommel's entire artillery forces opened fire with a simultaneous earsplitting crash. Another wave of Stukas came over, then another: there were hundreds of bombers.

Von Mellenthin said: "Fantastic. Kesselring really did it."

It was the wrong thing to say. Rommel snapped: "No credit to Kesselring: today we are directing the planes ourselves."

The Luftwaffe was putting on a good show, even so, von Mellenthin thought; but he did not say it.

Tobruk was a concentric fortress. The garrison itself was within a town, and the town was at the heart of a larger British-held area surrounded by a thirty-five-mile perimeter wire dotted with strongpoints. The Germans had to cross the wire, then penetrate the town, then take the garrison.

A cloud of orange smoke arose in the middle of the battlefield. Von Mellenthin said: "That's a signal from the assault engineers, telling the artillery to lengthen their range."

Rommel nodded. "Good. We're making progress."

Suddenly von Mellenthin was seized by optimism. There was booty in Tobruk: petrol, and dynamite, and tents, and trucks—already more than half Rommel's motorized transport consisted of captured British vehicles—and food. Von Mellenthin smiled and said: "Fresh fish for dinner?"

Rommel understood his train of thought. "Liver," he said. "Fried potatoes. Fresh bread."

"A real bed, with a feather pillow."

"In a house with stone walls to keep out the heat and the bugs."

A runner arrived with a signal. Von Mellenthin took it and read it. He tried to keep the excitement out of his voice as he said: "They've cut the wire at Strongpoint Sixty-nine. Group Menny is attacking with the infantry of the Afrika Korps."

"That's it," said Rommel. "We've opened a breach. Let's go."

It was ten-thirty in the morning when Lieutenant Colonel Reggie Bogge poked his head around the door of Vandam's office and said: "Tobruk is under siege."

It seemed pointless to work then. Vandam went on mechanically, reading reports from informants, considering the case of a lazy lieutenant who was due for promotion but did not deserve it, trying to think of a fresh approach to the Alex Wolff case; but everything seemed hopelessly trivial. The news became more depressing as the day wore on. The Germans breached the perimeter wire; they bridged the anti-tank ditch; they crossed the inner minefield; they reached the strategic road junction known as King's Cross.

Vandam went home at seven to have supper with Billy. He could not tell the boy about Tobruk: the news was not to be released at present. As they ate their lamb chops, Billy said that his English teacher, a young man with a lung condition who could not get into the Army, never stopped talking about how he would love to get out into the desert and have a bash at the Hun. "I don't believe him, though," Billy said. "Do you?"

"I expect he means it," Vandam said. "He just feels guilty."

Billy was at an argumentative age. "Guilty? He can't feel *guilty*—it's not his fault."

"Unconsciously he can."

"What's the difference?"

I walked into that one, Vandam thought. He considered

for a moment, then said: "When you've done something wrong, and you know it's wrong, and you feel bad about it, and you know why you feel bad, that's conscious guilt. Mr. Simkisson has done nothing wrong, but he *still* feels bad about it, and he doesn't know why he feels bad. That's unconscious guilt. It makes him feel better to talk about how much he wants to fight."

"Oh," said Billy.

Vandam did not know whether the boy had understood or not.

Billy went to bed with a new book. He said it was a "tec," by which he meant a detective story. It was called *Death on the Nile*.

Vandam went back to GHQ. The news was still bad. The 21st Panzers had entered the town of Tobruk and fired from the quay on to several British ships which were trying, belatedly, to escape to the open sea. A number of vessels had been sunk. Vandam thought of the men who made a ship, and the tons of precious steel that went into it, and the training of the sailors, and the welding of the crew into a team; and now the men were dead, the ship sunk, the effort wasted.

He spent the night in the officers' mess, waiting for news. He drank steadily and smoked so much that he gave himself a headache. Bulletins came down periodically from the Operations Room. During the night Ritchie, as commander of the Eighth Army, decided to abandon the frontier and retreat to Mersa Matruh. It was said that when Auchinleck, the commander in chief, heard this news he stalked out of the room with a face as black as thunder.

Toward dawn Vandam found himself thinking about his parents. Some of the ports on the south coast of England had suffered as much as London from the bombing, but his parents were a little way inland, in a village in the Dorset countryside. His father was postmaster at a small sorting office. Vandam looked at his watch: it would be four in the morning in England now, the old man would be putting on his cycle clips, climbing on his bike and riding to work in the dark. At sixty years of age he had the constitution of a teenage farmboy. Vandam's chapelgoing mother forbade smoking, drinking and all kinds of dissolute behavior, a term she used to encompass everything from darts matches to listening to the wireless. The regime seemed to suit her husband, but she herself was always ailing.

Eventually booze, fatigue and tedium sent Vandam into a doze. He dreamed he was in the garrison at Tobruk with Billy and Elene and his mother. He was running around closing all the windows. Outside, the Germans—who had turned into firemen—were leaning ladders against the wall and climbing up. Suddenly Vandam's mother stopped counting her forged banknotes and opened a window, pointing at Elene and screaming: "The Scarlet Woman!" Rommel came through the window in a fireman's helmet and turned a hose on Billy. The force of the jet pushed the boy over a parapet and he fell into the sea. Vandam knew he was to blame, but he could not figure out what he had done wrong. He began to weep bitterly. He woke up.

He was relieved to discover that he had not really been crying. The dream left him with an overwhelming sense of despair. He lit a cigarette. It tasted foul.

The sun rose. Vandam went around the mess turning out the lights, just for something to do. A breakfast cook came in with a pot of coffee. As Vandam was drinking his, a captain came down with another bulletin. He stood in the middle of the mess, waiting for silence.

He said: "General Klopper surrendered the garrison of Tobruk to Rommel at dawn today."

Vandam left the mess and walked through the streets of the city toward his house by the Nile. He felt impotent and useless, sitting in Cairo catching spies while out there in the desert his country was losing the war. It crossed his mind that Alex Wolff might have had something to do with Rommel's latest series of victories; but he dismissed the thought as somewhat farfetched. He felt so depressed that he wondered whether things could possibly get any worse, and he realized that, of course, they could.

When he got home he went to bed.

PART TWO

MERSA MATRUH

11

The Greek was a feeler.

Elene did not like feelers. She did not mind straightforward lust; in fact, she was rather partial to it. What she objected to was furtive, guilty, unsolicited groping.

After two hours in the shop she had disliked Mikis Aristopoulos. After two weeks she was ready to strangle him.

The shop itself was fine. She liked the spicy smells and the rows of gaily colored boxes and cans on the shelves in the back room. The work was easy and repetitive, but the time passed quickly enough. She amazed the customers by adding up their bills in her head very rapidly. From time to time she would buy some strange imported delicacy and take it home to try: a jar of liver paste, a Hershey bar, a bottle of Bovril, a can of baked beans. And for her it was novel to do an ordinary, dull, eight-hours-a-day job.

But the boss was a pain. Every chance he got he would touch her arm, her shoulder or her hip; each time he passed her, behind the counter or in the back room, he would brush against her breasts or her bottom. At first she had thought it was accidental, because he did not look the type: he was in his twenties, quite good-looking, with a big smile that showed his white teeth. He must have taken her silence for acquiescence. She would have to tread on him a little.

She did not need this. Her emotions were too confused already. She both liked and loathed William Vandam, who talked to her as an equal, then treated her like a whore; she was supposed to seduce Alex Wolff, whom she had never met; and she was being groped by Mikis Aristopoulos, for whom she felt nothing but scorn.

They all use me, she thought; it's the story of my life.

She wondered what Wolff would be like. It was easy for Vandam to tell her to befriend him, as if there were a button she could press which made her instantly irresistible. In reality a lot depended on the man. Some men liked her immediately. With others it was hard work. Sometimes it was impossible. Half of her hoped it would be impossible with Wolff. The other half remembered that he was a spy for the Germans, and Rommel was coming closer every day, and if the Nazis ever got to Cairo . . .

Aristopoulos brought a box of pasta out from the back room. Elene looked at her watch: it was almost time to go home. Aristopoulos dropped the box and opened it. On his way back, as he squeezed past her, he put his hands under her arms and touched her breasts. She moved away. She heard someone come into the shop. She thought: I'll teach the Greek a lesson. As he went into the back room, she called after him loudly, in Arabic: "If you touch me again I'll cut your cock off!"

There was a burst of laughter from the customer. She turned and looked at him. He was a European, but he must understand Arabic, she thought. She said: "Good afternoon."

He looked toward the back room and called out: "What have you been doing, Aristopoulos, you young goat?"

Aristopoulos poked his head around the door. "Good day, sir. This is my niece, Elene." His face showed embarrassment and something else which Elene could not read. He ducked back into the storeroom.

"Niece!" said the customer, looking at Elene. "A likely tale."

He was a big man in his thirties with dark hair, dark skin and dark eyes. He had a large hooked nose which might have been typically Arab or typically European-aristocratic. His mouth was thin-lipped, and when he smiled he showed small even teeth—like a cat's, Elene thought. She knew the signs of wealth and she saw them here: a silk shirt, a gold wristwatch, tailored cotton trousers with a crocodile belt, handmade shoes and a faint masculine cologne.

Elene said: "How can I help you?"

He looked at her as if he were contemplating several possible answers, then he said: "Let's start with some English marmalade."

"Yes." The marmalade was in the back room. She went there to get a jar.

"It's him!" Aristopoulos hissed.

"What are you talking about?" she asked in a normal voice. She was still mad at him.

"The bad-money man—Mr. Wolff—that's him!"

"Oh, God!" For a moment she had forgotten why she was here. Aristopoulos' panic infected her, and her mind went blank. "What shall I say to him? What should I do?"

"I don't know—give him the marmalade—I don't know—"

"Yes, the marmalade, right . . ." She took a jar of Cooper's Oxford from a shelf and returned to the shop. She forced herself to smile brightly at Wolff as she put the jar down on the counter. "What else?"

"Two pounds of the dark coffee, ground fine."

He was watching her while she weighed the coffee and put it through the grinder. Suddenly she was afraid of him. He was not like Charles, Johnnie and Claud, the men who had kept her. They had been soft, easygoing, guilty and pliable. Wolff seemed poised and confident: it would be hard to deceive him and impossible to thwart him, she guessed.

"Something else?"

"A tin of ham."

She moved around the shop, finding what he wanted and putting the goods on the counter. His eyes followed her everywhere. She thought: I must talk to him, I can't keep saying "Something else?" I'm supposed to befriend him. "Something else?" she said.

"A half case of champagne."

The cardboard box containing six full bottles was heavy. She dragged it out of the back room. "I expect you'd like us to deliver this order," she said. She tried to make it sound casual. She was slightly breathless with the effort of bending to drag the case, and she hoped this would cover her nervousness.

He seemed to look through her with his dark eyes. "Deliver?" he said. "No, thank you."

She looked at the heavy box. "I hope you live nearby."

"Close enough."

"You must be very strong."

"Strong enough."

"We have a thoroughly reliable delivery man—"

"No delivery," he said firmly.

She nodded. "As you wish." She had not really expected it to work, but she was disappointed all the same. "Something else?"

"I think that's all."

She began to add up the bill. Wolff said: "Aristopoulos must be doing well, to employ an assistant."

Elene said: "Five pounds twelve and six, you wouldn't say that if you knew what he pays me, five pounds thirteen and six, six pounds—"

"Don't you like the job?"

She gave him a direct look. "I'd do *anything* to get out of here."

"What did you have in mind?" He was very quick.

She shrugged, and went back to her addition. Eventually she said: "Thirteen pounds ten shillings and fourpence."

"How did you know I'd pay in sterling?"

He was *quick*. She was afraid she had given herself away. She felt herself begin to blush. She had an inspiration, and said: "You're a British officer, aren't you?"

He laughed loudly at that. He took out a roll of pound notes and gave her fourteen. She gave him his change in Egyptian coins. She was thinking: What else can I do? What else can I say? She began to pack his purchases into a brown-paper shopping bag.

She said: "Are you having a party? I love parties."

"What makes you ask?"

"The champagne."

"Ah. Well, life is one long party."

She thought: I've failed. He will go away now, and perhaps he won't come back for weeks, perhaps never; I've had him in my sights, I've talked to him, and now I have to let him walk away and disappear into the city.

She should have felt relieved, but instead she felt a sense of abject failure.

He lifted the case of champagne on to his left shoulder, and picked up the shopping bag with his right hand. "Good-bye," he said.

"Good-bye."

He turned around at the door. "Meet me at the Oasis Restaurant on Wednesday night at seven-thirty."

"All right!" she said jubilantly. But he was gone.

It took them most of the morning to get to the Hill of Jesus. Jakes sat in the front next to the driver; Vandam and Bogge sat in the back. Vandam was exultant. An Australian company had taken the hill in the night, and they had captured—almost intact—a German wireless listening post. It was the first good news Vandam had heard for months.

Jakes turned around and shouted over the noise of the engine. "Apparently the Aussies charged in their socks, to surprise 'em," he said. "Most of the Italians were taken prisoner in their pajamas."

Vandam had heard the same story. "The Germans weren't sleeping, though," he said. "It was quite a rough show."

They took the main road to Alexandria, then the coast road to El Alamein, where they turned on to a barrel track—a route through the desert marked with barrels. Nearly all the traffic was going in the opposite direction, retreating. Nobody knew what was happening. They stopped at a supply dump to fill up with petrol, and Bogge had to pull rank on the officer in charge to get a chitty.

Their driver asked for directions to the hill. "Bottle track," the officer said brusquely. The tracks, created by and for the Army, were named Bottle, Boot, Moon and Star, the symbols for which were cut into the empty barrels and petrol cans along the routes. At night little lights were placed in the barrels to illuminate the symbols.

Bogge asked the officer: "What's happening out here? Everything seems to be heading back east."

"Nobody tells me anything," said the officer.

They got a cup of tea and a bully-beef sandwich from the NAAFI truck. When they moved on they went through a recent battlefield, littered with wrecked and burned-out tanks, where a graveyard detail was desultorily collecting corpses. The barrels disappeared, but the driver picked them up again on the far side of the gravel plain.

They found the hill at midday. There was a battle going on not far away: they could hear the guns and see clouds of dust rising to the west. Vandam realized he had not been this near the fighting before. The overall impression was one of dirt, panic and confusion. They reported to the command vehicle and were directed to the captured German radio trucks.

Field intelligence men were already at work. Prisoners were being interrogated in a small tent, one at a time, while the others waited in the blazing sun. Enemy ordnance experts were examining weapons and vehicles, noting manufacturers' serial numbers. The Y Service was there looking for wavelengths and codes. It was the task of Bogge's little squad to investigate how much the Germans had been learning in advance about Allied movements.

They took a truck each. Like most people in Intelligence, Vandam had a smattering of German. He knew a couple of hundred words, most of them military terms, so that while he could not have told the difference between a love letter and a laundry list, he could read army orders and reports.

There was a lot of material to be examined: the captured post was a great prize for Intelligence. Most of the stuff would have to be boxed, transported to Cairo and perused at length by a large team. Today's job was a preliminary overview.

Vandam's truck was a mess. The Germans had begun to destroy their papers when they realized the battle was lost. Boxes had been emptied and a small fire started, but the damage had been arrested quickly. There was blood on a cardboard folder: someone had died defending his secrets.

Vandam went to work. They would have tried to destroy the important papers first, so he began with the half-burned pile. There were many Allied radio signals, intercepted and in some cases decoded. Most of it was routine—most of everything was routine—but as he worked Vandam began to realize that German Intelligence's wireless interception was picking up an awful lot of useful information. They were better than Vandam had imagined—and Allied wireless security was very bad.

At the bottom of the half-burned pile was a book, a novel in English. Vandam frowned. He opened the book and read the first line: "Last night I dreamt I went to Manderley again." The book was called *Rebecca*, and it was by Daphne du Maurier. The title was vaguely familiar. Vandam thought his wife might have read it. It seemed to be about a young woman living in an English country house.

Vandam scratched his head. It was, to say the least, peculiar reading for the Afrika Korps.

And why was it in English?

It might have been taken from a captured English soldier, but Vandam thought that unlikely: in his experience soldiers read pornography, hard-boiled private eye stories and the Bible. Somehow he could not imagine the Desert Rats getting interested in the problems of the mistress of Manderley.

No, the book was here for a purpose. What purpose? Vandam could think of only one possibility: it was the basis of a code.

A book code was a variation on the one-time pad. A one-time pad had letters and numbers randomly printed in five-character groups. Only two copies of each pad were made: one for the sender and one for the recipient of the signals. Each sheet of the pad was used for one message, then torn off and destroyed. Because each sheet was used only once the code could not be broken. A book code used the pages of a printed book in the same way, except that the sheets were not necessarily destroyed after use.

There was one big advantage which a book had over a pad. A pad was unmistakably for the purpose of encipherment, but a book looked quite innocent. In the battlefield this did not matter; but it did matter to an agent behind enemy lines.

This might also explain why the book was in English. German soldiers signaling to one another would use a book in German, if they used a book at all, but a spy in British territory would need to carry a book in English.

Vandam examined the book more closely. The price had been written in pencil on the endpaper, then rubbed out with an eraser. That might mean the book had been bought second-hand. Vandam held it up to the light, trying to read the impression the pencil had made in the paper. He made out the number 50, followed by some letters. Was it *eic*? It might be *erc*, or *esc*. It was *esc*, he realized—fifty escudos. The book had been bought in Portugal. Portugal was neutral territory, with both German and British embassies, and it was a hive of low-level espionage.

As soon as he got back to Cairo he would send a message to the Secret Intelligence Service station in Lisbon. They could check the English-language bookshops in Portugal—there could not be very many—and try to find out where the book had been bought, and if possible by whom.

At least two copies would have been bought, and a bookseller might remember such a sale. The interesting question was, where was the other copy? Vandam was pretty sure it was in Cairo, and he thought he knew who was using it.

He decided he had better show his find to Lieutenant Colonel Bogge. He picked up the book and stepped out of the truck.

Bogge was coming to find him.

Vandam stared at him. He was white-faced, and angry to the point of hysteria. He came stomping across the dusty sand, a sheet of paper in his hand.

Vandam thought: What the devil has got into him?

Bogge shouted: "What do you do all day, anyway?"

Vandam said nothing. Bogge handed him the sheet of paper. Vandam looked at it.

It was a coded radio signal, with the decrypt written between the lines of code. It was timed at midnight on June 3. The sender used the call sign Sphinx. The message, after the usual preliminaries about signal strength, bore the heading OPERATION ABERDEEN.

Vandam was thunderstruck. Operation Aberdeen had taken place on June 5, and the Germans had received a signal about it on June 3.

Vandam said: "Jesus Christ Almighty, this is a disaster."

"Of course it's a bloody disaster!" Bogge yelled. "It means Rommel is getting full details of our attacks before they bloody begin!"

Vandam read the rest of the signal. "Full details" was right. The message named the brigades involved, the timing of various stages of the attack, and the overall strategy.

"No wonder Rommel's winning," Vandam muttered.

"Don't make bloody jokes!" Bogge screamed.

Jakes appeared at Vandam's side, accompanied by a full colonel from the Australian brigade that had taken the hill, and said to Vandam: "Excuse me, sir—"

Vandam said abruptly: "Not now, Jakes."

"Stay here, Jakes," Bogge countermanded. "This concerns you, too."

Vandam handed the sheet of paper to Jakes. Vandam felt as if someone had struck him a physical blow. The information was so good that it had to have originated in GHQ.

Jakes said softly: "Bloody hell."

Bogge said: "They must be getting this stuff from an English officer, you realize that, do you?"

"Yes," Vandam said.

"What do you mean, *yes?* Your job is personnel security—this is your bloody responsibility!"

"I realize that, sir."

"Do you also realize that a leak of this magnitude will have to be reported to the commander in chief?"

The Australian colonel, who did not appreciate the scale of the catastrophe, was embarrassed to see an officer getting a public dressing down. He said: "Let's save the recriminations for later, Bogge. I doubt the thing is the fault of any one individual. Your first job is to discover the extent of the damage and make a preliminary report to your superiors."

It was clear that Bogge was not through ranting yet; but he was outranked. He suppressed his wrath with a visible effort, and said: "Right, get on with it, Vandam." He stumped off, and the colonel went away in the other direction.

Vandam sat down on the step of the truck. He lit a cigarette with a shaking hand. The news seemed worse as it sunk in. Not only had Alex Wolff penetrated Cairo and evaded Vandam's net, he had gained access to high-level secrets.

Vandam thought: Who is this man?

In just a few days he had selected his target, laid his groundwork, and then bribed, blackmailed or corrupted the target into treachery.

Who was the target; who was giving Wolff the information? Literally hundreds of people had the information: the generals, their aides, the secretaries who typed written messages, the men who encoded radio messages, the officers who carried verbal messages, all Intelligence staff, all inter-service liaison people . . .

Somehow, Vandam assumed, Wolff had found one among those hundreds of people who was prepared to betray his country for money, or out of political conviction, or under pressure of blackmail. Of course it was possible that Wolff had nothing to do with it—but Vandam thought that unlikely, for a traitor needed a channel of communication with the enemy, and Wolff had such a channel, and it was hard to believe there might be two like Wolff in Cairo.

Jakes was standing beside Vandam, looking dazed. Vandam said: "Not only is this information getting through, but Rommel is using it. If you recall the fighting on five June—"

"Yes, I do," Jakes said. "It was a massacre."

And it was my fault, Vandam thought. Bogge had been right about that: Vandam's job was to stop secrets getting out, and when secrets got out it was Vandam's responsibility.

One man could not win the war, but one man could lose it. Vandam did not want to be that man.

He stood up. "All right, Jakes, you heard what Bogge said. Let's get on with it."

Jakes snapped his fingers. "I forgot what I came to tell you: you're wanted on the field telephone. It's GHQ. Apparently there's an Egyptian woman in your office, asking for you, refusing to leave. She says she has an urgent message and she won't take no for an answer."

Vandam thought: Elene!

Maybe she made contact with Wolff. She must have—why else would she be desperate to speak to Vandam? Vandam ran to the command vehicle, with Jakes hard on his heels.

The major in charge of communications handed him the phone. "Make it snappy, Vandam, we're using that thing."

. Vandam had swallowed enough abuse for one day. He snatched the phone, thrust his face into the major's face, and said loudly: "I'll use it as long as I need it." He turned his back on the major and spoke into the phone. "Yes?"

"William?"

"Elene!" He wanted to tell her how good it was to hear her voice, but instead he said: "What happened?"

"He came into the shop."

"You saw him! Did you get his address?"

"No—but I've got a date with him."

"Well done!" Vandam was full of savage delight—he would catch the bastard now. "Where and when?"

"Tomorrow night, seven-thirty, at the Oasis Restaurant."

Vandam picked up a pencil and a scrap of paper. "Oasis Restaurant, seven-thirty," he repeated. "I'll be there."

"Good."

"Elene . . ."

"Yes?"

"I can't tell you how grateful I am. Thank you."

"Until tomorrow."

"Good-bye." Vandam put down the phone.

Bogge was standing behind him, with the major in charge of communications. Bogge said: "What the devil do you mean by using the field telephone to make dates with your bloody girl friends?"

Vandam gave him a sunny smile. "That wasn't a girl friend, it was an informant," he said. "She's made contact with the spy. I expect to arrest him tomorrow night."

12

Wolff watched Sonja eat. The liver was underdone, pink and soft, just as she liked it. She ate with relish, as usual. He thought how alike the two of them were. In their work they were competent, professional and highly successful. They both lived in the shadows of childhood shocks: her father's death, his mother's remarriage into an Arab family. Neither of them had ever come close to marrying, for they were too fond of themselves to love another person. What brought them together was not love, not even affection, but shared lusts. The most important thing in life, for both of them, was the indulgence of their appetites. They both knew that Wolff was taking a small but unnecessary risk by eating in a restaurant, and they both felt the risk was worth it, for life would hardly be worth living without good food.

She finished her liver and the waiter brought an ice-cream dessert. She was always very hungry after performing at the Cha-Cha Club. It was not surprising: she used a great deal of energy in her act. But when, finally, she quit dancing, she would grow fat. Wolff imagined her in twenty years' time: she would have three chins and a vast bosom, her hair would be brittle and graying, she would walk flat-footed and be breathless after climbing the stairs.

"What are you smiling at?" Sonja said.

"I was picturing you as an old woman, wearing a shapeless black dress and a veil."

"I won't be like that. I shall be very rich, and live in a palace surrounded by naked young men and women eager to gratify my slightest whim. What about you?"

Wolff smiled. "I think I shall be Hitler's ambassador to Egypt, and wear an SS uniform to the mosque."

"You'd have to take off your jackboots."

"Shall I visit you in your palace?"

"Yes, please—wearing your uniform."

"Would I have to take off my jackboots in your presence?"

"No. Everything else, but not the boots."

Wolff laughed. Sonja was in a rare gay mood. He called the waiter and asked for coffee, brandy and the bill. He said to Sonja: "There's some good news. I've been saving it. I think I've found another Fawzi."

She was suddenly very still, looking at him intently. "Who is she?" she said quietly.

"I went to the grocer's yesterday. Aristopoulos has his niece working with him."

"A shopgirl!"

"She's a real beauty. She has a lovely, innocent face and a slightly wicked smile."

"How old?"

"Hard to say. Around twenty, I think. She has such a girl-ish body."

Sonja licked her lips. "And you think she will . . . ?"

"I think so. She's dying to get away from Aristopoulos, and she practically threw herself at me."

"When?"

"I'm taking her to dinner tomorrow night."

"Will you bring her home?"

"Maybe. I have to feel her out. She's so perfect, I don't want to spoil everything by rushing her."

"You mean you want to have her first."

"If necessary."

"Do you think she's a virgin?"

"It's possible."

"If she is . . ."

"Then I'll save her for you. You were so good with Major Smith, you deserve a treat." Wolff sat back, studying Sonja. Her face was a mask of sexual greed as she anticipated the corruption of someone beautiful and innocent. Wolff sipped his brandy. A warm glow spread in his stomach. He felt good: full of food and wine, his mission going remarkably well and a new sexual adventure in view.

The bill came, and he paid it with English pound notes.

It was a small restaurant, but a successful one. Ibrahim managed it and his brother did the cooking. They had learned the trade in a French hotel in Tunisia, their home; and when their father died they had sold the sheep and come to Cairo to seek their fortune. Ibrahim's philosophy was simple: they knew only French-Arab cuisine, so that was all they offered. They might, perhaps, have attracted more customers if the menu in the window had offered spaghetti bolognaise or roast beef and Yorkshire pudding; but those customers would not have returned, and anyhow Ibrahim had his pride.

The formula worked. They were making a good living, more money than their father had ever seen. The war had brought even more business. But wealth had not made Ibrahim careless.

Two days earlier he had taken coffee with a friend who was a cashier at the Metropolitan Hotel. The friend had told him how the British paymaster general had refused to exchange four of the English pound notes which had been passed in the hotel bar. The notes were counterfeit, according to the British. What was so unfair was that they had confiscated the money.

This was not going to happen to Ibrahim.

About half his customers were British, and many of them paid in sterling. Since he heard the news he had been checking carefully every pound note before putting it into the till. His friend from the Metropolitan had told him how to spot the forgeries.

It was typical of the British. They did not make a public announcement to help the businessmen of Cairo to avoid being cheated. They simply sat back and confiscated the dud notes. The businessmen of Cairo were used to this kind of treatment, and they stuck together. The grapevine worked well.

When Ibrahim received the counterfeit notes from the tall European who was dining with the famous belly dancer, he was not sure what to do next. The notes were all crisp and new, and bore the identical fault. Ibrahim double-checked them against one of the good notes in his till: there was no doubt. Should he, perhaps, explain the matter quietly to the customer? The man might take offense, or at least pretend to; and he would probably leave without paying. His bill was a heavy one—he had taken the most expensive dishes, plus imported wine—and Ibrahim did not want to risk such a loss.

He would call the police, he decided. They would prevent the customer running off, and might help persuade him to pay by check, or at least leave an IOU.

But which police? The Egyptian police would probably argue that it was not their responsibility, take an hour to get here, and then require a bribe. The customer was presumably an Englishman—why else would he have sterling?—and was probably an officer, and it was British money that had been counterfeited. Ibrahim decided he would call the military.

He went over to their table, carrying the brandy bottle. He gave them a smile. "Monsieur, madame, I hope you have enjoyed your meal."

"It was excellent," said the man. He talked like a British officer.

Ibrahim turned to the woman. "It is an honor to serve the greatest dancer in the world."

She gave a regal nod.

Ibrahim said: "I hope you will accept a glass of brandy, with the compliments of the house."

"Very kind," said the man.

Ibrahim poured them more brandy and bowed away. That should keep them sitting still for a while longer, he thought. He left by the back door and went to the house of a neighbor who had a telephone.

If I had a restaurant, Wolff thought, I would do things like that. The two glasses of brandy cost the proprietor very little, in relation to Wolff's total bill, but the gesture was very effective in making the customer feel wanted. Wolff had often toyed with the idea of opening a restaurant, but it was a pipe dream: he knew there was too much hard work involved.

Sonja also enjoyed the special attention. She was positively glowing under the combined influences of flattery and liquor. Tonight in bed she would snore like a pig.

The proprietor had disappeared for a few minutes, then returned. Out of the corner of his eye, Wolff saw the man whispering to a waiter. He guessed they were talking about Sonja.

Wolff felt a pang of jealousy. There were places in Cairo where, because of his good custom and lavish tips, he was known by name and welcomed like royalty; but he had thought it wise not to go to places where he would be recognized, not while the British were hunting him. Now he wondered whether he could afford to relax his vigilance a little more.

Sonja yawned. It was time to put her to bed. Wolff waved to a waiter and said: "Please fetch Madame's wrap." The man went off, paused to mutter something to the proprietor, then continued on toward the cloakroom.

An alarm bell sounded, faint and distant, somewhere in the back of Wolff's mind.

He toyed with a spoon as he waited for Sonja's wrap. Sonja ate another petit four. The proprietor walked the length of the restaurant, went out of the front door, and came back in again. He approached their table and said: "May I get you a taxi?"

Wolff looked at Sonja. She said: "I don't mind."

Wolff said: "I'd like a breath of air. Let's walk a little way, then hail one."

"Okay."

Wolff looked at the proprietor. "No taxi."

"Very good, sir."

The waiter brought Sonja's wrap. The proprietor kept looking at the door. Wolff heard another alarm bell, this one louder. He said to the proprietor: "Is something the matter?"

The man looked very worried. "I must mention an extremely delicate problem, sir."

Wolff began to get irritated. "Well, what is it, man? We want to go home."

There was the sound of a vehicle noisily drawing up outside the restaurant.

Wolff took hold of the proprietor's lapels. "What is going on here?"

"The money with which you paid your bill, sir, is not good."

"You don't accept sterling? Then why didn't—"

"It's not that, sir. The money is counterfeit."

The restaurant door burst open and three military policemen marched in.

Wolff stared at them openmouthed. It was all happening so quickly, he couldn't catch his breath . . . Military police. Counterfeit money. He was suddenly afraid. He might go to jail. Those imbeciles in Berlin had given him forged notes, it was so *stupid,* he wanted to take Canaris by the throat and *squeeze—*

He shook his head. There was no time to be angry now. He had to keep calm and try to slide out of this mess—

The MPs marched up to the table. Two were British and the third was Australian. They wore heavy boots and steel helmets, and each of them had a small gun in a belt holster. One of the British said: "Is this the man?"

"Just a moment," Wolff said, and was astonished at how cool and suave his voice sounded. "The proprietor has, this very minute, told me that my money is no good. I don't believe this, but I'm prepared to humor him, and I'm sure we can make some arrangement which will satisfy him." He gave the proprietor a reproachful look. "It really wasn't necessary to call the police."

The senior MP said: "It's an offense to pass forged money."

"Knowingly," Wolff said. "It is an offense *knowingly* to pass forged money." As he listened to his own voice, quiet and persuasive, his confidence grew. "Now, then, what I propose is this. I have here my checkbook and some Egyptian money. I will write a check to cover my bill, and use the Egyptian money for the tip. Tomorrow I will take the allegedly counterfeit notes to the British paymaster general for examination, and if they really are forgeries I will surrender them." He smiled at the group surrounding him. "I imagine that should satisfy everyone."

The proprietor said: "I would prefer if you could pay entirely in cash, sir."

Wolff wanted to hit him in the face.

Sonja said: "I may have enough Egyptian money."

Wolff thought: Thank God.

Sonja opened her bag.

The senior MP said: "All the same, sir, I'm going to ask you to come with me."

Wolff's heart sank again. "Why?"

"We'll need to ask you some questions."

"Fine. Why don't you call on me tomorrow morning. I live—"

"You'll have to come with me. Those are my orders."

"From whom?"

"The assistant provost marshal."

"Very well, then," said Wolff. He stood up. He could feel the fear pumping desperate strength into his arms. "But either you or the provost will be in very deep trouble in the morning." Then he picked up the table and threw it at the MP.

He had planned and calculated the move in a couple of seconds. It was a small circular table of solid wood. Its edge struck the MP on the bridge of the nose, and as he fell back the table landed on top of him.

Table and MP were on Wolff's left. On his right was the proprietor. Sonja was opposite him, still sitting, and the other two MPs were on either side of her and slightly behind her.

Wolff grabbed the proprietor and pushed him at one of the MPs. Then he jumped at the other MP, the Australian, and punched his face. He hoped to get past the two of them and run away. It did not work. The MPs were chosen for their size, belligerence and brutality, and they were used to dealing with soldiers desert-hardened and fighting drunk. The Australian took the punch and staggered back a pace, but he did not fall over. Wolff kicked him in the knee and punched his face again; then the other MP, the second Englishman, pushed the proprietor out of the way and kicked Wolff's feet from under him.

Wolff landed heavily. His chest and his cheek hit the tiled floor. His face stung, he was momentarily winded and he saw stars. He was kicked again, in the side; the pain made him jerk convulsively and roll away from the blow. The MP jumped on him, beating him about the head. He struggled to push the man off. Someone else sat on Wolff's feet. Then Wolff saw, above him and behind the English MP on his chest, Sonja's face, twisted with rage. The thought flashed through his mind that she was remembering another beating that had been administered by British soldiers. Then he saw that she was raising high in the air the chair she had been sitting on. The MP on Wolff's chest glimpsed her, turned around, looked up, and raised his arms to ward off the blow. She brought the heavy chair down with all her might. A corner of the seat struck the MP's mouth, and he gave a shout of pain and anger as blood spurted from his lip.

The Australian got off Wolff's feet and grabbed Sonja from behind, pinning her arms. Wolff flexed his body and threw off the wounded Englishman, then scrambled to his feet.

He reached inside his shirt and whipped out his knife.

The Australian threw Sonja aside, took a pace forward, saw the knife and stopped. He and Wolff stared into each other's eyes for an instant. Wolff saw the other man's eyes flicker to one side, then the other, seeing his two partners lying on the floor. The Australian's hand went to his holster.

Wolff turned and dashed for the door. One of his eyes was closing: he could not see well. The door was closed. He grabbed for the handle and missed. He felt like screaming. He found the handle and flung the door open wide. It hit the wall with a crash. A shot rang out.

Vandam drove the motorcycle through the streets at a dangerous speed. He had ripped the blackout mask off the headlight—nobody in Cairo took the blackout seriously anyway—and he drove with his thumb on the horn. The streets were still busy, with taxis, gharries, army trucks, donkeys and camels. The pavements were crowded and the shops were bright with electric lights, oil lamps and candles. Vandam weaved recklessly through the traffic, ignoring the outraged hooting of the cars, the raised fists of the gharry drivers, and the blown whistle of an Egyptian policeman.

The assistant provost marshal had called him at home. "Ah, Vandam, wasn't it you who sent up the balloon about this funny money? Because we've just had a call from a restaurant where a European is trying to pass—"

"*Where?*"

The APM gave him the address, and Vandam ran out of the house.

He skidded around a corner, dragging a heel in the dusty road for traction. It had occurred to him that, with so much counterfeit money in circulation, some of it must have got into the hands of other Europeans, and the man in the restaurant might well be an innocent victim. He hoped not. He wanted desperately to get his hands on Alex Wolff. Wolff had outwitted and humiliated him and now, with his access to

secrets and his direct line to Rommel, he threatened to bring
about the fall of Egypt; but it was not just that. Vandam was
consumed with curiosity about Wolff. He wanted to see the
man and touch him, to find out how he would move and
speak. Was he clever, or just lucky? Courageous, or fool-
hardy? Determined, or stubborn? Did he have a handsome
face and a warm smile, or beady eyes and an oily grin?
Would he fight or come quietly? Vandam wanted to know.
And, most of all, Vandam wanted to take him by the throat
and drag him off to jail, chain him to the wall and lock the
door and throw away the key.

He swerved to avoid a pothole, then opened the throttle
and roared down a quiet street. The address was a little out
of the city center, toward the Old Town: Vandam was ac-
quainted with the street but not with the restaurant. He
turned two more corners, and almost hit an old man riding
an ass with his wife walking along behind. He found the
street he was looking for.

It was narrow and dark, with high buildings on either side.
At ground level there were some shop fronts and some house
entrances. Vandam pulled up beside two small boys playing
in the gutter and said the name of the restaurant. They
pointed vaguely along the street.

Vandam cruised along, pausing to look wherever he noticed a lit window. He was half way down the street when he
heard the *crack!* of a small firearm, slightly muffled, and the
sound of glass shattering. His head jerked around toward the
source of the noise. Light from a broken window glinted off
shards of falling glass, and as he looked a tall man ran out of
a door into the street.

It had to be Wolff.

He ran in the opposite direction.

Vandam felt a surge of savagery. He twisted the throttle of
the motorcycle and roared after the running man. As he
passed the restaurant an MP ran out and fired three shots.
The fugitive's pace did not falter.

Vandam caught him in the beam of the headlight. He was
running strongly, steadily, his arms and legs pumping rhyth-
mically. When the light hit him he glanced back over his
shoulder without breaking his stride, and Vandam glimpsed a

hawk nose and a strong chin, and a mustache above a mouth open and panting.

Vandam could have shot him, but officers at GHQ did not carry guns.

The motorcycle gained fast. When they were almost level Wolff suddenly turned a corner. Vandam braked and went into a back-wheel skid, leaning the bike against the direction of the skid to keep his balance. He came to a stop, jerked upright and shot forward again.

He saw the back of Wolff disappear into a narrow alleyway. Without slowing down, Vandam turned the corner and drove into the alley. The bike shot out into empty space. Vandam's stomach turned over. The white cone of his headlight illuminated nothing. He thought he was falling into a pit. He gave an involuntary shout of fear. The back wheel hit something. The front wheel went down, down, then hit. The headlight showed a flight of steps. The bike bounced, and landed again. Vandam fought desperately to keep the front wheel straight. The bike descended the steps in a series of spine-jarring bumps, and with each bump Vandam was sure he would lose control and crash. He saw Wolff at the bottom of the stairs, still running.

Vandam reached the foot of the staircase and felt incredibly lucky. He saw Wolff turn another corner, and followed. They were in a maze of alleys. Wolff ran up a short flight of steps.

Vandam thought: Jesus, no.

He had no choice. He accelerated and headed squarely for the steps. A moment before hitting the bottom step he jerked the handlebars with all his might. The front wheel lifted. The bike hit the steps, bucked like a wild thing and tried to throw him. He hung on grimly. The bike bumped crazily up. Vandam fought it. He reached the top.

He found himself in a long passage with high, blank walls on either side. Wolff was still in front of him, still running. Vandam thought he could catch him before Wolff reached the end of the passage. He shot forward.

Wolff looked back over his shoulder, ran on, and looked again. His pace was flagging, Vandam could see. His stride was no longer steady and rhythmic: his arms flew out to either side and he ran raggedly. Glimpsing Wolff's face, Vandam saw that it was taut with strain.

Wolff put on a burst of speed, but it was not enough. Vandam drew level, eased ahead, then braked sharply and twisted the handlebars. The back wheel skidded and the front wheel hit the wall. Vandam leaped off as the bike fell to the ground. Vandam landed on his feet, facing Wolff. The smashed headlight threw a shaft of light into the darkness of the passage. There was no point in Wolff's turning and running the other way, for Vandam was fresh and could easily catch him. Without pausing in his stride Wolff jumped over the bike, his body passing through the pillar of light from the headlight like a knife slicing a flame, and crashed into Vandam. Vandam, still unsteady, stumbled backward and fell. Wolff staggered and took another step forward. Vandam reached out blindly in the dark, found Wolff's ankle, gripped and yanked. Wolff crashed to the ground.

The broken headlight gave a little light to the rest of the alley. The engine of the bike had cut out, and in the silence Vandam could hear Wolff's breathing, ragged and hoarse. He could smell him, too: a smell of booze and perspiration and fear. But he could not see his face.

There was a split second when the two of them lay on the ground, one exhausted and the other momentarily stunned. Then they both scrambled to their feet. Vandam jumped at Wolff, and they grappled.

Wolff was strong. Vandam tried to pin his arms, but he could not hold on to him. Suddenly he let go and threw a punch. It landed somewhere soft, and Wolf said: "Ooff." Vandam punched again, this time aiming for the face; but Wolff dodged, and the fist hit empty space. Suddenly something in Wolff's hand glinted in the dim light.

Vandam thought: A knife!

The blade flashed toward his throat. He jerked back reflexively. There was a searing pain all across his cheek. His hand flew to his face. He felt a gush of hot blood. Suddenly the pain was unbearable. He pressed on the wound and his fingers touched something hard. He realized he was feeling his own teeth, and that the knife had sliced right through the flesh of his cheek; and then he felt himself falling, and he heard Wolff running away, and everything turned black.

13

Wolff took a handkerchief from his trousers pocket and wiped the blood from the blade of the knife. He examined the blade in the dim light, then wiped it again. He walked along, polishing the thin steel vigorously. He stopped, and thought: What am I doing? It's clean already. He threw away the handkerchief and replaced the knife in the sheath under his arm. He emerged from the alley into the street, got his bearings, and headed for the Old City.

He imagined a prison cell. It was six feet long by four feet wide, and half of it was taken up by a bed. Beneath the bed was a chamber pot. The walls were of smooth gray stone. A small light bulb hung from the ceiling by a cord. In one end of the cell was a door. In the other end was a small square window, set just above eye level: through it he could see the bright blue sky. He imagined that he woke up in the morning and saw all this, and remembered that he had been here for a year, and he would be here for another nine years. He used the chamberpot, then washed his hands in the tin bowl in the corner. There was no soap. A dish of cold porridge was pushed through the hatch in the door. He picked up the spoon and took a mouthful, but he was unable to swallow, for he was weeping.

He shook his head to clear it of nightmare visions. He thought: I got away, didn't I? *I got away*. He realized that some of the people on the street were staring at him as they passed. He saw a mirror in a shop window, and examined himself in it. His hair was awry, one side of his face was bruised and swollen, his sleeve was ripped and there was blood on his collar. He was still panting from the exertion of running and fighting. He thought: I look dangerous. He walked on, and turned at the next corner to take an indirect route which would avoid the main streets.

Those imbeciles in Berlin had given him counterfeit money! No wonder they were so generous with it—they were printing it themselves. It was so foolish that Wolff wondered if it might be more than foolishness. The Abwehr was run by the military, not by the Nazi Party; its chief, Canaris, was not the staunchest of Hitler's supporters.

When I get back to Berlin there will be such a purge . . .

How had it caught up with him, here in Cairo? He had been spending money fast. The forgeries had got into circulation. The banks had spotted the dud notes—no, not the banks, the paymaster general. Anyway, someone had begun to refuse the money, and word had got around Cairo. The proprietor of the restaurant had noticed that Wolff's money was fake and had called the military. Wolff grinned ruefully to himself when he recalled how flattered he had been by the proprietor's complimentary brandy—it had been no more than a ruse to keep him there until the MPs arrived.

He thought about the man on the motorcycle. He must be a determined bastard, to ride the bike around those alleys and up and down the steps. He had no gun, Wolff guessed: if he had, he would surely have used it. Nor had he a tin hat, so presumably he was not an MP. Someone from Intelligence, perhaps? Major Vandam, even?

Wolff hoped so.

I cut the man, he thought. Quite badly, probably. I wonder where? The face?

I hope it was Vandam.

He turned his mind to his immediate problem. They had Sonja. She would tell them she hardly knew Wolff—she would make up some story about a quick pickup in the Cha-Cha Club. They would not be able to hold her for long, because she was famous, a star, a kind of hero among the Egyptians, and to imprison her would cause a great deal of trouble. So they would let her go quite soon. However, she would have to give them her address; which meant that Wolff could not go back to the houseboat, not yet. But he was exhausted, bruised and disheveled: he had to clean himself up and get a few hours' rest, somewhere.

He thought: I've been here before—wandering the city, tired and hunted, with nowhere to go.

This time he would have to fall back on Abdullah.

He had been heading for the Old City, knowing all along, in the back of his mind, that Abdullah was all he had left; and now he found himself a few steps from the old thief's house. He ducked under an arch, went along a short dark passage and climbed a stone spiral staircase to Abdullah's home.

Abdullah was sitting on the floor with another man. A nargileh stood between them, and the air was full of the herbal smell of hashish. Abdullah looked up at Wolff and gave a slow, sleepy smile. He spoke in Arabic. "Here is my friend Achmed, also called Alex. Welcome, Achmed-Alex."

Wolff sat on the floor with them and greeted them in Arabic.

Abdullah said: "My brother Yasef here would like to ask you a riddle, something that has been puzzling him and me for some hours now, ever since we started the hubble-bubble, speaking of which . . ." He passed the pipe across, and Wolff took a lungful.

Yasef said: "Achmed-Alex, friend of my brother, welcome. Tell me this: Why do the British call us wogs?"

Yasef and Abdullah collapsed into giggles. Wolff realized they were heavily under the influence of hashish: they must have been smoking all evening. He drew on the pipe again, and pushed it over to Yasef. It was strong stuff. Abdullah always had the best. Wolff said: "As it happens, I know the answer. Egyptian men working on the Suez Canal were issued with special shirts, to show that they had the right to be on British property. They were Working On Government Service, so on the backs of their shirts were printed the letters W.O.G.S."

Yasef and Abdullah giggled all over again. Abdullah said: "My friend Achmed-Alex is clever. He is as clever as an Arab, almost, because he is almost an Arab. He is the only European who has ever got the better of me, Abdullah."

"I believe this to be untrue," Wolff said slipping into their stoned style of speech. "I would never try to outwit my friend Abdullah, for who can cheat the devil?"

Yasef smiled and nodded his appreciation of this witticism.

Abdullah said: "Listen, my brother, and I will tell you."
He frowned, collecting his doped thoughts. "Achmed-Alex
asked me to steal something for him. That way I would take
the risk and he would get the reward. Of course, he did not
outwit me so simply. I stole the thing—it was a case—and of
course my intention was to take its contents for myself, since
the thief is entitled to the proceeds of his crime, according to
the laws of God. Therefore I should have outwitted him,
should I not?"

"Indeed," said Yasef, "although I do not recall the passage
of Holy Scripture which says that a thief is entitled to the
proceeds of his crime. However . . ."

"Perhaps not," said Abdullah. "Of what was I speaking?"

Wolff, who was still more or less compos mentis, told him:
"You should have outwitted me, because you opened the case
yourself."

"Indeed! But wait. There was nothing of value in the case,
so Achmed-Alex had outwitted me. But wait! I made him pay
me for rendering this service; therefore I got one hundred
pounds and he got nothing."

Yasef frowned. "You, then, got the better of him."

"No." Abdullah shook his head sadly. "He paid me in
forged banknotes."

Yasef stared at Abdullah. Abdullah stared back. They both
burst out laughing. They slapped each other's shoulders,
stamped their feet on the floor and rolled around on the
cushions, laughing until the tears came to their eyes.

Wolff forced a smile. It was just the kind of funny story
that appealed to Arab businessmen, with its chain of double
crosses. Abdullah would be telling it for years. But it sent a
chill through Wolff. So Abdullah, too, knew about the counterfeit notes. How many others did? Wolff felt as if the hunting pack had formed a circle around him, so that every way
he ran he came up against one of them, and the circle drew
tighter every day.

Abdullah seemed to notice Wolff's appearance for the first
time. He immediately became very concerned. "What has
happened to you? Have you been robbed?" He picked up a
tiny silver bell and rang it. Almost immediately, a sleepy
woman came in from the next room. "Get some hot water,"

Abdullah told her. "Bathe my friend's wounds. Give him my European shirt. Bring a comb. Bring coffee. Quickly!"

In a European house Wolff would have protested at the women being roused, after midnight, to attend to him; but here such a protest would have been very discourteous. The women existed to serve the men, and they would be neither surprised nor annoyed by Abdullah's peremptory demands.

Wolff explained: "The British tried to arrest me, and I was obliged to fight with them before I could get away. Sadly, I think they may now know where I have been living, and this is a problem."

"Ah." Abdullah drew on the nargileh, and passed it around again. Wolff began to feel the effects of the hashish: he was relaxed, slow-thinking, a little sleepy. Time slowed down. Two of Abdullah's wives fussed over him, bathing his face and combing his hair. He found their ministrations very pleasant indeed.

Abdullah seemed to doze for a while, then he opened his eyes and said: "You must stay here. My house is yours. I will hide you from the British."

"You are a true friend," Wolff said. It was odd, he thought. He had planned to offer Abdullah money to hide him. Then Abdullah had revealed that he knew the money was no good, and Wolff had been wondering what else he could do. Now Abdullah was going to hide him for nothing. A true friend. What was odd was that Abdullah was not a true friend. There were no friends in Abdullah's world: there was the family, for whom he would do anything, and the rest, for whom he would do nothing. How have I earned this special treatment? Wolff thought sleepily.

His alarm bell was sounding again. He forced himself to think: it was not easy after the hashish. Take it one step at a time, he told himself. Abdullah asks me to stay here. Why? Because I am in trouble. Because I am his friend. Because I have outwitted him.

Because I have outwitted him. That story was not finished. Abdullah would want to add another double cross to the chain. How? By betraying Wolff to the British. That was it. As soon as Wolff fell asleep, Abdullah would send a message to Major Vandam. Wolff would be picked up. The British would pay Abdullah for the information, and the story could be told to Abdullah's credit at last.

Damn.

A wife brought a white European shirt. Wolff stood up and took off his torn and bloody shirt. The wife averted her eyes from his bare chest.

Abdullah said: "He doesn't need it yet. Give it to him in the morning."

Wolff took the shirt from the woman and put it on.

Abdullah said: "Perhaps it would be undignified for you to sleep in the house of an Arab, my friend Achmed?"

Wolff said: "The British have a proverb: He who sups with the devil must use a long spoon."

Abdullah grinned, showing his steel tooth. He knew that Wolff had guessed his plan. "Almost an Arab," he said.

"Good-bye, my friends," said Wolff.

"Until the next time," Abdullah replied.

Wolff went out into the cold night, wondering where he could go now.

In the hospital a nurse froze half of Vandam's face with a local anesthetic, then Dr. Abuthnot stitched up his cheek with her long, sensitive, clinical hands. She put on a protective dressing and secured it by a long strip of bandage tied around his head.

"I must look like a toothache cartoon," he said.

She looked grave. She did not have a big sense of humor. She said: "You won't be so chirpy when the anesthetic wears off. Your face is going to hurt badly. I'm going to give you a painkiller."

"No, thanks," said Vandam.

"Don't be a tough guy, Major," she said. "You'll regret it."

He looked at her, in her white hospital coat and her sensible flat-heeled shoes, and wondered how he had ever found her even faintly desirable. She was pleasant enough, even pretty, but she was also cold, superior and antiseptic. Not like—

Not like Elene.

"A pain-killer will send me to sleep," he told her.

"And a jolly good thing, too," she said. "If you sleep we can be sure the stitches will be undisturbed for a few hours."

"I'd love to, but I have some important work that won't wait."

"You can't *work*. You shouldn't really walk around. You should talk as little as possible. You're weak from loss of blood, and a wound like this is mentally as well as physically traumatic—in a few hours you'll feel the backlash, and you'll be dizzy, nauseous, exhausted and confused."

"I'll be worse if the Germans take Cairo," he said. He stood up.

Dr. Abuthnot looked cross. Vandam thought how well it suited her to be in a position to tell people what to do. She was not sure how to handle outright disobedience. "You're a silly boy," she said.

"No doubt. Can I eat?"

"No. Take glucose dissolved in warm water."

I might try it in warm gin, he thought. He shook her hand. It was cold and dry.

Jakes was waiting outside the hospital with a car. "I knew they wouldn't be able to keep you long, sir," he said. "Shall I drive you home?"

"No." Vandam's watch had stopped. "What's the time?"

"Five past two."

"I presume Wolff wasn't dining alone."

"No, sir. His companion is under arrest at GHQ."

"Drive me there."

"If you're sure . . ."

"Yes."

The car pulled away. Vandam said: "Have you notified the hierarchy?"

"About this evening's events? No, sir."

"Good. Tomorrow will be soon enough." Vandam did not say what they both knew: that the department, already under a cloud for letting Wolff gather intelligence, would be in utter disgrace for letting him slip through their fingers.

Vandam said: "I presume Wolff's dinner date was a woman."

"Very much so, if I may say so, sir. A real dish. Name of Sonja."

"The dancer?"

"No less."

They drove on in silence. Wolff was a cool customer, Vandam thought, to go out with the most famous belly dancer in Egypt in between stealing British military secrets. Well, he would not be so cool now. That was unfortunate in a way: having been warned by this incident that the British were on to him, he would be more careful from now on. Never scare them, just catch them.

They arrived at GHQ and got out of the car. Vandam said: "What's been done with her since she arrived?"

"The no-treatment treatment," Jakes said. "A bare cell, no food, no drink, no questions."

"Good." It was a pity, all the same, that she had been given time to collect her thoughts. Vandam knew from prisoner-of-war interrogations that the best results were achieved immediately after the capture, when the prisoner was still frightened of being killed. Later on, when he had been herded here and there and given food and drink, he began to think of himself as a prisoner rather than as a soldier, and remembered that he had new rights and duties; and then he was better able to keep his mouth shut. Vandam should have interviewed Sonja immediately after the fight in the restaurant. As that was not possible, the next best thing was for her to be kept in isolation and given no information until he arrived.

Jakes led the way along a corridor to the interview room. Vandam looked in through the judas. It was a square room, without windows but bright with electric light. There were a table, two upright chairs and an ashtray. To one side was a doorless cubicle with a toilet.

Sonja sat on one of the chairs facing the door. Jakes was right, Vandam thought; she's a dish. However she was by no means *pretty*. She was something of an Amazon, with her ripe, voluptuous body and strong, well-proportioned features. The young women in Egypt generally had a slender, leggy grace, like downy young deer: Sonja was more like . . . Vandam frowned, then thought: a tigress. She wore a long gown of bright yellow which was garish to Vandam but would be quite *à la mode* in the Cha-Cha Club. He watched her for a minute or two. She was sitting quite still, not fidgeting, not darting nervous glances around the bare cell, not smoking or biting her nails. He thought: She will be a tough nut to crack. Then the expression on her handsome face changed, and she stood up and began pacing up and down, and Van-dam thought: Not so tough.

He opened the door and went in.

He sat down at the table without speaking. This left her standing, which was a psychological disadvantage for a woman: Score the first point to me, he thought. He heard Jakes come in behind him and close the door. He looked up at Sonja. "Sit down."

She stood gazing at him, and a slow smile spread across her face. She pointed at his bandages. "Did he do that to you?" she said.

Score the second point to her.

"Sit down."

"Thank you." She sat.

"Who is 'he'?"

"Alex Wolff, the man you *tried* to beat up tonight."

"And who is Alex Wolff?"

"A wealthy patron of the Cha-Cha Club."

"How long have you known him?"

She looked at her watch. "Five hours."

"What is your relationship with him?"

She shrugged. "He was a date."

"How did you meet?"

"The usual way. After my act, a waiter brought a message inviting me to sit at Mr. Wolff's table."

"Which one?"

"Which table?"

"Which *waiter*."

"I don't remember."

"Go on."

"Mr. Wolff gave me a glass of champagne and asked me to have dinner with him. I accepted, we went to the restaurant, and you know the rest."

"Do you usually sit with members of the audience after your act?"

"Yes, it's a custom."

"Do you usually go to dinner with them?"

"Occasionally."

"Why did you accept this time?"

"Mr. Wolff seemed like an unusual sort of man." She

looked at Vandam's bandage again, and grinned. "He was an unusual sort of man."

"What is your full name?"

"Sonja el-Aram."

"Address?"

"*Jihan,* Zamalek. It's a houseboat."

"Age?"

"How discourteous."

"Age?"

"I refuse to answer."

"You're on dangerous ground——"

"No, *you* are on dangerous ground." Suddenly she startled Vandam by letting her feelings show, and he realized that all this time she had been suppressing a fury. She wagged a finger in his face. "At least ten people saw your uniformed bullies arrest me in the restaurant. By midday tomorrow half of Cairo will know that the British have put Sonja in jail. If I don't appear at the Cha-Cha tomorrow night there will be a riot. My people will burn the city. You'll have to bring troops back from the desert to deal with it. And if I leave here with a single bruise or scratch, I'll show it to the world onstage tomorrow night, and the result will be the same. No, mister, it isn't me who's on dangerous ground."

Vandam looked at her blankly throughout the tirade, then spoke as if she had said nothing extraordinary. He had to ignore what she said, because she was right, and he could not deny it. "Let's go over this again," he said mildly. "You say you met Wolff at the Cha-Cha——"

"No," she interrupted. "I won't go over it again. I'll cooperate with you, and I'll answer questions, but I will not be interrogated." She stood up, turned her chair around, and sat down with her back to Vandam.

Vandam stared at the back of her head for a moment. She had well and truly outmaneuvered him. He was angry with himself for letting it happen, but his anger was mixed with a sneaking admiration for her for the way she had done it. Abruptly, he got up and left the room. Jakes followed.

Out in the corridor Jakes said: "What do you think?"

"We'll have to let her go."

Jakes went to give instructions. While he waited, Vandam thought about Sonja. He wondered from what source she had been drawing the strength to defy him. Whether her story was true or false, she should have been frightened, confused, intimidated and ultimately compliant. It was true that her fame gave her some protection; but, in threatening him with her fame, she ought to have been blustering, unsure and a little desperate, for an isolation cell normally frightened anyone—especially celebrities, because the sudden excommunication from the familiar glittering world made them wonder even more than usually whether that familiar glittering world could possibly be real.

What gave her strength? He ran over the conversation in his mind. The question she had balked at had been the one about her age. Clearly her talent had enabled her to keep going past the age at which run-of-the-mill dancers retired, so perhaps she was living in fear of the passing years. No clues there. Otherwise she had been calm, expressionless and blank, except when she had smiled at his wound. Then, at the end she had allowed herself to explode, but even then she had used her fury, she had not been controlled by it. He called to mind her face as she had raged at him. What had he seen there? Not just anger. Not fear.

Then he had it. It had been hatred.

She hated him. But he was nothing to her, nothing but a British officer. Therefore she hated the British. And her hatred had given her strength.

Suddenly Vandam was tired. He sat down heavily on a bench in the corridor. From where was *he* to draw strength? It was easy to be strong if you were insane, and in Sonja's hatred there had been a hint of something a little crazy. He had no such refuge. Calmly, rationally, he considered what was at stake. He imagined the Nazis marching into Cairo; the Gestapo in the streets; the Egyptian Jews herded into concentration camps; the Fascist propaganda on the wireless . . .

People like Sonja looked at Egypt under British rule and felt that the Nazis had already arrived. It was not true, but if one tried for a moment to see the British through Sonja's eyes it had a certain plausibility: the Nazis said that Jews were sub-human, and the British said that blacks were like children; there was no freedom of the press in Germany, but there was none in Egypt either; and the British, like the Germans, had their political police. Before the war Vandam had sometimes heard Hitler's politics warmly endorsed in the officers' mess: they disliked him, not because he was a Fascist, but because he had been a corporal in the Army and a house painter in civilian life. There were brutes everywhere, and sometimes they got into power, and then you had to fight them.

It was a more rational philosophy than Sonja's, but it just was not inspirational.

The anesthetic in his face was wearing off. He could feel a sharp, clear line of pain across his cheek, like a new burn. He realized he also had a headache. He hoped Jakes would be a long time arranging Sonja's release, so that he could sit on the bench a little while longer.

He thought of Billy. He did not want the boy to miss him at breakfast. Perhaps I'll stay awake until morning, then take him to school, then go home and sleep, he thought. What would Billy's life be like under the Nazis? They would teach him to despise the Arabs. His present teachers were no great admirers of African culture, but at least Vandam could do a little to make his son realize that people who were different were not necessarily stupid. What would happen in the Nazi classroom when he put up his hand and said: "Please, sir, my dad says a dumb Englishman is no smarter than a dumb Arab"?

He thought of Elene. Now she was a kept woman, but at least she could choose her lovers, and if she didn't like what they wanted to do in bed she could kick them out. In the brothel of a concentration camp she would have no such choice . . . He shuddered.

Yes. We're not very admirable, especially in our colonies, but the Nazis are worse, whether the Egyptians know it or not. It is worth fighting. In England decency is making slow progress; in Germany it's taking a big step backward. Think about the people you love, and the issues become clearer.

Draw strength from that. Stay awake a little longer. Stand up.

He stood up.

Jakes came back.

Vandam said: "She's an Anglophobe."

"I beg your pardon, sir?"

"Sonja. She hates the British. I don't believe Wolff was a casual pickup. Let's go."

They walked out of the building together. Outside it was still dark. Jakes said: "Sir, you're very tired—"

"Yes. I'm very tired. But I'm still thinking straight, Jakes. Take me to the main police station."

"Sir."

They pulled away. Vandam handed his cigarette case and lighter to Jakes, who drove one-handed while he lit Vandam's cigarette. Vandam had trouble sucking: he could hold the cigarette between his lips and breathe the smoke, but he could not draw on it hard enough to light it. Jakes handed him the lit cigarette. Vandam thought: I'd like a martini to go with it.

Jakes stopped the car outside police headquarters. Vandam said: "We want the chief of detectives, whatever they call him."

"I shouldn't think he'll be there at this hour—"

"No. Get his address. We'll wake him up."

Jakes went into the building. Vandam stared ahead through the windshield. Dawn was on its way. The stars had winked out, and now the sky was gray rather than black. There were a few people about. He saw a man leading two donkeys loaded with vegetables, presumably going to market. The muezzins had not yet called the first prayer of the day.

Jakes came back. "Gezira," he said as he put the car in gear and let in the clutch.

Vandam thought about Jakes. Someone had told Vandam that Jakes had a terrific sense of humor. Vandam had always found him pleasant and cheerful, but he had never seen any evidence of actual humor. Am I such a tyrant, Vandam thought, that my staff are terrified of cracking a joke in my presence? Nobody makes me laugh, he thought.

Except Elene.

"You never tell *me* jokes, Jakes."

"Sir?"

"They say you have a terrific sense of humor, but you never tell me jokes."

"No, sir."

"Would you care to be candid for a moment and tell me why?"

There was a pause, then Jakes said: "You don't invite familiarity, sir."

Vandam nodded. How would they know how much he liked to throw back his head and roar with laughter? He said: "Very tactfully put, Jakes. The subject is closed."

The Wolff business is getting to me, he thought. I wonder whether perhaps I've never really been any good at my job, and then I wonder if I'm any good for anything at all. And my face hurts.

They crossed the bridge to the island. The sky turned from slate-gray to pearl. Jakes said: "I'd like to say, sir, that, if you'll pardon me, you're far and away the best superior officer I've ever had."

"Oh." Vandam was quite taken aback. "Good Lord. Well, thank you, Jakes. Thank you."

"Not at all, sir. We're there."

He stopped the car outside a small, pretty single-story house with a well-watered garden. Vandam guessed that the chief of detectives was doing well enough out of his bribes, but not too well. A cautious man, perhaps: it was a good sign.

They walked up the path and hammered on the door. After a couple of minutes a head looked out of a window and spoke in Arabic.

Jakes put on his sergeant major's voice. "Military Intelligence—open up the bloody door!"

A minute later a small, handsome Arab opened up, still belting his trousers. He said in English: "What's going on?"

Vandam took charge. "An emergency. Let us in, will you?"

"Of course." The detective stood aside and they entered. He led them into a small living room. "What has happened?" He seemed frightened, and Vandam thought: Who wouldn't be? The knock on the door in the middle of the night . . .

Vandam said: "There's nothing to panic about, but we want you to set up a surveillance, and we need it right away."

"Of course. Please sit down." The detective found a notebook and pencil. "Who is the subject?"

"Sonja el-Aram."

"The dancer?"

"Yes. I want you to put a twenty-four-hour watch on her home, which is a houseboat called *Jihan* in Zamalek."

As the detective wrote down the details, Vandam wished he did not have to use the Egyptian police for this work. However, he had no choice: it was impossible, in an African country, to use conspicuous, white-skinned, English-speaking people for surveillance.

The detective said: "And what is the nature of the crime?"

I'm not telling *you*, Vandam thought. He said: "We think she may be an associate of whoever is passing counterfeit sterling in Cairo."

"So you want to know who comes and goes, whether they carry anything, whether meetings are held aboard the boat . . ."

"Yes. And there is a particular man that we're interested in. He is Alex Wolff, the man suspected of the Assyut knife murder; you should have his description already."

"Of course. Daily reports?"

"Yes, except that if Wolff is seen I want to know immediately. You can reach Captain Jakes or me at GHQ during the day. Give him our home phone numbers, Jakes."

"I know these houseboats," the detective said. "The towpath is a popular evening walk, I think, especially for sweethearts."

Jakes said: "That's right."

Vandam raised an eyebrow at Jakes.

The detective went on: "A good place, perhaps, for a beggar to sit. Nobody ever sees a beggar. At night . . . well, there are bushes. Also popular with sweethearts."

Vandam said: "Is that right, Jakes?"

"I wouldn't know, sir." He realized he was being ribbed, and he smiled. He gave the detective a piece of paper with the phone numbers written on it.

A little boy in pajamas walked into the room, rubbing his eyes. He was about five or six years old. He looked around the room sleepily, then went to the detective.

"My son," the detective said proudly.

"I think we can leave you now," Vandam said. "Unless you want us to drop you in the city?"

"No, thank you, I have a car, and I should like to put on my jacket and tie and comb my hair."

"Very well, but make it fast." Vandam stood up. Suddenly he could not see straight. It was as if his eyelids were closing involuntarily, yet he knew he had his eyes wide open. He felt himself losing his balance. Then Jakes was beside him, holding his arm.

"All right, sir?"

His vision returned slowly. "All right now," he said.

"You've had a nasty injury," the detective said sympathetically.

They went to the door. The detective said: "Gentlemen, be assured that I will handle this surveillance personally. They won't get a mouse aboard that houseboat without your knowing it." He was still holding the little boy, and now he shifted him on to his left hip and held out his right hand.

"Good-bye," Vandam said. He shook hands. "By the way, I'm Major Vandam."

The detective gave a little bow. "Superintendent Kemel, at your service, sir."

14

Sonja brooded. She had half expected Wolff to be at the houseboat when she returned toward dawn, but she had found the place cold and empty. She was not sure how she felt about that. At first, when they had arrested her, she had felt nothing but rage toward Wolff for running away and leaving her at the mercy of the British thugs. Being alone, being a woman and being an accomplice of sorts in Wolff's spying, she was terrified of what they might do to her. She thought Wolff should have stayed to look after her. Then she had realized that that would not have been smart. By abandoning her he had diverted suspicion away from her. It was hard to take, but it was for the best. Sitting alone in the bare little room at GHQ, she had turned her anger away from Wolff and toward the British.

She had defied them, and they had backed down.

At the time she had not been sure that the man who interrogated her had been Major Vandam, but later, when she was being released, the clerk had let the name slip. The confirmation had delighted her. She smiled again when she thought of the grotesque bandage on Vandam's face. Wolff must have cut him with the knife. He should have killed him. But all the same, what a night, what a glorious night!

She wondered where Wolff was now. He would have gone to ground somewhere in the city. He would emerge when he thought the coast was clear. There was nothing she could do. She would have liked him here, though, to share the triumph.

She put on her nightdress. She knew she ought to go to bed, but she did not feel sleepy. Perhaps a drink would help.

175

She found a bottle of scotch whiskey, poured some into a glass, and added water. As she was tasting it she heard footsteps on the gangplank. Without thinking she called: "Achmed . . . ?" Then she realized the step was not his, it was too light and quick. She stood at the foot of the ladder in her nightdress, with the drink in her hand. The hatch was lifted and an Arab face looked in.

"Sonja?"

"Yes—"

"You were expecting someone else, I think." The man climbed down the ladder. Sonja watched him, thinking: What now? He stepped off the ladder and stood in front of her. He was a small man with a handsome face and quick, neat movements. He wore European clothes: dark trousers, polished black shoes and a short-sleeved white shirt. "I am Detective Superintendent Kemel, and I am honored to meet you." He held out his hand.

Sonja turned away, walked across to the divan and sat down. She thought she had dealt with the police. Now the Egyptians wanted to get in on the act. It would probably come down to a bribe in the end, she reassured herself. She sipped her drink, staring at Kemel. Finally she said: "What do you want?"

Kemel sat down uninvited. "I am interested in your friend, Alex Wolff."

"He's not my friend."

Kemel ignored that. "The British have told me two things about Mr. Wolff: one, that he knifed a soldier in Assyut; two, that he tried to pass counterfeit English banknotes in a restaurant in Cairo. Already the story is a little curious. Why was he in Assyut? Why did he kill the soldier? And where did he get the forged money?"

"I don't know anything about the man," said Sonja, hoping he would not come home right now.

"I do, though," said Kemel. "I have other information that the British may or may not possess. I know who Alex Wolff is. His stepfather was a lawyer, here in Cairo. His mother was German. I know, too, that Wolff is a nationalist. I know that he used to be your lover. And I know that you are a nationalist."

Sonja had gone cold. She sat still, her drink untouched,

watching the sly detective unreel the evidence against her. She said nothing.

Kemel went on: "Where did he get the forged money? Not in Egypt. I don't think there is a printer in Egypt capable of doing the work; and if there were, I think he would make Egyptian currency. Therefore the money came from Europe. Now Wolff, also known as Achmed Rahmha, quietly disappeared a couple of years ago. Where did he go? Europe? He came back—via Assyut. Why? Did he want to sneak into the country unnoticed? Perhaps he teamed up with an English counterfeiting gang, and has now returned with his share of the profits; but I don't think so, for he is not a poor man, nor is he a criminal. So, there is a mystery."

He knows, Sonja thought. Dear God, he knows.

"Now the British have asked me to put a watch on this houseboat, and tell them of everyone who comes and goes here. Wolff will come here, they hope; and then they will arrest him; and then they will have the answers. Unless I solve the puzzle first."

A watch on the boat! He could never come back. But—but why, she thought, is Kemel telling me?

"The key, I think, lies in Wolff's nature: he is both a German and an Egyptian." Kemel stood up, and crossed the floor to sit beside Sonja and look into her face. "I think he is fighting in this war. I think he is fighting for Germany and for Egypt. I think the forged money comes from the Germans. I think Wolff is a spy."

Sonja thought: But you don't know where to find him. That's why you're here. Kemel was staring at her. She looked away, afraid that he might read her thoughts in her face.

Kemel said: "If he is a spy, I can catch him. Or I can save him."

Sonja jerked her head around to look at him. "What does that mean?"

"I want to meet him. Secretly."

"But why?"

Kemel smiled his sly, knowing smile. "Sonja, you are not the only one who wants Egypt to be free. There are many of us. We want to see the British defeated, and we are not fastidious about who does the defeating. We want to work with the Germans. We want to contact them. We want to talk to Rommel."

"And you think Achmed can help you?"

"If he is a spy, he must have a way of getting messages to the Germans."

Sonja's mind was in a turmoil. From being her accuser, Kemel had turned into a co-conspirator—unless this was a trap. She did not know whether to trust him or not. She did not have enough time to think about it. She did not know what to say, so she said nothing.

Kemel persisted gently. "Can you arrange a meeting?"

She could not possibly make such a decision on the spur of the moment. "No," she said.

"Remember the watch on the houseboat," he said. "The surveillance reports will come to me before being passed on to Major Vandam. If there is a chance, just a chance, that you might be able to arrange a meeting, I in turn can make sure that the reports which go to Vandam are carefully edited so as to contain nothing . . . embarrassing."

Sonja had forgotten the surveillance. When Wolff came back—and he would, sooner or later—the watchers would report it, and Vandam would know, unless Kemel fixed it. This changed everything. She had no choice. "I'll arrange a meeting," she said.

"Good." He stood up. "Call the main police station and leave a message saying that Sirhan wants to see me. When I get that message I'll contact you to arrange date and time."

"Very well."

He went to the ladder, then came back. "By the way." He took a wallet from his trousers pocket and extracted a small photograph. He handed it to Sonja. It was a picture of her. "Would you sign this for my wife? She's a great fan of yours." He handed her a pen. "Her name is Hesther."

Sonja wrote: "To Hesther, with all good wishes, Sonja." She gave him the photograph, thinking: This is incredible.

"Thank you so much. She will be overjoyed."

Incredible.

Sonja said: "I'll get in touch just as soon as I can."

"Thank you." He held out his hand. This time she shook it. He went up the ladder and out, closing the hatch behind him.

Sonja relaxed. Somehow she had handled it right. She was

still not completely convinced of Kemel's sincerity; but if there was a trap she could not see it.

She felt tired. She finished the whiskey in the glass, then went through the curtains into the bedroom. She still had her nightdress on, and she was quite cold. She went to the bed and pulled back the covers. She heard a tapping sound. Her heart missed a beat. She whirled around to look at the porthole on the far side of the boat, the side that faced across the river. There was a head behind the glass.

She screamed.

The face disappeared.

She realized it had been Wolff.

She ran up the ladder and out on to the deck. Looking over the side, she saw him in the water. He appeared to be naked. He clambered up the side of the little boat, using the portholes for handholds. She reached for his arm and pulled him on to the deck. He knelt there on all fours for a moment, glancing up and down the river bank like an alert water rat; then he scampered down the hatch. She followed him.

He stood on the carpet, dripping and shivering. He *was* naked. She said: "What happened?"

"Run me a bath," he said.

She went through the bedroom into the bathroom. There was a small tub with an electric water heater. She turned the taps on and threw a handful of scented crystals into the water. Wolff got in and let the water rise around him.

"What happened?" Sonja repeated.

He controlled his shivering. "I didn't want to risk coming down the towpath, so I took off my clothes on the opposite bank and swam across. I looked in, and saw that man with you—I suppose he was another policeman."

"Yes."

"So I had to wait in the water until he went away."

She laughed. "You poor thing."

"It's not funny. My God, I'm cold. The fucking Abwehr gave me dud money. Somebody will be strangled for that, next time I'm in Germany."

"Why did they do it?"

"I don't know whether it's incompetence or disloyalty. Canaris has always been lukewarm on Hitler. Turn off the water, will you?" He began to wash the river mud off his legs.

"You'll have to use your own money," she said.

"I can't get at it. You can be sure the bank has instructions to call the police the moment I show my face. I could pay the occasional bill by check, but even that might help them get a line on me. I could sell some of my stocks and shares, or even the villa, but there again the money has to come through a bank . . ."

So you will have to use my money, Sonja thought. You won't ask, though: you'll just take it. She filed the thought for further consideration. "That detective is putting a watch on the boat—on Vandam's instructions."

Wolff grinned. "So it was Vandam."

"Did you cut him?"

"Yes, but I wasn't sure where. It was dark."

"The face. He had a huge bandage."

Wolff laughed aloud. "I wish I could see him." He became sober, and asked: "Did he question you?"

"Yes."

"What did you tell him?"

"That I hardly knew you."

"Good girl." He looked at her appraisingly, and she knew that he was pleased, and a little surprised, that she had kept her head. He said: "Did he believe you?"

"Presumably not, since he ordered this surveillance."

Wolff frowned. "That's going to be awkward. I can't swim the river every time I want to come home . . ."

"Don't worry," Sonja said. "I've fixed it."

"*You* fixed it?"

It was not quite so, Sonja knew, but it sounded good. "The detective is one of us," she explained.

"A nationalist?"

"Yes. He wants to use your radio."

"How does he know I've got one?" There was a threatening note in Wolff's voice.

"He doesn't," Sonja said calmly. "From what the British have told him he deduces that you're a spy; and he presumes a spy has a means of communicating with the Germans. The nationalists want to send a message to Rommel."

Wolff shook his head. "I'd rather not get involved."

She would not have him go back on a bargain she had made. "You've got to get involved," she said sharply.

"I suppose I do," he said wearily.

She felt an odd sense of power. It was as if she were taking control. She found it exhilarating.

Wolff said: "They're closing in. I don't want any more surprises like last night. I'd like to leave this boat, but I don't know where to go. Abdullah knows my money's no good—he'd like to turn me over to the British. Damn."

"You'll be safe here, while you string the detective along."

"I haven't any choice."

She sat on the edge of the bathtub, looking at his naked body. He seemed . . . not defeated, but at least cornered. His face was lined with tension, and there was in his voice a faint note of panic. She guessed that for the first time he was wondering whether he could hold out until Rommel arrived. And, also for the first time, he was dependent on her. He needed her money, he needed her home. Last night he had depended on her silence under interrogation, and—he now believed—he had been saved by her deal with the nationalist detective. He was slipping into her power. The thought intrigued her. She felt a little horny.

Wolff said: "I wonder if I should keep my date with that girl, Elene, tonight."

"Why not? She's nothing to do with the British. You picked her up in a shop!"

"Maybe. I just feel it might be safer to lie low. I don't know."

"No," said Sonja firmly. "I want her."

He looked up at her through narrowed eyes. She wondered whether he was considering the issue or thinking about her newfound strength of will. "All right," he said finally. "I'll just have to take precautions."

He had given in. She had tested her strength against his, and she had won. It gave her a kind of thrill. She shivered.

"I'm still cold," Wolf said. "Put some more hot water in."

"No." Without removing her nightdress, Sonja got into the bath. She knelt astride him, facing him, her knees jammed against the sides of the narrow tub. She lifted the wet hem of the nightdress to the level of her waist. She said: "Eat me."

He did.

Vandam was in high spirits as he sat in the Oasis Restaurant, sipping a cold martini, with Jakes beside him. He had slept all day and had woken up feeling battered but ready to fight back. He had gone to the hospital, where Dr. Abuthnot had told him he was a fool to be up and about, but a lucky fool, for his wound was mending. She had changed his dressing for a smaller, neater one that did not have to be secured by a yard of bandage around his head. Now it was a quarter past seven, and in a few minutes he would catch Alex Wolff.

Vandam and Jakes were at the back of the restaurant, in a position from which they could see the whole place. The table nearest to the entrance was occupied by two hefty sergeants eating fried chicken paid for by Intelligence. Outside, in an unmarked car parked across the road, were two MPs in civilian clothes with their handguns in their jacket pockets. The trap was set: all that was missing was the bait. Elene would arrive at any minute.

Billy had been shocked by the bandage at breakfast that morning. Vandam had sworn the boy to secrecy, then told him the truth. "I had a fight with a German spy. He had a knife. He got away, but I think I may catch him tonight." It was a breach of security, but what the hell, the boy needed to know why his father was wounded. After hearing the story Billy had not been worried anymore, but thrilled. Gaafar had been awestruck, and inclined to move around softly and talk in whispers, as if there had been a death in the family.

With Jakes, he found that last night's impulsive intimacy had left no overt trace. Their formal relationship had returned: Jakes took orders, called him sir, and did not offer opinions without being asked. It was just as well, Vandam thought: they were a good team as things were, so why make changes?

He looked at his wristwatch. It was seven-thirty. He lit another cigarette. At any moment now Alex Wolff would walk through the door. Vandam felt sure he would recognize Wolff—a tall, hawk-nosed European with brown hair and brown eyes, a strong, fit man—but he would make no move until Elene came in and sat by Wolff. Then Vandam and Jakes would move in. If Wolff fled the two sergeants would block the door, and in the unlikely event that he got past them, the MPs outside would shoot at him.

Seven thirty-five. Vandam was looking forward to interrogating Wolff. What a battle of wills that would be. But Vandam would win it, for he would have all the advantages. He would feel Wolff out, find the weak points, and then apply pressure until the prisoner cracked.

Seven thirty-nine. Wolff was late. Of course it was possible that he would not come at all. God forbid. Vandam shuddered when he recalled how superciliously he had said to Bogge: "I expect to arrest him tomorrow night." Vandam's section was in very bad odor at the moment, and only the prompt arrest of Wolff would enable them to come up smelling of roses. But suppose that, after last night's scare, Wolff had decided to lie low for a while, wherever it was that he was lying? Somehow Vandam felt that lying low was not Wolff's style. He hoped not.

At seven-forty the restaurant door opened and Elene walked in. Vandam heard Jakes whistle under his breath. She looked stunning. She wore a silk dress the color of clotted cream. Its simple lines drew attention to her slender figure, and its color and texture flattered her smooth tan skin: Vandam felt a sudden urge to stroke her.

She looked around the restaurant, obviously searching for Wolff and not finding him. Her eyes met Vandam's and moved on without hesitating. The headwaiter approached, and she spoke to him. He seated her at a table for two close to the door.

Vandam caught the eye of one of the sergeants and inclined his head in Elene's direction. The sergeant gave a little nod of acknowledgment and checked his watch.

Where was Wolff?

Vandam lit a cigarette and began to worry. He had assumed that Wolff, being a gentleman, would arrive a little early; and Elene would arrive a little late. According to that scenario the arrest would have taken place the moment she sat down. It's going wrong, he thought, it's going bloody wrong.

A waiter brought Elene a drink. It was seven forty-five. She looked in Vandam's direction and gave a small, dainty shrug of her slight shoulders.

The door of the restaurant opened. Vandam froze with a cigarette half way to his lips, then relaxed again, disappointed: it was only a small boy. The boy handed a piece of paper to a waiter then went out again.

Vandam decided to order another drink.

He saw the waiter go to Elene's table and hand her the piece of paper.

Vandam frowned. What was this? An apology from Wolff, saying he could not keep the date? Elene's face took on an expression of faint puzzlement. She looked at Vandam and gave that little shrug again.

Vandam considered whether to go over and ask her what was going on—but that would have spoiled the ambush, for what if Wolff should walk in while Elene was talking to Vandam? Wolff could turn around at the door and run, and he would have only the MPs to get past, two people instead of six.

Vandam murmured to Jakes: "Wait."

Elene picked up her clutch bag from the chair beside her and stood up. She looked at Vandam again, then turned around. Vandam thought she was going to the ladies' room. Instead she went to the door and opened it.

Vandam and Jakes got to their feet together. One of the sergeants half rose, looking at Vandam, and Vandam waved him down: no point in arresting Elene. Vandam and Jakes hurried across the restaurant to the door.

As they passed the sergeants Vandam said: "Follow me."

They went through the door into the street. Vandam looked around. There was a blind beggar sitting against the wall, holding out a cracked dish with a few piasters in it. Three soldiers in uniform staggered along the pavement, already drunk, arms around each other's shoulders, singing a vulgar song. A group of Egyptians had met just outside the restaurant and were vigorously shaking hands. A street vendor offered Vandam cheap razor blades. A few yards away Elene was getting into a taxi.

Vandam broke into a run.

The door of the taxi slammed and it pulled away.

Across the street, the MPs' car roared, shot forward and collided with a bus.

Vandam caught up with the taxi and leaped on to the run-

ning board. The car swerved suddenly. Vandam lost his grip,
hit the road running and fell down.

He got to his feet. His face blazed with pain: his wound
was bleeding again, and he could feel the sticky warmth under the dressing. Jakes and the two sergeants gathered around
him. Across the road the MPs were arguing with the bus
driver.

The taxi had disappeared.

15

Elene was terrified. It had all gone wrong. Wolff was supposed to have been arrested in the restaurant, and now he was here, in a taxi with her, smiling a feral smile. She sat still, her mind a blank.

"Who was he?" Wolff said, still smiling.

Elene could not think. She looked at Wolff, looked away again, and said: "What?"

"That man who ran after us. He jumped on the running board. I couldn't see him properly, but I thought he was a European. Who was he?"

Elene fought down her fear. *He's William Vandam, and he was supposed to arrest you.* She had to make up a story. Why would someone follow her out of a restaurant and try to get into her taxi? "He . . . I don't know him. He was in the restaurant." Suddenly she was inspired. "He was bothering me. I was alone. It's your fault, you were late."

"I'm so sorry," he said quickly.

Elene had an access of confidence after he swallowed her story so readily. "And why are we in a taxi?" she demanded. "What's it all about? Why aren't we having dinner?" She heard a whining note in her voice, and hated it.

"I had a wonderful idea." He smiled again, and Elene suppressed a shudder. "We're going to have a picnic. There's a basket in the trunk."

She did not know whether to believe him. Why had he pulled that stunt at the restaurant, sending a boy in with the message "Come outside.—A.W." unless he suspected a trap? What would he do now, take her into the desert and knife her? She had a sudden urge to leap out of the speeding car. She closed her eyes and forced herself to think calmly. If he suspected a trap, why did he come at all? No, it had to be more complex than that. He seemed to have believed her about the man on the running board—but she could not be sure what was going on behind his smile.

She said: "Where are we going?"

"A few miles out of town, to a little spot on the riverbank where we can watch the sun go down. It's going to be a lovely evening."

"I don't want to go."

"What's the matter?"

"I hardly know you."

"Don't be silly. The driver will be with us all the time— and I'm a gentleman."

"I should get out of the car."

"Please don't." He touched her arm lightly. "I have some smoked salmon, and a cold chicken, and a bottle of champagne. I get so bored with restaurants."

Elene considered. She could leave him now, and she would be safe—she would never see him again. That was what she wanted, to get away from the man forever. She thought: But I'm Vandam's only hope. What do I care for Vandam? I'd be happy never to see him again, and go back to the old peaceful life—

The old life.

She *did* care for Vandam, she realized; at least enough for her to hate the thought of letting him down. She *had* to stay with Wolff, cultivate him, angle for another date, try to find out where he lived.

Impulsively she said: "Let's go to your place."

He raised his eyebrows. "That's a sudden change of heart."

She realized she had made a mistake. "I'm confused," she said. "You sprung a surprise on me. Why didn't you ask me first?"

"I only thought of the idea an hour ago. It didn't occur to me that it might scare you."

Elene realized that she was, unintentionally, fulfilling her role as a dizzy girl. She decided not to overplay her hand. "All right," she said. She tried to relax.

Wolff was studying her. He said: "You're not quite as vulnerable as you seem, are you?"

"I don't know."

"I remember what you said to Aristopoulos, that first day I saw you in the shop."

Elene remembered: she had threatened to cut off Mikis' cock if he touched her again. She should have blushed, but she could not do so voluntarily. "I was so angry," she said.

Wolff chuckled. "You sounded it," he said. "Try to bear in mind that I am not Aristopoulos."

She gave him a weak smile. "Okay."

He turned his attention to the driver. They were out of the city, and Wolff began to give directions. Elene wondered where he had found this taxi: by Egyptian standards it was luxurious. It was some kind of American car, with big soft seats and lots of room, and it seemed only a few years old.

They passed through a series of villages, then turned on to an unmade road. The car followed the winding track up a small hill and emerged on a little plateau atop a bluff. The river was immediately below them, and on its far side Elene could see the neat patchwork of cultivated fields stretching into the distance until they met the sharp tan-colored line of the edge of the desert.

Wolff said: "Isn't this a lovely spot?"

Elene had to agree. A flight of swifts rising from the far bank of the river drew her eye upward, and she saw that the evening clouds were already edged in pink. A young girl was walking away from the river with a huge water jug on her head. A lone felucca sailed upstream, propelled by a light breeze.

The driver got out of the car and walked fifty yards away. He sat down, pointedly turning his back on them, lit a cigarette and unfolded a newspaper.

Wolff got a picnic hamper out of the trunk and set it on the floor of the car between them. As he began to unpack the food, Elene asked him: "How did you discover this place?"

"My mother brought me here when I was a boy." He handed her a glass of wine. "After my father died, my mother married an Egyptian. From time to time she would find the Muslim household oppressive, so she would bring me here in a gharry and tell me about . . . Europe, and so on."

"Did you enjoy it?"

He hesitated. "My mother had a way of spoiling things like that. She was always interrupting the fun. She used to say:

'You're so selfish, just like your father.' At that age I preferred my Arab family. My stepbrothers were wicked, and nobody tried to control them. We used to steal oranges from other people's gardens, throw stones at horses to make them bolt, puncture bicycle tires . . . Only my mother minded, and all she could do was warn us that we'd get punished eventually. She was always saying that—'They'll catch you one day, Alex!' "

The mother was right, Elene thought: they would catch Alex one day.

She was relaxing. She wondered whether Wolff was carrying the knife he had used in Assyut, and that made her tense again. The situation was so normal—a charming man taking a girl on a picnic beside the river—that for a moment she had forgotten she wanted something from him.

She said: "Where do you live now?"

"My house has been . . . commandeered by the British. I'm living with friends." He handed her a slice of smoked salmon on a china plate, then sliced a lemon in half with a kitchen knife. Elene watched his deft hands. She wondered what *he* wanted from *her*, that he should work so hard to please her.

Vandam felt very low. His face hurt, and so did his pride. The great arrest had been a fiasco. He had failed professionally, he had been outwitted by Alex Wolff and he had sent Elene into danger.

He sat at home, his cheek newly bandaged, drinking gin to ease the pain. Wolff had evaded him so damn *easily*. Vandam was sure the spy had not really known about the ambush—otherwise he would not have turned up at all. No, he had just been taking precautions; and the precautions had worked beautifully.

They had a good description of the taxi. It had been a distinctive car, quite new, and Jakes had read the number plate. Every policeman and MP in the city was looking out for it, and had orders to stop it on sight and arrest all the occupants. They would find it, sooner or later, and Vandam felt sure it would be too late. Nevertheless he was sitting by the phone.

What was Elene doing now? Perhaps she was in a candlelit restaurant, drinking wine and laughing at Wolff's jokes. Vandam pictured her, in the cream-colored dress, holding a glass, smiling her special, impish smile, the one that promised you anything you wanted. Vandam checked his watch. Perhaps they had finished dinner by now. What would they do then? It was traditional to go and look at the pyramids by moonlight: the black sky, the stars, the endless flat desert and the clean triangular planes of the pharaohs' tombs. The area would be deserted, except perhaps for another pair of lovers. They might climb a few levels, he springing up ahead and then reaching down to lift her; but soon she would be exhausted, her hair and her dress a little awry, and she would say that these shoes were not designed for mountaineering; so they would sit on the great stones, still warm from the sun, and breathe the mild night air while they watched the stars. Walking back to the taxi, she would shiver in her sleeveless evening gown, and he might put an arm around her shoulders to keep her warm. Would he kiss her in the taxi? No, he was too old for that. When he made his pass, it would be in some sophisticated manner. Would he suggest going back to his place, or hers? Vandam did not know which to hope for. If they went to his place, Elene would report in the morning, and Vandam would be able to arrest Wolff at home, with his radio, his code book and perhaps even his back traffic. Professionally, that would be better—but it would also mean that Elene would spend a night with Wolff, and that thought made Vandam more angry than it should have done. Alternatively, if they went to her place, where Jakes was waiting with ten men and three cars, Wolff would be grabbed before he got a chance to—

Vandam got up and paced the room. Idly, he picked up the book *Rebecca*, the one he thought Wolff was using as the basis of his code. He read the first line: "Last night I dreamt I went to Manderley again." He put the book down, then opened it again and read on. The story of the vulnerable, bullied girl was a welcome distraction from his own worries. When he realized that the girl would marry the glamorous, older widower, and that the marriage would be blighted by the ghostly presence of the man's first wife, he closed the book and put it down again. What was the age difference between himself and Elene? How long would he be haunted by Angela? She, too, had been coldly perfect; Elene, too, was young, impulsive and in need of rescue from the life she was living. These thoughts irritated him, for he was not going to marry Elene. He lit a cigarette. Why did the time pass so slowly? Why did the phone not ring? How could he have let Wolff slip through his fingers twice in two days? Where was Elene?

Where was Elene?

He had sent a woman into danger once before. It had happened after his other great fiasco, when Rashid Ali had slipped out of Turkey under Vandam's nose. Vandam had sent a woman agent to pick up the German agent, the man who had changed clothes with Ali and enabled him to escape. He had hoped to salvage something from the shambles by finding out all about the man. But next day the woman had been found dead in a hotel bed. It was a chilling parallel.

There was no point in staying in the house. He could not possibly sleep, and there was nothing else he could do there. He would go and join Jakes and the others, despite Dr. Abuthnot's orders. He put on a coat and his uniform cap, went outside, and wheeled his motorcycle out of the garage.

Elene and Wolff stood together, close to the edge of the bluff, looking at the distant lights of Cairo and the nearer, flickering glimmers of peasant fires in dark villages. Elene was thinking of an imaginary peasant—hardworking, poverty-stricken, superstitious—laying a straw mattress on the earth floor, pulling a rough blanket around him, and finding consolation in the arms of his wife. Elene had left poverty behind, she hoped forever, but sometimes it seemed to her that she had left something else behind with it, something she could not do without. In Alexandria when she was a child people would put blue palm prints on the red mud walls, hand shapes to ward off evil. Elene did not believe in the efficacy of the palm prints; but despite the rats, despite the nightly screams as the moneylender beat both of his wives, despite the ticks that infested everyone, despite the early death of many babies, she believed there had been *something* there that warded off evil. She had been looking for that something when she took men home, took them into her bed, accepted their gifts and their caresses and their money; but she had never found it.

She did not want to do that anymore. She had spent too much of her life looking for love in the wrong places. In particular, she did not want to do it with Alex Wolff. Several times she had said to herself: "Why not do it just once more?" That was Vandam's coldly reasonable point of view. But, each time she contemplated making love with Wolff, she saw again the daydream that had plagued her for the last few weeks, the daydream of seducing William Vandam. She knew *just* how Vandam would be: he would look at her with innocent wonder, and touch her with wide-eyed delight; thinking of it, she felt momentarily helpless with desire. She knew how Wolff would be, too. He would be knowing, selfish, skillful and unshockable.

Without speaking she turned from the view and walked back toward the car. It was time for him to make his pass. They had finished the meal, emptied the champagne bottle and the flask of coffee, picked clean the chicken and the bunch of grapes. Now he would expect his just reward. From the back seat of the car she watched him. He stayed a moment longer on the edge of the bluff, then walked toward her, calling to the driver. He had the confident grace that height often seemed to give to men. He was an attractive man, much more glamorous than any of Elene's lovers had been, but she was afraid of him, and her fear came not just from what she knew about him, his history and his secrets and his knife, but from an intuitive understanding of his nature: somehow she knew that his charm was not spontaneous but manipulative, and that if he was kind it was because he wanted to use her.

She had been used enough.

Wolff got in beside her. "Did you enjoy the picnic?"

She made an effort to be bright. "Yes, it was lovely. Thank you."

The car pulled away. Either he would invite her to his place or he would take her to her flat and ask for a nightcap. She would have to find an encouraging way to refuse him. This struck her as ridiculous: she was behaving like a frightened virgin. She thought: What am I doing—saving myself for Mr. Right?

She had been silent for too long. She was supposed to be witty and engaging. She should talk to him. "Have you heard the war news?" she asked, and realized at once it was not the most lighthearted of topics.

"The Germans are still winning," he said. "Of course."

"Why 'of course'?"

He smiled condescendingly at her. "The world is divided into masters and slaves, Elene." He spoke as if he were explaining simple facts to a schoolboy. "The British have been masters too long. They've gone soft, and now it will be someone else's turn."

"And the Egyptians—are they masters, or slaves?" She knew she should shut up, she was walking on thin ice, but his complacency infuriated her.

"The Bedouin are masters," he said. "But the average Egyptian is a born slave."

She thought: He means every word of it. She shuddered.

They reached the outskirts of the city. It was after midnight, and the suburbs were quiet, although downtown would still be buzzing. Wolff said: "Where do you live?"

She told him. So it was to be her place.

Wolff said: "We must do this again."

"I'd like that."

They reached the Sharia Abbas, and he told the driver to stop. Elene wondered what was going to happen now. Wolff turned to her and said: "Thank you for a lovely evening. I'll see you soon." He got out of the car.

She stared in astonishment. He bent down by the driver's window, gave the man some money and told him Elene's address. The driver nodded. Wolff banged on the roof of the car, and the driver pulled away. Elene looked back and saw Wolff waving. As the car began to turn a corner, Wolff started walking toward the river.

She thought: What do you make of that?

No pass, no invitation to his place, no nightcap, not even a good-night kiss—what game was he playing, hard-to-get?

She puzzled over the whole thing as the taxi took her home. Perhaps it was Wolff's technique to try to intrigue a woman. Perhaps he was just eccentric. Whatever the reason, she was very grateful. She sat back and relaxed. She was not obliged to choose between fighting him off and going to bed with him. Thank God.

The taxi drew up outside her building. Suddenly, from nowhere, three cars roared up. One stopped right in front of the taxi, one close behind, and one alongside. Men materialized out of the shadows. All four doors of the taxi were flung open, and four guns pointed in. Elene screamed.

Then a head was poked into the car, and Elene recognized Vandam.

"Gone?" Vandam said.

Elene realized what was happening. "I thought you were going to shoot me," she said.

"Where did you leave him?"

"Sharia Abbas."

"How long ago?"

"Five or ten minutes. May I get out of the car?"

He gave her a hand, and she stepped on to the pavement. He said: "I'm sorry we scared you."

"This is called slamming the stable door after the horse has bolted."

"Quite." He looked utterly defeated.

She felt a surge of affection for him. She touched his arm. "You've no idea how happy I am to see your face," she said.

He gave her an odd look, as if he was not sure whether to believe her.

She said: "Why don't you send your men home and come and talk inside?"

He hesitated. "All right." He turned to one of his men, a captain. "Jakes, I want you to interrogate the taxi driver, see what you can get out of him. Let the men go. I'll see you at GHQ in an hour or so."

"Very good, sir."

Elene led the way inside. It was so good to enter her own apartment, slump on the sofa, and kick off her shoes. The trial was over, Wolff had gone, and Vandam was here. She said: "Help yourself to a drink."

"No, thanks."

"What went wrong, anyway?"

Vandam sat down opposite her and took out his cigarettes. "We expected him to walk into the trap all unawares—but he was suspicious, or at least cautious, and we missed him. What happened then?"

She rested her head against the back of the sofa, closed her eyes, and told him in a few words about the picnic. She left out her thoughts about going to bed with Wolff, and she did not tell Vandam that Wolff had hardly touched her all evening. She spoke abruptly: she wanted to forget, not remember. When she had told him the story she said: "Make me a drink, even if you won't have one."

He went to the cupboard. Elene could see that he was angry. She looked at the bandage on his face. She had seen it in the restaurant, and again a few minutes ago when she arrived, but now she had time to wonder what it was. She said: "What happened to your face?"

"We almost caught Wolff last night."

"Oh, no." So he had failed twice in twenty-four hours: no wonder he looked defeated. She wanted to console him, to put her arms around him, to lay his head in her lap and stroke his hair; the longing was like an ache. She decided— impulsively, the way she always decided things—that she would take him to her bed tonight.

He gave her a drink. He had made one for himself after all. As he stooped to hand her the glass she reached up, touched his chin with her fingertips and turned his head so that she could look at his cheek. He let her look, just for a second, then moved his head away.

She had not seen him as tense as this before. He crossed the room and sat opposite her, holding himself upright on the edge of the chair. He was full of a suppressed emotion, something like rage, but when she looked into his eyes she saw not anger but pain.

He said: "How did Wolff strike you?"

She was not sure what he was getting at. "Charming. Intelligent. Dangerous."

"His appearance?"

"Clean hands, a silk shirt, a mustache that doesn't suit him. What are you fishing for?"

He shook his head irritably. "Nothing. Everything." He lit another cigarette.

She could not reach him in this mood. She wanted him to come and sit beside her, and tell her she was beautiful and brave and she had done well; but she knew it was no use asking. All the same she said: "How did I do?"

"I don't know," he said. "*What* did you do?"

"You know what I did."

"Yes. I'm most grateful."

He smiled, and she knew the smile was insincere. What was the matter with him? There was something familiar in his anger, something she would understand as soon as she put her finger on it. It was not just that he felt he had failed. It was his attitude to her, the way he spoke to her, the way he sat across from her and especially the way he looked at her. His expression was one of . . . it was almost one of disgust.

"He said he would see you again?" Vandam asked.

"Yes."

"I hope he does." He put his chin in his hands. His face was strained with tension. Wisps of smoke rose from his cigarette. "Christ, I hope he does."

"He also said: 'We must do this again,' or something like that," Elene told him.

"I see. 'We must do this again,' eh?"

"Something like that."

"What do you think he had in mind, exactly?"

She shrugged. "Another picnic, another date—damn it, William, what has got into you?"

"I'm just curious," he said. His face wore a twisted grin, one she had never seen on him before. "I'd like to know what the two of you did, other than eat and drink, in the back of that big taxi, and on the riverbank: you know, all that time together, in the dark, a man and a woman—"

"Shut up." She closed her eyes. Now she understood; now she knew. Without opening her eyes she said: "I'm going to bed. You can see yourself out."

A few seconds later the front door slammed.

She went to the window and looked down to the street. She saw him leave the building, and get on his motorcycle. He kicked the engine into life and roared off down the road at a breakneck speed and took the corner at the end as if he were in a race. Elene was very tired, and a little sad that she would be spending the night alone after all, but she was not unhappy, for she had understood his anger, she knew the cause of it, and that gave her hope. As he disappeared from sight she smiled faintly and said softly: "William Vandam, I do believe you're jealous."

16

By the time Major Smith made his third lunchtime visit to the houseboat, Wolff and Sonja had gotten into a slick routine. Wolff hid in the cupboard when the major approached. Sonja met him in the living room with a drink in her hand ready for him. She made him sit down there, ensuring that his briefcase was put down before they went into the bedroom. After a minute or two she began kissing him. By this time she could do what she liked with him, for he was paralyzed by lust. She contrived to get his shorts off, then soon afterward took him into the bedroom.

It was clear to Wolff that nothing like this had ever happened to the major before: he was Sonja's slave as long as she allowed him to make love to her. Wolff was grateful: things would not have been quite so easy with a more strong-minded man.

As soon as Wolff heard the bed creak he came out of the cupboard. He took the key out of the shorts pocket and opened the case. His notebook and pencil were beside him, ready.

Smith's second visit had been disappointing, leading Wolff to wonder whether perhaps it was only occasionally that Smith saw battle plans. However, this time he struck gold again.

General Sir Claude Auchinleck, the C in C Middle East, had taken over direct control of the Eighth Army from General Neil Ritchie. As a sign of Allied panic, that alone would be welcome news to Rommel. It might also help Wolff, for it meant that battles were now being planned in Cairo rather than in the desert, in which case Smith was more likely to get copies.

The Allies had retreated to a new defense line at Mersa Matruh, and the most important paper in Smith's briefcase was a summary of the new dispositions.

The new line began at the coastal village of Matruh and stretched south into the desert as far as an escarpment called Sidi Hamza. Tenth Corps was at Matruh; then there was a heavy minefield fifteen miles long; then a lighter minefield for ten miles; then the escarpment, the 13th Corps; then, south of the escarpment, the 13th Corps.

With half an ear on the noises from the bedroom, Wolff considered the position. The picture was fairly clear: the Allied line was strong at either end and weak in the middle.

Rommel's likeliest move, according to Allied thinking, was a dash around the southern end of the line, a classic Rommel outflanking maneuver, made more feasible by his capture of an estimated 500 tons of fuel at Tobruk. Such an advance would be repelled by the 13th Corps, which consisted of the strong 1st Armored Division and the 2nd New Zealand Division, the latter—the summary noted helpfully—freshly arrived from Syria.

However, armed with Wolff's information, Rommel could instead hit the soft center of the line and pour his forces through the gap like a stream bursting a dam at its weakest point.

Wolff smiled to himself. He felt he was playing a major role in the struggle for German domination of North Africa: he found it enormously satisfying.

In the bedroom, a cork popped.

Smith always surprised Wolff by the rapidity of his love-making. The cork popping was the sign that it was all over, and Wolff had a few minutes in which to tidy up before Smith came in search of his shorts.

He put the papers back in the case, locked it and put the key back in the shorts pocket. He no longer got back into the cupboard afterward—once had been enough. He put his shoes in his trousers pockets and tiptoed, soundlessly in his socks, up the ladder, across the deck, and down the gangplank to the towpath. Then he put his shoes on and went to lunch.

Kemel shook hands politely and said: "I hope your injury is healing rapidly, Major."

"Sit down," Vandam said. "The bandage is more damn nuisance than the wound. What have you got?"

Kemel sat down and crossed his legs, adjusting the crease of his black cotton trousers. "I thought I would bring the surveillance report myself, although I'm afraid there's nothing of interest in it."

Vandam took the proffered envelope and opened it. It contained a single typewritten sheet. He began to read.

Sonja had come home—presumably from the Cha-Cha Club—at eleven o'clock the previous night. She had been alone. She had surfaced at around ten the following morning, and had been seen on deck in a robe. The postman had come at one. Sonja had gone out at four and returned at six carrying a bag bearing the name of one of the more expensive dress shops in Cairo. At that hour the watcher had been relieved by the night man.

Yesterday Vandam had received by messenger a similar report from Kemel covering the first twelve hours of the surveillance. For two days, therefore, Sonja's behavior had been routine and wholly innocent, and neither Wolff nor anyone else had visited her on the houseboat.

Vandam was bitterly disappointed.

Kemel said: "The men I am using are completely reliable, and they are reporting directly to me."

Vandam grunted, then roused himself to be courteous. "Yes, I'm sure," he said. "Thank you for coming in."

Kemel stood up. "No trouble," he said. "Good-bye." He went out.

Vandam sat brooding. He read Kemel's report again, as if there might have been clues between the lines. If Sonja was connected with Wolff—and Vandam still believed she was, somehow—clearly the association was not a close one. If she was meeting anyone, the meetings must be taking place away from the houseboat.

Vandam went to the door and called: "Jakes!"

"Sir!"

Vandam sat down again and Jakes came in. Vandam said: "From now on I want you to spend your evenings at the Cha-Cha Club. Watch Sonja, and observe whom she sits with

after the show. Also, bribe a waiter to tell you whether anyone goes to her dressing room."

"Very good, sir."

Vandam nodded dismissal, and added with a smile: "Per-
mission to enjoy yourself is granted."

The smile was a mistake: it hurt. At least he was no longer
trying to live on glucose dissolved in warm water: Gaafar
was giving him mashed potatoes and gravy, which he could
eat from a spoon and swallow without chewing. He was exist-
ing on that and gin. Dr. Abuthnot had also told him he drank
too much and smoked too much, and he had promised to cut
down—after the war. Privately he thought: After I've caught
Wolff.

If Sonja was not going to lead him to Wolff, only Elene
could. Vandam was ashamed of his outburst at Elene's apartment. He had been angry at his own failure, and the thought
of her with Wolff had maddened him. His behavior could be
described only as a fit of bad temper. Elene was a lovely girl
who was risking her neck to help him, and courtesy was the
least he owed her.

Wolff had said he would see Elene again. Vandam hoped
he would contact her soon. He still felt irrationally angry at
the thought of the two of them together; but now that the
houseboat angle had turned out to be a dead end, Elene was
his only hope. He sat at his desk, waiting for the phone to
ring, dreading the very thing he wanted most.

Elene went shopping in the late afternoon. Her apartment
had come to seem claustrophobic after she had spent most of
the day pacing around, unable to concentrate on anything, alternately miserable and happy; so she put on a cheerful
striped dress and went out into the sunshine.

She liked the fruit-and-vegetable market. It was a lively
place, especially at this end of the day when the tradesmen
were trying to get rid of the last of their produce. She
stopped to buy tomatoes. The man who served her picked up
one with a slight bruise, and threw it away dramatically before filling a paper bag with undamaged specimens. Elene
laughed, for she knew that the bruised tomato would be re-
trieved, as soon as she was out of sight, and put back on the
display so that the whole pantomime could be performed

again for the next customer. She haggled briefly over the price, but the vendor could tell that her heart was not in it, and she ended up paying almost what he had asked originally.

She bought eggs, too, having decided to make an omelet for supper. It was good, to be carrying a basket of food, more food than she could eat at one meal: it made her feel safe. She could remember days when there had been no supper.

She left the market and went window shopping for dresses. She bought most of her clothes on impulse: she had firm ideas about what she liked, and if she planned a trip to buy something special, she could never find it. She wanted one day to have her own dressmaker.

She thought: I wonder if William Vandam could afford that for his wife?

When she thought of Vandam she was happy, until she thought of Wolff.

She knew she could escape, if she wished, simply by refusing to see Wolff, refusing to make a date with him, refusing to answer his message. She was under no obligation to act as the bait in a trap for a knife murderer. She kept returning to this idea, worrying at it like a loose tooth: I don't have to.

She suddenly lost interest in dresses, and headed for home. She wished she could make omelet for two, but omelet for one was something to be thankful for. There was a certain unforgettable pain in the stomach which came when, having gone to bed with no supper, you woke up in the morning to no breakfast. The ten-year-old Elene had wondered, secretly, how long people took to starve to death. She was sure Vandam's childhood had not suffered such worries.

When she turned into the entrance to her apartment block, a voice said: "Abigail."

She froze with shock. It was the voice of a ghost. She did not dare to look. The voice came again.

"Abigail."

She made herself turn around. A figure came out of the shadows: an old Jew, shabbily dressed, with a matted beard, veined feet in rubber-tire sandals . . .

Elene said: "Father."

He stood in front of her, as if afraid to touch her, just looking. He said: "So beautiful still, and not poor . . ."

Impulsively, she stepped forward, kissed his cheek, then stepped back again. She did not know what to say.

He said: "Your grandfather, my father, has died."

She took his arm and led him up the stairs. It was all unreal, irrational, like a dream.

Inside the apartment she said: "You should eat," and took him into the kitchen. She put a pan on to heat and began to beat the eggs. With her back to her father she said: "How did you find me?"

"I've always known where you were," he said. "Your friend Esme writes to her father, who sometimes I see."

Esme was an acquaintance, rather than a friend, but Elene ran into her every two or three months. She had never let on that she was writing home. Elene said: "I didn't want you to ask me to come back."

"And what would I have said to you? 'Come home, it is your duty to starve with your family.' No. But I knew where you were."

She sliced tomatoes into the omelet. "You would have said it was better to starve than to live immorally."

"Yes, I would have said that. And would I have been wrong?"

She turned to look at him. The glaucoma which had taken the sight of his left eye years ago was now spreading to the right. He was fifty-five, she calculated: he looked seventy. "Yes, you would have been wrong," she said. "It is always better to live."

"Perhaps it is."

Her surprise must have shown on her face, for he explained: "I'm not as certain of these things as I used to be. I'm getting old."

Elene halved the omelet and slid it on to two plates. She put bread on the table. Her father washed his hands, then blessed the bread. "Blessed art thou O Lord our God, King of the Universe . . ." Elene was surprised that the prayer did not drive her into a fury. In the blackest moments of her lonely life she had cursed and raged at her father and his religion for what it had driven her to. She had tried to cultivate an attitude of indifference, perhaps mild contempt; but she had not quite succeeded. Now, watching him pray, she thought: And what do I do, when this man whom I hate turns up on the doorstep? I kiss his cheek, and I bring him inside, and I give him supper.

They began to eat. Her father had been very hungry, and wolfed his food. Elene wondered why he had come. Was it just to tell her of the death of her grandfather? No. That was part of it, perhaps, but there would be more.

She asked about her sisters. After the death of their mother all four of them, in their different ways, had broken with their father. Two had gone to America, one had married the son of her father's greatest enemy, and the youngest, Naomi, had chosen the surest escape, and died. It dawned on Elene that her father was destroyed.

He asked her what she was doing. She decided to tell him the truth. "The British are trying to catch a man, a German, they think is a spy. It's my job to befriend him . . . I'm the bait in a snare. But . . . I think I may not help them anymore."

He had stopped eating. "Are you afraid?"

She nodded. "He's very dangerous. He killed a soldier with a knife. Last night . . . I was to meet him in a restaurant and the British were to arrest him there, but something went wrong and I spent the whole evening with him, I was so frightened, and when it was over, the Englishman . . ." She stopped, and took a deep breath. "Anyway, I may not help them anymore."

Her father went on eating. "Do you love this Englishman?"

"He isn't Jewish," she said defiantly.

"I've given up judging everyone," he said.

Elene could not take it all in. Was there *nothing* of the old man left?

They finished their meal, and Elene got up to make him a glass of tea. He said: "The Germans are coming. It will be very bad for Jews. I'm getting out."

She frowned. "Where will you go?"

"Jerusalem."

"How will you get there? The trains are full, there's a quota for Jews—"

"I am going to walk."

She stared at him, not believing he could be serious, not believing he would joke about such a thing. "Walk?"

He smiled. "It's been done before."

She saw that he meant it, and she was angry with him. "As I recall, Moses never made it."

"Perhaps I will be able to hitch a ride."

"It's crazy!"

"Haven't I always been a little crazy?"

"Yes!" she shouted. Suddenly her anger collapsed. "Yes, you've always been a little crazy, and I should know better than to try to change your mind."

"I will pray to God to preserve you. You will have a chance here—you're young and beautiful, and maybe they won't know you're Jewish. But me, a useless old man muttering Hebrew prayers . . . me they would send to a camp where I would surely die. It is always better to live. You said that."

She tried to persuade him to stay with her, for one night at least, but he would not. She gave him a sweater, and a scarf, and all the cash she had in the house, and told him that if he waited a day she could get more money from the bank, and buy him a good coat; but he was in a hurry. She cried, and dried her eyes, and cried again. When he left she looked out of her window and saw him walking along the street, an old man going up out of Egypt and into the wilderness, following in the footsteps of the Children of Israel. There *was* something of the old man left: his orthodoxy had mellowed, but he still had a will of iron. He disappeared into the crowd, and she left the window. When she thought of his courage, she knew she could not run out on Vandam.

"She's an intriguing girl," Wolff said. "I can't quite figure her out." He was sitting on the bed, watching Sonja get dressed. "She's a little jumpy. When I told her we were going on a picnic she acted quite scared, said she hardly knew me, as if she needed a chaperone."

"With you, she did," Sonja said.

"And yet she can be very earthy and direct."

"Just bring her home to me. I'll figure her out."

"It bothers me." Wolff frowned. He was thinking aloud. "Somebody tried to jump into the taxi with us."

"A beggar."

"No, he was a European."

"A European beggar." Sonja stopped brushing her hair to look at Wolff in the mirror. "This town is full of crazy people, you know that. Listen, if you have second thoughts, just picture her writhing on that bed with you and me on either side of her."

Wolff grinned. It was an appealing picture, but not an irresistible one: it was Sonja's fantasy, not his. His instinct told him to lay low now, and not to make dates with anyone. But Sonja was going to insist—and he still needed her.

Sonja said: "And when am I going to contact Kemel? He must know by now that you're living here."

Wolff sighed. Another date; another claim on him; another danger; also, another person whose protection he needed. "Call him tonight from the club. I'm not in a rush for this meeting, but we've got to keep him sweet."

"Okay." She was ready, and her taxi was waiting. "Make a date with Elene." She went out.

She was not in his power the way she had once been, Wolff realized. The walls you build to protect you also close you in. Could he afford to defy her? If there had been a clear and immediate danger, yes. But all he had was a vague nervousness, an intuitive inclination to keep his head down. And Sonja might be crazy enough to betray him if she really got angry. He was obliged to choose the lesser danger.

He got up from the bed, found a paper and a pen and sat down to write a note to Elene.

17

The message came the day after Elene's father left for Jerusalem. A small boy came to the door with an envelope. Elene tipped him and read the letter. It was short. "My dear Elene, let us meet at the Oasis Restaurant at eight o'clock next Thursday. I eagerly look forward to it. Fondly, Alex Wolff." Unlike his speech, his writing had a stiffness which seemed German—but perhaps it was her imagination. Thursday—that was the day after tomorrow. She did not know whether to be elated or scared. Her first thought was to telephone Vandam; then she hesitated.

She had become intensely curious about Vandam. She knew so little about him. What did he do when he was not catching spies? Did he listen to music, collect stamps, shoot duck? Was he interested in poetry or architecture or antique rugs? What was his home like? With whom did he live? What color were his pajamas?

She wanted to patch up their quarrel, and she wanted to see where he lived. She had an excuse to contact him now, but instead of telephoning she would go to his home.

She decided to change her dress, then she decided to take a bath first, then she decided to wash her hair as well. Sitting in the bath she thought about which dress to wear. She recalled the occasions she had seen Vandam, and tried to remember which clothes she had worn. He had never seen the pale pink one with puffed shoulders and buttons all down the front: that was very pretty.

She put on a little perfume, then the silk underwear Johnnie had given her, which always made her feel so feminine. Her short hair was dry already, and she sat in front of the mirror to comb it. The dark, fine locks gleamed after washing. I look ravishing, she thought, and she smiled at herself seductively.

She left the apartment, taking Wolff's note with her. Vandam would be interested to see his handwriting. He was interested in every little detail where Wolff was concerned, perhaps because they had never met face to face, except in the dark or at a distance. The handwriting was very neat, easily legible, almost like an artist's lettering: Vandam would draw some conclusion from that.

She headed for Garden City. It was seven o'clock, and Vandam worked until late, so she had time to spare. The sun was still strong, and she enjoyed the heat on her arms and legs as she walked. A bunch of soldiers whistled at her, and in her sunny mood she smiled at them, so they followed her for a few blocks before they got diverted into a bar.

She felt gay and reckless. What a good idea it was to go to his house—so much better than sitting alone at home. She had been alone too much. For her men, she had existed only when they had time to visit her; and she had made their attitudes her own, so that when they were not there she felt she had nothing to do, no role to play, no one to be. Now she had broken with all that. By doing this, by going to see him uninvited, she felt she was being herself instead of a person in someone else's dream. It made her almost giddy.

She found the house easily. It was a small French-colonial villa, all pillars and high windows, its white stone reflecting the evening sun with painful brilliance. She walked up the short drive, rang the bell and waited in the shadow of the portico.

An elderly, bald Egyptian came to the door. "Good evening, Madam," he said, speaking like an English butler.

Elene said: "I'd like to see Major Vandam. My name is Elene Fontana."

"The major has not yet returned home, Madam." The servant hesitated.

"Perhaps I could wait," Elene said.

"Of course, Madam." He stepped aside to admit her.

She crossed the threshold. She looked around with nervous eagerness. She was in a cool tiled hall with a high ceiling. Before she could take it all in the servant said: "This way,

Madam." He led her into a drawing room. "My name is
Gaafar. Please call me if there is anything you require."

"Thank you, Gaafar."

The servant went out. Elene was thrilled to be in Vandam's
house and left alone to look around. The drawing room had
a large marble fireplace and a lot of very English furniture:
somehow she thought he had not furnished it himself. Everything was clean and tidy and not very lived-in. What did this
say about his character? Perhaps nothing.

The door opened and a young boy walked in. He was very
good-looking, with curly brown hair and smooth, preadoles-
cent skin. He seemed about ten years old. He looked vaguely
familiar.

He said: "Hello, I'm Billy Vandam."

Elene stared at him in horror. A son—Vandam had a son!
She knew now why he seemed familiar: he resembled his
father. Why had it never occurred to her that Vandam might
be married? A man like that—charming, kind, handsome,
clever—was unlikely to have reached his late thirties without
getting hooked. What a fool she had been to think that she
might have been the first to desire him! She felt so stupid
that she blushed.

She shook Billy's hand. "How do you do," she said. "I'm
Elene Fontana."

"We never know what time Dad's coming home," Billy
said. "I hope you won't have to wait too long."

She had not yet recovered her composure. "Don't worry, I
don't mind, it doesn't matter a bit . . ."

"Would you like a drink, or anything?"

He was very polite, like his father, with a formality that
was somehow disarming. Elene said: "No, thank you."

"Well, I've got to have my supper. Sorry to leave you
alone."

"No, no . . ."

"If you need anything, just call Gaafar."

"Thank you."

The boy went out, and Elene sat down heavily. She was
disoriented, as if in her own home she had found a door to a
room she had not known was there. She noticed a photograph
on the marble mantelpiece, and got up to look at it. It was a
picture of a beautiful woman in her early twenties, a cool,

aristocratic-looking woman with a faintly supercilious smile. Elene admired the dress she was wearing, something silky and flowing, hanging in elegant folds from her slender figure. The woman's hair and makeup were perfect. The eyes were startlingly familiar, clear and perceptive and light in color: Elene realized that Billy had eyes like that. This, then, was Billy's mother—Vandam's wife. She was, of course, exactly the kind of woman who would be his wife, a classic English beauty with a superior air.

Elene felt she had been a fool. Women like that were queuing up to marry men like Vandam. As if he would have bypassed all of them only to fall for an Egyptian courtesan! She rehearsed the things that divided her from him: he was respectable and she was disreputable; he was British and she was Egyptian; he was Christian—presumably—and she was Jewish; he was well bred and she came out of the slums of Alexandria; he was almost forty and she was twenty-three . . . The list was long.

Tucked into the back of the photograph frame was a page torn from a magazine. The paper was old and yellowing. The page bore the same photograph. Elene saw that it had come from a magazine called *The Tatler*. She had heard of it: it was much read by the wives of colonels in Cairo, for it reported all the trivial events of London society—parties, balls, charity lunches, gallery openings and the activities of English royalty. The picture of Mrs. Vandam took up most of this page, and a paragraph of type beneath the picture reported that Angela, daughter of Sir Peter and Lady Beresford, was engaged to be married to Lieutenant William Vandam, son of Mr. and Mrs. John Vandam of Gately, Dorset. Elene refolded the cutting and put it back.

The family picture was complete. Attractive British officer, cool, self-assured English wife, intelligent charming son, beautiful home, money, class and happiness. Everything else was a dream.

She wandered around the room, wondering if it held any more shocks in store. The room had been furnished by Mrs. Vandam, of course, in perfect, bloodless taste. The decorous print of the curtains toned with the restrained hue of the upholstery and the elegant striped wallpaper. Elene wondered what their bedroom would be like. It too would be coolly tasteful, she guessed. Perhaps the main color would be blue-green, the shade they called eau de Nil although it was not a bit like the muddy water of the Nile. Would they have twin beds? She hoped so. She would never know.

Against one wall was a small upright piano. She wondered who played. Perhaps Mrs. Vandam sat here sometimes, in the evenings, filling the air with Chopin while Vandam sat in the armchair, over there, watching her fondly. Perhaps Vandam accompanied himself as he sang romantic ballads to her in a strong tenor. Perhaps Billy had a tutor, and fingered hesitant scales every afternoon when he came home from school. She looked through the pile of sheet music in the seat of the piano stool. She had been right about the Chopin: they had all the waltzes here in a book.

She picked up a novel from the top of the piano and opened it. She read the first line: "Last night I dreamt I went to Manderley again." The opening sentences intrigued her, and she wondered whether Vandam was reading the book. Perhaps she could borrow it: it would be good to have something of his. On the other hand, she had the feeling he was not a great reader of fiction. She did not want to borrow it from his wife.

Billy came in. Elene put the book down suddenly, feeling irrationally guilty, as if she had been prying. Billy saw the gesture. "That one's no good," he said. "It's about some silly girl who's afraid of her husband's housekeeper. There's no action."

Elene sat down, and Billy sat opposite her. Obviously he was going to entertain her. He was a miniature of his father, except for those clear gray eyes. She said: "You've read it, then?"

"*Rebecca*? Yes. But I didn't like it much. I always finish them, though."

"What *do* you like to read?"

"I like tecs best."

"Tecs?"

"Detectives. I've read all of Agatha Christie's and Dorothy Sayers'. But I like the American ones most of all—S.S. Van Dine and Raymond Chandler."

"Really?" Elene smiled. "I like detective stories too—I read them all the time."

"Oh! Who's your favorite tec?"

Elene considered. "Maigret."

"I've never heard of him. What's the author's name?"

"Georges Simenon. He writes in French, but now some of the books have been translated into English. They're set in Paris, mostly. They're very . . . complex."

"Would you lend me one? It's so hard to get new books, I've read all the ones in this house, and in the school library. And I swap with my friends but they like, you know, stories about children having adventures in the school holidays."

"All right," Elene said. "Let's swap. What have you got to lend me? I don't think I've read any American ones."

"I'll lend you a Chandler. The American ones are much more true to life, you know. I've gone off those stories about English country houses and people who probably couldn't murder a fly."

It was odd, Elene thought, that a boy for whom the English country house might be part of everyday life should find stories about American private eyes more "true to life." She hesitated, then asked: "Does your mother read detective stories?"

Billy said briskly: "My mother died last year in Crete."

"Oh!" Elene put her hand to her mouth; she felt the blood drain from her face. So Vandam was *not* married!

A moment later she felt ashamed that that had been her first thought, and sympathy for the child her second. She said: "Billy, how awful for you. I'm so sorry." Real death had suddenly intruded into their lighthearted talk of murder stories, and she felt embarrassed.

"It's all right," Billy said. "It's the war, you see."

And now he was like his father again. For a while, talking about books, he had been full of boyish enthusiasm, but now the mask was on, and it was a smaller version of the mask used by his father: courtesy, formality, the attitude of the considerate host. *It's the war, you see*: he had heard someone else say that, and had adopted it as his own defense. She wondered whether his preference for "true-to-life" murders, as opposed to implausible country-house killings, dated from the death of his mother. Now he was looking around him, searching for something, inspiration perhaps. In a moment he would offer her cigarettes, whiskey, tea. It was hard enough to know what to say to a bereaved adult: with Billy she felt helpless. She decided to talk of something else.

She said awkwardly: "I suppose, with your father working at GHQ, you get more news of the war than the rest of us."

"I suppose I do, but usually I don't really understand it. When he comes home in a bad mood I know we've lost another battle." He started to bite a fingernail, then stuffed his hands into his shorts pockets. "I wish I was *older*."

"You want to fight?"

He looked at her fiercely, as if he thought she was mocking him. "I'm not one of those kids who thinks it's all jolly good fun, like the cowboy films."

She murmured: "I'm sure you're not."

"It's just that I'm afraid the Germans will *win*."

Elene thought: Oh, Billy, if you were ten years older I'd fall in love with you, too. "It might not be so bad," she said. "They're not monsters."

He gave her a skeptical look: she should have known better than to soft-soap him. He said: "They'd only do to us what we've been doing to the Egyptians for fifty years."

It was another of his father's lines, she was sure.

Billy said: "But then it would all have been for nothing." He bit his nail again, and this time he did not stop himself. Elene wondered *what* would have been for nothing: the death of his mother? His own personal struggle to be brave? The two-year seesaw of the desert war? European civilization?

"Well, it hasn't happened yet," she said feebly.

Billy looked at the clock on the mantelpiece. "I'm supposed to go to bed at nine." Suddenly he was a child again.

"I suppose you'd better go, then."

"Yes." He stood up.

"May I come and say good night to you, in a few minutes?"

"If you like." He went out.

What kind of life did they lead in this house? Elene wondered. The man, the boy and the old servant lived here together, each with his own concerns. Was there laughter, and kindness, and affection? Did they have time to play games and sing songs and go on picnics? By comparison with her own childhood Billy's was enormously privileged; nevertheless she feared this might be a terribly adult household for a boy to grow up in. His young-old wisdom was charming, but he seemed like a child who did not have much fun. She experienced a rush of compassion for him, a motherless child in an alien country besieged by foreign armies.

She left the drawing room and went upstairs. There seemed to be three or four bedrooms on the second floor, with a narrow staircase leading up to a third floor where, presumably Gaafar slept. One of the bedroom doors was open, and she went in.

It did not look much like a small boy's bedroom. Elene did not know a lot about small boys—she had had four sisters— but she was expecting to see model airplanes, jigsaw puzzles, a train set, sports gear and perhaps an old, neglected teddy bear. She would not have been surprised to see clothes on the floor, a construction set on the bed and a pair of dirty football boots on the polished surface of a desk. But the place might almost have been the bedroom of an adult. The clothes were folded neatly on a chair, the top of the chest of drawers was clear, schoolbooks were stacked tidily on the desk and the only toy in evidence was a cardboard model of a tank. Billy was in bed, his striped pajama top buttoned to the neck, a book on the blanket beside him.

"I like your room," Elene said deceitfully.

Billy said: "It's fine."

"What are you reading?"

"*The Greek Coffin Mystery.*"

She sat on the edge of the bed. "Well, don't stay awake too late."

"I've to put out the light at nine-thirty."

She leaned forward suddenly and kissed his cheek.

At that moment the door opened and Vandam walked in.

It was the familiarity of the scene that was so shocking: the boy in bed with his book, the light from the bedside lamp falling just so, the woman leaning forward to kiss the boy good night. Vandam stood and stared, feeling like one who knows he is in a dream but still cannot wake up.

Elene stood up and said: "Hello, William."

"Hello, Elene."

"Good night, Billy."

"Good night, Miss Fontana."

She went past Vandam and left the room. Vandam sat on the edge of the bed, in the dip in the covers which she had vacated. He said: "Been entertaining our guest?"

"Yes."

"Good man."

"I like her—she reads detective stories. We're going to swap books."

"That's grand. Have you done your prep?"

"Yes—French vocab."

"Want me to test you?"

"It's all right, Gaafar tested me. I say, she's ever so pretty, isn't she."

"Yes. She's working on something for me—it's a bit hush-hush, so . . ."

"My lips are sealed."

Vandam smiled. "That's the stuff."

Billy lowered his voice. "Is she, you know, a secret agent?"

Vandam put a finger to his lips. "Walls have ears."

The boy looked suspicious. "You're having me on."

Vandam shook his head silently.

Billy said: "Gosh!"

Vandam stood up. "Lights out at nine-thirty."

"Right-ho. Good night."

"Good night, Billy." Vandam went out. As he closed the door it occurred to him that Elene's good-night kiss had probably done Billy a lot more good than his father's man-to-man chat.

He found Elene in the drawing room, shaking martinis. He felt he should have resented more than he did the way she had made herself at home in his house, but he was too tired to strike attitudes. He sank gratefully into a chair and accepted a drink.

Elene said: "Busy day?"

Vandam's whole section had been working on the new wireless security procedures that were being introduced following the capture of the German listening unit at the Hill of Jesus, but Vandam was not going to tell Elene that. Also, he felt she was playacting the role of housewife, and she had no right to do that. He said: "What made you come here?"

"I've got a date with Wolff."

"Wonderful!" Vandam immediately forgot all lesser concerns. "When?"

"Thursday." She handed him a sheet of paper.

He studied the message. It was a peremptory summons written in a clear, stylish script. "How did this come?"

"A boy brought it to my door."

"Did you question the boy? Where he was given the message and by whom, and so on?"

She was crestfallen. "I never thought to do that."

"Never mind." Wolff would have taken precautions, anyway; the boy would have known nothing of value.

"What will we do?" Elene asked.

"The same as last time, only better." Vandam tried to sound more confident than he felt. It should have been simple. The man makes a date with a girl, so you go to the meeting place and arrest the man when he turns up. But Wolff was unpredictable. He would not get away with the taxi trick again: Vandam would have the restaurant surrounded, twenty or thirty men and several cars, roadblocks in readiness and so on. But he might try a different trick. Vandam could not imagine what—and that was the problem.

As if she were reading his mind Elene said: "I don't want to spend another evening with him."

"Why?"

"He frightens me."

Vandam felt guilty—*remember Istanbul*—and suppressed his sympathy. "But last time he did you no harm."

"He didn't try to seduce me, so I didn't have to say no. But he will, and I'm afraid he won't take no for an answer."

"We've learned our lesson," Vandam said with false assurance. "There'll be no mistakes this time." Secretly he was surprised by her simple determination not to go to bed with Wolff. He had assumed that such things did not matter much, one way or the other, to her. He had misjudged her, then. Seeing her in this new light somehow made him very cheerful. He decided he must be honest with her. "I should rephrase that," he said. "I'll do everything in my power to make sure that there are no mistakes this time."

Gaafar came in and said: "Dinner is served, sir." Vandam smiled: Gaafar was doing his English-butler act in honor of the feminine company.

Vandam said to Elene: "Have you eaten?"

"No."

"What have we got, Gaafar?"

"For you, sir, clear soup, scrambled eggs and yoghurt. But I took the liberty of grilling a chop for Miss Fontana."

Elene said to Vandam: "Do you always eat like that?"

"No, it's because of my cheek, I can't chew." He stood up.

As they went into the dining room Elene said: "Does it still hurt?"

"Only when I laugh. It's true—I can't stretch the muscles on that side. I've got into the habit of smiling with one side of my face."

They sat down, and Gaafar served the soup.

Elene said: "I like your son very much."

"So do I," Vandam said.

"He's old beyond his years."

"Do you think that's a bad thing?"

She shrugged. "Who knows?"

"He's been through a couple of things that ought to be reserved for adults."

"Yes." Elene hesitated. "When did your wife die?"

"May the twenty-eighth, nineteen-forty-one, in the evening."

"Billy told me it happened in Crete."

"Yes. She worked on cryptanalysis for the Air Force. She was on a temporary posting to Crete at the time the Germans invaded the island. May twenty-eighth was the day the British realized they had lost the battle and decided to get out. Apparently she was hit by a stray shell and killed instantly. Of course, we were trying to get live people away then, not bodies, so . . . There's no grave, you see. No memorial. Nothing left."

Elene said quietly: "Do you still love her?"

"I think I'll always be in love with her. I believe it's like that with people you really love. If they go away, or die, it makes no difference. If ever I were to marry again, I would still love Angela."

"Were you very happy?"

"We . . ." He hesitated, unwilling to answer, then he realized that the hesitation was an answer in itself. "Ours wasn't an idyllic marriage. It was I who was *devoted* . . . Angela was fond of me."

"Do you think you will marry again?"

"Well. The English in Cairo keep thrusting replicas of Angela at me." He shrugged. He did not know the answer to the question. Elene seemed to understand, for she fell silent and began to eat her dessert.

Afterward Gaafar brought them coffee in the drawing room. It was at this time of day that Vandam usually began to hit the bottle seriously, but tonight he did not want to drink. He sent Gaafar to bed, and they drank their coffee. Vandam smoked a cigarette.

He felt the desire for music. He had loved music, at one time, although lately it had gone out of his life. Now, with the mild night air coming in through the open windows and the smoke curling up from his cigarette, he wanted to hear clear, delightful notes, and sweet harmonies, and subtle rhythms. He went to the piano and looked at the music. Elene watched him in silence. He began to play "Für Elise." The first few notes sounded, with Beethoven's characteristic, devastating simplicity; then the hesitation; then the rolling tune. The ability to play came back to him instantly, almost as if he had never stopped. His hands knew what to do in a way he always felt was miraculous.

When the song was over he went back to Elene, sat next to her, and kissed her cheek. Her face was wet with tears. She said: "William, I love you with all my heart."

They whisper.

She says, "I like your ears."

He says, "Nobody has ever licked them before."

She giggles. "Do you like it?"

"Yes, yes." He sighs. "Can I . . . ?"

"Undo the buttons—here—that's right—aah."

"I'll put out the light."

"No, I want to see you—"

"There's a moon." *Click.* "There, see? The moonlight is enough."

"Come back here quickly—"

"I'm here."

"Kiss me again, William."

They do not speak for a while. Then:

"Can I take this thing off?" he says.

"Let me help . . . there."

"Oh! Oh, they're so *pretty*."

"I'm so glad you like them . . . would you do that harder . . . suck a little . . . aah, God—"

And a little later she says:

"Let me feel *your* chest. Damn buttons—I've ripped your shirt—"

"The hell with that."

"Ah, I knew it would be like this . . . Look."

"What?"

"Our skins in the moonlight—you're so pale and I'm nearly black, look—"

"Yes."

"Touch me. Stroke me. Squeeze, and pinch, and explore, I want to feel your hands all over me—"

"Yes—"

"—everywhere, your hands, there, yes, especially there, oh, you *know*, you know *exactly* where, oh!"

"You're so soft inside."

"This is a dream."

"No, it's real."

"I never want to wake up."

"So soft . . ."

"And you're so hard . . . Can I kiss it?"

"Yes, please . . . Ah . . . Jesus it feels good—*Jesus*—"

"William?"

"Yes?"

"Now, William?"

"Oh, yes."

". . . Take them off."

"Silk."

"Yes. Be quick."

"Yes."

"I've wanted this for so long—"

She gasps, and he makes a sound like a sob, and then there is only their breathing for many minutes, until finally he begins to shout aloud, and she smothers his cries with her kisses and then she, too, feels it, and she turns her face into the cushion and opens her mouth and screams into the cushion, and he not being used to this thinks something is wrong and says:

"It's all right, it's all right, it's all right—"

—and finally she goes limp, and lies with her eyes closed for a while, perspiring, until her breathing returns to normal, then she looks up at him and says:

"So *that's* how it's supposed to be!"

And he laughs, and she looks quizzically at him, so he explains:

"That's exactly what I was thinking."

Then they both laugh, and he says:

"I've done a lot of things after . . . you know, afterwards . . . but I don't think I've ever laughed."

"I'm so glad," she says. "Oh, William, I'm so glad."

18

Rommel could smell the sea. At Tobruk the heat and the dust and the flies were as bad as they had been in the desert, but it was all made bearable by that occasional whiff of salty dampness in the faint breeze.

Von Mellenthin came into the command vehicle with his intelligence report. "Good evening, Field Marshal."

Rommel smiled. He had been promoted after the victory at Tobruk, and he had not yet gotten used to the new title. "Anything new?"

"A signal from the spy in Cairo. He says the Mersa Matruh Line is weak in the middle."

Rommel took the report and began to glance over it. He smiled when he read that the Allies anticipated he would try a dash around the southern end of the line: it seemed they were beginning to understand his thinking. He said: "So the minefield gets thinner at this point . . . but there the line is defended by two columns. What is a column?"

"It's a new term they're using. According to one of our prisoners of war, a column is a brigade group that has been twice overrun by Panzers."

"A weak force, then."

"Yes."

Rommel tapped the report with his forefinger. "If this is correct, we can burst through the Mersa Matruh Line as soon as we get there."

"I'll be doing my best to check the spy's report over the next day or two, of course," said von Mellenthin. "But he was right last time."

The door to the vehicle flew open and Kesselring came in.

Rommel was startled. "Field Marshal!" he said. "I thought you were in Sicily."

"I was," Kesselring said. He stamped the dust off his hand-made boots. "I've just flown here to see you. Damn it, Rommel, this has got to stop. Your orders are quite clear: you were to advance to Tobruk and no farther."

Rommel sat back in his canvas chair. He had hoped to keep Kesselring out of this argument. "The circumstances have changed," he said.

"But your original orders have been confirmed by the Italian Supreme Command," said Kesselring. "And what was your reaction? You declined the 'advice' and invited Bastico to lunch with you in Cairo!"

Nothing infuriated Rommel more than orders from Italians. "The Italians have done *nothing* in this war," he said angrily.

"That is irrelevant. Your air and sea support is now needed for the attack on Malta. After we have taken Malta your communications will be secure for the advance to Egypt."

"You people have learned nothing!" Rommel said. He made an effort to lower his voice. "While we are digging in the enemy, too, will be digging in. I did not get this far by playing the old game of advance, consolidate, then advance again. When they attack, I dodge; when they defend a position I go around that position; and when they retreat I chase them. They are running now, and now is the time to take Egypt."

Kesselring remained calm. "I have a copy of your cable to Mussolini." He took a piece of paper from his pocket and read: "The state and morale of the troops, the present supply position owing to captured dumps and the present weakness of the enemy permit our pursuing him into the depths of the Egyptian area." He folded the sheet of paper and turned to von Mellenthin. "How many German tanks and men do we have?"

Rommel suppressed the urge to tell von Mellenthin not to answer: he knew this was a weak point.

"Sixty tanks, Field Marshal, and two thousand five hundred men."

"And the Italians?"

"Six thousand men and fourteen tanks."

Kesselring turned back to Rommel. "And you're going to take Egypt with a total of seventy-four tanks? Von Mellenthin, what is our estimate of the enemy's strength?"

"The Allied forces are approximately three times as numerous as ours, but——"

"There you are."

Von Mellenthin went on: "——but we are very well supplied with food, clothing, trucks and armored cars, and fuel; and the men are in tremendous spirits."

Rommel said: "Von Mellenthin, go to the communications truck and see what has arrived."

Von Mellenthin frowned, but Rommel did not explain, so he went out.

Rommel said: "The Allies are regrouping at Mersa Matruh. They expect us to move around the southern end of their line. Instead we will hit the middle, where they are weakest——"

"How do you know all this?" Kesselring interrupted.

"Our intelligence assessment——"

"On what is the assessment based?"

"Primarily on a spy report——"

"My God!" For the first time Kesselring raised his voice. "You've no tanks, but you have your spy!"

"He was right last time."

Von Mellenthin came back in.

Kesselring said: "All this makes no difference. I am here to confirm the Fuehrer's orders: you are to advance no farther."

Rommel smiled. "I have sent a personal envoy to the Fuehrer."

"You . . . ?"

"I am a Field Marshall now, I have direct access to Hitler."

"Of course."

"I think von Mellenthin may have the Fuehrer's reply."

"Yes," said von Mellenthin. He read from a sheet of paper. "It is only once in a lifetime that the Goddess of Victory smiles. Onward to Cairo. Adolf Hitler."

There was a silence.

Kesselring walked out.

19

When Vandam got to his office he learned that, the previous evening, Rommel had advanced to within sixty miles of Alexandria.

Rommel seemed unstoppable. The Mersa Matruh Line had broken in half like a matchstick. In the south, the 13th Corps had retreated in a panic, and in the north the fortress of Mersa Matruh had capitulated. The Allies had fallen back once again—but this would be the last time. The new line of defense stretched across a thirty-mile gap between the sea and the impassable Qattara Depression, and if that line fell there would be no more defenses, Egypt would be Rommel's.

The news was not enough to dampen Vandam's elation. It was more than twenty-four hours since he had awakened at dawn, on the sofa in his drawing room, with Elene in his arms. Since then he had been suffused with a kind of adolescent glee. He kept remembering little details: how small and brown her nipples were, the taste of her skin, her sharp fingernails digging into his thighs. In the office he had been behaving a little out of character, he knew. He had given back a letter to his typist, saying: "There are seven errors in this, you'd better do it again," and smiled at her sunnily. She had nearly fallen off her chair. He thought of Elene, and he thought: "Why not? Why the hell not?" and there was no reply.

He was visited early by an officer from the Special Liaison Unit. Anybody with his ear to the ground in GHQ now knew that the SLUs had a very special, ultra-secret source of intelligence. Opinions differed as to how good the intelligence was, and evaluation was always difficult because they would

223

never tell you the source. Brown, who held the rank of captain but was quite plainly not a military man, leaned on the edge of the table and spoke around the stem of his pipe. "Are you being evacuated, Vandam?"

These chaps lived in a world of their own, and there was no point in telling them that a captain had to call a major "sir." Vandam said: "What? Evacuated? Why?"

"Our lot's off to Jerusalem. So's everyone who knows too much. Keep people out of enemy hands, you know."

"The brass is getting nervous, then." It was logical, really: Rommel could cover sixty miles in a day.

"There'll be riots at the station, you'll see—half Cairo's trying to get out and the other half is preening itself ready for the liberation. Ha!"

"You won't tell too many people that you're going . . ."

"No, no, no. Now, then, I've got a little snippet for you. We all know Rommel's got a spy in Cairo."

"How did you know?" Vandam said.

"Stuff comes through from London, old boy. Anyhow, the chap has been identified as, and I quote, 'the hero of the Rashid Ali affair.' Mean anything to you?"

Vandam was thunderstruck. "It does!" he said.

"Well, that's it." Brown got off the table.

"Just a minute," Vandam said. "Is that *all*?"

"I'm afraid so."

"What is this, a decrypt or an agent report?"

"Suffice it to say that the source is reliable."

"You always say that."

"Yes. Well, I may not see you for a while. Good luck."

"Thanks." Vandam muttered distractedly.

"Toodle-oo!" Brown went out, puffing smoke.

The hero of the Rashid Ali affair. It was incredible that Wolff should have been the man who outwitted Vandam in Istanbul. Yet it made sense: Vandam recalled the odd feeling he had had about Wolff's *style*, as if it were familiar. The girl whom Vandam had sent to pick up the mystery man had had her throat cut.

And now Vandam was sending Elene in against the same man.

A corporal came in with an order. Vandam read it with mounting disbelief. All departments were to extract from their files those papers which might be dangerous in enemy hands, and burn them. Just about anything in the files of an intelligence section might be dangerous in enemy hands. We might as well burn the whole damn lot, Vandam thought. And how would departments operate afterward? Clearly the brass thought the departments would not be operating at all for very much longer. Of course it was a precaution, but it was a very drastic one: they would not destroy the accumulated results of years of work unless they thought there was a very strong chance indeed of the Germans taking Egypt.

It's going to pieces, he thought; it's falling apart.

It was unthinkable. Vandam had given three years of his life to the defense of Egypt. Thousands of men had died in the desert. After all that, was it possible that we could lose? Actually give up, and turn and run away? It did not bear contemplating.

He called Jakes in and watched him read the order. Jakes just nodded, as if he had been expecting it. Vandam said: "Bit drastic, isn't it?"

"It's rather like what's been happening in the desert, sir," Jakes replied. "We establish huge supply dumps at enormous cost, then as we retreat we blow them up to keep them out of enemy hands."

Vandam nodded. "All right, you'd better get on with it. Try and play it down a bit, for the sake of morale—you know, brass getting the wind up unnecessarily, that sort of thing."

"Yes, sir. We'll have the bonfire in the yard at the back, shall we?"

"Yes. Find an old dustbin and poke holes in its bottom. Make sure the stuff burns up properly."

"What about your own files?"

"I'll go through them now."

"Very good, sir." Jakes went out.

Vandam opened his file drawer and began to sort through his papers. Countless times over the last three years he had thought: I don't need to remember that, I can always look it up. There were names and addresses, security reports on individuals, details of codes, systems of communication of orders, case notes and a little file of jottings about Alex Wolff. Jakes brought in a big cardboard box with "Lipton's Tea" printed on its side, and Vandam began to dump papers into it, thinking: This is what it is like to be the losers.

The box was half full when Vandam's corporal opened the door and said: "Major Smith to see you, sir."

"Send him in." Vandam did not know a Major Smith.

The major was a small, thin man in his forties with bulbous blue eyes and an air of being rather pleased with himself. He shook hands and said: "Sandy Smith, S.I.S."

Vandam said: "What can I do for the Secret Intelligence Service?"

"I'm sort of the liaison man between S.I.S. and the General Staff," Smith explained. "You made an inquiry about a book called *Rebecca* . . ."

"Yes."

"The answer got routed through us." Smith produced a piece of paper with a flourish.

Vandam read the message. The S.I.S. Head of Station in Portugal had followed up the query about *Rebecca* by sending one of his men to visit all the English-language bookshops in the country. In the holiday area of Estoril he had found a bookseller who recalled selling his entire stock—six copies—of *Rebecca* to one woman. On further investigation the woman had turned out to be the wife of the German military attaché in Lisbon.

Vandam said: "This confirms something I suspected. Thank you for taking the trouble to bring it over."

"No trouble," Smith said. "I'm over here every morning anyway. Glad to be able to help." He went out.

Vandam reflected on the news while he went on with his work. There was only one plausible explanation of the fact that the book had found its way from Estoril to the Sahara. Undoubtedly it was the basis of a code—and, unless there were two successful German spies in Cairo, it was Alex Wolff who was using that code.

The information would be useful, sooner or later. It was a pity the key to the code had not been captured along with the book and the decrypt. That thought reminded him of the importance of burning his secret papers, and he determined to be more ruthless about what he destroyed.

At the end he considered his files on pay and promotion of subordinates, and decided to burn those too since they might help enemy interrogation teams fix their priorities. The cardboard box was full. He hefted it on to his shoulder and went outside.

Jakes had the fire going in a rusty steel water tank propped up on bricks. A corporal was feeding papers to the flames. Vandam dumped his box and watched the blaze for a while. It reminded him of Guy Fawkes Night in England, fireworks and baked potatoes and the burning effigy of a seventeenth-century traitor. Charred scraps of paper floated up on a pillar of hot air. Vandam turned away.

He wanted to think, so he decided to walk. He left GHQ and headed downtown. His cheek was hurting. He thought he should welcome the pain, for it was supposed to be a sign of healing. He was growing a beard to cover the wound so that he would look a little less unsightly when the dressing came off. Every day he enjoyed not having to shave in the morning.

He thought of Elene, and remembered her with her back arched and perspiration glistening on her naked breasts. He had been shocked by what had happened after he had kissed her—shocked, but thrilled. It had been a night of firsts for him: first time he had made love anywhere other than on a bed, first time he had seen a woman have a climax like a man's, first time sex had been a mutual indulgence rather than the imposition of his will on a more or less reluctant woman. It was, of course, a disaster that he and Elene had fallen so joyfully in love. His parents, his friends and the Army would be aghast at the idea of his marrying a wog. His mother would also feel bound to explain why the Jews were wrong to reject Jesus. Vandam decided not to worry over all that. He and Elene might be dead within a few days. We'll bask in the sunshine while it lasts, he thought, and to hell with the future.

His thoughts kept returning to the girl whose throat had been cut, apparently by Wolff, in Istanbul. He was terrified that something might go wrong on Thursday and Elene might find herself alone with Wolff again.

Looking around him, he realized that there was a festive feeling in the air. He passed a hairdresser's salon and noticed that it was packed out, with women standing waiting. The dress shops seemed to be doing good business. A woman

came out of a grocer's with a basket full of canned food, and
Vandam saw that there was a queue stretching out of the
shop and along the pavement. A sign in the window of the
next shop said, in hasty scribble: "Sorry, no makeup." Vandam realized that the Egyptians were preparing to be liber-
ated, and looking forward to it.

He could not escape a sense of impending doom. Even the
sky seemed dark. He looked up: the sky *was* dark. There
seemed to be a gray swirling mist, dotted with particles, over
the city. He realized that it was smoke mixed with charred
paper. All across Cairo the British were burning their files,
and the sooty smoke had blotted out the sun.

Vandam was suddenly furious with himself and the rest of
the Allied armies for preparing so equably for defeat. Where
was the spirit of the Battle of Britain? What had happened to
that famous mixture of obstinacy, ingenuity and courage
which was supposed to characterize the nation? What, Vandam asked himself, are *you* planning to do about it?

He turned around and walked back toward Garden City,
where GHQ was billeted in commandeered villas. He visualized the map of the El Alamein Line, where the Allies would
make their last stand. This was one line Rommel could not
circumvent, for at its southern end was the vast impassable
Qattara Depression. So Rommel would have to break the
line.

Where would he try to break through? If he came through
the northern end, he would then have to choose between
dashing straight for Alexandria and wheeling around and attacking the Allied forces from behind. If he came through
the southern end he must either dash for Cairo or, again,
wheel around and destroy the remains of the Allied forces.

Immediately behind the line was the Alam Halfa ridge,
which Vandam knew was heavily fortified. Clearly it would
be better for the Allies if Rommel wheeled around after
breaking through the line, for then he might well spend his
strength attacking Alam Halfa.

There was one more factor. The southern approach to
Alam Halfa was through treacherous soft sand. It was unlikely that Rommel knew about the quicksand, for he had
never penetrated this far east before, and only the Allies had
good maps of the desert.

So, Vandam thought, my duty is to prevent Alex Wolff telling Rommel that Alam Halfa is well defended and cannot be attacked from the south.

It was a depressingly negative plan.

Vandam had come, without consciously intending it, to the Villa les Oliviers, Wolff's house. He sat in the little park opposite it, under the olive trees, and stared at the building as if it might tell him where Wolff was. He thought idly: If only Wolff would make a mistake, and encourage Rommel to attack Alam Halfa from the south.

Then it hit him.

Suppose I do capture Wolff. Suppose I also get his radio. Suppose I even find the key to his code.

Then I could impersonate Wolff, get on the radio to Rommel, and tell him to attack Alam Halfa from the south.

The idea blossomed rapidly in his mind, and he began to feel elated. By now Rommel was convinced, quite rightly, that Wolff's information was good. Suppose he got a message from Wolff saying the El Alamein Line was weak at the southern end, that the southern approach to Alam Halfa was hard going, and that Alam Halfa itself was weakly defended.

The temptation would be too much for Rommel to resist.

He would break through the line at the southern end and then swing northward, expecting to take Alam Halfa without much trouble. Then he would hit the quicksand. While he was struggling through it, our artillery would decimate his forces. When he reached Alam Halfa he would find it heavily defended. At that point we would bring in more forces from the front line and squeeze the enemy like a nutcracker.

If the ambush worked well, it might not only save Egypt but annihilate the Afrika Korps.

He thought: I've got to put this idea up to the brass.

It would not be easy. His standing was not very high just now—in fact his professional reputation was in ruins on account of Alex Wolff. But surely they would see the merit of the idea.

He got up from the bench and headed for his office. Suddenly the future looked different. Perhaps the jackboot would not ring out on the tiled floors of the mosques. Perhaps the treasures of the Egyptian Museum would not be shipped to

Berlin. Perhaps Billy would not have to join the Hitler Youth. Perhaps Elene would not be sent to Dachau.

We could all be saved, he thought.

If I catch Wolff.

PART THREE

ALAM HALFA

20

One of these days, Vandam thought, I'm going to punch Bogge on the nose.

Today Lieutenant Colonel Bogge was at his worst: indecisive, sarcastic and touchy. He had a nervous cough which he used when he was afraid to speak, and he was coughing a lot now. He was also fidgeting: tidying piles of papers on his desk, crossing and uncrossing his legs and polishing his wretched cricket ball.

Vandam sat still and quiet, waiting for him to tie himself up in knots.

"Now look here, Vandam, strategy is for Auchinleck. Your job is personnel security—and you're not doing very well."

"Nor is Auchinleck," Vandam said.

Bogge pretended not to hear. He picked up Vandam's memo. Vandam had written out his deception plan and formally submitted it to Bogge, with a copy to the brigadier. "For one thing, this is full of holes," Bogge said.

Vandam said nothing.

"Full of holes." Bogge coughed. "For one thing, it involves letting old Rommel through the line, doesn't it?"

Vandam said: "Perhaps the plan could be made contingent on his getting through."

"Yes. Now, you see? This is the kind of thing I mean. If you put up a plan that's full of holes like that, given that your reputation is at a pretty damn low point around here at the moment, well, you'll be laughed out of Cairo. Now." He coughed. "You want to encourage Rommel to attack the line at its weakest point—giving him a better chance of getting through! You see?"

"Yes. Some parts of the line are weaker than others, and since Rommel has air reconnaissance there's a chance he'll know which parts."

"And you want to turn a chance into a certainty."

"For the sake of the subsequent ambush, yes."

"Now, it seems to me that we want old Rommel to attack the *strongest* part of the line, so that he won't get through at all."

"But if we repel him, he'll just regroup and hit us again. Whereas if we trap him we could finish him off finally."

"No, no, no. Risky. Risky. This is our last line of defense, laddie." Bogge laughed. "After his, there's nothing but one little canal between him and Cairo. You don't seem to realize—"

"I realize very well, sir. Let me put it this way. One: if Rommel gets through the line he must be diverted to Alam Halfa by the false prospect of an easy victory. Two: it is preferable that he attack Alam Halfa from the south, because of the quicksand. Three: either we must wait and see which end of the line he attacks, and take the risk that he will go north; or we must encourage him to go south, and take the risk that we will thereby increase his chances of breaking through the line in the first place."

"Well," said Bogge, "now that we've rephrased it, the plan is beginning to make a bit more sense. Now look here: you're going to have to leave it with me for a while. When I've got a moment I'll go through the thing with a fine-toothed comb, and see if I can knock it into shape. Then perhaps we'll put it up to the brass."

I see, Vandam thought: the object of the exercise is to make it Bogge's plan. Well, what the hell? If Bogge can be bothered to play politics at this stage, good luck to him. It's winning that matters, not getting the credit.

Vandam said: "Very good, sir. If I might just emphasize the time factor . . . If the plan is to be put into operation, it must be done quickly."

"I think I'm the best judge of its urgency, Major, don't you?"

"Yes, sir."

"And, after all, everything depends on catching the damn

spy, something at which you have not so far been entirely successful, am I right?"

"Yes, sir."

"I'll be taking charge of tonight's operation myself, to ensure that there are no further foul-ups. Let me have your proposals this afternoon, and we'll go over them together—"

There was a knock at the door and the brigadier walked in. Vandam and Bogge stood up.

Bogge said: "Good morning, sir."

"At ease, gentlemen," the brigadier said. "I've been looking for you, Vandam."

Bogge said: "We were just working on an idea we had for a deception plan—"

"Yes, I saw the memo."

"Ah, Vandam sent you a copy," Bogge said. Vandam did not look at Bogge, but he knew the lieutenant colonel was furious with him.

"Yes, indeed," said the brigadier. He turned to Vandam. "You're supposed to be catching spies, Major, not advising generals on strategy. Perhaps if you spent less time telling us how to win the war you might be a better security officer."

Vandam's heart sank.

Bogge said: "I was just saying—"

The brigadier interrupted him. "However, since you have done this, and since it's such a splendid plan, I want you to come with me and sell it to Auchinleck. You can spare him, Bogge, can't you?"

"Of course, sir," Bogge said through clenched teeth.

"All right, Vandam. The conference will be starting any minute. Let's go."

Vandam followed the brigadier out and shut the door very softly on Bogge.

On the day that Wolff was to see Elene again, Major Smith came to the houseboat at lunchtime.

The information he brought with him was the most valuable yet.

Wolff and Sonja went through their now-familiar routine. Wolff felt like an actor in a French farce, who has to hide in the same stage wardrobe night after night. Sonja and Smith, following the script, began on the couch and moved into the bedroom. When Wolff emerged from the cupboard the curtains were closed, and there on the floor were Smith's briefcase, his shoes and his shorts with the key ring poking out of the pocket.

Wolff opened the briefcase and began to read.

Once again Smith had come to the houseboat straight from the morning conference at GHQ, at which Auchinleck and his staff discussed Allied strategy and decided what to do.

After a few minutes' reading Wolff realized that what he held in his hand was a complete rundown of the Allies' last-ditch defense on the El Alamein Line.

The line consisted of artillery on the ridges, tanks on the level ground and minefields all along. The Alam Halfa ridge, five miles behind the center of the line, was also heavily fortified. Wolff noted that the southern end of the line was weaker, both in troops and mines.

Smith's briefcase also contained an enemy-position paper. Allied Intelligence thought Rommel would probably try to break through the line at the southern end, but noted that the northern end was possible.

Beneath this, written in pencil in what was presumably Smith's handwriting, was a note which Wolff found more exciting than all the rest of the stuff put together. It read: "Major Vandam proposes deception plan. Encourage Rommel to break through at southern end, lure him toward Alam Halfa, catch him in quicksand, then nutcracker. Plan accepted by Auk."

"Auk" was Auchinleck, no doubt. What a discovery this was! Not only did Wolff hold in his hand the details of the Allied defense line—he also knew what they expected Rommel to do, *and* he knew their deception plan.

And the deception plan was Vandam's!

This would be remembered as the greatest espionage coup of the century. Wolff himself would be responsible for assuring Rommel's victory in North Africa.

They should make me King of Egypt for this, he thought, and he smiled.

He looked up and saw Smith standing between the curtains, staring down at him.

Smith roared: "Who the devil are you?"

Wolff realized angrily that he had not been paying attention to the noises from the bedroom. Something had gone wrong, the script had not been followed, there had been no champagne-cork warning. He had been totally absorbed in the strategic appreciation. The endless names of divisions and brigades, the numbers of men and tanks, the quantities of fuel and supplies, the ridges and depressions and quicksands had monopolized his attention to the exclusion of local sounds. He was suddenly terribly afraid that he might be thwarted in his moment of triumph.

Smith said: "That's my bloody briefcase!"

He took a step forward.

Wolff reached out, caught Smith's foot, and heaved sideways. The major toppled over and hit the floor with a heavy thud.

Sonja screamed.

Wolff and Smith both scrambled to their feet.

Smith was a small, thin man, ten years older than Wolff and in poor shape. He stepped backward, fear showing in his face. He bumped into a shelf, glanced sideways, saw a cut-glass fruit bowl on the shelf, picked it up and hurled it at Wolff.

It missed, fell into the kitchen sink, and shattered loudly.

The noise, Wolff thought: if he makes any more noise people will come to investigate. He moved toward Smith.

Smith, with his back to the wall, yelled: "Help!"

Wolff hit him once, on the point of the jaw, and he collapsed, sliding down the wall to sit, unconscious, on the floor.

Sonja came out and stared at him.

Wolff rubbed his knuckles. "It's the first time I've ever done that," he said.

"What?"

"Hit somebody on the chin and knocked him out. I thought only boxers could do that."

"Never mind that, what are we going to do about him?"

"I don't know." Wolff considered the possibilities. To kill Smith would be dangerous, for the death of an officer—and the disappearance of his briefcase—would now cause a terrific rumpus throughout the city. There would be the problem of what to do with the body. And Smith would bring home no more secrets.

Smith groaned and stirred.

Wolff wondered whether it might be possible to let him go.
After all, if Smith were to reveal what had been going on in
the houseboat he would implicate himself. Not only would it
ruin his career, he would probably be thrown in jail. He did
not look like the kind of man to sacrifice himself for a higher
cause.

Let him go free? No, the chance was too much to take. To
know that there was a British officer in the city who
possessed all of Wolff's secrets . . . Impossible.

Smith had his eyes open. "You . . ." he said. "You're
Slavenburg . . ." He looked at Sonja, then back at Wolff. "It
was you who introduced . . . in the Cha-Cha . . . this was
all planned . . ."

"Shut up," Wolf said mildly. Kill him or let him go: what
other options were there? Only one: to keep him here, bound
and gagged, until Rommel reached Cairo.

"You're damned spies," Smith said. His face was white.

Sonja said nastily: "And you thought I was crazy for your
miserable body."

"Yes." Smith was recovering. "I should have known better
than to trust a wog bitch."

Sonja stepped forward and kicked his face with her bare
foot.

"Stop it!" Wolff said. "We've got to think what to do with
him. Have we got any rope to tie him with?"

Sonja thought for a moment. "Up on deck, in that locker
at the forward end."

Wolff took from the kitchen drawer the heavy steel he used
for sharpening the carving knife. He gave the steel to Sonja.
"If he moves, hit him with that," he said. He did not think
Smith would move.

He was about to go up the ladder to the deck when he
heard footsteps on the gangplank.

Sonja said: "Postman!"

Wolff knelt in front of Smith and drew his knife. "Open
your mouth."

Smith began to say something, and Wolff slid the knife between Smith's teeth.

Wolff said: "Now, if you move or speak, I'll cut out your
tongue."

Smith sat dead still, staring at Wolff with a horrified look.

Wolff realized that Sonja was stark naked. "Put something on, quickly!"

She pulled a sheet off the bed and wrapped it around her as she went to the foot of the ladder. The hatch was opening. Wolff knew that he and Smith could be seen from the hatch. Sonja let the sheet slide down a little as she reached up to take the letter from the postman's outstretched hand.

"Good morning!" the postman said. His eyes were riveted on Sonja's half-exposed breasts.

She went farther up the ladder toward him, so that he had to back away, and let the sheet slip even more. "Thank you," she simpered. She reached for the hatch and pulled it shut.

Wolff breathed again.

The postman's footsteps crossed the deck and descended the gangplank.

Wolff said to Sonja: "Give me that sheet."

She unwrapped herself and stood naked again.

Wolff withdrew the knife from Smith's mouth and used it to cut off a foot or two of the sheet. He crumpled the cotton into a ball and stuffed it into Smith's mouth. Smith did not resist. Wolff slid the knife into its underarm sheath. He stood up. Smith closed his eyes. He seemed limp, defeated.

Sonja picked up the sharpening steel and stood ready to hit Smith while Wolff went up the ladder and on to the deck. The locker Sonja had mentioned was in the riser of a step in the prow. Wolff opened it. Inside was a coil of slender rope. It had perhaps been used to tie up the vessel in the days before she became a houseboat. Wolff took the rope out. It was strong, but not too thick: ideal for tying someone's hands and feet.

He heard Sonja's voice, from below, raised in a shout. There was a clatter of feet on the ladder.

Wolff dropped the rope and whirled around.

Smith, wearing only his underpants, came up through the hatch at a run.

He had not been as defeated as he looked—and Sonja must have missed him with the steel.

Wolff dashed across the deck to the gangplank to head him off.

Smith turned, ran to the other side of the boat, and jumped into the water.

Wolff said: "Shit!"

He looked all around quickly. There was no one on the decks of the other houseboats—it was the hour of the siesta. The towpath was deserted except for the "beggar"—Kemel would have to deal with him—and one man in the distance walking away. On the river there were a couple of feluccas, at least a quarter of a mile away, and a slow-moving steam barge beyond them.

Wolff ran to the edge. Smith surfaced, gasping for air. He wiped his eyes and looked around to get his bearings. He was clumsy in the water, splashing a lot. He began to swim, inexpertly, away from the houseboat.

Wolff stepped back several paces and took a running jump into the river.

He landed, feet first, on Smith's head.

For several seconds all was confusion. Wolff went underwater in a tangle of arms and legs—his and Smith's—and struggled to reach the surface and push Smith down at the same time. When he could hold his breath no longer he wriggled away from Smith and came up.

He sucked air and wiped his eyes. Smith's head bobbed up in front of him, coughing and spluttering. Wolff reached forward with both hands, grabbed Smith's head. and pulled it toward himself and down. Smith wriggled like a fish. Wolff got him around the neck and pushed down. Wolff himself went under the water, then came up again a moment later. Smith was still under, still struggling.

Wolff thought: How long does it take a man to drown?

Smith gave a convulsive jerk and freed himself. His head came up and he heaved a great lungful of air. Wolff tried to punch him. The blow landed, but it had no force. Smith was coughing and retching between shuddering gasps. Wolff himself had taken in water. Wolff reached for Smith again. This time he got behind the major and crooked one arm around the man's throat while he used the other to push down on the top of his head.

He thought: Christ, I hope no one is watching.

Smith went under. He was facedown in the water now, with Wolff's knees in his back, and his head held in a firm grip. He continued to thrash around under water, turning, jerking, flailing his arms, kicking his legs and trying to twist his body. Wolff tightened his grip and held him under.

Drown, you bastard, drown!

He felt Smith's jaws open and knew the man was at last breathing water. The convulsions grew more frantic. Wolff felt he was going to have to let go. Smith's struggle pulled Wolff under. Wolff squeezed his eyes shut and held his breath. It seemed Smith was weakening. By now his lungs must be half full of water, Wolff thought. After a few seconds Wolff himself began to need air.

Smith's movements became feeble. Holding the major less tightly, Wolff kicked himself upward and found air. For a minute he just breathed. Smith became a dead weight. Wolff used his legs to swim toward the houseboat, pulling Smith with him. Smith's head came up out of the water, but there was no sign of life.

Wolff reached the side of the boat. Sonja was up on deck, wearing a robe, staring over the side.

Wolff said: "Did anybody see?"

"I don't think so. Is he dead?"

"Yes."

Wolff thought: What the hell do I do now?

He held Smith against the side of the boat. If I let him go, he'll just float, he thought. The body will be found near here and there will be a house-to-house search. But I can't carry a body half across Cairo to get rid of it.

Suddenly Smith jerked and spewed water.

"Jesus Christ, he's alive!" Wolff said.

He pushed Smith under again. This was no good, it took too long. He let Smith go, pulled out his knife, and lunged. Smith was underwater, moving feebly. Wolff could not direct the knife. He slashed wildly. The water hampered him. Smith thrashed about. The foaming water turned pink. At last Wolff was able to grab Smith by the hair and hold his head still while he cut his throat.

Now he was dead.

Wolff let Smith go while he sheathed the knife again. The river water turned muddy red all around him. I'm swimming in blood, he thought, and he was suddenly filled with disgust.

The body was drifting away. Wolff pulled it back. He realized, too late, that a drowned major might simply have fallen

in the river, but a major with his throat cut had unquestion-
ably been murdered. Now he *had* to hide the body.

He looked up. "Sonja!"

"I feel ill."

"Never mind that. We have to make the body sink to the
bottom."

"Oh, God, the water's all bloody."

"Listen to me!" He wanted to yell at her, to make her snap
out of it, but he had to keep his voice low. "Get . . . get that
rope. Go on!"

She disappeared from view for a moment, and returned
with the rope. She was helpless, Wolff decided: he would
have to tell her exactly what to do.

"Now—get Smith's briefcase and put something heavy in
it."

"Something heavy . . . but what?"

"Jesus Christ . . . What have we got that's heavy? What's
heavy? Um . . . books, books are heavy, no, that might not
be enough . . . I know, bottles. Full bottles—champagne
bottles. Fill his briefcase with full bottles of champagne."

"Why?"

"My God, stop dithering, do what I tell you!"

She went away again. Through the porthole he could see
her coming down the ladder and into the living room. She
was moving very slowly, like a sleepwalker.

Hurry, you fat bitch, hurry!

She looked around her dazedly. Still moving in slow mo-
tion, she picked up the briefcase from the floor. She took it to
the kitchen area and opened the icebox. She looked in, as if
she were deciding what to have for dinner.

Come *on.*

She took out a champagne bottle. She stood with the bottle
in one hand and the briefcase in the other, and she frowned,
as if she could not remember what she was supposed to be
doing with them. At last her expression cleared and she put
the bottle in the case, laying it flat. She took another bottle
out.

Wolff thought: Lay them head to toe, idiot, so you get
more in.

She put the second bottle in, looked at it, then took it out
and turned it the other way.

Brilliant, Wolff thought.

She managed to get four bottles in. She closed the icebox and looked around for something else to add to the weight. She picked up the sharpening steel and a glass paperweight. She put those into the briefcase and fastened it. Then she came up on deck.

"What now?" she said.

"Tie the end of the rope around the handle of the briefcase."

She was coming out of her daze. Her fingers moved more quickly.

"Tie it very tight," Wolff said.

"Okay."

"Is there anyone around?"

She glanced to left and right. "No."

"Hurry."

She finished the knot.

"Throw me the rope," Wolff said.

She threw down the other end of the rope and he caught it. He was tiring with the effort of keeping himself afloat and holding on to the corpse at the same time. He had to let Smith go for a moment because he needed both hands for the rope, which meant he had to tread water furiously to stay up. He threaded the rope under the dead man's armpits and pulled it through. He wound it around the torso twice, then tied a knot. Several times during the operation he found himself sinking, and once he took a revolting mouthful of bloody water.

At last the job was done.

"Test your knot," he told Sonja.

"It's tight."

"Throw the briefcase into the water—throw it as far out as you can."

She heaved the briefcase over the side. It splashed a couple of yards away from the houseboat—it had been too heavy for her to throw far—and went down. Slowly the rope followed the case. The length of rope between Smith and the case became taut, then the body went under. Wolff watched the surface. The knots were holding. He kicked his legs, underwater where the body had gone down: they did not contact anything. The body had sunk deep.

Wolff muttered: "*Liebe Gott*, what a shambles."

He climbed on deck. Looking back down, he saw that the pink tinge was rapidly disappearing from the water.

A voice said: "Good morning!"

Wolff and Sonja whirled around to face the towpath.

"Good morning!" Sonja replied. She muttered to Wolff in an undertone: "A neighbor."

The neighbor was a half-caste woman of middle age, carrying a shopping basket. She said: "I heard a lot of splashing—is there anything wrong?"

"Um . . . no," Sonja said. "My little dog fell in the water, and Mr. Robinson here had to rescue him."

"How gallant!" the woman said. "I didn't know you had a dog."

"He's a puppy, a gift."

"What kind?"

Wolff wanted to scream: Go away, you stupid old woman!

"A poodle," Sonja replied.

"I'd love to see him."

"Tomorrow, perhaps—he's been locked up as a punishment now."

"Poor thing."

Wolff said: "I'd better change my wet clothes."

Sonja said to the neighbor: "Until tomorrow."

"Lovely to meet you, Mr. Robinson," the neighbor said.

Wolff and Sonja went below.

Sonja slumped on the couch and closed her eyes. Wolff stripped off his wet clothes.

Sonja said: "It's the worst thing that's ever happened to me."

"You'll survive," Wolff said.

"At least it was an Englishman."

"Yes. You should be jumping for joy."

"I will when my stomach settles."

Wolff went into the bathroom and turned on the taps of the tub. When he came back Sonja said: "Was it worth it?"

"Yes." Wolff pointed to the military papers which were still on the floor, where he had dropped them when Smith surprised him. "That stuff is red-hot—the best he's ever brought us. With that, Rommel can win the war."

"When will you send it?"

"Tonight, at midnight."

"Tonight you're going to bring Elene here."

He stared at her. "How can you think of that when we've just killed a man and sunk his body?"

She stared at him defiantly. "I don't know, I just know it makes me feel very sexy."

"My God."

"You *will* bring her home tonight. You owe it to me."

Wolff hesitated. "I'd have to make the broadcast while she's here."

"I'll keep her busy while you're on the radio."

"I don't know—"

"Damn it, Alex, you *owe* me!"

"All right."

"Thank you."

Wolff went into the bathroom. Sonja was unbelievable, he thought. She took depravity to new heights of sophistication. He got into the hot water.

She called from the bedroom: "But now Smith won't be bringing you any more secrets."

"I don't think we'll need them, after the next battle," Wolff replied. "He's served his purpose."

He picked up the soap and began to wash off the blood.

21

Vandam knocked at the door of Elene's flat an hour before she was due to meet Alex Wolff.

She came to the door wearing a black cocktail dress and high-heeled black shoes with silk stockings. Around her neck was a slender gold chain. Her face was made up, and her hair gleamed. She had been expecting Vandam.

He smiled at her, seeing someone familiar yet at the same time astonishingly beautiful. "Hello."

"Come in." She led him into the living room. "Sit down."

He had wanted to kiss her, but she had not given him the chance. He sat on the couch. "I wanted to tell you the details for tonight."

"Okay." She sat on a chair opposite him. "Do you want a drink?"

"Sure."

"Help yourself."

He stared at her. "Is something wrong?"

"Nothing. Give yourself a drink, then brief me."

Vandam frowned. "What is this?"

"Nothing. We've got work to do, so let's do it."

He stood up, went across to her, and knelt in front of her chair. "Elene. What are you doing?"

She glared at him. She seemed close to tears. She said loudly: "Where have you been for the last two days?"

He looked away from her, thinking. "I've been at work."

"And where do you think I've been?"

"Here, I suppose."

"Exactly!"

He did not understand what that meant. It crossed his

246

mind that he had fallen in love with a woman he hardly knew. He said: "I've been working, and you've been here, and so you're mad at me?"

She shouted: "Yes!"

Vandam said: "Calm down. I don't understand why you're so cross, and I want you to explain it to me."

"No!"

"Then I don't know what to say." Vandam sat on the floor with his back to her and lit a cigarette. He truly did not know what had upset her, but there was an element of will-fulness in his attitude: he was ready to be humble, to apologize for whatever he had done, and to make amends—but he was not willing to play guessing games.

They sat in silence for a minute, not looking at one an-other.

Elene sniffed. Vandam could not see her, but he knew the kind of sniff that came from weeping. She said: "You could have sent me a note, or even a bunch of bloody flowers!"

"A note? What for? You knew we were to meet tonight."

"Oh, my God."

"Flowers? What do you want with flowers? We don't need to play that game anymore."

"Oh, really?"

"What do you want me to say?"

"Listen. We made love the night before last, in case you've forgotten—"

"Don't be silly—"

"You brought me home and kissed me good-bye. Then—nothing."

He drew on his cigarette. "In case *you* have forgotten, a certain Erwin Rommel is knocking at the gates with a bunch of Nazis in tow, and I'm one of the people who's trying to keep him out."

"Five minutes, that's all it would have taken to send me a note."

"What *for*?"

"Well, exactly, what for? I'm a loose woman, am I not? I give myself to a man the way I take a drink of water. An hour later I've forgotten—is that what you think? Because that's how it seems to me! Damn you, William Vandam, you make me feel cheap!"

It made no more sense than it had at the start, but now he could hear the pain in her voice. He turned to face her. "You're the most wonderful thing that's happened to me for a long time, perhaps ever. Please forgive me for being a fool." He took her hand in his own.

She looked toward the window, biting her lip, fighting back tears. "Yes, you are," she said. She looked down at him and touched his hair. "You bloody, bloody fool," she whispered, stroking his head. Her eyes spilled tears.

"I've such a lot to learn about you," he said.

"And I about you."

He looked away, thinking aloud. "People resent my equanimity—always have. Those who work for me don't, they like it. They know that when they feel like panicking, when they feel they can't cope, they can come to me and tell me about the dilemma; and if I can't see a way through it, I'll tell them what is the best thing to do, the lesser evil; and because I say it in a calm voice, because I see that it's a dilemma and I don't panic, they go away reassured and do what they have to do. All I do is clarify the problem and refuse to be frightened by it; but that's just what they need. However . . . exactly the same attitude often infuriates other people—my superiors, my friends, Angela, you . . . I've never understood why."

"Because sometimes you *should* panic, fool," she said softly. "Sometimes you should show that you are frightened, or obsessed, or crazy for something. It's human, and it's a sign that you care. When you're so calm all the time we think it's because you don't give a damn."

Vandam said: "Well, people should know better. Lovers should know better, and so should friends, and bosses if they're any good." He said this honestly, but in the back of his mind he realized that there was indeed an element of ruthlessness, of cold-heartedness, in his famous equanimity.

"And if they don't know better . . . ?" She had stopped crying now.

"I should be different? No." He wanted to be honest with her now. He could have told her a lie to make her happy: Yes, you're right, I'll try to be different. But what was the point? If he could not be *himself* with her, it was all worthless, he would be manipulating her the way all men had manipulated her, the way he manipulated people he did not love. So he told her the truth. "You see, this is the way I win. I mean, win everything . . . the game of life—so to speak." He gave a wry grin. "I *am* detached. I look at everything from a distance. I *do* care, but I refuse to do pointless things, symbolic gestures, empty fits of rage. Either we love each other or we don't, and all the flowers in the world won't make any difference. But the work I did today could affect whether we live or die. I *did* think of you, all day; but each time I thought of you, I turned my mind to more urgent things. I work efficiently, I set priorities and I don't worry about you when I know you're okay. Can you imagine yourself getting used to that?"

She gave him a watery smile. "I'll try."

And all the time, in the back of his mind, he was thinking: For how long? Do I want this woman forever? What if I don't?

He pushed the thought down. Right now it was low priority. "What I want to say, after all that, is: Forget about tonight, don't go, we'll manage without you. But I can't. We need you, and it's terribly important."

"That's okay, I understand."

"But first of all, may I kiss you hello?"

"Yes, please."

Kneeling beside the arm of her chair, he took her face in his big hand, and kissed her lips. Her mouth was soft and yielding, and slightly moist. He savored the feel and the taste of her. Never had he felt like this, as though he could go on kissing, just so, all night and never get tired.

Eventually she drew back, took a deep breath, and said: "My, my, I do believe you mean it."

"You may be sure of that."

She laughed. "When you said that, you were the old Major Vandam for a moment—the one I used to know before I knew you."

"And your 'My, my,' in that provocative voice was the old Elene."

"Brief me, Major."

"I'll have to get out of kissing distance."

"Sit over there and cross your legs. Anyway, what *were* you doing today?"

Vandam crossed the room to the drinks cupboard and found the gin. "A major in Intelligence has disappeared—along with a briefcase full of secrets."

"Wolff?"

"Could be. It turns out that this major has been disappearing at lunchtime, a couple of times a week, and nobody knows where he's been going. I've a hunch that he might have been meeting Wolff."

"So why would he disappear?"

Vandam shrugged. "Something went wrong."

"What was in his briefcase today?"

Vandam wondered how much to tell her. "A rundown of our defenses which was so complete that we think it could alter the result of the next battle." Smith had also been in possession of Vandam's proposed deception plan, but Vandam did not tell Elene this: he trusted her all the way, but he also had security instincts. He finished: "So, we'd better catch Wolff tonight."

"But it might be too late already!"

"No. We found the decrypt of one of Wolff's signals, a while back. It was timed at midnight. Spies have a set time for reporting, generally the same time every day. At other times their masters won't be listening—at least, not on the right wavelength—so even if they do signal nobody picks it up. Therefore, I think Wolff will send this information tonight at midnight—unless I catch him first." He hesitated, then changed his mind about security and decided she ought to know the full importance of what she was doing. "There's something else. He's using a code based on a novel called *Rebecca*. I've got a copy of the novel. If I can get the key to the code—"

"What's that?"

"Just a piece of paper telling him how to use the book to encode signals."

"Go on."

"If I can get the key to the *Rebecca* code, I can impersonate Wolff over the radio and send false information to Rommel. It could turn the tables completely—it could save Egypt. But I must have the key."

"All right. What's tonight's plan?"

"It's the same as before, only more so. I'll be in the restaurant with Jakes, and we'll both have pistols."

Her eyes widened. "You've got a gun?"

"I haven't got it now. Jakes is bringing it to the restaurant. Anyway, there will be two other men in the restaurant, and six more outside on the pavement, trying to look inconspicuous. There will also be civilian cars ready to block all exits from the street at the sound of a whistle. No matter what Wolff does tonight, if he wants to see you he's going to be caught."

There was a knock at the apartment door.

Vandam said: "What's that?"

"The door—"

"Yes, I know, are you expecting someone? Or something?"

"No, of course not, it's almost time for me to leave."

Vandam frowned. Alarm bells were sounding. "I don't like this. Don't answer."

"All right," Elene said. Then she changed her mind. "I have to answer. It might be my father. Or news of him."

"Okay, answer it."

Elene went out of the living room. Vandam sat listening. The knock came again, then she opened the door.

Vandam heard her say: "Alex!"

Vandam whispered: "Christ!"

He heard Wolff's voice. "You're all ready. How delightful." It was a deep, confident voice, the drawled English spoken with only the faintest trace of an unidentifiable accent.

Elene said: "Of course . . ."

"I know. May I come in?"

Vandam leaped over the back of the sofa and lay on the floor behind it.

"Elene said: "Of course . . ."

Wolff's voice came closer. "My dear, you look exquisite tonight."

Vandam thought: Smooth bastard.

The front door slammed shut.

Wolff said: "This way?"

"Um . . . yes . . ."

Vandam heard the two of them enter the room. Wolff said: "What a lovely apartment. Mikis Aristopoulos must pay you well."

"Oh, I don't work there regularly. He's a distant relation, it's family, I help out."

"Uncle. He must be your uncle."

"Oh . . . great-uncle, second cousin, something. He calls me his niece for simplicity."

"Well. These are for you."

"Oh, flowers. Thank you."

Vandam thought: Fuck that.

Wolff said: "May I sit down?"

"Of course."

Vandam felt the sofa shift as Wolff lowered his weight onto it. Wolff was a big man. Vandam remembered grappling with him in the alley. He also remembered the knife, and his hand went to the wound on his cheek. He thought: What can I do?

He could jump Wolff now. The spy was here, practically in his hands! They were about the same weight, and evenly matched—except for the knife. Wolff had had the knife that night when he had been dining with Sonja, so presumably he took it everywhere with him, and had it now.

If they fought, and Wolff had the advantage of the knife, Wolff would win. It had happened before, in the alley. Vandam touched his cheek again.

He thought: Why didn't I bring the gun here?

If they fought, and Wolff won, what would happen then? Seeing Vandam in Elene's apartment, Wolff would know she had been trying to trap him. What would he do to her? In Istanbul, in a similar situation, he had slit the girl's throat.

Vandam blinked to shut out the awful image.

Wolff said: "I see you were having a drink before I arrived. May I join you?"

"Of course," Elene said again. "What would you like?"

"What's that?" Wolff sniffed. "Oh, a little gin would be very nice."

Vandam thought: That was my drink. Thank God Elene didn't have a drink as well—two glasses would have given the game away. He heard ice clink.

"Cheers!" Wolff said.

"Cheers."

"You don't seem to like it."

"The ice has melted."

Vandam knew why she had made a face when she sipped his drink: it had been straight gin. She was coping so well with the situation, he thought. What did she think he, Vandam, was planning to do? She must have guessed by now where he was hiding. She would be trying desperately not to look in this direction. Poor Elene! Once again she had got more than she bargained for.

Vandam hoped she would be passive, take the line of least resistance and trust him.

Did Wolff still plan to go to the Oasis Restaurant? Perhaps he did. If only I could be sure of that, Vandam thought, I could leave it all to Jakes.

Wolff said: "You seem nervous, Elene. Did I confuse your plans by coming here? If you want to go and finish getting ready, or something—not that you look a whit less than perfect right now—just leave me here with the gin bottle."

"No, no . . . Well, we did say we'd meet at the restaurant . . ."

"And here I am, altering everything at the last minute again. To be truthful, I'm bored with restaurants, and yet they are, so to speak, the conventional meeting place; so I arrange to have dinner with people, then when the time comes I can't face it, and I think of something else to do."

So they're not going to the Oasis, Vandam thought. Damn.

Elene said: "What do you want to do?"

"May I surprise you again?"

Vandam thought: Make him tell you!

Elene said: "All right."

Vandam groaned inwardly. If Wolff would reveal where they were going, Vandam could contact Jakes and have the whole ambush moved to the new venue. Elene was not thinking the right way. It was understandable: she sounded terrified.

Wolff said: "Shall we go?"

"All right."

The sofa creaked as Wolff got up. Vandam thought: I could go for him now!

Too risky.

He heard them leave the room. He stayed where he was for a moment. He heard Wolff, in the hallway, say: "After you." Then the front door was slammed shut.

Vandam stood up. He would have to follow them, and

take the first available opportunity of calling GHQ and contacting Jakes. Elene did not have a telephone, not many
people did in Cairo. Even if she had there was no time now.
He went to the front door and listened. He heard nothing. He
opened it a fraction: they had gone. He went out, closed the
door and hurried along the corridor and down the stairs.

As he stepped out of the building he saw them on the
other side of the road. Wolff was holding open a car door for
Elene to get in. It was not a taxi: Wolff must have rented,
borrowed or stolen a car for the evening. Wolff closed the
door on Elene and walked around to the driver's side. Elene
looked out of the window and caught Vandam's eye. She
stared at him. He looked away from her, afraid to make any
kind of gesture in case Wolff should see it.

Vandam walked to his motorcycle, climbed on and started
the engine.

Wolff's car pulled away, and Vandam followed.

The city traffic was still heavy. Vandam was able to keep
five or six cars between himself and Wolff without risking losing Wolff. It was dusk, but few cars had their lights on.

Vandam wondered where Wolff was going. They were sure
to stop somewhere, unless the man intended to drive around
all night. If only they would stop someplace where there was
a telephone . . .

They headed out of the city, toward Giza. Darkness fell
and Wolff illuminated the lights of the car. Vandam left his
motorcycle lights off, so that Wolff would not be able to see
that he was being followed.

It was a nightmare ride. Even in daylight, in the city, riding a motorcycle was a little hair-raising: the roads were
strewn with bumps, potholes and treacherous patches of oil,
and Vandam found he had to watch the surface as much as
the traffic. The desert road was worse, and yet he now had to
drive without lights and keep an eye on the car ahead. Three
or four times he almost came off the bike.

He was cold. Not anticipating this ride, he had worn only
a short-sleeved uniform shirt, and at speed the wind cut
through it. How far was Wolff planning to go?

The pyramids loomed ahead.

Vandam thought: No phone there.

Wolff's car slowed down. They were going to picnic by the

pyramids. Vandam cut the motorcycle engine and coasted to a halt. Before Wolff had a chance to get out of the car, Vandam wheeled his bike off the road on to the sand. The desert was not level, except when seen from a distance, and he found a rocky hump behind which to lay down the motorcycle. He lay in the sand beside the hump and watched the car.

Nothing happened.

The car stayed still, its engine off, its interior dark. What where they doing in there? Vandam was seized by jealousy. He told himself not to be stupid—they were eating, that was all. Elene had told him about the last picnic: the smoked salmon, the cold chicken, the champagne. You could not kiss a girl with a mouthful of fish. Still, their fingers would touch as he handed her the wine . . .

Shut up.

He decided to risk a cigarette. He moved behind the hump to light it, then cupped it in his hand, army fashion, to hide the glow as he returned to his vantage point.

Five cigarettes later the car doors opened.

The cloud had cleared and the moon was out. The whole landscape was dark blue and silver, the complex shadow work of the pyramids rising out of shining sand. Two dark figures got out of the car and walked toward the nearest of the ancient tombs. Vandam could see that Elene walked with her arms folded across her chest, as if she were cold, or perhaps because she did not want to hold Wolff's hand. Wolff put an arm lightly across her shoulders, and she made no move to resist him.

They stopped at the base of the monument and talked. Wolff pointed upward, and Elene seemed to shake her head: Vandam guessed she did not want to climb. They walked around the base and disappeared behind the pyramid.

Vandam waited for them to emerge on the other side. They seemed to take a very long time. What were they doing behind there? The urge to go and see was almost irresistible.

He could get to the car now. He toyed with the idea of sabotaging it, rushing back to the city, and returning with his team. But Wolff would not be here when Vandam got back; it would be impossible to search the desert at night; by the morning Wolff might be miles away.

It was almost unbearable to watch and wait and do nothing, but Vandam knew it was the best course.

At last Wolff and Elene came back into view. He still had his arm around her. They returned to the car, and stood beside the door. Wolff put his hands on Elene's shoulders, said something, and leaned forward to kiss her.

Vandam stood up.

Elene gave Wolff her cheek, then turned away, slipping out of his grasp, and got into the car.

Vandam lay down on the sand again.

The desert silence was broken by the roar of Wolff's car. Vandam watched it turn in a wide circle and take the road. The headlights came on, and Vandam ducked his head involuntarily, although he was well concealed. The car passed him, heading toward Cairo.

Vandam jumped up, wheeled his cycle on to the road and kicked the starter. The engine would not turn over. Vandam cursed: he was terrified he might have gotten sand in the carburetor. He tried again, and this time it fired. He got on and followed the car.

The moonlight made it easier for him to spot the holes and bumps in the road surface, but it also made him more visible. He stayed well behind Wolff's car, knowing there was nowhere to go but Cairo. He wondered what Wolff planned next. Would he take Elene home? If so, where would he go afterward? He might lead Vandam to his base.

Vandam thought: I wish I had that gun.

Would Wolf take Elene to *his* home? The man had to be staying somewhere, had to have a bed in a room in a building in the city. Vandam was sure Wolff was planning to seduce Elene. Wolff had been rather patient and gentlemanly with her, but Vandam knew that in reality he was a man who liked to get his way quickly. Seduction might be the least of the dangers Elene faced. Vandam thought: What wouldn't I give for a phone!

They reached the outskirts of the city, and Vandam was obliged to pull up closer to the car, but fortunately there was plenty of traffic about. He contemplated stopping and giving a message to a policeman, or an officer, but Wolff was driving fast, and anyway, what would the message say? Vandam still did not know where Wolff was going.

He began to suspect the answer when they crossed the bridge to Zamalek. This was where the dancer, Sonja, had her houseboat. It was surely not possible that Wolff was living there, Vandam thought, for the place had been under surveillance for days. But perhaps he was reluctant to take Elene to his real home, and so was borrowing the houseboat.

Wolff parked in a street and got out. Vandam stood his motorcycle against a wall and hurriedly chained the wheel to prevent theft—he might need the bike again tonight.

He followed Wolff and Elene from the street to the towpath. From behind a bush he watched as they walked a short distance along the path. He wondered what Elene was thinking. Had she expected to be rescued before this? Would she trust that Vandam was still watching her? Would she now lose hope?

They stopped beside one of the boats—Vandam noted carefully which one—and Wolff helped Elene on to the gangplank. Vandam thought: Has it not occurred to Wolff that the houseboat might be under surveillance? Obviously not. Wolff followed Elene on to the deck, then opened a hatch. The two of them disappeared below.

Vandam thought: What now? This was surely his best chance to fetch help. Wolff must be intending to spend some time on the boat. But supposing that did not happen? Suppose, while Vandam was dashing to a phone, something went wrong—Elene insisted on being taken home, Wolff changed his plans, or they decided to go to a nightclub?

I could still lose the bastard, Vandam thought.

There must be a policeman around here somewhere.

"Hey!" he said in a stage whisper. "Is anybody there? Police? This is Major Vandam. Hey, where are—"

A dark figure materialized from behind a tree. An Arab voice said: "Yes?"

"Hello. I'm Major Vandam. Are you the police officer watching the houseboat?"

"Yes, sir."

"Okay, listen. The man we're chasing is on the boat now. Do you have a gun?"

"No, sir."

"Damn." Vandam considered whether he and the Arab could raid the boat on their own, and decided they could not:

the Arab could not be trusted to fight enthusiastically, and in that confined space Wolff's knife could wreak havoc. "Right, I want you to go to the nearest telephone, ring GHQ, and get a message through to Captain Jakes or Colonel Bogge, absolutely top priority: they are to come here in force and raid the houseboat immediately. Is that clear?"

"Captain Jakes or Colonel Bogge, GHQ, they are to raid the houseboat immediately. Yes, sir."

"All right. Be quick!"

The Arab left at a trot.

Vandam found a position in which he was concealed from view but could still watch the houseboat and the towpath. A few minutes later the figure of a woman came along the path. Vandam thought she looked familiar. She boarded the houseboat, and Vandam realized she was Sonja.

He was relieved: at least Wolff could not molest Elene while there was another woman on the boat.

He settled down to wait.

22

The Arab was worried. "Go to the nearest telephone," the Englishman had said. Well, there were telephones in some of the nearby houses. But houses with phones were occupied by Europeans, who would not take kindly to an Egyptian—even a police officer—banging on their doors at eleven o'clock at night and demanding to use the phone. They would almost certainly refuse, with oaths and curses: it would be a humiliating experience. He was not in uniform, not even wearing his usual plainclothes outfit of white shirt and black trousers, but was dressed like a fellah. They would not even believe he was a policeman.

There were no public phones on Zamalek that he knew of. That left him only one option: to phone from the station house. He headed that way, still trotting.

He was also worried about calling GHQ. It was an unwritten rule for Egyptian officials in Cairo that no one ever voluntarily contacted the British. It always meant trouble. The switchboard at GHQ would refuse to put through the call, or they would leave the message until morning—then deny they had ever received it—or they would tell him to call back later. And if anything went wrong there would be hell to pay. How, anyway, did he know that the man on the towpath had been genuine? He did not know Major Vandam from Adam, and anyone could put on the uniform shirt of a major. Suppose it was a hoax? There was a certain type of young English officer who just loved to play practical jokes on well-meaning Egyptians.

He had a standard response to situations like this: pass the buck. Anyway, he had been instructed to report to his su-

perior officer and no one else on this case. He would go to
the station house and from there, he decided, he would call
Superintendent Kemel at home.

Kemel would know what to do.

Elene stepped off the ladder and looked nervously around the
interior of the houseboat. She had expected the decor to be
sparse and nautical. In fact it was luxurious, if a little over-
ripe. There were thick rugs, low divans, a couple of elegant
occasional tables, and rich velvet floor-to-ceiling curtains
which divided this area from the other half of the boat,
which was presumably the bedroom. Opposite the curtains,
where the boat narrowed to what had been its stern, was a
tiny kitchen with small but modern fittings.

"Is this yours?" she asked Wolff.

"It belongs to a friend," he said. "Do sit down."

Elene felt trapped. Where the hell was William Vandam?
Several times during the evening she had thought there was a
motorcycle behind the car, but she had been unable to look
carefully for fear of alerting Wolff. Every second, she had
been expecting soldiers to surround the car, arrest Wolff and
set her free; and as the seconds turned into hours she had begun to wonder if it was all a dream, if William Vandam existed at all.

Now Wolff was going to the icebox, taking out a bottle of
champagne, finding two glasses, unwrapping the silver foil
from the top of the bottle, unwinding the wire fastening, pulling the cork with a loud pop and pouring the champagne into
the glasses and *where the hell was William?*

She was terrified of Wolff. She had had many liaisons with
men, some of them casual, but she had always trusted the
man, always known he would be kind, or if not kind, at least
considerate. It was her body she was frightened for: if she let
Wolff play with her body, what kind of games would he in-
vent? Her skin was sensitive, she was soft inside, so easy to
hurt, so vulnerable lying on her back with her legs apart . . .
To be like that with someone who loved her, someone who
would be as gentle with her body as she herself, would be a
joy—but with Wolff, who wanted only to *use* her body . . .
she shuddered.

"Are you cold?" Wolff said as he handed her a glass.

"No, I wasn't shivering . . ."

He raised his glass. "Your health."

Her mouth was dry. She sipped the cold wine, then took a gulp. It made her feel a little better.

He sat beside her on the couch and twisted around to look at her. "What a super evening," he said. "I enjoy your company so much. You're an enchantress."

Here it comes, she thought.

He put his hand on her knee.

She froze.

"You're enigmatic," he said. "Desirable, rather aloof, very beautiful, sometimes naïve and sometimes so knowing . . . will you tell me something?"

"I expect so." She did not look at him.

With his fingertip he traced the silhouette of her face: forehead, nose, lips, chin. He said: "Why do you go out with me?"

What did he mean? Was is possible he suspected what she was really doing? Or was this just the next move in the game?

She looked at him and said: "You're a very attractive man."

"I'm glad you think so." He put his hand on her knee again, and leaned forward to kiss her. She offered him her cheek, as she had done once before this evening. His lips brushed her skin, then he whispered: "Why are you frightened of me?"

There was a noise up on deck—quick, light footsteps—and then the hatch opened.

Elene thought: William!

A high-heeled shoe and a woman's foot appeared. The woman came down, closing the hatch above her, and stepped off the ladder. Elene saw her face and recognized her as Sonja, the belly dancer.

She thought: What on earth is going on?

"All right, Sergeant," Kemel said into the telephone. "You did exactly the right thing in contacting me. I'll deal with everything myself. In fact, you may go off duty now."

"Thank you, sir," said the sergeant. "Good night."

"Good night." Kemel hung up. This was a catastrophe. The British had followed Alex Wolff to the houseboat, and

Vandam was trying to organize a raid. The consequences would be two-fold. First, the prospect of the Free Officers using the German's radio would vanish, and then there would be no possibility of negotiations with the Reich before Rommel conquered Egypt. Second, once the British discovered that the houseboat was a nest of spies, they would quickly figure out that Kemel had been concealing the facts and protecting the agents. Kemel regretted that he had not pushed Sonja harder, forced her to arrange a meeting within hours instead of days; but it was too late for regrets. What was he going to do now?

He went back into the bedroom and dressed quickly. From the bed his wife said softly: "What is it?"

"Work," he whispered.

"Oh, no." She turned over.

He took his pistol from the locked drawer in the desk and put it in his jacket pocket, then he kissed his wife and left the house quietly. He got into his car and started the engine. He sat thinking for a minute. He had to consult Sadat about this, but that would take time. In the meanwhile Vandam might grow impatient, waiting at the houseboat, and do something precipitate. Vandam would have to be dealt with first, quickly; then he could go to Sadat's house.

Kemel pulled away, heading for Zamalek. He wanted time to think, slowly and clearly, but time was what he lacked. Should he kill Vandam? He had never killed a man and did not know whether he would be capable of it. It was years since he had so much as hit anyone. And how would he cover up his involvement in all this? It might be days yet before the Germans reached Cairo—indeed it was possible, even at this stage, that they might be repulsed. Then there would be an investigation into what had happened on the towpath tonight, and sooner or later the blame would be laid at Kemel's door. He would probably be shot.

"Courage," he said aloud, remembering the way Imam's stolen plane had burst into flames as it crash-landed in the desert.

He parked near the towpath. From the trunk of the car he took a length of rope. He stuffed the rope into the pocket of his jacket, and carried the gun in his right hand.

He held the gun reversed, for clubbing. How long since he

had used it? Six years, he thought, not counting occasional target practice.

He reached the riverbank. He looked at the silver Nile, the black shapes of the houseboats, the dim line of the towpath and the darkness of the bushes. Vandam would be in the bushes somewhere. Kemel stepped forward, walking softly.

Vandam looked at his wristwatch in the glow of his cigarette. It was eleven-thirty. Clearly something had gone wrong. Either the Arab policeman had given the wrong message, or GHQ had been unable to locate Jakes, or Bogge had somehow fouled everything up. Vandam could not take the chance of letting Wolff get on the radio with the information he had now. There was nothing for it but to go aboard the houseboat himself, and risk everything.

He put out his cigarette, then he heard a footstep somewhere in the bushes. "Who is it?" he hissed. "Jakes?"

A dark figure emerged and whispered: "It's me."

Vandam could not recognize the whispered voice, nor could he see the face. "Who?"

The figure stepped nearer and raised an arm. Vandam said: "Who—" then he realized that the arm was sweeping down in a blow. He jerked sideways, and something hit the side of his head and bounced on his shoulder. Vandam shouted with pain, and his right arm went numb. The arm was lifted again. Vandam stepped forward, reaching clumsily for his assailant with his left hand. The figure stepped back and struck again, and this time the blow landed squarely on top of Vandam's head. There was a moment of intense pain, then Vandam lost consciousness.

Kemel pocketed the gun and knelt beside Vandam's prone figure. First he touched Vandam's chest, and was relieved to feel a strong heartbeat. Working quickly, he took off Vandam's sandals, removed the socks, rolled them into a ball and stuffed them into the unconscious man's mouth. That should stop him from calling out. Next he rolled Vandam over, crossed his wrists behind his back, and tied them together with the rope. With the other end of the rope he bound Vandam's ankles. Finally he tied the rope to a tree.

Vandam would come round in a few minutes, but he

would find it impossible to move. Nor could he cry out. He would remain there until somebody stumbled on him. How soon was that likely to happen? Normally there might have been people in these bushes, young men with their sweethearts and soldiers with their girls, but tonight there had surely been enough comings and goings here to frighten them away. There was a chance that a latecoming couple would see Vandam, or perhaps hear him groaning . . . Kemel would have to take that chance, there was no point standing around and worrying.

He decided to take a quick look at the houseboat. He walked light-footedly along the towpath to the *Jihan*. There were lights on inside, but little curtains were drawn across the portholes. He was tempted to go aboard, but he wanted to consult with Sadat first, for he was not sure what should be done.

He turned around and headed back toward his car.

Sonja said: "Alex has told me all about you, Elene." She smiled.

Elene smiled back. Was this the friend of Wolff's who owned the houseboat? Was Wolff living with her? Had he not expected her back so early? Why was neither of them angry, or puzzled, or embarrassed? Just for something to say, Elene asked her: "Have you just come from the Cha-Cha Club?"

"Yes."

"How was it?"

"As always—exhausting, thrilling, successful."

Sonja was not a humble woman, clearly.

Wolff handed Sonja a glass of champagne. She took it without looking at him, and said to Elene: "So you work in Mikis' shop?"

"No, I don't," Elene said, thinking: Are you really interested in this? "I helped him for a few days, that's all. We're related."

"So you're Greek?"

"That's right." The small talk was giving Elene confidence. Her fear receded. Whatever happened, Wolff was not likely to rape her at knifepoint in front of one of the most famous women in Egypt. Sonja gave her a breathing space, at least.

William was determined to capture Wolff before midnight—

Midnight!

She had almost forgotten. At midnight Wolff was to contact the enemy by wireless, and hand over the details of the defense line. But where was the radio? Was it here, on the boat? If it was somewhere else, Wolff would have to leave soon. If it was here, would he send his message in front of Elene and Sonja? What was in his mind?

He sat down beside Elene. She felt vaguely threatened, with the two of them on either side of her. Wolff said: "What a lucky man I am, to be sitting here with the two most beautiful women in Cairo."

Elene looked straight ahead, not knowing what to say.

Wolff said: "Isn't she beautiful, Sonja?"

"Oh, yes." Sonja touched Elene's face, then took her chin and turned her head. "Do you think I'm beautiful, Elene?"

"Of course." Elene frowned. This was getting weird. It was almost as if—

"I'm so glad," Sonja said, and she put her hand on Elene's knee.

And then Elene understood.

Everything fell into place: Wolff's patience, his phony courtliness, the houseboat, the unexpected appearance of Sonja . . . Elene realized she was not safe at all. Her fear of Wolff came back, stronger than before. The pair of them wanted to use her, and she would have no choice, she would have to lie there, mute and unresisting, while they did whatever they wanted, Wolff with the knife in one hand—

Stop it.

I won't be afraid. I can stand being mauled about by a pair of depraved old fools. There's more at stake here. Forget about your precious little body, think about the radio, and how to stop Wolff using it.

This threesome might be turned to advantage.

She looked furtively at her wristwatch. It was a quarter to midnight. Too late, now, to rely on William. She, Elene, was the only one who could stop Wolff.

And she thought she knew how.

A look passed between Sonja and Wolff like a signal. Each with a hand on one of Elene's thighs, they leaned across her and kissed each other in front of her eyes.

She looked at them. It was a long, lascivious kiss. She thought: What do they expect me to do?

They drew apart.

Wolff kissed Elene the same way. Elene was unresistant. Then she felt Sonja's hand on her chin. Sonja turned Elene's face toward her and kissed her lips.

Elene closed her eyes, thinking: It won't hurt me, it won't hurt.

It did not hurt, but it was *strange*, to be kissed so tenderly by a woman's mouth.

Elene thought: Somehow I have to get control of this scene.

Sonja pulled open her own blouse. She had big brown breasts. Wolff bent his head and took a nipple into his mouth. Elene felt Sonja pushing her head down. She realized she was supposed to follow Wolff's example. She did so. Sonja moaned.

All this was for Sonja's benefit: it was clearly her fantasy, her kink; she was the one who was panting and groaning now, not Wolff. Elene was afraid that any minute now Wolff might break away and go to his radio. As she went mechanically through the motions of making love to Sonja, she cast about in her mind for ways to drive Wolff out of his mind with lust.

But the whole scene was so silly, so farcical, that everything she thought of doing seemed merely comical.

I've got to keep Wolff from that radio.

What's the *key* to all this? What do they *really* want?

She moved her face away from Sonja and kissed Wolff. He turned his mouth to hers. She found his hand, and pressed it between her thighs. He breathed deeply, and Elene thought: At least he's interested.

Sonja tried to push them apart.

Wolff looked at Sonja, then slapped her face, hard.

Elene gasped with surprise. Was this the key? It must be a game they play, it must be.

Wolff turned his attention back to Elene. Sonja tried to get between them again.

This time Elene slapped her.

Sonja moaned deep in her throat.

Elene thought: I've done it, I've guessed the game, I'm in *control*.

She saw Wolff look at his wristwatch.

Suddenly she stood up. They both stared at her. She lifted her arms then, slowly, she pulled her dress up over her head, threw it to one side, and stood there in her black underwear and stockings. She touched herself, lightly, running her hands between her thighs and across her breasts. She saw Wolff's face change: his look of composure vanished, and he gazed at her, wide-eyed with desire. He was tense, mesmerized. He licked his lips. Elene raised her left foot, planted a high-heeled shoe between Sonja's breasts and pushed Sonja backward. Then she grasped Wolff's head and drew it to her belly.

Sonja started kissing Elene's foot.

Wolff made a sound between a groan and a sigh, and buried his face between Elene's thighs.

Elene looked at her watch.

It was midnight.

23

Elene lay on her back in the bed, naked. She was quite still, rigid, her muscles tense, staring straight up at the blank ceiling. On her right was Sonja, facedown, arms and legs spread all ways over the sheets, fast asleep, snoring. Sonja's right hand rested limply on Elene's hip. Wolff was on Elene's left. He lay on his side, facing her, sleepily stroking her body.

Elene was thinking: Well, it didn't kill me.

The game had been all about rejecting and accepting Sonja. The more Elene and Wolff rejected her and abused her, the more passionate she became, until in the dénouement Wolff rejected Elene and made love to Sonja. It was a script that Wolff and Sonja obviously knew well: they had played it before.

It had given Elene very little pleasure, but she was not sickened or humiliated or disgusted. What she felt was that she had been betrayed, and betrayed by herself. It was like pawning a jewel given by a lover, or having your long hair cut off to sell for money, or sending a small child to work in a mill. She had abused herself. Worst of all, what she had done was the logical culmination of the life she had been living: in the eight years since she had left home she had been on the slippery slope that ended in prostitution, and now she felt she had arrived there.

The stroking stopped, and she glanced sideways at Wolff's face. His eyes were closed. He was falling asleep.

She wondered what had happened to Vandam.

Something had gone wrong. Perhaps Vandam had lost sight of Wolff's car in Cairo. Maybe he had had an accident in the traffic. Whatever the reason, Vandam was no longer watching over her. She was on her own.

She had succeeded in making Wolff forget his midnight transmission to Rommel—but what now was to stop him sending the message another night? Elene would have to get to GHQ and tell Jakes where Wolff was to be found. She would have to slip away, right now, find Jakes, get him to pull his team out of bed . . .

It would take too long. Wolff might wake, find she was gone, and vanish again.

Was his radio here, on the houseboat, or somewhere else? That might make all the difference.

She remembered something Vandam had said last evening—was it really only a few hours ago? "If I can get the key to the *Rebecca* code, I can impersonate him over the radio . . . it could turn the tables completely . . ."

Elene thought: Perhaps I can find the key.

He had said it was a sheet of paper explaining how to use the book to encode messages.

Elene realized that she now had a chance to locate the radio and the key to the code.

She had to search the houseboat.

She did not move. She was frightened again. If Wolff should discover her searching . . . She remembered his theory of human nature: the world is divided into masters and slaves. A slave's life was worth nothing.

No, she thought; I'll leave here in the morning, quite normally, and then I'll tell the British where Wolff is to be found, and they'll raid the houseboat, and—

And what if Wolff had gone by then? What if the radio was not here?

Then it would all have been for nothing.

Wolff's breathing was now slow and even: he was fast asleep. Elene reached down, gently picked up Sonja's limp hand, and moved it from her thigh on to the sheet. Sonja did not stir.

Now neither of them was touching Elene. It was a great relief.

Slowly, she sat upright.

The shift of weight on the mattress disturbed both of the other two. Sonja grunted, lifted her head, turned it the other

way, and fell to snoring again. Wolff rolled over on his back
without opening his eyes.

Moving slowly, wincing with every movement of the
mattress, Elene turned around so that she was on her hands
and knees, facing the head of the bed. She began painfully to
crawl backward: right knee, left hand, left knee, right hand.
She watched the two sleeping faces. The foot of the bed
seemed miles away. The silence rang in her ears like thunder.
The houseboat itself rocked from side to side on the wash of
a passing barge, and Elene backed off the bed quickly under
cover of the disturbance. She stood there, rooted to the spot,
watching the other two, until the boat stopped moving. They
stayed asleep.

Where should the search start? Elene decided to be me-
thodical, and begin at the front and work backward. In the
prow of the boat was the bathroom. Suddenly she realized
she had to go there anyway. She tiptoed across the bedroom
and went into the tiny bathroom.

Sitting on the toilet, she looked around. Where might a radio be hidden? She did not really know how big it would be:
the size of a suitcase? A briefcase? A handbag? Here there
were a basin, a small tub and a cupboard on the wall. She
stood up and opened the cupboard. It contained shaving gear,
pills and a small roll of bandage.

The radio was not in the bathroom.

She did not have the courage to search the bedroom while
they slept, not yet. She crossed it and passed through the curtains into the living room. She looked quickly all around. She
felt the need to hurry, and forced herself to be calm and
careful. She began on the starboard side. Here there was a divan couch. She tapped its base gently: it seemed hollow. The
radio might be underneath. She tried to lift it, and could not.
Looking around its edge, she saw that it was screwed to the
floor. The screws were tight. The radio would not be there.
Next there was a tall cupboard. She opened it gently. It
squeaked a little, and she froze. She heard a grunt from the
bedroom. She waited for Wolff to come bounding through the
curtains and catch her red-handed. Nothing happened.

She looked in the cupboard. There was a broom, and some
dusters, and cleaning materials, and a flashlight. No radio.
She closed the door. It squeaked again.

She moved into the kitchen area. She had to open six smaller cupboards. They contained crockery, tinned food, saucepans, glasses, supplies of coffee and rice and tea, and towels. Under the sink there was a bucket for kitchen waste. Elene looked in the icebox. It contained one bottle of champagne. There were several drawers. Would the radio be small enough to fit in a drawer? She opened one. The rattle of cutlery shredded her nerves. No radio. Another: a massive selection of bottled spices and flavorings, from vanilla essence to curry powder—somebody liked to cook. Another drawer: kitchen knives.

Next to the kitchen was a small escritoire with a fold-down desk top. Beneath it was a small suitcase. Elene picked up the suitcase. It was heavy. She opened it. There was the radio.

Her heart skipped.

It was an ordinary, plain suitcase, with two catches, a leather handle and reinforced corners. The radio fitted inside exactly, as if it had been designed that way. The recessed lid left a little room on top of the radio, and here there was a book. Its board covers had been torn off to make it fit into the space in the lid. Elene picked up the book and looked inside. She read: "Last night I dreamt I went to Manderley again." It was *Rebecca*.

She flicked the pages of the book. In the middle there was something between the pages. She let the book fall open and a sheet of paper dropped to the floor. She bent down and picked it up. It was a list of numbers and dates, with some words in German. This was surely the key to the code.

She held in her hand what Vandam needed to turn the tide of the war.

Suddenly the responsibility weighed her down.

Without this, she thought, Wolff cannot send messages to Rommel—or if he sends messages in plain language the Germans will suspect their authenticity and also worry that the Allies have overheard them . . . Without this, Wolff is useless. With this, Vandam can win the war.

She had to run away, now, taking the key with her.

She remembered that she was stark naked.

She broke out of her trance. Her dress was on the couch, crumpled and wrinkled. She crossed the boat, put down the

book and the key to the code, picked up her dress and
slipped it over her head.

The bed creaked.

From behind the curtains came the unmistakable sound of
someone getting up, someone heavy, it had to be him. Elene
stood still, paralyzed. She heard Wolff walk toward the curtains, then away again. She heard the bathroom door.

There was no time to put her panties on. She picked up
her bag, her shoes, and the book with the key inside. She
heard Wolff come out of the bathroom. She went to the ladder and ran up it, wincing as her bare feet cut into the edges
of the narrow wooden steps. Glancing down, she saw Wolff
appear between the curtains and glance up at her in astonishment. His eyes went to the suitcase opened on the floor.
Elene looked away from him to the hatch. It was secured on
the inside with two bolts. She slid them both back. From the
corner of her eye she saw Wolff dash to the ladder. She
pushed up the hatch and scrambled out. As she stood upright
on the deck she saw Wolff scrambling up the ladder. She bent
swiftly and lifted the heavy wooden hatch. As Wolff's right
hand grasped the rim of the opening, Elene slammed the
hatch down on his fingers with all her might. There was a
roar of pain. Elene ran across the deck and down the gangplank.

It was just that: a plank, leading from the deck to the
riverbank. She stooped, picked up the end of the plank, and
threw it into the river.

Wolff came up through the hatch, his face a mask of pain
and fury.

Elene panicked as she saw him come across the deck at a
run. She thought: he's naked, he can't chase me! He took a
flying jump over the rail of the boat.

He can't make it.

He landed on the very edge of the riverbank, his arms
windmilling for balance. With a sudden access of courage
Elene ran at him and, while he was still off balance, pushed
him backward into the water.

She turned and ran along the towpath.

When she reached the lower end of the pathway that led to
the street, she stopped and looked back. Already her heart
was pounding and she was breathing in long, shuddering

gasps. She felt elated when she saw Wolff, dripping wet and naked, climbing out of the water up the muddy riverbank. It was getting light: he could not chase her far in that state. She spun around toward the street, broke into a run and crashed into someone.

Strong arms caught her in a tight grip. She struggled desperately, got free and was seized again. She slumped in defeat: after all that, she thought; after all that.

She was turned around, grasped by the arms and marched toward the houseboat. She saw Wolff walking toward her. She struggled again, and the man holding her got an arm around her throat. She opened her mouth to scream for help, but before she could make a sound the man had thrust his fingers down her throat, making her retch.

Wolff came up and said: "Who are you?"

"I'm Kemel. You must be Wolff."

"Thank God you were there."

"You're in trouble, Wolff," said the man called Kemel.

"You'd better come aboard—oh, shit, she threw away the fucking plank." Wolff looked down at the river and saw the plank floating beside the houseboat. "I can't get any wetter," he said. He slid down the bank and into the water, grabbed the plank, shoved it up on to the bank and climbed up after it. He picked it up again and laid it across the gap between the houseboat and the bank.

"This way," he said.

Kemel marched Elene across the plank, over the deck and down the ladder.

"Put her over there," Wolff said, pointing to the couch.

Kemel pushed Elene over to the couch, not ungently, and made her sit down.

Wolff went through the curtains and came back a moment later with a big towel. He proceeded to rub himself dry with it. He seemed quite unembarrassed by his nakedness.

Elene was surprised to see that Kemel was quite a small man. From the way he had grabbed her, she had imagined he was Wolff's build. He was a handsome, dark-skinned Arab. He was looking away from Wolff uneasily.

Wolff wrapped the towel around his waist and sat down. He examined his hand. "She nearly broke my fingers," he said. He looked at Elene with a mixture of anger and amusement.

Kemel said: "Where's Sonja?"

"In bed," Wolff said, jerking his head toward the curtains. "She sleeps through earthquakes, especially after a night of lust."

Kemel was uncomfortable with such talk, Elene observed, and perhaps also impatient with Wolff's levity. "You're in trouble," he said again.

"I know," Wolff said. "I suppose she's working for Vandam."

"I don't know about that. I got a call in the middle of the night from my man on the towpath. Vandam had come along and sent my man to fetch help."

Wolff was shocked. "We came close!" he said. He looked worried. "Where's Vandam now?"

"Out there still. I knocked him on the head and tied him up."

Elene's heart sank. Vandam was out there in the bushes, hurt and incapacitated—and nobody else knew where she was. It had all been for nothing, after all.

Wolff nodded. "Vandam followed her here. That's two people who know about this place. If I stay here I'll have to kill them both."

Elene shuddered: he talked of killing people so lightly. Masters and slaves, she remembered.

"Not good enough," Kemel said. "If you kill Vandam the murder will eventually be blamed on me. You can go away, but I have to live in this town." He paused, watching Wolff with narrowed eyes. "And if you were to kill me, that would still leave the man who called me last night."

"So . . ." Wolff frowned and made an angry noise. "There's no choice. I have to go. Damn."

Kemel nodded. "If you disappear, I think I can cover up. But I want something from you. Remember the reason we've been helping you."

"You want to talk to Rommel."

"Yes."

"I'll be sending a message tomorrow night—tonight, I mean, damn, I've hardly slept. Tell me what you want to say, and I'll—"

"Not good enough," Kemel interrupted. "We want to do it ourselves. We want your radio."

Wolff frowned. Elene realized that Kemel was a nationalist rebel, cooperating or trying to cooperate with the Germans.

Kemel added: "We could send your message for you . . ."

"Not necessary," Wolff said. He seemed to have reached a decision. "I have another radio."

"It's agreed, then."

"There's the radio." Wolff pointed to the open case, still on the floor where Elene had left it. "It's already tuned to the correct wavelength. All you have to do is broadcast at midnight, any night."

Kemel went over to the radio and examined it. Elene wondered why Wolff had said nothing about the *Rebecca* code. Wolff did not care whether Kemel got through to Rommel or not, she decided; and to give him the code would be to risk that he might give it to someone else. Wolff was playing safe again.

Wolff said: "Where does Vandam live?"

Kemel told him the address.

Elene thought: *Now* what is he after?

Wolff said: "He's married, I suppose."

"No."

"A bachelor. Damn."

"Not a bachelor," Kemel said, still looking at the wireless transmitter. "A widower. His wife was killed in Crete last year."

"Any children?"

"Yes," Kemel said. "A small boy called Billy, so I'm told. Why?"

Wolff shrugged. "I'm interested, a little obsessed, with the man who's come so close to catching me."

Elene was sure he was lying.

Kemel closed the suitcase, apparently satisfied. Wolff said to him: "Keep an eye on her for a minute, would you?"

"Of course."

Wolff turned away, then turned back. He had noticed that Elene still had *Rebecca* in her hand. He reached down and took it from her. He disappeared through the curtains.

Elene thought: If I tell Kemel about the code, then maybe

Kemel will make Wolff give it to him, and maybe then Vandam will get it from Wolff—but what will happen to me?

Kemel said to her: "What—" He stopped abruptly as Wolff came back, carrying his clothes, and began to dress.

Kemel said to him: "Do you have a call sign?"

"Sphinx," Wolff said shortly.

"A code?"

"No code."

"What was in that book?"

Wolff looked angry. "A code," he said. "But you can't have it."

"We need it."

"I can't give it to you," Wolff said. "You'll have to take your chance, and broadcast in clear."

Kemel nodded.

Suddenly Wolff's knife was in his hand. "Don't argue," he said. "I know you've got a gun in your pocket. Remember, if you shoot, you'll have to explain the bullet to the British. You'd better go now."

Kemel turned, without speaking, and went up the ladder and through the hatch. Elene heard his footsteps above. Wolff went to the porthole and watched him walk away along the towpath.

Wolff put his knife away and buttoned his shirt over the sheath. He put on his shoes and laced them tightly. He got the book from the next room, extracted from it the sheet of paper bearing the key to the code, crumpled the paper, dropped it into a large glass ashtray, took a box of matches from a kitchen drawer and set fire to the paper.

He must have another key with the other radio, Elene thought.

Wolff watched the flames to make sure the paper was entirely burned. He looked at the book, as if contemplating burning that too, then he opened a porthole and dropped it into the river.

He took a small suitcase from a cupboard and began to pack a few things into it.

"Where are you going?" Elene said.

"You'll find out—you're coming."

"Oh, no." What would he do with her? He had caught her deceiving him—had he dreamed up some appropriate punishment? She felt very weary and afraid. Nothing she had done had turned out well. At one time she had been afraid merely that she would have to have sex with him. How much more there was to fear now. She thought of trying again to run away—she had almost made it last time—but she no longer had the spirit.

Wolff continued packing his case. Elene saw some of her own clothes on the floor, and remembered that she had not dressed properly. There were her panties, her stockings and her brassiere. She decided to put them on. She stood up and pulled her dress over her head. She bent down to pick up her underwear. As she stood up Wolff embraced her. He pressed a rough kiss against her lips, not seeming to care that she was completely unresponsive. He reached between her legs and thrust a finger inside her. He withdrew his finger from her vagina and shoved it into her anus. She tensed. He pushed his finger in farther, and she gasped with pain.

He looked into her eyes. "Do you know, I think I'd take you with me even if I didn't have a use for you."

She closed her eyes, humiliated. He turned from her abruptly and returned to his packing.

She put on her clothes.

When he was ready, he took a last look around and said: "Let's go."

Elene followed him up on to the deck, wondering what he planned to do about Sonja.

As if he knew what she was thinking, he said: "I hate to disturb Sonja's beauty sleep." He grinned. "Get moving."

They walked along the towpath. Why was he leaving Sonja behind? Elene wondered. She could not figure it out, but she knew it was callous. Wolff was a completely unscrupulous man, she decided; and the thought made her shudder, for she was in his power.

She wondered whether she could kill him.

He carried his case in his left hand and gripped her arm with his right. They turned on to the footpath, walked to the street, and went to his car. He unlocked the door on the driver's side and made her climb in over the gear stick to the passenger side. He got in beside her and started the car.

It was a miracle the car was still in one piece after being left on the road all night: normally anything detachable would have been stolen, including wheels. He gets all the luck there is, Elene thought.

They drove away. Elene wondered where they were going. Wherever it was, Wolff's second radio was there, along with another copy of *Rebecca* and another key to the code. When we get there, I'll have to try again, she thought wearily. It was all up to her now. Wolff had left the houseboat, so there was nothing Vandam could do even after somebody untied him. Elene, on her own, had to try to stop Wolff from contacting Rommel, and if possible steal the key to the code. The idea was ridiculous, shooting for the moon. All she really wanted was to get away from this evil, dangerous man, to go home, to forget about spies and codes and war, to feel safe again.

She thought of her father, walking to Jerusalem, and she knew she had to try.

Wolff stopped the car. Elene realized where they were. She said: "This is Vandam's house!"

"Yes."

She gazed at Wolff, trying to read the expression on his face. She said: "But Vandam isn't there."

"No." Wolff smiled bleakly. "But Billy is."

24

Anwar el-Sadat was delighted with the radio.

"It's a Hallicrafter/Skychallenger," he told Kemel. "American." He plugged it in to test it, and pronounced it very powerful.

Kemel explained that he had to broadcast at midnight on the preset wavelength, and that the call sign was Sphinx. He said that Wolff had refused to give him the code, and that they would have to take the risk of broadcasting in clear.

They hid the radio in the oven in the kitchen of the little house.

Kemel left Sadat's home and drove from Kubri al-Qubbah back to Zamalek. On the way he considered how he was to cover up his role in the events of the night.

His story would have to tally with that of the sergeant whom Vandam had sent for help, so he would have to admit that he had received the phone call. Perhaps he would say that, before alerting the British, he had gone to the houseboat himself to investigate, in case "Major Vandam" was an impostor. What then? He had searched the towpath and the bushes for Vandam, and then he, too, had been knocked on the head. The snag was that he would not have stayed unconscious all these hours. So he would have to say that he had been tied up. Yes, he would say he had been tied up and had just managed to free himself. Then he and Vandam would board the houseboat—and find it empty.

It would serve.

He parked his car and went cautiously down to the towpath. Looking into the shrubbery, he figured out roughly where he had left Vandam. He went into the bushes thirty or

forty yards away from that spot. He lay down on the ground
and rolled over, to make his clothes dirty, then he rubbed
some of the sandy soil on his face and ran his fingers through
his hair. Then, rubbing his wrists to make them look sore, he
went in search of Vandam.

He found him exactly where he had left him. The bonds
were still tight and the gag still in place. Vandam looked at
Kemel with wide, staring eyes.

Kemel said: "My God, they got you, too!"

He bent down, removed the gag, and began to untie Vandam. "The sergeant contacted me," he explained. "I came
down here looking for you, and the next thing I knew, I
woke up bound and gagged with a headache. That was hours
ago. I just got free."

Vandam said nothing.

Kemel threw the rope aside. Vandam stood up stiffly. Kemel said: "How do you feel?"

"I'm all right."

"Let's board the houseboat and see what we can find," Kemel said. He turned around.

As soon as Kemel turned his back, Vandam stepped forward
and hit him as hard as he possibly could with an edge-of-the-
hand blow to the back of the neck. It might have killed Kemel, but Vandam did not care. Vandam had been bound and
gagged, and he had been unable to see the towpath; but he
had been able to hear: "I'm Kemel. You must be Wolff."
That was how he knew that Kemel had betrayed him. Kemel
had not thought of that possibility, obviously. Since overhear-
ing those words, Vandam had been seething, and all his
pent-up anger had gone into the blow.

Kemel lay on the ground, stunned. Vandam rolled him
over, searched him and found the gun. He used the rope that
had bound his own hands to tie Kemel's hands behind his
back. Then he slapped Kemel's face until he came around.

"Get up," Vandam said.

Kemel looked blank, then fear came into his eyes. "What
are you doing?"

Vandam kicked him. "Kicking you," he said. "Get up."

Kemel struggled to his feet.

"Turn around."

Kemel turned around. Vandam took hold of Kemel's collar with his left hand, keeping the gun in his right.

"Move."

They walked to the houseboat. Vandam pushed Kemel ahead, up the gangplank and across the deck.

"Open the hatch."

Kemel put the toe of his shoe into the handle of the hatch and lifted it open.

"Go down."

Awkwardly, with his hands tied, Kemel descended the ladder. Vandam bent down to look inside. There was nobody there. He went quickly down the ladder. Pushing Kemel to one side, he pulled back the curtain, covering the space behind with the gun.

He saw Sonja in bed, sleeping.

"Get in there," he told Kemel.

Kemel went through and stood beside the head of the bed.

"Wake her."

Kemel touched Sonja with his foot. She turned over, rolling away from him, without opening her eyes. Vandam realized vaguely that she was naked. He reached over and tweaked her nose. She opened her eyes and sat up immediately, looking cross. She recognized Kemel, then she saw Vandam with the gun.

She said: "What's going on?"

Then she and Vandam said simultaneously: "Where's Wolff?"

Vandam was quite sure she was not dissembling. It was clear now that Kemel had warned Wolff, and Wolff had fled without waking Sonja. Presumably he had taken Elene with him—although Vandam could not imagine why.

Vandam put the gun to Sonja's chest, just below her left breast. He spoke to Kemel. "I'm going to ask you a question. If you give the wrong answer, she dies. Understand?"

Kemel nodded tensely.

Vandam said: "Did Wolff send a radio message at midnight last night?"

"No!" Sonja screamed. "No, he didn't, he didn't!"

"What *did* happen here?" Vandam asked, dreading the answer.

"We went to bed."

"Who did?"

"Wolff, Elene and me."

"Together?"

"Yes."

So that was it. And Vandam had thought she was safe, because there was another woman around! That explained Wolff's continuing interest in Elene: they had wanted her for their threesome. Vandam was sick with disgust, not because of what they had done, but because he had caused Elene to be forced to be part of it.

He put the thought out of his mind. Was Sonja telling the truth—had Wolff failed to radio Rommel last night? Vandam could not think of a way to check. He could only hope it was true.

"Get dressed," he told Sonja.

She got off the bed and hurriedly put on a dress. Keeping both of them covered with the gun, Vandam went to the prow of the boat and looked through the little doorway. He saw a tiny bathroom with two small portholes.

"Get in there, both of you."

Kemel and Sonja went into the bathroom. Vandam closed the door on them and began to search the houseboat. He opened all the cupboards and drawers, throwing their contents on the floor. He stripped the bed. With a sharp knife from the kitchen he slashed the mattress and the upholstery of the couch. He went through all the papers in the escritoire. He found a large glass ashtray full of charred paper and poked through it, but all of the paper was completely burned up. He emptied the icebox. He went up on deck and cleaned out the lockers. He checked all around the outside of the hull, looking for a rope dangling into the water.

After half an hour he was sure that the houseboat contained no radio, no copy of *Rebecca* and no code key.

He got the two prisoners out of the bathroom. In one of the deck lockers he had found a length of rope. He tied Sonja's hands, then roped Sonja and Kemel together.

He marched them off the boat, along the towpath and up to the street. They walked to the bridge, where he hailed a taxi. He put Sonja and Kemel in the back then, keeping the gun pointed at them, he got in the front beside the wide-eyed, frightened Arab driver.

"GHQ," he told the driver.

The two prisoners would have to be interrogated, but really there were only two questions to be asked:

Where was Wolff?

And where was Elene?

Sitting in the car, Wolff took hold of Elene's wrist. She tried to pull away but his grip was too strong. He drew out his knife and ran its blade lightly across the back of her hand. The knife was very sharp. Elene stared at her hand in horror. At first there was just a line like a pencil mark. Then blood welled up in the cut, and there was a sharp pain. She gasped.

Wolff said: "You're to stay very close to me and say nothing."

Suddenly Elene hated him. She looked into his eyes. "Otherwise you'll cut me?" she said with all the scorn she could muster.

"No," he said. "Otherwise I'll cut Billy."

He released her wrist and got out of the car. Elene sat still, feeling helpless. What could she do against this strong, ruthless man? She took a little handkerchief from her bag and wrapped it around her bleeding hand.

Impatiently, Wolff came around to her side of the car and pulled open the door. He took hold of her upper arm and made her get out of the car. Then, still holding her, he crossed the road to Vandam's house.

They walked up the short drive and rang the bell. Elene remembered the last time she had stood in this portico waiting for the door to open. It seemed years ago, but it was only days. Since then she had learned that Vandam had been married, and that his wife had died; and she had made love to Vandam; and he had failed to send her flowers—how could she have made such a fuss about that?—and they had found Wolff; and—

The door opened. Elene recognized Gaafar. The servant remembered her, too, and said: "Good morning, Miss Fontana."

"Hello, Gaafar."

Wolff said: "Good morning, Gaafar. I'm Captain Alexander. The major asked me to come round. Let us in, would you?"

"Of course, sir." Gaafar stood aside. Wolff, still gripping Elene's arm, stepped into the house. Gaafar closed the door. Elene remembered this tiled hall. Gaafar said: "I hope the major is all right . . ."

"Yes, he's fine," Wolff said. "But he can't get home this morning, so he asked me to come round, tell you that he's well, and drive Billy to school."

Elene was aghast. It was awful—Wolff was going to kidnap Billy. She should have guessed that as soon as Wolff mentioned the boy's name—but it was unthinkable, she must not let it happen! What could she do? She wanted to shout No, Gaafar, he's lying, take Billy and get away, run, run! But Wolff had the knife, and Gaafar was old, and Wolff would get Billy anyway.

Gaafar seemed to hesitate. Wolff said: "All right, Gaafar, snap it up. We haven't got all day."

"Yes, sir," Gaafar said, reacting with the reflex of an Egyptian servant addressed in an authoritative manner by a European. "Billy is just finishing his breakfast. Would you wait in here for a moment?" He opened the drawing-room door.

Wolff propelled Elene into the room and at last let go of her arm. Elene looked at the upholstery, the wallpaper, the marble fireplace and the *Tatler* photographs of Angela Vandam: these things had the eerie look of familiar objects seen in a nightmare. Angela would have known what to do, Elene thought miserably. "Don't be ridiculous!" she would have said; then, raising an imperious arm, she would have told Wolff to get out of her house. Elene shook her head to dispel the fantasy: Angela would have been as helpless as she.

Wolff sat down at the desk. He opened a drawer, took out a pad and a pencil, and began to write.

Elene wondered what Gaafar might do. Was it possible he might call GHQ to check with Billy's father? Egyptians were very reluctant to make phone calls to GHQ, Elene knew: Gaafar would have trouble getting past the switchboard operators and secretaries. She looked around, and saw that anyway the phone was here in this room, so that if Gaafar tried, Wolff would know and stop him.

"Why did you bring me here?" she cried. Frustration and fear made her voice shrill.

Wolff looked up from his writing. "To keep the boy quiet. We've got a long way to go."

"Leave Billy here," she pleaded. "He's a child."

"Vandam's child," Wolff said with a smile.

"You don't need him."

"Vandam may be able to guess where I'm going," Wolff said. "I want to make sure he doesn't come after me."

"Do you really think he'll sit at home while you have his son?"

Wolff appeared to consider the point. "I hope so," he said finally. "Anyway, what have I got to lose? If I don't take the boy he'll definitely come after me."

Elene fought back tears. "Haven't you got any *pity?*"

"Pity is a decadent emotion," Wolff said with a gleam in his eye. "Scepticism regarding morality is what is decisive. The end of the moral interpretation of the world, which no longer has any sanction . . ." He seemed to be quoting.

Elene said: "I don't think you're doing this to make Vandam stay home. I think you're doing it out of spite. You're thinking about the anguish you'll cause him, and you love it. You're a crude, twisted, loathsome man."

"Perhaps you're right."

"You're sick."

"That's enough!" Wolff reddened slightly. He appeared to calm himself with an effort. "Shut up while I'm writing."

Elene forced herself to concentrate. They were going on a long journey. He was afraid Vandam would follow them. He had told Kemel he had another wireless set. Vandam might be able to guess where they were going. At the end of the journey, surely, there was the spare radio, with a copy of *Rebecca* and a copy of the key to the code. Somehow she had to help Vandam follow them, so that he could rescue them and capture the key. If Vandam could guess the destination, Elene thought, then so could I. Where would Wolff have kept a spare radio? It was a long journey away. He might have hidden one somewhere before he reached Cairo. It might be somewhere in the desert, or somewhere between here and Assyut. Maybe—

Billy came in. "Hello," he said to Elene. "Did you bring me that book?"

She did not know what he was talking about. "Book?" She

stared at him, thinking that he was still very much a child, despite his grown-up ways. He wore gray flannel shorts and a white shirt, and there was no hair on the smooth skin of his bare forearm. He was carrying a school satchel and wearing a school tie.

"You forgot," he said, and looked betrayed. "You were going to lend me a detective story by Simenon."

"I did forget. I'm sorry."

"Will you bring it next time you come?"

"Of course."

Wolff had been staring at Billy all this time, like a miser looking into his treasure chest. Now he stood up. "Hello, Billy," he said with a smile. "I'm Captain Alexander."

Billy shook hands and said: "How do you do, sir."

"Your father asked me to tell you that he's very busy indeed."

"He always comes home for breakfast," Billy said.

"Not today. He's pretty busy coping with old Rommel, you know."

"Has he been in another fight?"

Wolff hesitated. "Matter of fact he has, but he's okay. He got a bump on the head."

Billy seemed more proud than worried, Elene observed.

Gaafar came in and spoke to Wolff. "You are sure, sir, that the major said you were to take the boy to school?"

He *is* suspicious, Elene thought.

"Of course," Wolff said. "Is something wrong?"

"No, but I am responsible for Billy, and we don't actually know you . . ."

"But you know Miss Fontana," Wolff said. "She was with me when Major Vandam spoke to me, weren't you, Elene?" Wolff stared at her and touched himself under the left arm, where the knife was sheathed.

"Yes," Elene said miserably.

Wolff said: "However, you're quite right to be cautious, Gaafar. Perhaps you should call GHQ and speak to the major yourself." He indicated the phone.

Elene thought: No, don't Gaafar, he'll kill you before you finish dialing.

Gaafar hesitated, then said: "I'm sure that won't be necessary, sir. As you say, we know Miss Fontana."

Elene thought: It's all my fault.

Gaafar went out.

Wolff spoke to Elene in rapid Arabic. "Keep the boy quiet for a minute." He continued writing.

Elene looked at Billy's satchel, and had the glimmer of an idea. "Show me your schoolbooks," she said.

Billy looked at her as if she were crazy.

"Come on," she said. The satchel was open, and an atlas stuck out. She reached for it. "What are you doing in geography?"

"The Norwegian fjords."

Elene saw Wolff finish writing and put the sheet of paper in an envelope. He licked the flap, sealed the envelope, and put it in his pocket.

"Let's find Norway," Elene said. She flipped the pages of the atlas.

Wolff picked up the telephone and dialed. He looked at Elene, then looked away, out of the window.

Elene found the map of Egypt.

Billy said: "But that's—"

Quickly, Elene touched his lips with her finger. He stopped speaking and frowned at her.

She thought: Please, little boy, be quiet and leave this to me.

She said: "Scandinavia, yes, but Norway is in Scandinavia, look." She unwrapped the handkerchief from around her hand. Billy stared at the cut. With her fingernail Elene opened the cut and made it bleed again. Billy turned white. He seemed about to speak, so Elene touched his lips and shook her head with a pleading look.

Elene was sure Wolff was going to Assyut. It was a likely guess, and Wolff had said he was afraid Vandam would correctly guess their destination. As she thought this, she heard Wolff say into the phone: "Hello? Give me the time of the train to Assyut."

I was right! she thought. She dipped her finger in the blood from her hand. With three strokes, she drew an arrow in blood on the map of Egypt, with the point of the arrow on the town of Assyut, three hundred miles south of Cairo. She closed the atlas. She used her handkerchief to smear blood on the cover of the book, then pushed the book behind her.

Wolff said: "Yes—and what time does it arrive?"

Elene said: "But why are there fjords in Norway and not in Egypt?"

Billy seemed dumbstruck. He was staring at her hand. She had to make him snap out of it before he gave her away. She said: "Listen, did you ever read an Agatha Christie story called *The Clue of the Bloodstained Atlas?*"

"No, there's no such—"

"It's very clever, the way the detective is able to figure everything out on the basis of *that one clue.*"

He frowned at her, but instead of the frown of the utterly amazed, it was the frown of one who is working something out.

Wolff put down the phone and stood up. "Let's go," he said. "You don't want to be late for school, Billy." He went to the door and opened it.

Billy picked up his satchel and went out. Elene stood up, dreading that Wolff would spot the atlas.

"Come on," he said impatiently.

She went through the door and he followed her. Billy was on the porch already. There was a little pile of letters on a kidney-shaped table in the hall. Elene saw Wolff drop his envelope on top of the pile.

They went out through the front door.

Wolff asked Elene: "Can you drive?"

"Yes," she answered, then cursed herself for thinking slowly—she should have said no.

"You two get in the front," Wolff instructed. He got in the back.

As she pulled away, Elene saw Wolff lean forward. He said: "See this?"

She looked down. He was showing the knife to Billy.

"Yes," Billy said in an unsteady voice.

Wolff said: "If you make trouble, I'll cut your head off."

Billy began to cry.

25

"Stand to attention!" Jakes barked in his sergeant major's voice.

Kemel stood to attention.

The interrogation room was bare but for a table. Vandam followed Jakes in, carrying a chair in one hand and a cup of tea in the other. He sat down.

Vandam said: "Where is Alex Wolff?"

"I don't know," said Kemel, relaxing slightly.

"Attention!" Jakes yelled. "Stand straight, boy!"

Kemel came to attention again.

Vandam sipped his tea. It was part of the act, a way of saying that he had all the time in the world and was not very concerned about anything, whereas the prisoner was in real trouble. It was the reverse of the truth.

He said: "Last night you received a call from the officer on surveillance at houseboat *Jihan*."

Jakes shouted: "Answer the major!"

"Yes," Kemel said.

"What did he say to you?"

"He said that Major Vandam had come to the towpath and sent him to summon assistance."

"Sir!" said Jakes. "To summon assistance, sir!"

"To summon assistance, sir."

Vandam said: "And what did you do?"

"I went personally to the towpath to investigate, sir."

"And then?"

"I was struck on the head and knocked unconscious. When I recovered I was bound hand and foot. It took me several

289

hours to free myself. Then I freed Major Vandam, whereupon he attacked me."

Jakes went close to Kemel. "You're a bloody lying little
bloody wog!" Kemel took a pace back. "Stand forward!"
Jakes shouted. "You're a lying little wog, what are you?" Kemel said nothing.

Vandam said: "Listen, Kemel. As things stand you're going to be shot for spying. If you tell us all you know, you
could get off with a prison sentence. Be sensible. Now, you
came to the towpath and knocked me out, didn't you?"

"No, sir."

Vandam sighed. Kemel had his story and he was sticking
to it. Even if he knew, or could guess, where Wolff had gone,
he would not reveal it while he was pretending innocence.

Vandam said: "What is your wife's involvement in all
this?"

Kemel said nothing, but he looked scared.

Vandam said: "If you won't answer my questions, I'll have
to ask her."

Kemel's lips were pressed together in a hard line.

Vandam stood up. "All right, Jakes," he said. "Bring in the
wife on suspicion of spying."

Kemel said: "Typical British justice."

Vandam looked at him. "Where is Wolff?"

"I don't know."

Vandam went out. He waited outside the door for Jakes.
When the captain came out, Vandam said: "He's a police-
man, he knows the techniques. He'll break, but not today."
And Vandam had to find Wolff today.

Jakes asked: "Do you want me to arrest the wife?"

"Not yet. Maybe later." And where was Elene?

They walked a few yards to another cell. Vandam said: "Is
everything ready here?"

"Yes."

"Okay." He opened the door and went in. This room was
not so bare. Sonja sat on a hard chair, wearing a coarse gray
prison dress. Beside her stood a woman army officer who
would have scared Vandam, had he been her prisoner. She
was short and stout, with a hard masculine face and short
gray hair. There was a cot in one corner of the cell and a
cold-water basin in the other.

As Vandam walked in the woman officer said: "Stand up!"

Vandam and Jakes sat down. Vandam said: "Sit down, Sonja."

The woman officer pushed Sonja into the chair.

Vandam studied Sonja for a minute. He had interrogated her once before, and she had been stronger than he. It would be different this time: Elene's safety was in the balance, and Vandam had few scruples left.

He said: "Where is Alex Wolff?"

"I don't know."

"Where is Elene Fontana?"

"I don't know."

"Wolff is a German spy, and you have been helping him."

"Ridiculous."

"You're in trouble."

She said nothing. Vandam watched her face. She was proud, confident, unafraid. Vandam wondered what, exactly, had happened on the houseboat this morning. Surely, Wolff had gone off without warning Sonja. Did she not feel betrayed?

"Wolff betrayed you," Vandam said. "Kemel, the policeman, warned Wolff of the danger; but Wolff left you sleeping and went off with another woman. Are you going to protect him after that?"

She said nothing.

"Wolff kept his radio on your boat. He sent messages to Rommel at midnight. You knew this, so you were an accessory to espionage. You're going to be shot for spying."

"All Cairo will riot! You wouldn't dare!"

"You think so? What do we care if Cairo riots now? The Germans are at the gates—let them put down the rebellion."

"You dare not touch me."

"Where has Wolff gone?"

"I don't know."

"Can you guess?"

"No."

"You're not being helpful, Sonja. It will make things worse for you."

"You can't touch me."

"I think I'd better prove to you that I can." Vandam nodded to the woman officer.

The woman held Sonja still while Jakes tied her to the chair. She struggled for a moment, but it was hopeless. She looked at Vandam, and for the first time there was a hint of fear in her eyes. She said: "What are you doing, you bastards?"

The woman officer took a large pair of scissors from her bag. She lifted a hank of Sonja's long, thick hair and cut it off.

"You can't do this!" Sonja shrieked.

Swiftly, the woman cut Sonja's hair. As the heavy locks fell away the woman dropped them in Sonja's lap. Sonja screamed, cursing Vandam and Jakes and the British in language which Vandam had never heard from a woman.

The woman officer took a smaller pair of scissors and cropped Sonja's hair close to the scalp.

Sonja's screams subsided into tears. When he could be heard Vandam said: "You see, we don't care much about legality and justice anymore, nor do we care about Egyptian public opinion. We've got our backs to the wall. We may all be killed soon. We're desperate."

The woman took soap and a shaving brush and lathered Sonja's head, then began to shave her scalp.

Vandam said: "Wolff was getting information from someone at GHQ. Who?"

"You're evil," said Sonja.

Finally the woman officer took a mirror from her bag and held it in front of Sonja's face. At first Sonja would not look in the glass, but after a moment she gave in. She gasped when she saw the reflection of her totally bald head. "No," she said. "It's not me." She burst into tears.

All the hatred was gone, now; she was completely demoralized. Vandam said softly: "Where was Wolff getting his information?"

"From Major Smith," Sonja replied.

Vandam heaved a sigh of relief. She had broken: thank God.

"First name?" he asked.

"Sandy Smith."

Vandam glanced at Jakes. That was the name of the major from MI6 who had disappeared—it was as they had feared.

"How did he get the information?"

"Sandy came to the houseboat in his lunch break to visit me. While we were in bed Alex went through his briefcase."

As simple as that, Vandam thought. Jesus, I feel tired. Smith was liaison man between the Secret Intelligence Service—also known as MI6—and GHQ, and in that role he had been privy to all strategic planning, for MI6 needed to know what the Army was doing so that it could tell its spies what information to look for. Smith had been going straight from the morning conferences at GHQ to the houseboat, with a briefcase full of secrets. Vandam had already learned that Smith had been telling people at GHQ he was lunching at the MI6 office, and telling his superiors at MI6 he was lunching at GHQ, so that nobody would know he was screwing a dancer. Vandam had previously assumed Wolff was bribing or blackmailing someone: it had never occurred to him that Wolff might be getting information from someone without that someone's knowledge.

Vandam said: "Where is Smith now?"

"He caught Alex going through his briefcase. Alex killed him."

"Where's the body?"

"In the river by the houseboat."

Vandam nodded to Jakes, and Jakes went out.

Vandam said to Sonja: "Tell me about Kemel."

She was in full flood now, eager to tell all she knew, her resistance quite crushed; she would do anything to make people be nice to her. "He came and told me you had asked him to have the houseboat watched. He said he would censor his surveillance reports if I would arrange a meeting between Alex and Sadat."

"Alex and whom?"

"Anwar el-Sadat. He's a captain in the Army."

"Why did he want to meet Wolff?"

"So the Free Officers could send a message to Rommel."

Vandam thought: there are elements to this that I never thought of. He said: "Where does Sadat live?"

"Kubri al-Qubbah."

"The address?"

"I don't know."

Vandam said to the woman officer: "Go and find out the exact address of Captain Anwar el-Sadat."

"Yes, sir." The woman's face broke into a smile that was astonishingly pretty. She went out.

Vandam said: "Wolff kept his radio on your houseboat."

"Yes."

"He used a code for his messages."

"Yes, he had an English novel which he used to use to make up the code words."

"*Rebecca.*"

"Yes."

"And he had a key to the code."

"A key?"

"A piece of paper telling him which pages of the book to use."

She nodded slowly. "Yes, I think he did."

"The radio, the book and the key have gone. Do you know where?"

"No," she said. She got scared. "Honestly, no, I don't know, I'm telling the truth—"

"It's all right, I believe you. Do you know where Wolff might have gone?"

"He has a house . . . Villa les Oliviers."

"Good idea. Any other suggestions?"

"Abdullah. He might have gone to Abdullah."

"Yes. Any more?"

"His cousins, in the desert."

"And where would they be found?"

"No one knows. They're nomads."

"Might Wolff know their movements?"

"I suppose he might."

Vandam sat looking at her for a little while longer. She was no actress: she could not have faked this. She was totally broken down, not only willing but eager to betray her friends and tell all her secrets. She was telling the truth.

"I'll see you again," Vandam said, and went out.

The woman officer handed him a slip of paper with Sadat's address on it, then went into the cell. Vandam hurried to the muster room. Jakes was waiting. "The Navy is lending us a couple of divers," Jakes said. "They'll be here in a few minutes."

"Good." Vandam lit a cigarette. "I want you to raid Abdullah's place. I'm going to arrest this Sadat fellow. Send a small team to the Villa les Oliviers, just in case—I don't suppose they'll find anything. Has everyone been briefed?"

Jakes nodded. "They know we're looking for a wireless transmitter, a copy of *Rebecca*, and a set of coding instructions."

Vandam looked around, and noticed for the first time that there were Egyptian policemen in the room. "Why have we got bloody Arabs on the team?" he said angrily.

"Protocol, sir," Jakes replied formally. "Colonel Bogge's idea."

Vandam bit back a retort. "After you've done Abdullah, meet me at the houseboat."

"Yes, sir."

Vandam stubbed his cigarette. "Let's go."

They went out into the morning sunshine. A dozen or more jeeps were lined up, their engines idling. Jakes gave instructions to the sergeants in the raiding parties, then nodded to Vandam. The men boarded the jeeps, and the teams pulled out.

Sadat lived in a suburb three miles out of Cairo in the direction of Heliopolis. His home was an ordinary family house in a small garden. Four jeeps roared up outside, and the soldiers immediately surrounded the house and began to search the garden. Vandam rapped on the front door. A dog began to bark loudly. Vandam knocked again. The door was opened.

"Captain Anwar el-Sadat?"

"Yes."

Sadat was a thin, serious young man of medium height. His curly brown hair was already receding. He wore his captain's uniform and fez, as if he was about to go out.

"You're under arrest," Vandam said, and pushed past him into the house. Another young man appeared in a doorway. "Who is he?" Vandam demanded.

"My brother, Tal'at," said Sadat.

Vandam looked at Sadat. The Arab was calm and dignified, but he was hiding some tension. He's afraid, Vandam thought; but he's not afraid of me, and he's not afraid of going to prison; he's afraid of something else.

What kind of deal had Kemel done with Wolff this morn-

ing? The rebels needed Wolff to help them get in touch with
Rommel. Were they hiding Wolff somewhere?

Vandam said: "Which is your room, Captain?"

Sadat pointed. Vandam went into the room. It was a
simple bedroom, with a mattress on the floor and a galabiya
hanging from a hook. Vandam pointed to two British soldiers
and an Egyptian policeman, and said: "All right, go ahead."
They began to search the room.

"What is the meaning of this?" Sadat said quietly.

"You know Alex Wolff," Vandam said.

"No."

"He also calls himself Achmed Rahmha, but he's a European."

"I've never heard of him."

Clearly Sadat was a fairly tough personality, not the kind
to break down and confess everything just because a few
burly soldiers started messing up his house. Vandam pointed
across the hall. "What's that room?"

"My study—"

Vandam went to the door.

Sadat said: "But the women of the family are in there, you
must let me warn them—"

"They know we're here. Open the door."

Vandam let Sadat enter the room first. There were no
women inside, but a back door was open as if someone had
just stepped out. That was okay: the garden was full of soldiers, no one would escape. Vandam saw an army pistol on
the desk holding down some sheets of paper covered with Arabic script. He went to the bookshelf and examined the
books: *Rebecca* was not there.

A shout came from another part of the house: "Major
Vandam!"

Vandam followed the sound into the kitchen. A sergeant
MP was standing beside the oven, with the house dog yap-
ping at his booted feet. The oven door stood open, and the
sergeant lifted out a suitcase-radio.

Vandam looked at Sadat, who had followed him into the
kitchen. The Arab's face was twisted with bitterness and disappointment. So this was the deal they had done: they
warned Wolff, and in exchange they got his radio. Did that

mean he had another? Or had Wolff arranged to come here, to Sadat's house, to broadcast?

Vandam spoke to his sergeant. "Well done. Take Captain Sadat to GHQ."

"I protest," Sadat said. "The law states that officers in the Egyptian Army may be detained only in the officers' mess and must be guarded by a fellow officer."

The senior Egyptian policeman was standing nearby. "This is correct," he said.

Once again Vandam cursed Bogge for bringing the Egyptians into this. "The law also states that spies are to be shot," he told Sadat. He turned to the sergeant. "Send out my driver. Finish searching the house. Then have Sadat charged with espionage."

He looked again at Sadat. The bitterness and disappointment had gone from his face, to be replaced by a calculating look. He's figuring out how to make the most of all this, Vandam thought; he's preparing to play martyr. He's very adaptable—he should be a politician.

Vandam left the house and went out to the jeep. A few moments later his driver came running out and jumped into the seat beside him. Vandam said: "To Zamalek."

"Yes, sir." The driver started the jeep and pulled away.

When Vandam reached the houseboat the divers had done their work and were standing on the towpath getting out of their gear. Two soldiers were hauling something extremely grisly out of the Nile. The divers had attached ropes to the body they had found on the bottom and then washed their hands of the affair.

Jakes came over to Vandam. "Look at this, sir." He handed him a waterlogged book. The board covers had been torn off. Vandam examined the book: it was *Rebecca*.

The radio went to Sadat; the code book went into the river. Vandam remembered the ashtray full of charred paper in the houseboat: had Wolff burned the key to the code?

Why had he gotten rid of the radio, the book and the key, when he had a vital message to send to Rommel? The conclusion was inescapable: he had *another* radio, book and key hidden away somewhere.

The soldiers got the body on to the bank and then stepped back as if they wanted nothing more to do with it. Vandam stood over it. The throat had been cut and the head was almost severed from the body. A briefcase was roped to the waist. Vandam bent down and gingerly opened the case. It was full of bottles of champagne.

Jakes said: "My God."

"Ugly, isn't it," Vandam said. "Throat cut, then dumped in the river with a case of champagne to weigh him down."

"Cool bastard."

"And damn quick with that knife." Vandam touched his cheek: the dressing had been taken off, now, and several days' growth of beard hid the wound. *But not Elene, not with the knife, please.* "I gather you haven't found him."

"I haven't found anything. I've had Abdullah brought in, just on general principles, but there was nothing at his house. And I called in at the Villa les Oliviers on the way back—same story."

"And at Captain Sadat's house." Suddenly Vandam felt utterly drained. It seemed that Wolff outwitted him at every turn. It occurred to him that he might simply not be smart enough to catch this sly, evasive spy. "Perhaps we've lost," he said. He rubbed his face. He had not slept in the last twenty-four hours. He wondered what he was doing here, standing over the hideous corpse of Major Sandy Smith. There was no more to be learned from it. "I think I'll go home and sleep for an hour," he said. Jakes looked surprised. Vandam added: "It might help me think more clearly. This afternoon we'll interrogate all the prisoners again."

"Very good, sir."

Vandam walked back to his vehicle. Driving across the bridge from Zamalek to the mainland, he recalled that Sonja had mentioned one other possibility: Wolff's nomad cousins. He looked at the boats on the wide, slow river. The current took them downstream and the wind blew them upstream—a coincidence of enormous importance to Egypt. The boatmen were still using the single triangular sail, a design which had been perfected . . . How long ago? Thousands of years, perhaps. So many things in this country were done the way they had been done for thousands of years. Vandam closed his eyes and saw Wolff, in a felucca, sailing upriver, manipulating the triangular sail with one hand while with the other he tapped out messages to Rommel on the transmitter. The car

stopped suddenly and Vandam opened his eyes, realizing he
had been daydreaming, or dozing. Why would Wolff go upriver? To find his nomad cousins. But who could tell where
they would be? Wolff might be able to find them, if they followed some annual pattern in their wanderings.

The jeep had stopped outside Vandam's house. He got out.
"I want you to wait for me," he told the driver. "You'd better
come in." He led the way into the house, then directed the
driver to the kitchen. "My servant, Gaafar, will give you
something to eat, so long as you don't treat him like a wog."

"Thank you very much, sir," said the driver.

There was a small stack of mail on the hall table. The top
envelope had no stamp, and was addressed to Vandam in a
vaguely familiar hand. It had "Urgent" scribbled in the top
left-hand corner. Vandam picked it up.

There was more he should do, he realized. Wolff could
well be heading south now. Roadblocks should be set up at
all major towns on the route. There should be someone at every stop on the railway line, looking for Wolff. And the river
itself . . . There had to be some way of checking the river, in
case Wolff really had gone by boat, as in the daydream. Vandam was finding it hard to concentrate. We could set up
riverblocks on the same principle as roadblocks, he thought;
why not? None of it would be any good if Wolff had simply
gone to ground in Cairo. Suppose he were hiding in the cem-
eteries? Many Muslims buried their dead in tiny houses, and
there were acres of such empty buildings in the city: Vandam
would have needed a thousand men to search them all. Perhaps I should do it anyway, he thought. But Wolff might
have gone north, toward Alexandria; or east or west into the
desert . . .

He went into the drawing room, looking for a letter
opener. Somehow the search had to be narrowed down. Vandam did not have thousands of men at his disposal—they
were all in the desert, fighting. He had to decide what was
the best bet. He remembered where all this had started: Assyut. Perhaps he should contact Captain Newman in Assyut.
That seemed to be where Wolff had come in from the desert,
so maybe he would go out that way. Maybe his cousins were
in that vicinity. Vandam looked indecisively at the telephone.

Where was that damned letter opener? He went to the door
and called: "Gaafar!" He came back into the room, and saw
Billy's school atlas on a chair. It looked mucky. The boy had
dropped it in a puddle, or something. He picked it up. It was
sticky. Vandam realized there was blood on it. He felt as if
he were in a nightmare. What was going on? No letter
opener, blood on the atlas, nomads at Assyut . . .

Gaafar came in. Vandam said: "What's this mess?"

Gaafar looked. "I'm sorry, sir, I don't know. They were
looking at it while Captain Alexander was here—"

"Who's they? Who's Captain Alexander?"

"The officer you sent to take Billy to school, sir. His name
was—"

"Stop." A terrible fear cleared Vandam's brain in an instant. "A British Army captain came here this morning and
took Billy away?"

"Yes, sir, he took him to school. He said you sent him—"

"Gaafar, *I sent nobody.*"

The servant's brown face turned gray.

Vandam said: "Didn't you check that he was genuine?"

"But, sir, Miss Fontana was with him, so it seemed all
right."

"Oh, my God." Vandam looked at the envelope in his
hand. Now he knew why the handwriting was familiar: it
was the same as that on the note that Wolff had sent to
Elene. He ripped open the envelope. Inside was a message in
the same hand:

Dear Major Vandam,

Billy is with me. Elene is taking care of him. He will
be quite all right as long as I am safe. I advise you to stay
where you are and do nothing. We do not make war on
children, and I have no wish to harm the boy. All the
same, the life of one child is as nothing beside the future
of my two nations, Egypt and Germany; so be assured
that if it suits my purpose I will kill Billy.

Yours truly,
Alex Wolff.

It was a letter from a madman: the polite salutations, the correct English, the semicolon, the attempt to justify the kidnapping of an innocent child . . . Now Vandam knew that, somewhere deep down inside, Wolff was insane.

And he had Billy.

Vandam handed the note to Gaafar, who put on his spectacles with a shaky hand. Wolff had taken Elene with him when he left the houseboat. It would not have been difficult to coerce her into helping him: all he had to do was threaten Billy, and she would have been helpless. But what was the point of the kidnap, really? And where had they gone? And why the blood?

Gaafar was weeping openly. Vandam said: "Who was hurt? Who was bleeding?"

"There was no violence," Gaafar said. "I think Miss Fontana had cut her hand."

And she had smeared blood on Billy's atlas and left it on the chair. It was a sign, a message of some kind. Vandam held the book in his hands and let it fall open. Immediately he saw the map of Egypt with a blotted red arrow roughly drawn. It pointed to Assyut.

Vandam picked up the phone and dialed GHQ. When the switchboard answered he hung up. He thought: If I report this, what will happen? Bogge will order a squad of light infantry to arrest Wolff at Assyut. There will be a fight. Wolff will know he has lost, know he is to be shot for spying, not to mention kidnapping and murder—and what will he do then?

He is insane, Vandam thought; he will kill my son.

He felt paralyzed by fear. Of course that was what Wolff wanted, that was his aim in taking Billy, to paralyze Vandam. That was how kidnapping worked.

If Vandam brought the Army in, there would be a shootout. Wolff might kill Billy out of mad spite. So there was only one option.

Vandam had to go after them alone.

"Get me two bottles of water," he told Gaafar. The servant went off. Vandam went into the hall and put on his motorcycle goggles, then found a scarf and wound it around his mouth and neck. Gaafar came from the kitchen with the bottles of water. Vandam left the house and went to his motorcycle. He put the bottles in the pannier and climbed on the

bike. He kicked it into life and revved the engine. The fuel
tank was full. Gaafar stood beside him, still weeping. Vandam touched the old man's shoulder. "I'll bring them back,"
he said. He rocked the bike off its stand, drove into the street
and turned south.

26

My God, the station was a shambles. I suppose everyone wants to get out of Cairo in case it gets bombed. No first-class seats on the trains to Palestine—not even standing room. The wives and children of the British are running like rats. Fortunately southbound trains are less in demand. The booking office still claimed there were no seats, but they always say that; a few piasters here and a few more there always gets a seat, or three. I was afraid I might lose Elene and the boy on the platform, among all the hundreds of peasants, barefoot in their dirty galabiyas, carrying boxes tied with string, chickens in crates, sitting on the platform eating their breakfast, a fat mother in black handing out boiled eggs and pita bread and caked rice to her husband and sons, cousins and daughters and in-laws; smart idea of mine, to hold the boy's hand—if I keep him close by, Elene will follow; smart idea, I have smart ideas, Christ I'm smart, smarter than Vandam, eat your heart out, Major Vandam, I've got your son. Somebody had a goat on a lead. Fancy taking a goat on a train ride. I never had to travel economy with the peasants and their goats. What a job, to clean the economy coach at the end of the journey, I wonder who does it, some poor fellah, a different breed, a different race, born slaves, thank God we got first-class seats, I travel first class through life, I hate dirt, God that station was dirty. Vendors on the platform: cigarettes, newspapers, a man with a huge basket of bread on his head. I like the women when they carry baskets on their heads, looking so graceful and proud, makes you want to do it to them there and then, standing up, I like women when they like to do it, when they lose their minds with pleasure, when they scream, Gesundheit! Look at Elene, sitting there beside the boy, so frightened, so beautiful, I want to do it with her again soon, forget Sonja, I'd like to do it with Elene right now, here on the train, in front of all these people, humiliate her, with Vandam's son watching, terrified, ha! Look at the mud-brick suburbs, houses leaning against one another for support, cows and sheep in the narrow dusty streets, I always wondered what they ate, those city sheep with their fat tails, where do they graze? No plumbing in those dark little houses beside the railway line. Women in the doorways peeling vegetables, sitting cross-legged on the dusty ground. Cats. So graceful, the cats. European cats are different, slower and much fatter; no wonder cats are sacred here, they are so beautiful, a kitten brings luck. The English like dogs. Disgusting animals, dogs: unclean, undignified, slobbering, fawning, sniffing. A cat is superior, and knows it. It is so important to be superior. One is a master or a slave. I hold my head up, like a cat; I walk about, ignoring the hoi polloi, intent on my own mysterious tasks, using people the way a cat uses its owner, giving no thanks and accepting no affection, taking what they offer as a right, not a gift. I'm a master, a German Nazi, an Egyptian Bedouin, a born ruler. How many hours to Assyut, eight, ten? Must move fast. Find Ishmael. He should be at the well, or not far away. Pick up the radio. Broadcast at midnight tonight. Complete British defense, what a coup, they'll give me medals. Germans in charge in Cairo. Oh, boy, we'll get the place into shape. What a combination, Germans and Egyptians, efficiency by day and sensuality by night, Teutonic technology and Bedouin savagery, Beethoven and hashish. If I can survive, make it to Assyut, contact Rommel; then Rommel can cross the last bridge, destroy the last line of defense, dash to Cairo, annihilate the British, what a victory that will be. If I can make it. What a triumph! What a triumph! What a triumph!

I *will* not be *sick*, I *will* not be *sick*, I *will* not be *sick*. The train says it for me, rattling on the tracks. I'm too old to throw up on trains now, I used to do that when I was eight. Dad took me to Alexandria, bought me candy and oranges and lemonade, I ate too much, don't think about it, it makes me ill to think about it, Dad said it wasn't my fault it was

his, but I always used to feel sick even if I didn't eat, today
Elene bought chocolate but I said no, thanks, I'm pretty
grown-up to say no to chocolate, kids never say no to chocolate, look, I can see the pyramids, one, two, and the little one
makes three, this must be Giza. Where are we going? He was
supposed to take me to school. Then he got out the knife. It's
curved. He'll cut off my head, where's Dad? I should be in
school, we have geography in the first period today, a test on
the Norwegian fjords, I learned it all last night, I needn't
have bothered, I've missed the test. They've already finished it
by now, Mr. Johnstone collecting up the papers, *You call
that a map, Higgins? Looks more like a drawing of your ear,
boy!* Everybody laughs. *Smythe can't spell Moskenstraumen.
Write it fifty times, lad.* Everyone is glad he isn't Smythe. Old
Johnstone opens the textbook. *Next, the Arctic tundra.* I wish
I was in school. I wish Elene would put her arm round me. I
wish the man would stop looking at me, staring at me like
that, so pleased with himself, I think he's crazy, where's Dad?
If I don't think about the knife, it will be just as if it wasn't
there. I mustn't think about the knife. If I concentrate on not
thinking about the knife, that's the same as thinking about
the knife. It's impossible to deliberately not think about something. How does anyone stop thinking of something? Accidentally. Accidental thoughts. All thoughts are accidental.
There, I stopped thinking about the knife for a second. If I
see a policeman, I'll rush up to him and yell Save me, save
me! I'll be so quick that *he* won't be able to stop me. I can
run like the wind, I'm quick. I might see an officer. I might
see a general. I'll shout, Good morning, General! He'll look
at me, surprised, and say Well, young fellow-me-lad, you're a
fine boy! Pardon me, sir, I'll say, I'm Major Vandam's son,
and this man is taking me away, and my father doesn't know,
I'm sorry to trouble you, but I need help. What? says the general. Look here, sir, you can't do this to the son of a British
officer! Not cricket, you know! Just clear off, d'you hear?
Who the devil d'you think you are? And you needn't flash
that little penknife at me, I've got a pistol! You're a brave
lad, Billy. I'm a brave lad. All day men get killed in the
desert. Bombs fall, Back Home. Ships in the Atlantic get
sunk by U-boats, men fall into the icy water and drown.
RAF chaps shot down over France. Everybody is brave. Chin

up! Damn this war. That's what they say: Damn this war.
Then they climb into the cockpit, hurry down the air-raid
shelter, attack the next dune, fire torpedoes at the U-boats,
write letters home. I used to think it was exciting. Now I
know better. It isn't exciting at all. It makes you feel sick.

Billy is so pale. He looks it. He's trying to be brave. He
shouldn't, he should act like a child, he should scream and
cry and throw a tantrum, Wolff couldn't cope with that; but
he won't, of course, for he has been taught to be tough, to
bite back the cry, to suppress the tears, to have self-control.
He knows how his father would be, what else does a boy do
but copy his father? Look at Egypt. A canal alongside the
railway line. A grove of date palms. A man crouching in a
field, his galabiya hitched up above his long white under-
shorts, doing something to the crops; an ass grazing, so much
healthier than the miserable specimens you see pulling carts
in the city; three women sitting beside the canal, washing
clothes, pounding them on stones to get them clean; a man
on horseback, galloping, must be the local effendi, only the
richest peasants have horses; in the distance, the lush green
countryside ends abruptly in a range of dusty tan hills. Egypt
is only thirty miles wide, really: the rest is desert. What am I
going to do? That chill, deep in my chest, every time I look
at Wolff. The way he stares at Billy. The gleam in his eye.
His restlessness: the way he looks out of the window, then
around the carriage, then at Billy, then at me, then at Billy
again, always with that gleam in his eye, the look of triumph.
I should comfort Billy. I wish I knew more about boys, I had
four sisters. What a poor stepmother I should be for Billy. I'd
like to touch him, put my arm around him, give him a quick
squeeze, or even a cuddle, but I'm not sure that's what he
wants, it might make him feel worse. Perhaps I could take his
mind off things by playing a game. What a ridiculous idea.
Perhaps not so ridiculous. Here is his school satchel. Here is
an exercise book. He looks at me curiously. What game?
Noughts and crosses. Four lines for the grid; my cross in the
center. The way he looks at me as he takes the pencil, I do
believe he's going along with this crazy idea in order to comfort me! His nought in the corner. Wolff snatches the book,
looks at it, shrugs, and gives it back. My cross, Billy's nought;

it will be a drawn game. I should let him win next time. I
can play this game without thinking, more's the pity. Wolff
has a spare radio at Assyut. Perhaps I should stay with him,
and try to prevent him using the radio. Some hope! I have to
get Billy away, then contact Vandam and tell him where I
am. I hope Vandam saw the atlas. Perhaps the servant saw it,
and called GHQ. Perhaps it will lie on the chair all day, unnoticed. Perhaps Vandam will not go home today. I have to
get Billy away from Wolff, away from that knife. Billy makes
a cross in the center of a new grid. I make a nought, then
scribble hastily: *We must escape—be ready*. Billy makes another cross, and: *OK*. My nought. Billy's cross and *When?*
My nought and *Next station*. Billy's third cross makes a line.
He scores through the line of crosses, then smiles up at me
jubilantly. He has won. The train slows down.

Vandam knew the train was still ahead of him. He had
stopped at the station at Giza, close to the pyramids, to ask
how long ago the train had passed through; then he had
stopped and asked the same question at three subsequent sta-
tions. Now, after traveling for an hour, he had no need to
stop and ask, for the road and the railway line ran parallel,
on either side of a canal, and he would see the train when he
caught up with it.

Each time he stopped he had taken a drink of water. With
his uniform cap, his goggles and the scarf around his mouth
and neck, he was protected from the worst of the dust; but
the sun was terribly hot and he was continually thirsty. Eventually he realized he was running a slight fever. He thought
he must have caught cold, last night, lying on the ground
beside the river for hours. His breath was hot in his throat,
and the muscles of his back ached.

He had to concentrate on the road. It was the only road
which ran the length of Egypt, from Cairo to Aswan, and
consequently much of it was paved; and in recent months the
Army had done some repair work: but he still had to watch
for bumps and potholes. Fortunately the road ran straight as
an arrow, so he could see, far ahead, the hazards of cattle,
wagons, camel trains and flocks of sheep. He drove very fast,
except through the villages and towns, where at any moment

people might wander out into the road: he would not kill a child to save a child, not even to save his own child.

So far he had passed only two cars—a ponderous Rolls-Royce and a battered Ford. The Rolls had been driven by a uniformed chauffeur, with an elderly English couple in the back seat; and the old Ford had contained at least a dozen Arabs. By now Vandam was fairly sure Wolff was traveling by train.

Suddenly he heard a distant hoot. Looking ahead and to his left he saw, at least a mile away, a rising plume of white smoke which was unmistakably that of a steam engine. Billy! he thought. Elene! He went faster.

Paradoxically, the engine smoke made him think of England, of gentle slopes, endless green fields, a square church tower peeping over the tops of a cluster of oak trees, and a railway line through the valley with a puffing engine disappearing into the distance. For a moment he was in that English valley, tasting the damp air of morning; then the vision passed, and he saw again the steel-blue African sky, the paddy fields, the palm trees and the far brown cliffs.

The train was coming into a town. Vandam did not know the names of the places anymore: his geography was not that good, and he had rather lost track of the distance he had traveled. It was a small town. It would have three or four brick buildings and a market.

The train was going to get there before him. He had made his plans, he knew what he was going to do: but he needed time, it was impossible for him to rush into the station and jump on the train without making preparations. He reached the town and slowed right down. The street was blocked by a small flock of sheep. From a doorway an old man smoking a hookah watched Vandam: a European on a motorcycle would be a rare, but not unknown, sight. An ass tied to a tree snarled at the bike. A water buffalo drinking from a bucket did not even look up. Two filthy children in rags ran alongside, holding imaginary handlebars and saying "Brrrm, brrrm," in imitation. Vandam saw the station. From the square he could not see the platform, for that was obscured by a long, low station building; but he could observe the exit and see anyone who came out. He would wait outside until the train left, just in case Wolff got off; then he would go ahead, and reach the next stop in plenty of time. He brought the motorcycle to a halt and killed the engine.

The train rolled slowly over a level crossing. Elene saw the patient faces of the people behind the gate, waiting for the train to pass so that they could cross the line: a fat man on a donkey, a very small boy leading a camel, a horse-drawn cab, a group of silent old women. The camel couched, the boy began to beat it about the face with a stick and then the scene slid sideways out of view. In a moment the train would be in the station. Elene's courage deserted her. Not this time, she thought. I haven't had time to think of a plan. The next station, let me leave it until the next station. But she had told Billy they would try to get away at this station. If she did nothing he would not trust her any longer. It had to be this time.

She tried to devise a plan. What was her priority? To get Billy away from Wolff. That was the only thing that counted. Give Billy a chance to run, then try to prevent Wolff from giving chase. She had a sudden, vivid memory of a childhood fight in a filthy slum street in Alexandria: a big boy, a bully, hitting her, and another boy intervening and struggling with the bully, the smaller boy shouting to her "Run, run!" while she stood watching the fight, horrified but fascinated. She could not remember how it had ended.

She looked around. Think quickly! They were in an open carriage, with fifteen or twenty rows of seats. She and Billy sat side by side, facing forward. Wolff was opposite them. Beside him was an empty seat. Behind him was the exit door to the platform. The other passengers were a mixture of Europeans and wealthy Egyptians, all of them in Western clothing. Everyone was hot, weary and enervated. Several people were asleep. The trainmaster was serving tea in glasses to a group of Egyptian Army officers at the far end of the carriage.

Through the window she saw a small mosque, then a French courthouse, then the station. A few trees grew in the dusty soil beside the concrete platform. An old man sat cross-legged beneath a tree, smoking a cigarette. Six boyish-looking Arab soldiers were crowded on to one small bench. A pregnant woman carried a baby in her arms. The train stopped.

Not yet, Elene thought; not yet. The time to move would be when the train was about to pull out again—that would give Wolff less time to catch them. She sat feverishly still. There was a clock on the platform with roman numerals. It had stopped at five to five. A man came to the window offering fruit drinks, and Wolff waved him away.

A priest in Coptic robes boarded the train and took the seat next to Wolff, saying politely: *"Vous permettez, m'sieur?"*

Wolff smiled charmingly and replied: *"Je vous en prie."*

Elene murmured to Billy: "When the whistle blows, run for the door and get off the train." Her heart beat faster: now she was committed.

Billy said nothing. Wolff said: "What was that?" Elene looked away. The whistle blew.

Billy looked at Elene, hesitating.

Wolff frowned.

Elene threw herself at Wolff, reaching for his face with her hands. She was suddenly possessed by rage and hatred toward him for the humiliation, anxiety and pain he had inflicted on her. He put up his arms protectively, but they did not stop her rush. Her strength astonished her. She raked his face with her fingernails, and saw blood spurt.

The priest gave a shout of surprise.

Over the back of Wolff's seat she saw Billy run to the door and struggle to open it.

She collapsed on Wolff, banging her face against his forehead. She lifted herself again and tried to scratch his eyes.

At last he found his voice, and roared with anger. He pushed himself out of his seat, driving Elene backward. She grabbed at him and caught hold of his shirt front with both hands. Then he hit her. His hand came up from below his waist, bunched into a fist, then struck the side of her jaw. She had not known a punch could hurt so much. For an instant she could not see. She lost her grip on Wolff's shirt, and fell back into her seat. Her vision returned and she saw him heading for the door. She stood up.

Billy had got the door open. She saw him fling it wide and

jump on to the platform. Wolff leaped after him. Elene ran to the door.

Billy was racing along the platform, running like the wind. Wolff was charging after him. The few Egyptians standing around were looking on, mildly astonished, and doing nothing. Elene stepped down from the train and ran after Wolff. The train shuddered, about to move. Wolff put on a burst of speed. Elene yelled: "Run, Billy, run!" Billy looked over his shoulder. He was almost at the exit now. A ticket collector in a raincoat stood there, looking on openmouthed. Elene thought: They won't let him out, he has no ticket. It did not matter, she realized, for the train was now inching forward, and Wolff had to get back on it. Wolff looked at the train, but did not slow his pace. Elene saw that Wolff was not going to catch Billy, and she thought: We did it! Then Billy fell.

He had slipped on something, a patch of sand or a leaf. He lost his balance completely, and went flying through the air, carried by the momentum of his running, to hit the ground hard. Wolff was on him in a flash, bending to lift him. Elene caught up with them and jumped on Wolff's back. Wolff stumbled, losing his grip on Billy. Elene clung to Wolff. The train was moving slowly but steadily. Wolff grabbed Elene's arms, broke her grip, and shook his wide shoulders, throwing her to the ground.

For a moment she lay stunned. Looking up, she saw that Wolff had thrown Billy across his shoulder. The boy was yelling and hammering on Wolff's back, without effect. Wolff ran alongside the moving train for a few paces, then jumped in through an open door. Elene wanted to stay where she was, never to see Wolff again; but she could not leave Billy. She struggled to her feet.

She ran, stumbling, alongside the train. Someone reached out a hand to her. She took it, and jumped. She was aboard.

She had failed miserably. She was back where she started. She felt crushed.

She followed Wolff through the carriages back to their seats. She did not look at the faces of the people she passed. She saw Wolff give Billy one sharp smack on the bottom and dump him into his seat. The boy was crying silently.

Wolff turned to Elene. "You're a silly, crazy girl," he said loudly, for the benefit of the other passengers. He grabbed

her arm and pulled her closer to him. He slapped her face
with the palm of his hand, then with the back, then with the
palm, again and again. It hurt, but Elene had no energy to
resist. At last the priest stood up, touched Wolff's shoulder,
and said something.

Wolff let her go and sat down. She looked around. They
were all staring at her. None of them would help her, for she
was not just an Egyptian, she was an Egyptian woman, and
women, like camels, had to be beaten from time to time. As
she met the eyes of the other passengers they looked away,
embarrassed, and turned to their newspapers, their books and
the view from the windows. No one spoke to her.

She fell into her seat. Useless, impotent rage boiled within
her. Almost, they had almost escaped.

She put her arm around the child and pulled him close.
She began to stroke his hair. After a while he fell asleep.

27

Vandam heard the train puff, pull and puff again. It gathered speed and moved out of the station. Vandam took another drink of water. The bottle was empty. He put it back in his pannier. He drew on his cigarette and threw away the butt. No one but a few peasants had gotten off the train. Vandam kicked his motorcycle into life and drove away.

In a few moments he was out of the little town and back on the straight, narrow road beside the canal. Soon he had left the train behind. It was noon: the sunshine was so hot it seemed tangible. Vandam imagined that if he stuck out his arm the heat would drag on it like a viscous liquid. The road ahead stretched into a shimmering infinity. Vandam thought: If I were to drive straight into the canal, how cool and refreshing it would be!

Somewhere along the road he had made a decision. He had set out from Cairo with no thought in his mind but to rescue Billy; but at some point he had realized that that was not his only duty. There was still the war.

Vandam was almost certain that Wolff had been too busy at midnight last night to use his radio. This morning he had given away the radio, thrown the book in the river and burned the key to the code. It was likely that he had another radio, another copy of *Rebecca* and another key to the code; and that the place they were all hidden was Assyut. If Vandam's deception plan were to be implemented, he had to have the radio and the key—and that meant he had to let Wolff get to Assyut and retrieve his spare set.

It ought to have been an agonizing decision, but somehow Vandam had taken it with equanimity. He had to rescue Billy and Elene, yes; but *after* Wolff had picked up his spare radio. It would be tough on the boy, savagely tough, but the worst of it—the kidnapping—was already in the past and irreversible, and living under Nazi rule, with his father in a concentration camp, would also be savagely tough.

Having made the decision, and hardened his heart, Vandam needed to be certain that Wolff really was on that train. And in figuring out how to check, he had thought of a way to make things a little easier for Billy and Elene at the same time.

When he reached the next town he reckoned he was at least fifteen minutes ahead of the train. It was the same kind of place as the last town: same animals, same dusty streets, same slow-moving people, same handful of brick buildings. The police station was in a central square, opposite the railway station, flanked by a large mosque and a small church. Vandam pulled up outside and gave a series of peremptory blasts on the horn of his bike.

Two Arab policemen came out of the building: a gray-haired man in a white uniform with a pistol at his belt, and a boy of eighteen or twenty years who was unarmed. The older man was buttoning his shirt. Vandam got off the bike and bawled: "Attention!" Both men stood straight and saluted. Vandam returned the salute, then shook the older man's hand. "I'm chasing a dangerous criminal, and I need your help," he said dramatically. The man's eyes glittered. "Let's go inside."

Vandam led the way. He felt he needed to keep the initiative firmly in his own hands. He was by no means sure of his own status here, and if the policemen were to choose to be uncooperative there would be little he could do about it. He entered the building. Through a doorway he saw a table with a telephone. He went into that room, and the policemen followed him.

Vandam said to the older man: "Call British headquarters in Cairo." He gave him the number, and the man picked up the phone. Vandam turned to the younger policeman. "Did you see the motorcycle?"

"Yes, yes." He nodded violently.

"Could you ride it?"

The boy was thrilled by the idea. "I ride it very well."

"Go out and try it."

The boy looked doubtfully at his superior, who was shouting into the telephone.

"Go on," Vandam said.

The boy went out.

The older man held the phone out to Vandam. "This is GHQ."

Vandam spoke into the phone. "Connect me with Captain Jakes, fast." He waited.

Jakes' voice came on the line after a minute or two. "Hello, yes?"

"This is Vandam. I'm in the south, following a hunch."

"There's a right panic on here since the brass heard what happened last night—the brigadier's having kittens and Bogge is running around like a fart in a colander—where in buggeration are you, sir?"

"Never mind where exactly, I won't be here much longer and I have to work alone at the moment. In order to assure the maximal support of the indigenous constabulary—" He spoke like this so that the policeman would not be able to understand—"I want you to do your Dutch uncle act. Ready?"

"Yes, sir."

Vandam gave the phone to the gray-haired policeman and stood back. He could guess what Jakes was saying. The policeman unconsciously stood straighter and squared his shoulders as Jakes instructed him, in no uncertain terms, to do everything Vandam wanted and do it fast. "Yes, sir!" the policeman said, several times. Finally he said: "Please be assured, sir and gentleman, that we will do all in our power—" He stopped abruptly. Vandam guessed that Jakes had hung up. The policeman glanced at Vandam then said "Good-bye" to the empty wire.

Vandam went to the window and looked out. The young policeman was driving around and around the square on the motorcycle, hooting the horn and overrevving the engine. A small crowd had gathered to watch him, and a bunch of children were running behind the bike. The boy was grinning from ear to ear. He'll do, Vandam thought.

"Listen," he said. "I'm going to get on the Assyut train when it stops here in a few minutes. I'll get off at the next station. I want your boy to drive my bike to the next station and meet me there. Do you understand?"

"Yes, sir," said the man. "The train will stop here, then?"

"Doesn't it usually?"

"The Assyut train does not stop here usually."

"Then go to the station and tell them to stop it!"

"Yes, sir!" He went out at a run.

Vandam watched him cross the square. He could not hear the train yet. He had time for one more phone call. He picked up the receiver, waited for the operator, then asked for the army base in Assyut. It would be a miracle if the phone system worked properly twice in a row. It did. Assyut answered, and Vandam asked for Captain Newman. There was a long wait while they found him. At last he came on the line.

"This is Vandam. I think I'm on the trail of your knife man."

"Jolly good show, sir!" said Newman. "Anything I can do?"

"Well, now, listen. We have to go very softly. For all sorts of reasons which I'll explain to you later, I'm working entirely on my own, and to go after Wolff with a big squad of armed men would be worse than useless."

"Understood. What do you need from me?"

"I'll be arriving in Assyut in a couple of hours. I need a taxi, a large galabiya and a small boy. Will you meet me?"

"Of course, no problem. Are you coming by road?"

"I'll meet you at the city limits, how's that?"

"Fine." Vandam heard a distant chuff-chuff-chuff. "I have to go."

"I'll be waiting for you."

Vandam hung up. He put a five-pound note on the table beside the telephone: a little baksheesh never hurt. He went out into the square. Away to the north he could see the approaching smoke of the train. The younger policeman drove up to him on the bike. Vandam said: "I'm getting on the train. You drive the motorcycle to the next station and meet me there. Okay?"

"Okay, okay!" He was delighted.

Vandam took out a pound note and tore it in half. The

young policeman's eyes widened. Vandam gave him half the note. "You get the other half when you meet me."

"Okay!"

The train was almost in the station. Vandam ran across the square. The older policeman met him. "The stationmaster is stopping the train."

Vandam shook his hand. "Thank you. What's your name?"

"Sergeant Nesbah."

"I'll tell them about you in Cairo. Goodbye." Vandam hurried into the station. He ran south along the platform, away from the train, so that he could board it at the front end without any of the passengers seeing him through the windows.

The train came in, billowing smoke. The stationmaster came along the platform to where Vandam was standing. When the train stopped the stationmaster spoke to the engine driver and the footplateman. Vandam gave all three of them baksheesh and boarded the train.

He found himself in an economy carriage. Wolff would surely travel first class. He began to walk along the train, picking his way over the people sitting on the floor with their boxes and crates and animals. He noticed that it was mainly women and children on the floor: the slatted wooden seats were occupied by the men with their bottles of beer and their cigarettes. The carriages were unbearably hot and smelly. Some of the women were cooking on makeshift stoves: surely that was dangerous! Vandam almost trod on a tiny baby crawling on the filthy floor. He had a feeling that if he had not avoided the child in the nick of time they would have lynched him.

He passed through three economy carriages, then he was at the door to a first-class coach. He found a guard just outside, sitting on a little wooden stool, drinking tea from a glass. The guard stood up. "Some tea, General?"

"No, thank you." Vandam had to shout to make himself heard over the noise of the wheels beneath them. "I have to check the papers of all first-class passengers."

"All in order, all very good," said the guard, trying to be helpful.

"How many first-class carriages are there?"

"All in order—"

Vandam bent to shout in the man's ear. "How many first-class coaches?"

The guard held up two fingers.

Vandam nodded and unbent. He looked at the door. Suddenly he was not sure that he had the nerve to go through with this. He thought that Wolff had never got a good look at him—they had fought in the dark, in the alley—but he could not be absolutely sure. The gash on his cheek might have given him away, but it was almost completely covered now by his beard; still he should try to keep that side of his face away from Wolff. Billy was the real problem. Vandam had to warn his son, somehow, to keep quiet and pretend not to recognize his father. There was no way to plan it, that was the trouble. He just had to go in there and think on his feet.

He took a deep breath and opened the door.

Stepping through, he glanced quickly and nervously at the first few seats and did not recognize anyone. He turned his back to the carriage as he closed the door, then turned around again. His gaze swept the rows of seats quickly: no Billy.

He spoke to the passengers nearest him. "Your papers, please, gentlemen."

"What's this, Major?" said an Egyptian Army officer, a colonel.

"Routine check, sir," Vandam replied.

He moved slowly along the aisle, checking people's papers. By the time he was halfway down the carriage he had studied the passengers well enough to be sure that Wolff, Elene and Billy were not here. He felt he had to finish the pantomime of checking papers before going on to the next coach. He began to wonder whether his guesswork might have gone wrong. Perhaps they weren't on the train at all; perhaps they weren't even heading for Assyut; perhaps the atlas clue had been a trick . . .

He reached the end of the carriage and passed through the door into the space between the coaches. If Wolff is on the train, I'll see him now, he thought. If Billy is here—if Billy is here—

He opened the door.

He saw Billy immediately. He felt a pang of distress like a wound. The boy was asleep in his seat, his feet only just reaching the floor, his body slumped sideways, his hair falling over his forehead. His mouth was open, and his jaws were moving slightly: Vandam knew, for he had seen this before, that Billy was grinding his teeth in his sleep.

The woman who had her arm around him, and on whose bosom his head rested, was Elene. Vandam had a disorienting sense of déjà vu: it reminded him of the night he had come upon Elene kissing Billy good night . . .

Elene looked up.

She caught Vandam's eye. He saw her face begin to change expression: her eyes widening, her mouth coming open for a cry of surprise; and, because he was prepared for something like this, he was very quick to raise a finger to his lips in a hushing sign. She understood immediately, and dropped her eyes; but Wolff had caught her look, and he was turning his head to find out what she had seen.

They were on Vandam's left, and it was his left cheek which had been cut by Wolff's knife. Vandam turned around so that his back was to the carriage, then he spoke to the people on the side of the aisle opposite Wolff's. "Your papers, please."

He had not reckoned on Billy being asleep.

He had been ready to give the boy a quick sign, as he had done with Elene, and he had hoped that Billy was alert enough to mask his surprise rapidly, as Elene had done. But this was a different situation. If Billy were to wake up and see his father standing there, he would probably give the game away before he had time to collect his thoughts.

Vandam turned to Wolff and said: "Papers, please."

It was the first time he had seen his enemy face to face. Wolff was a handsome bastard. His big face had strong features: a wide forehead, a hooked nose, even white teeth, a broad jaw. Only around the eyes and the corners of the mouth was there a hint of weakness, of self-indulgence, of depravity. He handed over his papers then looked out of the window, bored. The papers identified him as Alex Wolff, of Villa les Oliviers, Garden City. The man had remarkable nerve.

Vandam said: "Where are you going, sir?"

"Assyut."

"On business?"

"To visit relations." The voice was strong and deep, and Vandam would not have noticed the accent if he had not been listening for it.

Vandam said: "Are you people together?"

"That's my son and his nanny," Wolff said.

Vandam took Elene's papers and glanced at them. He wanted to take Wolff by the throat and shake him until his bones rattled. *That's my son and his nanny.* You bastard.

He gave Elene her papers. "No need to wake the child," he said. He looked at the priest sitting next to Wolff, and took the proffered wallet.

Wolff said: "What's this about, Major?"

Vandam looked at him again, and noticed that he had a fresh scratch on his chin, a long one: perhaps Elene had put up some resistance. "Security, sir," Vandam replied.

The priest said: "I'm going to Assyut, too."

"I see," said Vandam. "To the convent?"

"Indeed. You've heard of it, then."

"The place where the Holy Family stayed after their sojourn in the desert."

"Quite. Have you been there?"

"Not yet—perhaps I'll make it this time."

"I hope so," said the priest.

Vandam handed back the papers. "Thank you." He backed away, along the aisle to the next row of seats, and continued to examine papers. When he looked up he met Wolff's eyes. Wolff was watching him expressionlessly. Vandam wondered whether he had done anything suspicious. Next time he looked up, Wolff was staring out of the window again.

What was Elene thinking? She must be wondering what I'm up to, Vandam thought. Perhaps she can guess my intentions. It must be hard for her all the same, to sit still and see me walk by without a word. At least now she knows she's not alone.

What was Wolff thinking? Perhaps he was impatient, or gloating, or frightened, or eager . . . No, he was none of those, Vandam realized; he was bored.

He reached the end of the carriage and examined the last of the papers. He was handing them back, about to retrace his steps along the aisle, when he heard a cry that pierced his heart:

"THAT'S MY DAD!"

He looked up. Billy was running along the aisle toward him, stumbling, swaying from side to side, bumping against the seats, his arms outstretched.

Oh, God.

Beyond Billy, Vandam could see Wolff and Elene standing up, watching; Wolff with intensity, Elene with fear. Vandam opened the door behind him, pretending to take no notice of Billy, and backed through it. Billy came flying through. Vandam slammed the door. He took Billy in his arms.

"It's all right," Vandam said. "It's all right."

Wolff would be coming to investigate.

"They took me away!" Billy said. "I missed geography and I was really really scared!"

"It's all right now." Vandam felt he could not leave Billy now; he would have to keep the boy and kill Wolff, he would have to abandon his deception plan and the radio and the key to the code . . . No, it had to be done, it *had* to be done . . . He fought down his instincts. "Listen," he said. "I'm here, and I'm watching over you, but I have to catch that man, and I don't want him to know who I am. He's the German spy I'm after, do you understand?"

"Yes, yes . . ."

"Listen. Can you pretend you made a mistake? Can you pretend I'm not your father? Can you go back to him?"

Billy stared, openmouthed. He said nothing but his whole expression said *No, no, no!*

Vandam said: "This is a real-life tec story, Billy, and we're in it, you and I. You have to go back to that man, and pretend you made a mistake; but remember, I'll be nearby, and together we'll catch the spy. Is that okay? Is it okay?"

Billy said nothing.

The door opened and Wolff came through.

"What's all this?" Wolff said.

Vandam made his face bland and forced a smile. "He seems to have woken up from a dream and mistaken me for his father. We're the same build, you and I . . . You did say you were his father, didn't you?"

Wolff looked at Billy. "What nonsense!" he said brusquely. "Come back to your seat at once."

Billy stood still.

Vandam put a hand on Billy's shoulder. "Come on, young man," he said. "Let's go and win the war."

The old catchphrase did the trick. Billy gave a brave grin. "I'm sorry, sir," he said. "I must have been dreaming."

Vandam felt as though his heart would break.

Billy turned away and went back inside the coach. Wolff went after him, and Vandam followed. As they walked along the aisle the train slowed down. Vandam realized they were already approaching the next station, where his motorcycle would be waiting. Billy reached his seat and sat down. Elene was staring at Vandam uncomprehendingly. Billy touched her arm and said: "It's okay, I made a mistake, I must have been dreaming." She looked at Billy, then at Vandam, and a strange light came into her eyes: she seemed on the point of tears.

Vandam did not want to walk past them. He wanted to sit down, to talk, to do anything to prolong the time he spent with them. Outside the train windows, another dusty little town appeared. Vandam yielded to temptation and paused at the carriage door. "Have a good trip," he said to Billy.

"Thank you, sir."

Vandam went out.

The train pulled into the station and stopped. Vandam got off and walked forward along the platform a little way. He stood in the shade of an awning and waited. Nobody else got off, but two or three people boarded the economy coaches. There was a whistle, and the train began to move. Vandam's eye was fixed on the window which he knew to be next to Billy's seat. As the window passed him, he saw Billy's face. Billy raised his hand in a little wave. Vandam waved back, and the face was gone.

Vandam realized he was trembling all over.

He watched the train recede into the hazy distance. When it was almost out of sight he left the station. There outside was his motorcycle, with the young policeman from the last town sitting astride it explaining its mysteries to a small crowd of admirers. Vandam gave him the other half of the pound note. The young man saluted.

Vandam climbed on the motorcycle and started it. He did not know how the policeman was going to get home, and he did not care. He drove out of town on the road south. The sun had passed its zenith, but the heat was still terrific.

Soon Vandam passed the train. He would reach Assyut thirty or forty minutes ahead of it, he calculated. Captain Newman would be there to meet him. Vandam knew in outline what he was going to do thereafter, but the details would have to be improvised as he went along.

He pulled ahead of the train which carried Billy and Elene, the only people he loved. He explained to himself again that he had done the right thing, the best thing for everyone, the best thing for Billy; but in the back of his mind a voice said: Cruel, cruel, cruel.

28

The train entered the station and stopped. Elene saw a sign which said, in Arabic and English, Assyut. She realized with a shock that they had arrived.

It had been an enormous relief to see Vandam's kind, worried face on the train. For a while she had been euphoric: surely, she had felt, it was all over. She had watched his pantomime with the papers, expecting him at any moment to pull a gun, reveal his identity, or attack Wolff. Gradually she had realized that it would not be that simple. She had been astonished, and rather horrified, at the icy nerve with which Vandam had sent his own son back to Wolff; and the courage of Billy himself had seemed incredible. Her spirits had plunged farther when she saw Vandam on the station platform, waving as the train pulled out. What game was he playing?

Of course, the *Rebecca* code was still on his mind. He must have some scheme to rescue her and Billy and also get the key to the code. She wished she knew how. Fortunately Billy did not seem to be troubled by such thoughts: his father had the situation under control, and apparently the boy did not even entertain the idea that his father's schemes could fail. He had perked up, taking an interest in the countryside through which the train was passing, and had even asked Wolff where he got his knife. Elene wished she had as much faith in William Vandam.

Wolff was also in good spirits. The incident with Billy had scared him, and he had looked at Vandam with hostility and anxiety; but he seemed reassured when Vandam got off the train. After that his mood had oscillated between boredom and nervous excitement, and now, arriving in Assyut, the excitement became dominant. Some kind of change had occurred in Wolff in the last twenty-four hours, she thought. When she first met him he had been a very poised, suave man. His face had rarely shown any spontaneous emotion other than a faint arrogance, his features had been generally rather still, his movements had been almost languid. Now all that had gone. He fidgeted, he looked about him restlessly, and every few seconds the corner of his mouth twitched almost imperceptibly, as if he were about to grin, or perhaps to grimace, at his thoughts. The poise which had once seemed to be part of his deepest nature now turned out to be a cracked façade. She guessed this was because his fight with Vandam had become vicious. What had begun as a deadly game had turned into a deadly battle. It was curious that Wolff, the ruthless one, was getting desperate while Vandam just got cooler.

Elene thought: Just so long as he doesn't get too damn cool.

Wolff stood up and took his case from the luggage rack. Elene and Billy followed him from the train and on to the platform. This town was bigger and busier than the others they had passed through, and the station was crowded. As they stepped down from the train they were jostled by people trying to get on. Wolff, a head higher than most of the people, looked around for the exit, spotted it, and began to carve a path through the throng. Suddenly a dirty boy in bare feet and green striped pajamas snatched Wolff's case, shouting: "I get taxi! I get taxi!" Wolff would not let go of the case, but neither would the boy. Wolff gave a good-humored shrug, touched with embarrassment, and let the boy pull him to the gate.

They showed their tickets and went out into the square. It was late afternoon, but here in the south the sun was still very hot. The square was lined with quite tall buildings, one of them called the Grand Hotel. Outside the station was a row of horse-drawn cabs. Elene looked around, half expecting a detachment of soldiery ready to arrest Wolff. There was no sign of Vandam. Wolff told the Arab boy: "Motor taxi, I want a motor taxi." There was one such car, an old Morris parked a few yards behind the horse cabs. The boy led them to it.

"Get in the front," Wolff told Elene. He gave the boy a coin and got into the back of the car with Billy. The driver wore dark glasses and an Arab headdress to keep the sun off. "Go south, toward the convent," Wolff told the driver in Arabic.

"Okay," the driver said.

Elene's heart missed a beat. She knew that voice. She stared at the driver. It was Vandam.

Vandam drove away from the station, thinking: So far, so good—except for the Arabic. It had not occurred to him that Wolff would speak to a taxi-driver in Arabic. Vandam's knowledge of the language was rudimentary, but he was able to give—and therefore to understand—directions. He could reply in monosyllables, or grunts, or even in English, for those Arabs who spoke a little English were always keen to use it, even when addressed by a European in Arabic. He would be all right as long as Wolff did not want to discuss the weather and the crops.

Captain Newman had come through with everything Vandam had asked for, including discretion. He had even loaned Vandam his revolver, a sixshot Enfield .380 which was now in the pocket of Vandam's trousers beneath his borrowed galabiya. While waiting for the train Vandam had studied Newman's map of Assyut and the surrounding area, so he had some idea of how to find the southbound road out of the city. He drove through the souk, honking his horn more or less continually in the Egyptian fashion, steering dangerously close to the great wooden wheels of the carts, nudging sheep out of the way with his fenders. From the buildings on either side shops, cafés and workshops spilled out into the street. The unpaved road was surfaced with dust, rubbish and dung. Glancing into his rear-view mirror Vandam saw that four or five children were riding his back bumper.

Wolff said something, and this time Vandam did not understand. He pretended not to have heard. Wolff repeated it. Vandam caught the word for petrol. Wolff was pointing to a garage. Vandam tapped the gauge on the dashboard, which showed a full tank. "Kifaya," he said. "Enough." Wolff seemed to accept that.

Pretending to adjust his mirror, Vandam stole a glance at

Billy, wondering if he had recognized his father. Billy was staring at the back of Vandam's head with an expression of delight. Vandam thought: Don't give the game away, for God's sake!

They left the town behind and headed south on a straight desert road. On their left were the irrigated fields and groves of trees; on their right, the wall of granite cliffs, colored beige by a layer of dusty sand. The atmosphere in the car was peculiar. Vandam could sense Elene's tension, Billy's euphoria and Wolff's impatience. He himself was very edgy. How much of all that was getting through to Wolff? The spy needed only to take one good look at the taxi driver to realize he was the man who had inspected papers on the train. Vandam hoped Wolff was preoccupied with thoughts of his radio.

Wolff said: *"Ruh alyaminak."*

Vandam knew this meant "Turn right." Up ahead he saw a turn-off which seemed to lead straight to the cliff. He slowed the car and took the turn, then saw that he was headed for a pass through the hills.

Vandam was surprised. Farther along the southbound road there were some villages and the famous convent, according to Newman's map; but beyond these hills there was nothing but the Western Desert. If Wolff had buried the radio in the sand he would never find it again. Surely he knew better? Vandam hoped so, for if Wolff's plans were to collapse, so would his.

The road began to climb, and the old car struggled to take the gradient. Vandam changed down once, then again. The car made the summit in second gear. Vandam looked out across an apparently endless desert. He wished he had a jeep. He wondered how far Wolff had to go. They had better get back to Assyut before nightfall. He could not ask Wolff questions for fear of revealing his ignorance of Arabic.

The road became a track. Vandam drove across the desert, going as fast as he dared, waiting for instructions from Wolff. Directly ahead, the sun rolled down the edge of the sky. After an hour they passed a small flock of sheep grazing on tufty, sparse camel thorn, guarded by a man and a boy. Wolff sat up in his seat and began to look about him. Soon

afterward the road intersected a wadi. Cautiously Vandam let
the car roll down the bank of the dried-up river.

Wolff said: *"Ruh ashshimalak."*

Vandam turned left. The going was firm. He was astonished to see groups of people, tents and animals in the wadi.
It was like a secret community. A mile farther on they saw
the explanation: a wellhead.

The mouth of the well was marked by a low circular wall
of mud brick. Four roughly dressed tree trunks leaned together over the hole, supporting a crude winding mechanism.
Four or five men hauled water continuously, emptying the
buckets into four radiating troughs around the wellhead.
Camels and women crowded around the troughs.

Vandam drove close to the well. Wolff said: *"Andak."*
Vandam stopped the car. The desert people were incurious,
although it must have been rare for them to see a motor vehicle: perhaps, Vandam thought, their hard lives left them no
time to investigate oddities. Wolff was asking questions of one
of the men in rapid Arabic. There was a short exchange. The
man pointed ahead. Wolff said to Vandam: *"Dughri."* Vandam drove on.

At last they came to a large encampment where Wolff
made Vandam stop. There were several tents in a cluster,
some penned sheep, several hobbled camels and a couple of
cooking fires. With a sudden quick movement Wolff reached
into the front of the car, switched off the engine and pulled
out the key. Without a word he got out.

Ishmael was sitting by the fire, making tea. He looked up and
said: "Peace be with you," as casually as if Wolff had
dropped in from the tent next door.

"And with you be health and God's mercy and blessing,"
Wolff replied formally.

"How is thy health?"

"God bless thee; I am well, thank God." Wolff squatted in
the sand.

Ishmael handed him a cup. "Take it."

"God increase thy good fortune," Wolff said.

"And thy good fortune also."

Wolff drank the tea. It was hot, sweet and very strong. He

remembered how this drink had fortified him during his trek through the desert . . . was it only two months ago?

When Wolff had drunk, Ishmael raised his hand to his head and said: "May it agree with thee, sir."

"God grant it may agree with thee."

The formalities were done. Ishmael said: "What of your friends?" He nodded toward the taxi, parked in the middle of the wadi, incongruous among the tents and camels.

"They are not friends," Wolff said.

Ishmael nodded. He was incurious. For all the polite inquiries about one's health, Wolff thought, the nomads were not really interested in what city people did: their lives were so different as to be incomprehensible.

Wolff said: "You still have my box?"

"Yes."

Ishmael would say yes, whether he had it or not, Wolff thought; that was the Arab way. Ishmael made no move to fetch the suitcase. He was incapable of hurrying. "Quickly" meant "within the next few days"; "immediately" meant "tomorrow."

Wolff said: "I must return to the city today."

"But you will sleep in my tent."

"Alas, no."

"Then you will join us in eating."

"Twice alas. Already the sun is low, and I must be back in the city before night falls."

Ishmael shook his head sadly, with the look of one who contemplates a hopeless case. "You have come for your box."

"Yes. Please fetch it, my cousin."

Ishmael spoke to a man standing behind him, who spoke to a younger man, who told a child to fetch the case. Ishmael offered Wolfe a cigarette. Wolff took it out of politeness. Ishmael lit the cigarettes with a twig from the fire. Wolff wondered where the cigarettes had come from. The child brought the case and offered it to Ishmael. Ishmael pointed to Wolff.

Wolff took the case and opened it. A great sense of relief flooded over him as he looked at the radio, the book and the key to the code. On the long and tedious train journey his euphoria had vanished, but now it came back, and he felt intoxicated with the sense of power and imminent victory. Once again he knew he was going to win the war. He closed the lid of the case. His hands were unsteady.

Ishmael was looking at him through narrowed eyes. "This is very important to you, this box."

"It's important to the world."

Ishmael said: "The sun rises, and the sun sets. Sometimes it rains. We live, then we die." He shrugged.

He would never understand, Wolff thought; but others would. He stood up. "I thank you, my cousin."

"Go in safety."

"May God protect thee."

Wolff turned around and walked toward the taxi.

Elene saw Wolff walk away from the fire with a suitcase in his hand. "He's coming back," she said. "What now?"

"He'll want to go back to Assyut," Vandam said, not looking at her. "Those radios have no batteries, they have to be plugged in, he has to go somewhere where there's electricity, and that means Assyut."

Billy said: "Can I come in the front?"

"No," Vandam said. "Quiet, now. Not much longer."

"I'm scared of him."

"So am I."

Elene shuddered. Wolff got into the car. "Assyut," he said. Vandam held out his hand, palm upward, and Wolff dropped the key in it. Vandam started the car and turned it around.

They went along the wadi, past the well, and turned onto the road. Elene was thinking about the case Wolff held on his knees. It contained the radio, the book and the key to the *Rebecca* code: how absurd it was that so much should hang on the question of who held that case in his hands, that she should have risked her life for it, that Vandam should have jeopardized his son for it. She felt very tired. The sun was low behind them now, and the smallest objects—boulders, bushes, tufts of grass—cast long shadows. Evening clouds were gathering over the hills ahead.

"Go faster," Wolff said in Arabic. "It's getting dark."

Vandam seemed to understand, for he increased speed. The car bounced and swayed on the unmade road. After a couple of minutes Billy said: "I feel sick."

Elene turned around to look at him. His face was pale and

tense, and he was sitting bolt upright. "Go slower." she said to Vandam, then she repeated it in Arabic, as if she had just recalled that he did not speak English.

Vandam slowed down for a moment, but Wolff said: "Go faster." He said to Elene: "Forget about the child."

Vandam went faster.

Elene looked at Billy again. He was as white as a sheet, and seemed to be on the brink of tears. "You bastard," she said to Wolff.

"Stop the car," Billy said.

Wolff ignored him, and Vandam had to pretend not to understand English.

There was a low hump in the road. Breasting it at speed, the car rose a few inches into the air, and came down again with a bump. Billy yelled: "Dad, stop the car! Dad!"

Vandam slammed on the brakes.

Elene braced herself against the dashboard and turned her head to look at Wolff.

For a split second he was stunned with shock. His eyes went to Vandam, then to Billy, then back to Vandam; and she saw in his expression first incomprehension, then astonishment, then fear. She knew he was thinking about the incident on the train, and the Arab boy at the railway station, and the kaffiyeh that covered the taxi driver's face; and then she saw that he knew, he had understood it all in a flash.

The car was screeching to a halt, throwing the passengers forward. Wolff regained his balance. With a rapid movement he threw his left arm around Billy and pulled the boy to him. Elene saw his hand go inside his shirt, and then he pulled out the knife.

The car stopped.

Vandam looked around. At the same moment, Elene saw, his hand went to the side slit of his galabiya—and froze there as he looked into the back seat. Elene turned too.

Wolff held the knife an inch from the soft skin of Billy's throat. Billy was wild-eyed with fear. Vandam looked stricken. At the corners of Wolff's mouth there was the hint of a mad smile.

"Damn it," Wolff said. "You almost had me."

They all stared at him in silence.

"Take off that foolish hat," he said to Vandam.

Vandam removed the kaffiyeh.

"Let me guess," said Wolff. "Major Vandam." He seemed to be enjoying the moment. "What a good thing I took your son for insurance."

"It's finished, Wolff," said Vandam. "Half the British Army is on your trail. You can let me take you alive, or let them kill you."

"I don't believe you're telling the truth," Wolff said. "You wouldn't have brought the Army to look for your son. You'd be afraid those cowboys would shoot the wrong people. I don't think your superiors even know where you are."

Elene felt sure Wolff was right, and she was gripped by despair. She had no idea what Wolff would do now, but she felt sure Vandam had lost the battle. She looked at Vandam, and saw defeat in his eyes.

Wolff said: "Underneath his galabiya, Major Vandam is wearing a pair of khaki trousers. In one of the pockets of the trousers, or possibly in the waistband, you will find a gun. Take it out."

Elene reached through the side slit of Vandam's galabiya and found the gun in his pocket. She thought: How did Wolff know? and then: He guessed. She took the gun out.

She looked at Wolff. He could not take the gun from her without releasing Billy, and if he released Billy, even for a moment, Vandam would do something.

But Wolff had thought of that. "Break the back of the gun, so that the barrel falls forward. Be careful not to pull the trigger by mistake."

She fiddled with the gun.

Wolff said: "You'll probably find a catch alongside the cylinder."

She found the catch and opened the gun.

"Take out the cartridges and drop them outside the car."

She did so.

"Put the gun on the floor of the car."

She put it down.

Wolff seemed relieved. Now, once again, the only weapon in the picture was his knife. He spoke to Vandam. "Get out of the car."

Vandam sat motionless.

"Get out," Wolff repeated. With a sudden precise movement he nicked the lobe of Billy's ear with the knife. A drop of blood welled out.

Vandam got out of the car.

Wolff said to Elene: "Get into the driving seat."

She climbed over the gear stick.

Vandam had left the car door open. Wolff said: "Close the door." Elene closed the door. Vandam stood beside the car, staring in.

"Drive," Wolff said.

The car had stalled. Elene put the gearshift into neutral and turned the key. The engine coughed and died. She hoped it would not go. She turned the key again; again the starter failed.

Wolff said: "Touch the accelerator pedal as you turn the key."

She did what he said. The engine caught and roared.

"Drive," Wolff said.

She pulled away.

"Faster."

She changed up.

Looking in the mirror she saw Wolff put the knife away and release Billy. Behind the car, already fifty yards away, Vandam stood on the desert road, his silhouette black against the sunset. He was quite still.

Elene said: "He's got no water!"

"No," Wolff replied.

Then Billy went berserk.

Elene heard him scream: "You can't leave him behind!" She turned around, forgetting about the road. Billy had leaped on Wolff like an enraged wildcat, punching and scratching and, somehow, kicking; yelling incoherently, his face a mask of childish rage, his body jerking convulsively like one in a fit. Wolff, who had relaxed, thinking the crisis was over, was momentarily powerless to resist. In the confined space, with Billy so close to him, he was unable to strike a proper blow, so he raised his arms to protect himself, and pushed against the boy.

Elene looked back to the road. While she was turning around, the car had gone off course, and now the left-hand front wheel was plowing through the sandy scrub beside the road. She struggled to turn the steering wheel but it seemed

to have a will of its own. She stamped on the brake, and the
rear of the car began to slide sideways. Too late, she saw a
deep rut running across the road immediately in front. The
skidding car hit the rut broadside with an impact that jarred
her bones. It seemed to bounce upward. Elene came up off
the seat momentarily, and when she came down again she
unintentionally trod on the accelerator pedal. The car shot
forward and began to skid in the other direction. Out of the
corner of her eye she saw that Wolff and Billy were being
tossed about helplessly, still fighting. The car went off the
road into the soft sand. It slowed abruptly, and Elene banged
her forehead on the rim of the steering wheel. The whole of
the car tilted sideways and seemed to be flying. She saw the
desert fall away beside her, and realized the car was in fact
rolling. She thought it would go over and over. She fell sideways, grabbing at the wheel and the gear stick. The car did
not turn turtle, but perched on its side like a coin dropped
edgeways into the sand. The gear shift came off in her hand.
She slumped against the door, banging her head again. The
car was still.

She got to her hands and knees, still holding the broken-off
gear stick, and looked into the rear of the car. Wolff and
Billy had fallen in a heap with Wolff on top. As she looked,
Wolff moved.

She had hoped he was dead.

She had one knee on the car door and the other on the
window. On her right the roof of the car stood up vertically.
On her left was the seat. She was looking through the gap between the top of the seat back and the roof.

Wolff got to his feet.

Billy seemed to be unconscious.

Elene felt disoriented and helpless, kneeling on the side
window of the car.

Wolff, standing on the inside of the left-hand rear door,
threw his weight against the floor of the car. The car rocked.
He did it again: the car rocked more. On his third try the car
tilted over and fell on all four wheels with a crash. Elene was
dizzy. She saw Wolff open the door and get out of the car.
He stood outside, crouched and drew his knife. She saw Vandam approaching.

She knelt on the seat, watching. She could not move until

her head stopped spinning. She saw Vandam crouch like Wolff, ready to spring, his hands raised protectively. He was red-faced and panting: he had run after the car. They circled. Wolff was limping slightly. The sun was a huge orange globe behind them.

Vandam moved forward, then seemed to hesitate curiously. Wolff lashed out with the knife, but he had been surprised by Vandam's hesitation, and his thrust missed. Vandam's fist lashed out. Wolff jerked back. Elene saw that Wolff's nose was bleeding.

They faced each other again, like boxers in a ring.

Vandam jumped forward again. This time Wolff dodged back. Vandam kicked out, but Wolff was out of range. Wolff jabbed with the knife. Elene saw it rip through Vandam's trousers and draw blood. Wolff stabbed again, but Vandam had stepped away. A dark stain appeared on his trouser leg.

Elene looked at Billy. The boy lay limply on the floor of the car, his eyes closed. Elene clambered over into the back and lifted him onto the seat. She could not tell whether he was dead or alive. She touched his face. He did not stir. "Billy," she said. "Oh, Billy."

She looked outside again. Vandam was down on one knee. His left arm hung limply from a shoulder covered with blood. He held his right arm out in a defensive gesture. Wolff approached him.

Elene jumped out of the car. She still had the broken-off gear stick in her hand. She saw Wolff bring back his arm, ready to slash at Vandam once more. She rushed up behind Wolff, stumbling in the sand. Wolff struck at Vandam. Vandam jerked sideways, dodging the blow. Elene raised the gear stick high in the air and brought it down with all her might on the back of Wolff's head. He seemed to stand still for a moment.

Elene said: "Oh, God."

Then she hit him again.

She hit him a third time.

He fell down.

She hit him again.

Then she dropped the gear stick and knelt beside Vandam.

"Well done," he said weakly.

"Can you stand up?"

He put a hand on her shoulder and struggled to his feet.
"It's not as bad as it looks," he said.

"Let me see."

"In a minute. Help me with this." Using his good arm, he
took hold of Wolff's leg and pulled him toward the car. Elene
grabbed the unconscious man's arm and heaved. When Wolff
was lying beside the car, Vandam lifted Wolff's limp arm and
placed the hand on the running board. palm down. Then he
lifted his foot and stamped on the elbow. Wolff's arm
snapped. Elene turned white. Vandam said: "That's to make
sure he's no trouble when he comes round."

He leaned into the back of the car and put a hand on
Billy's chest. "Alive," he said. "Thank God."

Billy's eyes opened.

"It's all over," Vandam said.

Billy closed his eyes.

Vandam got into the front seat of the car. "Where's the
gear stick?" he said.

"It broke off. That's what I hit him with."

Vandam turned the key. The car jerked. "Good—it's still
in gear," he said. He pressed the clutch and turned the key
again. The engine fired. He eased out the clutch and the car
moved forward. He switched off. "We're mobile," he said.
"What a piece of luck."

"What will we do with Wolff?"

"Put him in the boot."

Vandam took another look at Billy. He was conscious now,
his eyes wide open. "How are you, son?" said Vandam.

"I'm sorry," Billy said, "but I couldn't help feeling sick."

Vandam looked at Elene. "You'll have to drive," he said.
There were tears in his eyes.

29

There was the sudden, terrifying roar of nearby aircraft. Rommel glanced up and saw the British bombers approaching low from behind the nearest line of hills: the troops called them "Party Rally" bombers because they flew in the perfect formation of display aircraft at the prewar Nuremberg parades. "Take cover!" Rommel yelled. He ran to a slit trench and dived in.

The noise was so loud it was like silence. Rommel lay with his eyes closed. He had a pain in his stomach. They had sent him a doctor from Germany, but Rommel knew that the only medicine he needed was victory. He had lost a lot of weight: his uniform hung loosely on him now, and his shirt collars seemed too large. His hair was receding rapidly and turning white in places.

Today was September 1, and everything had gone terribly wrong. What had seemed to be the weak point in the Allied defense line was looking more and more like an ambush. The minefields were heavy where they should have been light, the ground beneath had been quicksand where hard going was expected, and the Alam Halfa ridge, which should have been taken easily, was being mightily defended. Rommel's strategy was wrong; his intelligence had been wrong; his spy had been wrong.

The bombers passed overhead. Rommel got out of the trench. His aides and officers emerged from cover and gathered around him again. He raised his field glasses and looked out over the desert. Scores of vehicles stood still in the sand, many of them blazing furiously. If the enemy would only charge, Rommel thought, we could fight him. But the

Allies sat tight, well dug in, picking off the Panzer tanks like fish in a barrel.

It was no good. His forward units were fifteen miles from Alexandria, but they were stuck. Fifteen miles, he thought. Another fifteen miles, and Egypt would have been mine. He looked at the officers around him. As always, their expressions reflected his own: he saw in their faces what they saw in his.

It was defeat.

He knew it was a nightmare, but he could not wake up.

The cell was six feet long by four feet wide, and half of it was taken up by a bed. Beneath the bed was a chamberpot. The walls were of smooth gray stone. A small light bulb hung from the ceiling by a cord. In one end of the cell was a door. In the other end was a small square window, set just above eye level: through it he could see the bright blue sky.

In his dream he thought: I'll wake up soon, then it will be all right. I'll wake up, and there will be a beautiful woman lying beside me on a silk sheet, and I will touch her breasts—and as he thought this he was filled with strong lust—and she will wake up and kiss me, and we will drink champagne . . . But he could not quite dream that, and the dream of the prison cell came back. Somewhere nearby a bass drum was beating steadily. Soldiers were marching to the rhythm outside. The beat was terrifying, terrifying, boom-boom, boom-boom, tramp-tramp, the drum and the soldiers and the close gray walls of the cell and that distant, tantalizing square of blue sky and he was so frightened, so horrified, that he forced his eyes open and he woke up.

He looked around him, not understanding. He was awake, wide awake, no question about it, the dream was over; yet he was still in a prison cell. It was six feet long by four feet wide, and half of it was taken up by a bed. He raised himself from the bed and looked underneath it. There was a chamberpot.

He stood upright. Then, quietly and calmly, he began to bang his head against the wall.

Jerusalem, 24 September 42
My dear Elene,

Today I went to the Western Wall, which is also called the Wailing Wall. I stood before it with many other Jews, and I prayed. I wrote a kvitlach and put it into a crack in the wall. May God grant my petition.

This is the most beautiful place in the world, Jerusalem. Of course I do not live well. I sleep on a mattress on the floor in a little room with five other men. Sometimes I get a little work, sweeping up in a workshop where one of my roommates, a young man, carries wood for the carpenters. I am very poor, like always, but now I am poor in Jerusalem, which is better than rich in Egypt.

I crossed the desert in a British Army truck. They asked me what I would have done if they had not picked me up, and when I said I would have walked, I believe they thought me mad. But this is the sanest thing I ever did.

I must tell you that I am dying. My illness is quite incurable, even if I could afford doctors, and I have only weeks left, perhaps a couple of months. Don't be sad. I have never been happier in my life.

I should tell you what I wrote in my kvitlach. I asked God to grant happiness to my daughter Elene. I believe he will. Farewell,

Your Father.

The smoked ham was sliced as thin as paper and rolled into dainty cylinders. The bread rolls were home-baked, fresh that morning. There was a glass jar of potato salad made with real mayonnaise and crisp chopped onion. There were a bottle of wine, another bottle of soda and a bag of oranges. And a packet of cigarettes, his brand.

Elene began to pack the food into the picnic basket.

She had just closed the lid when she heard the knock at the door. She took off her apron before going to open it.

Vandam stepped inside, closed the door behind him and kissed her. He put his arms around her and held her painfully tightly. He always did this, and it always hurt, but she never complained, for they had almost lost each other, and now when they were together they were just so grateful.

They went into the kitchen. Vandam hefted the picnic basket and said: "Lord, what have you got in here, the Crown Jewels?"

"What's the news?" Elene asked.

He knew she meant news of the war in the desert. He said: "Axis forces in full retreat, and I quote." She thought how relaxed he was these days. He even talked differently. A little gray was appearing in his hair, and he laughed a lot.

"I think you're one of those men who gets more good-looking as he gets older," she said.

"Wait till my teeth drop out."

They went out. The sky was curiously black, and Elene said "Oh!" in surprise as she stepped into the street.

"End of the world today," Vandam said.

"I've never seen it like this before," Elene said.

They got on the motorcycle and headed for Billy's school. The sky became even darker. The first rain fell as they were passing Shepheard's Hotel. Elene saw an Egyptian drape a handkerchief over his fez. The raindrops were enormous; each one soaked right through her dress to the skin. Vandam turned the bike around and parked in front of the hotel. As they dismounted the clouds burst.

They stood under the hotel canopy and watched the storm. The sheer quantity of water was incredible. Within minutes the gutters overflowed and the pavements were awash. Opposite the hotel the shopkeepers waded through the flood to put up shutters. The cars simply had to stop where they were.

"There's no main drainage in this town," Vandam remarked. "The water has nowhere to go but the Nile. Look at it." The street had turned into a river.

"What about the bike?" Elene said.

"Damn thing will float away," said Vandam. "I'll have to bring it under here." He hesitated, then dashed out on to the pavement, seized the bike by its handlebars and pushed it through the water to the steps of the hotel. When he regained the shelter of the canopy his clothes were thoroughly soaked and his hair was plastered around his head like a mop coming out of a bucket. Elene laughed at him.

The rain went on a long time. Elene said: "What about Billy?"

"They'll have to keep the kids at school until the rain stops."

Eventually they went into the hotel for a drink. Vandam ordered sherry: he had sworn off gin, and claimed he did not miss it.

At last the storm ended, and they went out again; but they had to wait a little longer for the flood to recede. Finally there was only an inch or so of water, and the sun came out. The motorists began to try to start their cars. The bike was not too wet, and it fired first time.

The sun came out and the roads began to steam as they drove to the school. Billy was waiting outside. "What a storm!" he said excitedly. He climbed on to the bike, sitting between Elene and Vandam.

They drove out into the desert. Holding on tightly, her eyes half closed, Elene did not see the miracle until Vandam stopped the bike. The three of them got off and looked around, speechless.

The desert was carpeted with flowers.

"It's the rain, obviously," said Vandam. "But . . ."

Millions of flying insects had also appeared from nowhere, and now butterflies and bees dashed frantically from bloom to bloom, reaping the sudden harvest.

Billy said: "The seeds must have been in the sand, waiting."

"That's it," Vandam said. "The seeds have been there for years, just waiting for this."

The flowers were all tiny, like miniatures, but very brightly colored. Billy walked a few paces from the road and bent down to examine one. Vandam put his arms around Elene and kissed her. It started as a peck on the cheek, but turned into a long, loving embrace.

Eventually she broke away from him, laughing. "You'll embarrass Billy," she said.

"He's going to have to get used to it," Vandam said.

Elene stopped laughing. "Is he?" she said. "Is he, really?"

Vandam smiled, and kissed her again.

**You are invited to enjoy the first chapter
of Ken Follett's riveting novel**
Night Over Water

Chapter 1

IT WAS THE MOST romantic plane ever made.

Standing on the dock at Southampton, at half past twelve on the day war was declared, Tom Luther peered into the sky, waiting for the plane with a heart full of eagerness and dread. Under his breath he hummed a few bars of Beethoven over and over again: the first movement of the *Emperor* Concerto, a stirring tune, appropriately warlike.

There was a crowd of sightseers around him: aircraft enthusiasts with binoculars, small boys and curiosity seekers. Luther reckoned this must be the ninth time the Pan American Clipper had landed on Southampton Water, but the novelty had not worn off. The plane was so fascinating, so enchanting, that people flocked to look at it even on the day their country went to war. Beside the same dock were two magnificent ocean liners, towering over people's heads, but he floating hotels had lost their magic: everyone was looking at the sky.

However, while they waited they were all talking about the war, in their English accents. The children were excited by the prospect; the men spoke knowingly in low tones about tanks and artillery; the women just looked grim. Luther was an American, and he hoped his country would stay out of the war: it was none of America's business. Besides, one thing you could say for the Nazis, they were tough on communism.

Luther was a businessman, manufacturing wool

cloth, and he had had a lot of trouble with Reds in his mills at one time. He had been at their mercy: they had almost ruined him. He still felt bitter about it. His father's menswear store had been run into the ground by Jews setting up in competition, and then Luther Woolens was threatened by the Commies— most of whom were Jews! Then Luther had met Ray Patriarca, and his life had changed. Patriarca's people knew what to do about Communists. There were some accidents. One hothead got his hand caught in a loom. A union recruiter was killed in a hit-and-run. Two men who complained about breaches of the safety regulations got into a fight in a bar and finished up in the hospital. A woman troublemaker dropped her lawsuit against the company after her house burned down. It only took a few weeks: since then there had been no unrest. Patriarca knew what Hitler knew: the way to deal with Communists was to crush them like cockroaches. Luther stamped his foot, still humming Beethoven.

A launch put out from the Imperial Airways flyingboat dock, across the estuary at Hythe, and made several passes along the splashdown zone, checking for floating debris. An eager murmur went up from the crowd: the plane must be approaching.

The first to spot it was a small boy with large new boots. He had no binoculars, but his eleven-year-old eyesight was better than lenses. "Here it comes!" he shrilled. "Here comes the Clipper!" He pointed southwest. Everyone looked that way. At first Luther could see only a vague shape that might have been a bird, but soon its outline resolved, and a buzz of excitement spread through the crowd as people told one another that the boy was right.

Everyone called it the Clipper, but technically it was a Boeing B-314. Pan American had commissioned Boeing to build a plane capable of carrying passengers across the Atlantic Ocean in total luxury, and this was the result: enormous, majestic, unbelievably powerful, an airborne palace. The airline had taken delivery of six and ordered another six. In comfort and elegance they were equal to the fabulous ocean liners that docked at Southampton, but the ships took four or five days to cross the Atlantic, whereas the Clipper could make the trip in twenty-five to thirty hours.

It looked like a winged whale, Luther thought as the plane came closer. It had a big blunt whale-like snout, a massive body and a tapering rear that culminated in twin high-mounted tailfins. The huge engines were built into the wings. Below the wings was a pair of stubby sea-wings, which served to stabilize the aircraft when it was in the water. The bottom of the plane had a sharp knife-edge like the hull of a fast ship.

Soon Luther could make out the big rectangular windows, in two irregular rows, marking the upper and lower decks. He had come to England on the Clipper exactly a week earlier, so he was familiar with its layout. The upper deck comprised the flight cabin and baggage holds and the lower was the passenger deck. Instead of seat rows, the passenger deck had a series of lounges with davenport couches. At mealtimes the main lounge became the dining room, and at night the couches were converted into beds.

Everything was done to insulate the passengers from the world and the weather outside the windows. There were thick carpets, soft lighting, velvet fabrics, soothing colors and deep upholstery. The heavy soundproofing reduced the roar of the mighty engines to a distant, reassuring hum. The captain was calmly authoritative, the crew clean-cut and smart in their Pan American uniforms, the stewards ever attentive. Every need was catered to; there was constant food and drink; whatever you wanted appeared as if by magic, just when you wanted it, curtained bunks at bedtime, fresh strawberries at breakfast. The world outside started to appear unreal, like a film projected onto the windows; and the interior of the aircraft seemed like the whole universe.

Such comfort did not come cheap. The round-trip fare was $675, half the price of a small house. The passengers were royalty, movie stars, chairmen of large corporations and presidents of small countries.

Tom Luther was none of those things. He was rich, but he had worked hard for his money, and he would not normally have squandered it on luxury. However, he had needed to familiarize himself with the plane. He had been asked to do a dangerous job for a power-ful man—very powerful indeed. He would not be paid for his work, but to be owed a favor by such a man was better than money.

The whole thing might yet be called off: Luther was waiting for a message giving him the final go-ahead. Half the time he was eager to get on with it; the other half, he hoped he would not have to do it.

The plane came down at an angle, its tail lower than its nose. It was quite close now, and Luther was struck again by its tremendous size. He knew that it was 109 feet long and 152 feet from one wingtip to the other, but the measurements were just numbers until you actually saw the goddam thing floating through the air.

For a moment it looked as if it were not flying but falling, and would crash into the sea like a dropped stone and sink to the bottom. Then it seemed to hang in the air, just above the surface, as if dangling on a string, for a long moment of suspense. At last it touched the water, skipping the surface, splashing across the tops of the waves like a stone thrown skim-wise, sending up small explosions of foam. But there was very little swell in the sheltered estuary, and a moment later, with an explosion of spray like the smoke from a bomb, the hull plunged into the water.

It cleaved the surface, plowing a white furrow in the green, sending twin curves of spray high in the air on either side; and Luther thought of a mallard coming down on a lake with spread wings and folded feet. The hull sank lower, enlarging the sail-shaped curtains of spray that flew up to left and right; then it began to tilt forward. The spray increased as the plane leveled out, submerging more and more of its whale's belly. Then at last its nose was down. Its speed slowed suddenly, the spray diminished to a wash, and the aircraft sailed the sea like the ship it was, as calmly as if it had never dared to reach for the sky.

Luther realized he had been holding his breath, and let it out in a long relieved sigh. He started humming again.

The plane taxied toward its berth. Luther had disembarked there a week ago. The dock was a specially designed raft with twin piers. In a few minutes, ropes would be attached to stanchions at the front and rear of the plane and it would be winched in, backward, to its parking slot between the piers. Then the privileged passengers would emerge, stepping from the door onto the broad surface of the seawing, then onto the raft, and from there up a gangway to dry land.

Luther turned away, then stopped suddenly. Standing at his shoulder was someone he had not seen before: a man of about his own height, dressed in a dark gray suit and a bowler hat, like a clerk on his way to the office. Luther was about to pass on, then he looked again. The face beneath the bowler hat was not that of a clerk. The man had a high forehead, bright blue eyes, a long jaw, and a thin, cruel mouth. He was older than Luther, about forty; but he was broad-shouldered and seemed fit. He looked handsome and dangerous. He stared into Luther's eyes.

Luther stopped humming.

The man said: "I am Henry Faber."

"Tom Luther."

"I have a message for you."

Luther's heart skipped a beat. He tried to hide his excitement, and spoke in the same clipped tones as the other man. "Good. Go ahead."

"The man you're so interested in will be on this plane on Wednesday when it leaves for New York."

"You're sure?"

The man looked hard at Luther and did not answer.

Luther nodded grimly. So the job was on. At least the suspense was over. "Thank you," he said.

"There's more."

"I'm listening."

"The second part of the message is: Don't let us down."

Luther took a deep breath. "Tell them not to worry," he said, with more confidence than he really felt. "The guy may leave Southampton, but he'll never reach New York."

Imperial Airways had a flying-boat facility just across the estuary from Southampton Docks. Imperial's mechanics serviced the Clipper, supervised by the Pan American flight engineer. On this trip the engineer was Eddie Deakin.

It was a big job, but they had three days. After discharging its passengers at Berth 108, the Clipper taxied across to Hythe. There, in the water, it was maneuvered onto a dolly, then it was winched up a slipway and towed, looking like a whale balanced on a baby carriage, into the enormous green hangar.

The transatlantic flight was a punishing task for the engines. On the longest leg, from Newfoundland to Ireland, the plane was in the air for nine hours (and on the return journey, against head winds, the same leg took sixteen and a half hours). Hour after hour the fuel flowed, the plugs sparked, the fourteen cylinders in each enormous engine pumped tirelessly up and down, and the fifteen-foot propellers chopped through clouds and rain and gales.

For Eddie that was the romance of engineering. It was wonderful, it was amazing that men could make engines that would work perfectly and precisely, hour after hour. There were so many things that might have gone wrong, so many moving parts that had to be precision-made and meticulously fitted together so that they would not snap, slip, get blocked or simply wear out while they carried a forty-one-ton airplane over thousands of miles.

By Wednesday morning the Clipper would be ready to do it again.

About the Author

Ken Follett was born in Cardiff, Wales. After taking a degree in philosophy at University College, London, he became a newspaper reporter, first with the *South Wales Echo* and later with the London *Evening News*. His first international best seller, *Eye of the Needle*, won the Edgar Award of the Mystery Writers of America. Follett is also the author of *Triple*, *The Key to Rebecca*, *The Man from St. Petersburg*, *On Wings of Eagles*, *The Pillars of the Earth*, and *Night Over Water*. He and his wife live in London, England.